PROPHECY
OF
DAYS

PROPHECY
OF
DAYS

BOOK I: THE DAYKEEPER'S GRIMOIRE

CHRISTY RAEDEKE

flux™
Woodbury, Minnesota

First Edition
First Printing, 2010

Cover design by Kevin R. Brown
Interior art by Llewellyn art department

Flux, an imprint of Llewellyn Worldwide Ltd.

Library of Congress Cataloging-in-Publication Data
Raedeke, Christy, 1966–
  Prophecy of days / Christy Raedeke.—1st ed.
    p. cm. — (The daykeeper's grimoire ; bk. 1)
  Summary: Caity Mac Fireland of San Francisco accompanies her parents to an isle off the coast of Scotland where she finds a Mayan relic and, guided by a motley crew of advisors, uncovers an incredible secret that an elite group of power-brokers will stop at nothing to control.
  ISBN 978-0-7387-1576-6
  [1. Prophecies—Fiction. 2. Conspiracies—Fiction.
3. Mayas—Antiquities—Fiction. 4. Indians of Central
America—Antiquities—Fiction. 5. Scotland—Fiction.] I. Title.
  PZ7.R1233Pro 2010
  [Fic]—dc22

                                                          2009030668

Flux
A Division of Llewellyn Worldwide Ltd.
2143 Wooddale Drive
Woodbury, MN 55125-2989
www.fluxnow.com

For Juliet

They must find it difficult...
Those who have taken authority as the truth,
Rather than truth as the authority.

—Gerald Massey

All of the prophecies of the world,
All the traditions, are converging now.
There is no time for games...
The world will not end. It will be transformed.

—Carlos Barrios, Mayan Elder

PREFACE

(OR: THE CLIFFSNOTES VERSION OF MY LIFE UP UNTIL NOW)

First off, I'm going to save you from reading seventy-two pages of how I got to a Scottish castle on the Isle of Huracan in the middle of a black churning sea. I need to tell it fast because if you read the long, drawn-out version you're going to think you've heard it all before. It has all the clichés: super-smart young girl ripped from her cushy life in San Francisco, taken away from her best friend Justine whom she's known since preschool, relocated to a dreary island castle in Scotland (inherited, of course!) for the summer before her junior year so her parents can see if they want to turn it into a bed and breakfast, even though they have not made bed nor breakfast for this super-smart girl in years. You've heard it a million times, right? Wait, there's more! The girl finds a secret room attached to her bedroom, because there just *has* to be a secret room.

And of course, there's a monkey. A small monkey that was abandoned at the castle years ago by a Chinese visitor.

PETA should give me a medal or something because I convinced Thomas, the whisky-soaked groundskeeper, to move him from the cold little shed behind the castle to the wood cubby by the kitchen fireplace. We lost two cooks over this, but that's okay. The new cook, Mrs. Findlay, is amazing and she has a beautiful grandson a year older than me who looks like he could be posing for a J. Crew ad every minute of the day. Because there has to be a boy, right? (Thank God!)

Anyway, this monkey knows how to do origami, so his highly original name is Mr. Papers. I know it sounds hard to believe, but he communicates through his origami—kind of like sign language but with paper.

Having a monkey at the castle was a bonus; I would never have been able to get one on my own because Mom is all righteous about caging up animals that live in the wild. You should have seen her face when Thomas first told her about Mr. Papers—I knew the minute she heard the words "monkey" and "origami" she was probably picturing the little guy in a Taiwan sweatshop cranking out origami ornaments for Walmart.

Speaking of my mom, I guess I should fill you in on my parents because they are anything but cliché, which also takes my story a bit further from the standard-model "inherited castle full of weird stuff" tale.

My mom is a professional safecracker. Yep, a safecracker. This puts me way too close to the word *crack*, a favorite of the incredibly immature, acne-covered boy species at the San Francisco Academy of Humanities, or the Academy of Cruelties as Justine and I refer to it. They call me Cracky Mac Cracken instead of Caity Mac Fireland, which unfortunately isn't vulgar enough to get them expelled.

Mom flies all over the world a few times a year to open up safes that no one else can. But believe me she's not like the safecracker babes you see on TV and in movies that slink under laser beams in lycra pants and stuff. There are only a few people in the world who can do what she does and she says her special weapon is her ability to *touch sound*. It may seem supernatural but it's not; she says it's like when you bend a Barbie knee and you get that satisfying sound and feeling at the same time. She actually has one of my Barbie legs in her pencil cup—she plucked one from a hip socket when she saw me tossing my Barbies out—and she will often do the knee-cracking thing for quite a while if she's thinking hard about something. I realize this makes her sound way freakier than she is. Just think of it like how some people bite their fingernails or pace, but she cracks a Barbie knee.

Anyway, she couldn't be that weird if my dad married her. He's got that George Clooney-ish early-gray-hair-but-dark-eyebrows-and-olive-skin thing. He's also really tall, which I inherited. All my friends' moms are in love with him, but I'm happy to report he is completely oblivious to this. He says he was a total geek as a kid, which explains the Ph.D. in Computer Science. He just sort of accidentally turned handsome later in life.

Dad is obsessed with making himself "untraceable by The Man," as he says. Seriously, no matter how many different ways you Googled his name you'd never get any info on him. This is nearly impossible in this day so it's a point of pride. He said he could see the writing on the wall when he first heard of the Internet, how corporations and the government would be able to amass tons of information about you. Plus his dad was a privacy nut.

So he enrolled in college under a different name, and now he does all his freelance work through an untraceable company he made up in the Bahamas. He pays taxes and doesn't do anything sketchy that would make him need some weird fake company, but he still insists. Mom just rolls with it; she thinks it makes him feel like James Bond and keeps telling me it's better than him buying a cheesy red sports car or having an affair. Like those are the only options? Whatever. I just accept it as part of his geek personality, along with his constant whistling and his huge collection of Japanese gashapon. Don't even ask about that last one…

You can tell he and Mom are still totally in love by how much they laugh at each other's bad jokes, but they are definitely not the kind of people who call each other "babe" or "sweetheart" or anything other than Fiona and Angus. And, lucky for me, they're not the kind of parents you find making out on the couch all the time.

Dad's the reason we own a small (Population: 144! Towns: 1!) Scottish island called the Isle of Huracan and Breidablik Castle that sits on it. His great-uncle Hamish left it to him and now he's what's called a "Laird" in Scotland. I thought it was something royal at first and hoped I would get to be a Countess or Lady, but Laird just means landowner. Not that having a "title" hasn't gone to his head anyway.

The island should have gone to my grandparents, but they both died in a car accident when Dad was in college. I never met my dad's parents, or Great Uncle Hamish. The only thing I knew about Hamish was that he'd lived out in the middle of nowhere in this castle and he'd never had children of his own. He loved that my parents named me Caitrina, with the Scottish spelling, and he sent me some weird baby gifts when I was born: a chunky silver circle with a strange symbol on it, an old Mexican plaque made out of clay, and a framed picture of the Milky Way (as in galaxy, not candy bar.) For obvious reasons I'd always thought he was a lunatic.

And me? All I want is to be discovered. I have a secret fantasy of being at a restaurant or the mall and having a Hollywood Agent walk up to me and say, "My God, child, why aren't you in the movies?" Or having some famous Art Critic come to an art show at the Academy of Cruelties and marvel at my grasp of light and shadow. "I'm a tonalist," I'll say, pointing out my minimal use of color. (I have special responses for almost anyone who could discover me.)

Because of my Discovery Fantasy I haven't spent much time focusing on what I want to do with my life. I guess I'm waiting to see whether it's a Talent Agent, Senate Page Scout, Art Critic, Filmmaker, or even Pageant Coach who discovers me. The last one might tip you off to the fact that I'm not very discriminating about what I get discovered for…

I've never said a word of this to anyone, of course, because it seems so conceited as if I could be world-class *anything*. But I also suspect that I'm not the only one with this fantasy.

So there you have it. I've saved you sixty-seven pages of reading and caught you up to now. And like my hippie fifth-grade teacher used to say, "Now is the present, and a present is a great gift." I never really got that, but it sounds kind of cool, doesn't it?

ONE

When you think *island* and *summer* you generally think of warm breezes and palm trees, but not here. Even in June, most days the wind sandblasts your face and the sea spits at you as it thrashes against the rocky shore. So this morning after breakfast when I can't take the cold any more, I grab Mr. Papers and go back to my bedroom to light a fire in my fireplace.

I don't have a fireplace in my room in San Francisco—we are pretty well off by most standards, but only the super-rich, I-have-my-own-helicopter-pad kind of kids have fireplaces in their bedrooms in the city. Every bedroom at Breidablik has one because it gets so cold here, and they're all really big, too; a mid-sized ten-year-old could probably stand upright in any one of them.

Actually, everything here is oversized. I remember when we first drove up I was shocked by how big this place was.

Breidablik Castle is definitely not one of those pretty, princessy castles that you see at Disneyland. It's more boxy. It looks like it was built in three pieces; on one side there's a big square stone tower, about ten stories high that is linked to the castle itself by a four-story wing. The main part of the castle ranges from about three stories to seven stories and it's all made out of a light grey stone. The roofline is all over the place, with some cone roofs and some steep pointy roofs.

You might even consider Breidablik ugly if the grounds were not so nice. There's a big stone wall around the whole castle that ivy is making a good attempt to take over. Metal gates close off the tall, rounded entrance to the inner courtyard and garden and immediately inside the wall a small stream, only about five feet wide, circles the castle. The driveway is made of tiny pebbles that make a nice crunch under your feet.

The word "Breidablik" is carved into the enormous front door that has lots of heavy iron straps. If you stand where the door is at the top of the stairs and turn around you get a good view of the large pond and the formal garden, where everything is super symmetrical and the bushes are cut so tightly they seem like sculptures.

The inside of the castle looks like a museum. There's lots of big wooden furniture, and tons of exotic rugs everywhere. The walls are covered with these twelve-foot-high portraits of men in kilts and white knee socks with their skinny little dogs and women who look like they've never seen sunlight, glowing ghost-white in their fancy clothes with their hair pulled back severely. Thank God bronzer and bangs were invented.

Thomas told us the best bedrooms were in the East Wing, so that's the part of the castle he had wired first by Scottish TeleCom (Dad's first priority, naturally). The East Wing is the bridge between the castle and the tower. Thomas encouraged me to take the room I'm in, but I think I would have chosen it anyway because the furniture is cartoonishly big.

Mom and Dad fell in love with the room next to mine; Mom was sold on the twenty-foot blue velvet curtains and Dad was attracted to the dangerous-looking fireplace tools. He picked up the heavy iron fire poker, did a quick fencing move and said, "Touché." That was our first hint that the Laird thing was going to his head.

So now I have this room the size of a basketball court with supersized furniture. The bed is so big that I have to use this mini staircase to even get into it.

The bedposts are as thick around as telephone poles and a purple tufted-velvet canopy and purple curtains drape the whole thing. It's *so* over the top. I love it though; when I get in bed and close all the curtains, I feel like I'm in a genie's bottle.

Anyway, as I wad up printer paper and stuff it under the logs to start a fire, Mr. Papers comes over to help. He probably thinks wadding up paper is my lame version of origami. It's hilarious to watch a monkey do human things, especially a monkey as cute as Mr. Papers. He's not as big as you'd expect—about the size of a small house cat. His fur is long and silky, coffee colored on his body but white around his neck and face with another little coffee-colored patch on the top of his head like a cap. He wears this strange outfit of striped shorts and a vest with diamond shapes on it that must've come from a doll. His humanlike hands are small like a newborn baby's, but the fingers are long and wrinkled, a contrast that often freaks me out. I Googled capuchin monkeys once I got here and found out they're the ones that get trained to be helpers for paraplegics. There are picture on the web of these little guys microwaving food and opening mail and stuff for people who have no use of their arms and legs. It's amazing.

Once Mr. Papers and I get the fire going, I sit down in one of the old leather chairs by the fireplace, but it's hard and cold. The funky lime-green velvet fainting couch in the secret room comes to mind.

Finding the secret chamber on my own was a pretty major discovery. I was looking at this carved wood panel in my room and saw a cool optical illusion of three rabbits, all joined at the ears. I drew them in my sketchbook because I love optical illusions. When I first started working with charcoal I went through a serious Escher phase; I could look at that "hands drawing hands drawing hands drawing hands" thing forever.

So as I was sketching these rabbits, I noticed that the ears looked a lot like the silver pendant that Hamish had sent as a baby gift. I never wore it around my neck because it's really bulky, but I had put it on a key chain and hung it on my backpack. It gives off a little Goth vibe because it's chunky and metal and looks hand carved.

Removing it from my backpack, I placed it over the rabbit's ears on the wall and found it was a perfect match! I was stunned that this thing I'd had since I was a baby, what had looked to me like a circle with random carvings on it, actually became rabbit's ears in this weird carved optical illusion. The most amazing part, though, was that when I pressed it in, I heard a slight *whoosh* and then the sound of a shell scraping the sidewalk as the panel slid to the side and revealed a short doorway.

It was all very exciting—isn't it every girl's dream to have a secret hideout?

The room behind the panel is the size of a small bedroom. The walls are covered in intricately carved wood and all that's in there is a big oriental rug, a side table that holds a magnifying glass and a lamp, and the green fainting couch. Which brings me back to why I was even explaining all of this in the first place: it's cold today and I want to replace my creaky leather chairs with the fainting couch so I can lounge by the fire.

Placing my key over the carving of the rabbit ears, I give it a good push and enter. When I turn on the lamp, Mr. Papers jumps off my shoulder and starts chattering, running around pointing excitedly to the carvings on the walls.

The first time I'd been in here I never really looked closely at the carvings. From far away it just looks decorative, but when I start looking closely at the wall I see there's definitely a pattern, and repetition. It's basically a series of symbols, almost like runes, but instead of being carved in rows or columns they're arranged into the shape of square spirals. Like if you wrote one big long sentence, but started it at the top of a piece of paper and kept turning the paper and kept writing on all four sides over and over again until it made a big square spiral.

"What is this?" I say out loud as I run my fingers over the carvings.

Mr. Papers scampers out of the room and goes to my desk for origami paper, then returns. He takes one piece and folds it in half like a book, and then he rolls up the other piece like a pencil and pretends to write in his book. He motions to the wall with his head.

"This is writing?" I ask as I mime that I'm writing on my hand. He nods.

Back in my room, I gather a pencil, a piece of tape, some white paper, and a few more sheets of origami paper for Mr. Papers and hurry back to the chamber. I hand Papers the small colored sheets to keep him occupied and then tape a piece of white paper over one of the middle spirals. Once it's secure, I run the pencil over the white sheets, like in art class at the Academy of Cruelties when we made wax rubbings of old gravestones at Mission Dolores. It seems magical when the symbols appear in negative space, white against the grey of the pencil marks.

I finish and look over at Mr. Papers, who is busy with some intricate origami. I've never seen him do something so complicated, so I sit on the fainting couch to watch. It takes him awhile to finish, then he hands me his work. It's incredible—a man wearing a long robe with a tiny monkey on his shoulder. He grabs it from me and takes it over by one of the spirals, sets it on the floor, and then points from it to the wall and back, like he's saying they are connected.

It still freaks me out that he communicates with origami and I have to rub my arms to get the goose bumps down. All of a sudden I want out, so I pick up Mr. Papers and the rubbing and rush out of the room, leaving the origami man in the chamber.

I sit on my bed looking at the paper with the symbols on it. For the first time since we arrived I feel like I have something interesting to do other than wander around the castle grounds. If I show this to Mom and Dad they will ask where the symbols came from, and then my secret room won't be secret anymore.

My best friend Justine's grandfather is a professor of Egyptology at Princeton and I suspect he may know enough about other old languages to decipher this. I scan the rubbing and then attach the scan to an email:

From: caitymacfireland@gmail.com
To: justinemiddleford@gmail.com
Subject: Need a favor…

Hi J, huge favor, please! Can you forward this rubbing
to your Grandpa at Princeton and ask him if he knows
what it says? It might be some kind of old language.
There's a bunch of these symbols carved into the walls
of this hidden room that's attached to my bedroom here
(yes, I have a hidden room AND a monkey, thank you
very much. I can officially die now…)

After I send the email I go back to stoke the fire. Mesmerized by the flames and the warmth, I poke mindlessly at
it until the new-mail chime on my computer startles me. It's
Justine.

From: justinemiddleford@gmail.com
To: caitymacfireland@gmail.com
Subject: RE: Need a favor…

Hi C—Got your attachment, weird! Doesn't look
anything like the reproduction Egyptian stuff Gramps
has at his house, but maybe he'll know what it is. I'll
email you the minute I hear. Cruelties is unbearable
without you and it's only the fourth day of summer
session. The only ray of sunshine in my bleak
existence is that I got paired with David von Kellerman
in chemistry. He's hotter than ever with his summer
tan and he smells oooooou good. We're always doing
experiments wrong even tho I know the right way
because I can't make myself correct him. Very un-
feminist of me, I'm like a 1950s housewife. You'd hate
me. "Yes David, sure David, I'll mix those two things
that I know will have a nasty chemical reaction for you

David, and may I cook you a meatloaf David?" Ewww.
I'm pitiful.

XO, Justine

Justine has to go to summer session just because she got a
B in Chemistry. At Cruelties if you retake a class in the summer, they will erase your other grade, which she has to do
because her parents won't allow anything less than As. But at
least she gets to sit next to David von Kellerman each day. A
pang of jealousy stabs me in the solar plexus.

To keep from checking my email every five minutes, I go
back in the room and take a few more rubbings of the spirals
on the wall. I'd love to do it all at once, but it's not super easy;
holding your arms up for that long while rubbing a pencil
over the paper is really hard.

I go about my day, bumping in to my parents and Thomas
and Mrs. Findlay as if nothing unusual has happened, as if I
haven't just stumbled upon the coolest thing ever.

It's not until the next morning that I get an email from
Justine:

From: justinemiddleford@gmail.com
To: caitymacfireland@gmail.com
Subject: That rubbing you took…

Hey C, Check out the reply from Gramps below. (Sorry,
I pretended I took the rubbing so he'd think I was into
this kind of thing—I guess I'll have to come clean now.)
So what's the big mystery anyway? Looks like you've
got all the old guys at Princeton pretty excited. Today
in Chem I splashed some water on my face while I
was washing out our beakers (so domestic!) and David

wiped it away with his thumb. Do you think he likes me? I mean, that's pretty unusual to use your thumb, isn't it?

Here's what Gramps has to say:

My Dearest Justine,

How wonderful that you are taking an interest in archaeology and antiquities! I found your rubbing absolutely fascinating, as I had never seen anything like it. I sent it on to Dr. Tenzo in Ancient Languages. He is very anxious to hear where you took the rubbing; so much so that he wanted your email address to reach you directly. I promise I won't sic Tenzo on you, but do tell me dear, where did you find those symbols?

Much love, Grandfather

It's exciting that some guy at Princeton may know what these symbols are, but I'm a little freaked out that they want more info. All I really needed was to know what it said. I guess I have to ask Justine to try to nip this in the bud.

From: caitymacfireland@gmail.com
To: justinemiddleford@gmail.com
Subject: RE: That rubbing you took...

Wow, so they think they know what it says but they won't tell you? And now they want more info? Yikes, let's just forget the whole thing Sorry I even got you involved... can we make it die?

And yes, wiping your face with his thumb is totally intimate—he'd only do that if he wanted part of his palm to touch your face too. Clearly: he's so into you.

I wish I could get an instant reply but based on the time difference I know Justine is asleep and I won't get one until tomorrow, which is frustrating.

Deciding to go back into the room to check out the symbols again, I use my rabbit-ears key to open the panel and then enter. I take a seat on the fainting couch to soak it all in, to try to see what the guy from Princeton saw. Mr. Papers goes over to the wall and slowly traces some carvings with his fingers. He seems almost sad; there's none of the excitement he had yesterday. He picks up his origami man and puts the little paper monkey that has fallen to the floor back on its shoulder. I guess he misses his friend in the robe.

I pick up the big antler-handled magnifying glass from the side table, surprised to find that it is much heavier than it looks. When Mr. Papers comes over to see what I'm doing I hold the glass up to my eye and look right at him. Seeing my magnified eyeball, he squawks and jumps back, knocking the side table over.

After a loud crack, the top of the table pops off the base and lands upside down to reveal a small leather-bound book attached to the underside. For a moment I wonder if it's a private journal and I try to resist opening it up; I would hate for someone to read my private journal, even if I were long gone. There's a small title on it, so I move the twine just enough to read it. Embossed in gold and slightly off-kilter like it was stamped by hand are the words: *The Daykeeper's Grimoire*.

I actually happen to know what grimoire means because Maddie La Fond from school carries a journal everywhere that says *Madison's Grimoire* in big swirly letters on the front. One day I made the mistake of asking her what it was and she told me that a grimoire is a book of symbols that work together; she said it's where she keeps track of society's subversive symbolism. Then she went into some big tirade about how the male society has hijacked the term grimoire and made it mean something pagan, blah blah blah. (The blah blah blah part is where I tuned her out for fear of having my brain explode. She's one of those girls who thinks she's ironic by being a punk rocker *and* treasurer of the Knitting Club; when those people with their made-up "complicatedness" go on tirades it makes me want to stick blunt pencils into my eardrums until their mouths stop moving.)

When I open the book I see it is a true grimoire. It's a book of symbols—the symbols that make up the square spirals on the wall. Each page is devoted to one symbol; on the left is a drawing of it and on the right the page is either blank or has the symbol's corresponding sound. The words *As Above, So Below* are written on the first page, in old-fashioned cursive that looks like it was written with the kind of pen that you dip into ink. The paper is old and yellowed around the edges; it feels like it might disintegrate if I crumple it up.

I count only seven decoded symbols. I wonder how long the person who made this book had been working on it to get those seven letters. This is just the kind of thing that Dad would be really good at, but I'm nervous to tell him about it yet. He and Mom would come in and totally take over, like every science project I've ever had. They're geeky in that way that puzzles and projects become all-consuming—I've had more than one teacher ask them to let me do my own work.

Overcome by a flash of inspiration, I realize how I can trick them in to helping me decode this. I take the rubbing that I did last night from my scanner, put another piece of paper over it, and trace the symbols. When I'm done it just looks like weird letters on paper instead of like a rubbing. At the bottom I write out the decoded symbols from the grimoire, then roll it up and secure it with a rubber band.

When I get to the kitchen, Mom and Dad are already there having breakfast. Dad looks up and says, "Well, stranger, what've you been up to? More monkey business?"

Mom flashes a cheesy smile and says, "Although we don't want to *pry, mate*…"

Dad immediately does the end-of-joke, "Badump bumb, chhaaahhh…" noise.

I give them a courtesy smile. "'Primate.' Funny. You guys should take this bit on the road, it's hilarious." This is when I wish I had a brother or sister; I'd love to have someone to roll my eyes with.

"We hardly saw you yesterday," Mom says. "What've you been doing with yourself?"

"Actually, I've been coming up with a puzzle for you," I reply.

"I'm intrigued," Dad says as he sets down his coffee mug. "Do tell."

"Well, your whole job is encryption, right? So you can make credit cards secure online and junk like that?"

"Thanks for qualifying what I do as junk, Caity," he says.

"So how good are you at decoding things?" I ask.

He shrugs and says, "I'd have to go with brilliant."

"He's almost as good as I am," Mom adds.

"Perfect, then you can both work on my puzzle. It will be

like a contest," I say. "I've come up with a set of symbols and I want to see if you guys can decode it."

"That's so sweet, honey," Mom says, looking at me with her head cocked to one side. "What an interesting little project." She is totally underestimating me.

"So here it is. This is one, uh, 'saying' I'd guess you'd call it. I'm giving you a head start with seven of the symbols already decoded on the other sheet of paper."

"Okay, Angus, it's on. I'll make a photocopy of this and we'll see who can finish first. No peeking at the decoded symbols, let's do it blind!"

Did I mention that my parents were competitive?

"Prepare for a crushing defeat, Fiona!" Dad says as he swipes the paper away and runs to the library where the copy machine is, Mom running behind him.

This ought to be interesting, I think to myself. I wonder if either could crack it even *with* the key I provided.

Two

While I'm waiting for my folks to work on the code, hoping they can get one or two words each so I can piece this thing together, I figure I should try to get some more information on the history of Breidablik. I want to find out more about Fergus, the guy who built this castle, and I figure Thomas is a good place to start. Mr. Papers and I track him down out by the pond where he is cleaning out some of the overgrown plants. Thomas is one of those tall, skinny balding guys with a big hook nose who can't help but look like a bird. His khaki pants are tucked into knee-high rubber boots and his checkered wool shirt is, as always, buttoned all the way up.

"Hey Thomas, how's it going?" I ask.

"Hello lassie, hello Papers," he says. "You two ever apart these days?"

"Nope," I say. "It's hard to believe I lived my whole life without a monkey."

He comes over and scratches Mr. Papers under the chin. "Aye, 'tis a treat."

I kick some pebbles around with my toe. "Hey Thomas, what do you know about my super-great-grandfather Fergus?"

"Not much, he died centuries ago. The castle has been through several generations since."

I look over at the tower. "So what's the deal with the tower?"

"Well, towers were built to defend land, so guards could stand atop 'em and see if the enemy was approaching."

"But this was never used as a fort or anything, right?"

Thomas leans on his long-handled net. "Aye, s'pose this tower is purely decorative. Odd thing is, the tower was built *before* the castle, by only Fergus and a Chinese man."

"What was a Chinese man doing here with Fergus two hundred years ago?" I ask.

"Well, Fergus came to the Isle of Huracan after some years exploring in China. He returned with a Chinese man and the two of them built the tower by themselves. Later they had help with the castle, of course."

"And who lived here on the island before him?"

"Nary a soul. Was an uninhabited isle. 'Fore Fergus came here, people thought the place was haunted; no one would set foot on it. 'Twas only after Fergus built the tower and had lived here for several years that anyone else would move here—most people who settled on Huracan were hired to help with the building of the castle."

"I can't believe that he and just one other guy built this tower," I say as Mr. Papers jumps off my shoulder and goes to the edge of the formal pond. He grabs a water cabbage and starts munching on it. I keep forgetting that he's an animal. I guess we all are, come to think of it.

He nods. "Backbreaking work, that. Took them five years of toil."

"So if no one lived here, then no one saw them build it?" I ask.

"Nae, he didn't want help. Folks speculated he had some new method of building from the East or something, but one look at this and you know it's pure Scot. Nothing unusual 'cept for the fact that you can't get to the center. Stairs just wind themselves over what seems to be a solid core."

I nod but don't agree. It just doesn't make sense to build a tower, basically a tall stone box, without any help, unless what's under it is something you don't want anyone else to see. It makes me think that the tower must hide something in its core.

"Can you show me around the tower sometime, Thomas?"

"Not much to it, lassie, just a big staircase that leads to a platform on top."

"I'd still love to see it."

Thomas walks me over to a small wooden door with a rounded top that we both have to duck to walk through it. Inside, cold stone stairs wind their way around the inner square core of the tower, and the only light comes in from the few slats in the wall. Thomas says that in a working tower, these would have been for archers to stand behind so they could shoot out while no one could shoot them back, but here they're just for ventilation. We climb and climb, and finally get to the top, which gives us a 360-degree view of the property. From up here everything looks so small, like a railroad set. The loch is glimmering with sunlight, the forest that surrounds the castle looks tidy and cute, and the low hills are rounded like sand dunes from eons of wind and rain. The dark sea in the distance looks ominous.

"So is there any way to get to the tower from inside the castle?" I ask.

"Nae. Was once, but it's been blocked off for ages," he says. "No reason to use this old tower anymore, 'cept for the view."

I look straight down and see water coming pouring out. "Why's there a stream coming out of the bottom of the tower?"

"'Tis a spring, actually. Overflow from the well," Thomas says. "Feeds the small *burn* that runs around the inside of the gate."

"Isn't it weird to have a moat *inside* the gate?"

Thomas laughs, "Nae, a *burn* is a stream. 'Tisn't more than three feet deep; wouldn't keep much of anybody out now would it? The *burn's* just part of the landscape design."

"So the tower is built over the source of the spring?" I ask.

"Aye, Fergus laid a nice stone canal for it in the foundation, so it just bubbles up from the ground and flows out here." He breathes in sharply from his nose and says, "I best be getting back to work, lassie. You want to come down now?"

Mr. Papers and I follow Thomas down, where we see our cook, Mrs. Findlay, walking to her car. "Got to fetch a lamb from Moody Farm," she yells over to us. "Caity, you and Mr. P want to go for a ride in the country?"

I shrug. "Sure, why not?" There's a lot of the island I don't think I've seen yet.

We're a few miles down the road when Mrs. Findlay casually mentions that her grandson Alex will be at the farm so I can finally meet him. I'd already seen him twice from afar; Thomas pointed him out once while we were driving through the island's one town called Brayne, and then another time I spied him from my window when he came to pick up Mrs. Findlay. He is spectacularly good looking. No, that's too mild. He is the ultimate. The be-all end-all. The yardstick by which all others will forever be measured.

For good reason, I am full of dread. This is the kind of meeting I would spend *a lot* of time preparing for. Hair, clothes, shoes, conversation—all of this should have been carefully planned out over the course of days, weeks maybe, with Justine. I'm just glad Mr. Papers is with me; an origami monkey seems like a natural ice breaker.

Whenever I drive around the island, I realize it's a lot bigger than I think it is. The landscape here is so different from what I'm used to. Other than a few clusters of small forests, the island is mostly just rolling hills of soft grass. When you're driving, it looks like the hills are covered in old felt, with patches torn out to reveal rocks that are the size of baseball diamonds. It seems like the kind of place that yard gnomes would play.

We pull up to an old barn. "Here we are," Mrs. Findlay says.

The barn looks ancient. The bottom half is made with stone and the top is made with wood. There are two enormous doors on the front that are both open. It looks dark inside except for a few bulbs dangling from wires.

"So Mr. Papers and I will wait in the car?" I ask, hoping I can avoid the meeting altogether.

"Heavens no, child. Alex will want to meet you."

I reluctantly follow her to the barn, which smells like animals and wet hay. It sounds gross, but I like it.

Mrs. Findlay yells in a singsong voice, "Al-ex! Al-ex!"

He walks out from behind a stable and I look around for the photographer, it's just too much like a J. Crew photo shoot. You know how they dress the models up all mismatched and rumpled as if they've actually been working outside? It's like that, but for real.

He has dark wavy hair that he keeps flipping back from his beautiful blue eyes that are so pale they have that wolf-like quality. He's a few inches taller than I am and very well built compared to the geeks at the Academy of Cruelties who think two hours with a Wiimote is a workout. His faded checkered shirt hangs open over a red T-shirt, and his worn jeans are tucked into Wellies that come up to his knees. He glances over and smiles at me. His teeth are white and perfect except one of his front teeth crosses over the other by a millimeter—just enough to make him look real instead of like a wax figure of The Perfect Human Male.

"Hello mate, I've been meaning to come 'round to the castle to meet you," he says as he pulls his right hand out of a leather glove and reaches out to shake. I'm embarrassed that my hand is clammy from being nervous. His big square hand is warm and dry. I don't want to let go.

I hadn't even factored in what the Scottish accent would do to the whole look. And yes, it does exactly what you'd expect it to. Times ten.

"Nice to meet you," I say, my voice coming out more childlike than I'd intended.

That's all I've got. I've already run out of things to say.

Mr. Papers starts bobbing up and down on my shoulder with excitement. Alex reaches in and his hand brushes my shoulder as he goes to pet Mr. Papers. I completely stiffen.

"Gram mentioned what good mates you and Mr. Papers are. If he's so fond of you, that's all the recommendation I need," he says.

I just smile like an idiot.

"You reckon the lamb's ready, son?" Mrs. Findlay asks, saving me from myself.

"'Tis, 'tis," he says. "I'll just go and get it."

When he walks off I look over at Mrs. Findlay, who has a grin on her face like she knows exactly what's going on in my head. I'm sure I am turning bright red.

"You two should get to know each other—if your parents decide to stay past the summer, at least you'll have a mate when school starts," she casually says to me.

"Great." I'm trying to seem low-key, but the way I am fidgeting with Mr. Papers is a dead giveaway. I was against staying in Scotland any longer than the summer until this moment.

Alex comes out of the barn straining to carry a box that looks larger than he is. God, he's beautiful *and* strong.

Mrs. Findlay opens the back of the Land Rover and Alex puts the big box in. "Well, he was a good lamb," he says as he pats the top.

I realize what's in the box was once a living creature and before I can stop myself I make a gasping noise, like a drain that's suddenly become unclogged. Alex looks at me like I'm the prissiest girl ever born and says, "Nothing to fret over, he'll be as useful on your plate as he was in the field—"

"Oh, yeah. I'm sure he'll taste great!" I say, not wanting to appear wimpy.

"Well, 'twas a pleasure to meet you, Caity." He shakes my hand one more time, then reaches up to scratch Mr. Papers' chin and says, "Bye mate."

All I can think to say is, "You too. See you around." Ugh. What a brilliant conversationalist.

As we drive off it takes all my willpower not to turn around and look.

The minute we get back to the castle, I have to go to my room and inspect myself with fresh eyes.

Full-Length Mirror Report/Top to Bottom: My curls are wild today, skipped the defrizzer because I didn't think anyone but a monkey would see me. Subtract three points. Note to self: Must use hair smoother every day! My hair is pretty shiny, though, from the great well water, and my shade of auburn looks good in direct sunlight, add a point. Freckles will always be a problem, subtract a point. Note: See if Mom's face powder tones them down a bit. Fortunately I'm addicted to this pink mint lip gloss, so the lips look alright. Add a point. Teeth are brushed, bonus points. I happened to put a snug cashmere v-neck sweater over my white T-shirt because I was chilly this morning, add two points. But I'm wearing these stupid cropped jeans that make me look even more freakishly tall than I am. Total mistake. Subtract 2,000 points. Note: Throw them away already!

I hear a knock and Mom pops her head in the door. "Got time for a chat, Caity?"

"Sure, Mom. What's up?"

She comes up behind me, wraps her arms around my waist, and looks in the mirror. Our similarities are only in our coloring: the auburn hair, green eyes, and pale skin. She came away unscathed by freckles and curly hair. They say I get the freckles from the Mac Fireland side, along with everything else. It's true; if I pulled my hair back until it hurts and then put on white makeup, I'd look surprisingly similar to all the pale women in the big paintings in the hall.

Mom lets go of my waist, turns me to face her, and says, "Your Dad and I have been busy on that code you made up. Did you just do that since you've been here?"

"Yep. What do you think?" I ask as I look over toward my bed. It's hard to look your mom in the eyes and not tell the truth.

"It's extraordinary, Caity. Neither of us had any luck without the key; now your Dad is trying it *with* the key. The whole thing is now in the computer; he's created a program that's working on decoding it."

"Oh, letting the computer do your work, huh?" I say, trying to lighten the mood since Mom is taking this way too seriously.

"So how did you come up with that code?"

I shrug. "I don't know, it was just something I was playing around with."

This is not enough. She's looking at me like there is more for me to explain.

"Why, what's the big deal?" I ask.

"Well, your dad and I were wondering if you think maybe you'd like to try a boarding school, a world-class school that would challenge you in new ways."

Suddenly it feels like work to keep my heart inside my chest. This is not what I expected. "What are you talking about?" I ask.

"The San Francisco Academy of Humanities is quite good, but you never produced anything of this caliber there," she says, her eyes looking straight into me like only a mom's can. "This code just shows an incredible aptitude for creativity, problem solving, and logic. Obviously you are a very, very bright girl. We always knew it, but this just blew us away."

I pull back from her intensity and go sit on the edge of my bed. "No, Mom. I'm fine where I am, honestly." I definitely don't want to be shipped off somewhere and I definitely don't want to have to live up to something I'm not, and believe me, I'm no genius! Clearly it's time to apply some parental guilt.

"You really want to ship me farther off, totally *alone*?" I ask. "Isn't it enough that you dragged me to the middle of nowhere, away from my entire life, for this bed and breakfast fantasy?"

"We've decided to go with 'Inn'," she replies.

I've thrown her so far off subject that even I don't know where she landed.

"What?" I ask.

"After looking at hundreds of bed and breakfast websites, we've decided to be an Inn instead. I refuse to hang frilly curtains and have lace bed skirts and striped wallpaper with cat borders. Inn sounds much more distinguished."

"Did you guys make the decision to stay without *me* in on the conversation? You just decided to stay and then ship me off?"

Mom comes over and sits next to me and puts her hand on my knee in the universal "consolation" pose. Not a good sign. Decisions have been made.

"Nothing has been written in stone yet," she says. "We're thinking that if we get this set up as an Inn, we may be able to hire someone to run it. Then we'll go back to the city, but still be able to keep this property in the family."

"But I'm *not* going to boarding school," I say.

"I know it's hard for a girl as independent as you to hear this, but it's really up to your dad and me. *We* decide what's in your best interest."

Mom never does this kind of parental domination. I feel like I've been slapped.

"Is this all just because of that code? It's seriously not that big of a deal."

"Yes, Caity, it is that big of a deal," she says as she puts her arm around my shoulders. "Look, we just don't want your brain to get squishy because you're not challenged."

"How about if I do some private study with you or Dad every night—in addition to any homework? You guys can teach me how to crack codes and stuff and—"

"I'll discuss it with Dad," she says, interrupting my spiel. As she gets up from my bed she adds, "But we are quite serious about this. Once we've made a decision about the Inn, we'll be better able to plan for your academics."

My head drops. She lifts my chin and looks at me with her head tilted. "To be honest, Caity, I didn't know you'd feel so strongly about staying with us. I'm flattered."

She kisses me on the cheek and turns to leave.

THREE

The next morning I start my computer to see if I have any new email. I see Justine is online so I IM her:

Caitym: Justine-u will not believe the boy I met yesterday. straight off CK billboard.

Justinem: ooo, pix?

Caitym: No, but will take covert one soon. he's the grandson of r cook.

Justinem: r age?

Caitym: 1 year older, but out of reach. way 2 cute 2 like me.

Justinem: NO!

Caitym: howz David von Hotnik?

Justinem: kinda over him.

Caitym: ??? What about the thumb move?

Justinem: Watching him struggle w/basic chem is total turnoff

Caitym: understandable. Hey did u get my last email about that rubbing?

Justinem: was just going to email u—Gramps called me about it last nite, had 2 tell him it was frm u

Caitym: did he tell u what it says?

Justinem: no, just said this guy Tenzo is all in a froth
about it.
Caitym: Y?
Justinem: Thinks it's a "major discovery" or something.
u have 2 tell me where u took it.
Caitym: did u already tell him where I live now?
Justinem: Gramps already knew, mom had told him
back when your parents first decided to go. anyway,
g-pa might email u
Caitym: *freaking out!*
Justinem: What's the big deal? r u mad?
Caitym: No, no—totally not mad, I'm the 1 who asked
for help
Justinem: it sucks here without u
Caitym: tell me about it. my only friend is a monkey.
omg, that looks so pathetic when it is typed out.
Justinem: god I would LOVE a monkey of my own.
anyone who says they wouldn't is lying.
Caitym: ha! tru. Hey gotta run, sleep well my friend. xo
Justinem: xo right back

God, I miss Justine. I look at the little framed photograph
on my desk of the two of us all dressed up to go to the Winter Dance at Cruelties. Justine is looking very elegant in her
floor-length red velvet sheath dress with her spotless skin and
long, super-shiny black hair that is so much her trademark,
you always expect to see a little ™ dangling from it. She is
smiling with both her mouth and her big brown eyes. I am
next to her in a dress I regret, a green silk number that sort
of poofs out at the bottom the same way my curly hair does.
When my hair is wet it's almost to the middle of my back, but
when it dries it curls up to my shoulders, despite all the goop
I put on it to make it more relaxed. I'd played soccer outside
that day and the winter sun had drawn out my freckles but

hadn't tanned my skin. Justine can look like a grown woman in the right clothes, but even when I am older, my freckles will probably still make me look like a child.

I put down the photo and snap from my past life to this new, stranger one when I see an email from Dr. Stephen Middleford, Justine's grandfather.

From: stephen@professormiddleford.com
To: caitymacfireland@gmail.com
Subject: Ancient text

Dear Caitrina,

This is Justine's grandfather, Stephen. Justine sent me a very interesting rubbing of an ancient artifact that has a few of us here at Princeton quite excited. Dear girl, could you please share with me the story of how and where you came upon this? You are quite astute to recognize its importance and to take a rubbing. Well done!

Best, Stephen Middleford

I feel sick. Both my stomach and my head hurt like after watching one of those IMAX flying movies. I should've stuck to having my parents try to crack this thing, now I have to make up something for him. Based on the time difference, I have a few hours before I need to email back. I should go see what Dad thinks about the code first.

When I get to the kitchen, Dad is sitting at the table in the same clothes he was wearing yesterday, looking rumpled. "What's up, Dad?" I ask.

He looks up from his coffee and shakes his head.

"Well, my little cipher, I've been up all night working on cracking your code."

"Oh yeah? Any luck?" I ask, trying to seem nonchalant.

"How did you come up with that? Did you crib that from a World War I code book or something?"

I avoid answering by asking, "Have you translated a word yet?"

"A single word? Do you know who I am? I'll have the whole thing done this morning! Got the software program I created working on a new angle."

"Really?" I say, realizing that I don't want him to know what the whole thing says before *I* do, I just wanted some words to piece together.

"Unfortunately I can't stay awake another minute. I'm going to bed. Mom was up all night with me, so we'll both be napping for a few hours."

Other kids may find it weird that their parents pull all-nighters, but it's nothing new to me. Standard computer-nerd behavior—if it's not coding it's gaming.

He pats my head and walks out of the kitchen. When I'm sure he's gone, I eat my oatmeal as quickly so I can get to the library. When I leave the kitchen, Mr. Papers looks at me like I'm abandoning him, but I don't want him to see this.

I have to do something drastic.

Dad has a whole wall of computers and servers glowing and humming. It looks totally out of place in this old-style library, with all the dark wood, musty books, and oil paintings. I find the screen that has lines and lines and lines of symbols quickly scrolling. The screen next to it has what I'm looking for: a few random words. This has to be the code being cracked.

I go back into the hallway and stand right outside the door to the library. From here I can still see the screen that's scrolling, and this way if anyone comes by I can just say I was heading up to my room. I stand watching from outside the doorway for nearly half an hour, with my entire body tense. This is the closest thing to Pilates I've done in weeks.

Finally the scrolling screen stops, so I figure it's done. I run in, print out the words, and quickly shove the paper in my pocket. I am totally shaking but force myself to remain calm. I hit the escape key on the machine that was decoding, make a note of the program's name (littlegenius.exe, ugh!), close it down, and go to the directory to find it.

Then I delete it. I delete the whole decoding program that Dad wrote from scratch. Then I empty the trash to cover my tracks.

I immediately feel like I'm going to throw up. This is the worst, most devious thing I've ever done. I'll rot in hell, that's for sure.

Now I have to make it all look legitimate. I go to the little shed where Mr. Papers used to live, where all the fuse boxes are. I find the one marked "Kitchen/Dining/Library" and switch it off. I hear a little pop and wonder for a moment if that is my brain exploding.

I take the long way back to the castle so no one will see me. When I walk into the dark kitchen, Mrs. Findlay is standing by the sink looking out the window.

"Caity, have you seen Thomas?" she asks.

"No, I haven't," I say casually. "Why do you have all the lights off?"

"Seems we've had a power outage. I need to find Thomas."

"I'll go look," I say, grabbing Mr. Papers and heading outside.

I see Thomas pull up in the Land Rover and I wave at him with both hands, air-traffic-controller style. He hops out of the car and says, "What's the matter, lass?"

"Something happened to the electricity," I say. "There's no power on the first floor and I don't want to wake Dad because he's been up all night."

"I reckon it's just a fuse. Nothing to worry about." He points to the shed and says, "Let me show you where the fuse box is in case this happens again."

"Fuse box?" I say.

"Oh, you big city girls wouldn't know about that now would you?"

I just shrug.

Thomas leads me to the shed and shows me the fuse box. I ask all sorts of dumb questions to make it seem like I've never seen one before. I'm scared about how all this lying is coming so easily to me and wonder at what stage it's labeled "pathological" because I might not be too far off.

My hand is on the piece of paper in my pocket and I can't stop playing with it and wondering if Dad was really able to decode those symbols into something readable. If so, what could it possibly say?

When Thomas finishes his fuse box lesson, I casually walk away until I am out of his sight and then I run as fast as

I can into the castle and up the stairs. Mr. Papers is jumping banisters to keep up.

At my desk, I lay the paper out flat to read it. There is no punctuation, just a string of words. I say them out loud as I read them to see if it makes any sense, "glory great the in usher will Caitrina." I stop at my name.

How could my name be in this thing carved on the wall? Maybe it was some kind of mistake. I read on, "named one but story the begin would who Fergus me tis table eastern far a round me to told fable prescient the in writ is as." Makes no sense, it's just a jumble of words.

I look at the part with my name again: "Glory great the in usher will Caitrina." I turn it upside down—that's what I do with word jumbles and it always works, the letters always seem to sort themselves out better that way. Then it becomes clear: it's backwards!

Caitrina will usher in the great glory.

That's it! It's just been input backwards, from the outside in instead of the inside out. I write the whole thing out the other direction and break it where it rhymes:

> *As is writ in the prescient fable*
> *Told to me 'round a far Eastern table*
> *'Tis me, Fergus who would begin the story*
> *But one named Caitrina will usher in the glory*

I find it hard to catch my breath, like when you stick your head out of a moving car window. How could this be? Is it a joke? I look all around the room trying to see if I'm on a hidden camera show or something. I reread it at least ten times to make sense of it.

Before this, the biggest shock of my life was being voted to high-level student government at school. The Academy of Humanities does not allow campaigning, so they spring the vote on you at an unscheduled assembly. They explain the qualities the person needs for each position and you just do a write-in; Justine and I were beyond surprised that I was voted not just Student Senator, but Speaker of the House! I mean, I didn't even nominate *myself.* Who knew the whole school thought I was "independent, fair, and someone people would listen to"?

And now my name comes up again, here in this poem.

Well, now I *have* to decode the rest. But after deleting Dad's program, I'm not sure what I can do to get him to decode the others. Maybe I blew it too early. God, I'm just not thinking ahead at all!

I need to get out of this room but I don't want to be downstairs when Dad realizes the blown fuse crashed his program. I'm jittery and don't know what to do with myself, so I pick up my sketchbook and start drawing because that always calms me and makes me lose track of time; sometimes I'll sketch for three hours and not even know that any time has passed. I decide to draw the entire carved panel over the secret door.

Mrs. Findlay's voice jolts me out of my sketching coma when she announces afternoon tea on the intercom. I hope that Dad is already downstairs, has discovered the "power outage," and has cooled off.

I pat my shoulder and Mr. Papers jumps on. He tugs at my ear lobe a little and squawks.

"We'll play after tea. You gotta stay cool, my friend."

Stopping outside the kitchen door, I crane my neck to listen to Mom and Dad talking.

"Just be grateful that you didn't lose any real work, Angus."

"But I was so close!" he says, slapping his hands on the table. "I had it, I know I did—we're talking a matter of *moments*..."

"Tell me the angle and we can work on it together," Mom says.

I shuffle my feet as I walk in so they'll hear me. Dad is slumped over a cup of coffee and Mom has her hand on his back. They both look up. "What's the matter?" I ask.

"We had a power outage this morning and your dad lost everything he was working on."

"Oh, no!" I say with horror. "I knew the power went off, but I totally forgot about the computers. Are you going to get in trouble at work?"

Dad shakes his head. "No, I didn't lose any work. But I did lose the program I wrote to decode your symbols. Fried. Disappeared completely. I don't know what happened—I must not have compiled and saved it correctly."

"Bummer!" I say, maybe with too much drama.

"I was so close. Now I have to start over and rewrite the program."

"Dad, don't worry about it. It was just a dumb game. I'll tell you what it said."

"That's not the point. The point is that it was a brilliant set of symbols you came up with, and I worked really hard on it and now it's all gone."

Thomas walks in and Mrs. Findlay takes him a cup of tea. "Well, you should be proud of Caity," he says to my parents. "She learned all about fuses today, didn't you Caity?"

"Um, yeah," I say, grabbing a piece of shortbread and stuffing it into my mouth.

"Caity has always been obsessed with the fuse box," Mom says proudly. "We have a vacation house at Lake Tahoe, and ever since she was a little tyke she's insisted on being the one to turn the fuses on and off when we come and go."

Thomas looks at me. "That right, lassie? And here I was thinking I taught you something new—"

"Oh you did, Thomas. It's all very different here in Scotland…" I can feel my face turning red and hot.

"Yes, yes. Of course," Thomas says, looking at me funny. He absolutely knows I'm lying.

"I'm not feeling well," I say. "Do you mind if I go upstairs?"

Mom puts her hand on my forehead. "You do seem a bit flushed, Caity. Need anything?"

"Nah, I'll be okay." As I leave I say, "Sorry about all your hard work, Dad."

"Thanks honey," he replies and Mom says, "I'll come check on you later."

Once in my room, I draw all the bed curtains and crash out to escape my new world of lies and deceit.

FOUR

knock on the door wakes me. I look at the window and see the sun is setting; I must have slept for hours. "Come on in," I say, expecting it to be Mom bringing up dinner for me after the fake sickness thing I pulled.

A stranger's voice says, "Caity? You in here?"

All of a sudden I place it—Alex.

"Um, yeah, just a minute," I say as I pat down my hair and work the sheet marks off my face. I open the door to see Alex holding a tray with food on it.

"They're having dinner down there and Gran asked me to bring yours up to you."

"That's nice of you, thanks. Want to put it on that table by the two chairs?"

"Aye," he says as he makes his way to the table.

"Is it really dinner time? I can't believe I slept that long."

He raises his eyebrows and says, "They said you've been sleeping all afternoon."

"Why does it matter to them how long I nap?" I snap,

instantly regretting using the word "nap" because it makes me sound like a toddler. "Sorry," I say, "didn't mean to shoot the messenger."

Alex waves it off. "I was eavesdropping, and just 'twixt you and me, they all think you've a touch of culture shock and that's why you're sleeping so much."

"Really?" I'm as surprised that they're talking about me as I am that he said "'twixt."

"Do you?" he asks.

"Do I what?"

"Have culture shock?"

"No!" I say with a laugh. "It's not like we moved to Mongolia. We all speak the same language and eat the same food. Except for that weird pork-and-beans-in-the-morning thing."

Alex laughs. "Aye, I didn't take you for the delicate constitution type."

Oh, so he thinks I'm not delicate? Of course, how could an Amazon girl be delicate? I hate those cropped jeans!

Alex walks over to the fireplace. "It's cold. Would you like me to start a fire for you?"

Anything to keep him here longer, I think. "Wow, that would be great," I say, turning away to wipe my mouth with the back of my hand, checking for any wayward nap drool.

Looking over at my digital camera, I'm tempted to take a picture of him as he builds a kindling teepee around a wad of newspaper. He lights the wood and the smell of smoke rises in the air and mingles with the shepherd's pie.

Taking a seat in the leather chair by the fire, I say, "So are you over here helping Thomas with something?"

"Aye, he wanted me to take a look at the fuse box."

"Are you an electrician?"

He smiles. "Nae, but my dad was. I worked by his side for five summers before he died."

"Oh, God, I'm so sorry…" Way to ruin the mood, Caity.

"That's okay, I like talking about him. 'Twas nice to sit and talk with your father, too."

"You talked to my dad?" I ask.

"They invited me to stay for dinner."

"Oh," I say, terrified that Mom pulled out naked baby pictures of me or something.

He gestures to the fireplace and says, "Well, the fire's going. Need anything else?"

I try to think of something to need so he will stay longer but I can't come up with anything. I shrug. "I guess not. Thanks so much for bringing up dinner."

He bows and makes a sweeping gesture with his arm. "'Twas a pleasure," he says, as if he's addressing the Queen. I smile and feel warm from the inside out, like hot chocolate on a frosty day.

Alex leaves and I daintily eat my shepherd's pie by the fire, pretending that he is sitting in the chair next to me warming his feet by the flames. When I'm finished eating and my Alex haze fades, I remember I have to answer Dr. Middleford's email. By now deception is second nature, so an answer comes to me right away. I sit down at my computer and open up my mail.

From: caitymacfireland@gmail.com
To: stephen@professormiddleford.com
Subject: RE: Ancient text

Dear Dr. Middleford,

Thanks for your email! It's nice to hear from you. I really
appreciate you taking a look at that rubbing for me,
but I'm afraid I might have wasted your time. I talked
to our groundskeeper Thomas about it and he told me
the story. Apparently the guy who carved it was crazy.
He had caught something as a child that messed up
his brain. Anyway, my super-great-grandfather Fergus,
the one who built the castle, was really nice and
hired him even though he wasn't all there. He just set
him free and let him carve, so these spirals are just
random decorations. I'm really sorry that I even got you
involved. I know you are very busy and I feel really silly
about this. Please give my apology to your friend Dr.
Tenzo as well. Have a fun summer!

Sincerely,
Caity

The minute I hit the send button I see that Justine has
come online and I IM her:

Caitym: hey! what r u doing?
Justinem: freaking out
Caitym: Y?
Justinem: David von Studley's mom called my mom and
  asked her if I would help tutor him in chem.
Caitym: Just like an arranged marriage…
Justinem: ha! but he is hopeless
Caitym: he's good in English, what's the prob?
Justinem: doesn't get science. Tragic. did u email
  Gramps?

Caitym: oh, yeah. Sorry about all that. I don't know
exactly what's going on with it, I'll fill u in when I
figure it out. sorry to get your grandfather involved.

Justinem: well, I guess Tenzo found a tie to some lost
language or something.

Caitym: No!!! must be a mistake.

Justinem: oh. ok, whatever. howz jcrew?

Caitym: HE BROUGHT DINNER TO MY ROOM
TONIGHT!

Justinem: WHAT???????

Caitym: yep, and he made me a fire and everything.

Justinem: romance^2 !!!!!!!!!

Caitym: can u imagine any guy from Cruelties doing
anything remotely gentlemanly?

Justinem: no! David won't even help me wash the chem
lab beakers! like that's "woman's work" or something.
u must send pix.

Caitym: will work on covert pix. not sure when I will see
him next. talk tomorrow?

Justinem: for me it IS tomorrow. or is it yesterday?

Caitym: I think u r behind-I just lived the day u are
waking up to.

Justinem: brain freeze.

Caitym: ha! nitey nite, J.

A tie to a lost language? You've got to be kidding me.
I wish I had known this before I'd emailed Dr. Middleford;
now they'll know I was making all that up about the insane
carver.

———

In the morning I awaken to Mr. Papers thumping on my
chest with his tiny fists. God, he's cute. I scratch his little
head, which always makes his legs twitch.

Dad walks in with a cup of hot chocolate. "Mr. Papers was worried about you—he hadn't seen you since teatime yesterday," he says.

Mr. Papers hops down, runs over to the carved wall, and tries to move the panel. "Hey, Mr. Papers, careful! That's an antique!" I say as I run over and pull him away, terrified that Dad might see the panel move.

"The more I know this monkey, the more I think he may answer you back one of these days," Dad says.

"That would be the ultimate!"

"Then there'd be no difference between us and them. It would be just like having a really small, really ugly friend."

"He's not ugly!"

Dad laughs, "Right. He's as cute as that young man who brought you dinner last night."

"Okay, maybe not that cute..."

"Nice guy, too. Did you know he's a bit of a math prodigy? He's doing some interesting work, has real potential. His old computer is slowing down his progress so I might give him one of mine; I could use an upgrade anyway."

"That's nice of you," I say, wondering how Alex could be that beautiful *and* be smart.

"Well, you should hear about the computer he's working on. It's all so... 1992 around here."

Suddenly I worry that if Alex becomes friendly with Dad, he'll think of me more as a sister than the potential love of his life. I know I'm getting ahead of myself, but a girl has to plot these things out. "Is Alex going to be *your* Mr. Papers, Dad?" I ask.

Dad looks confused. "What do you mean?"

"Are you adopting him?"

"Heavens no, Caity. I'm just offering him an old thing that I'd be getting rid of anyway."

I shrug. "Okay. That's cool."

"Glad I have your approval," he says, as if he's irritated. "Terrible tragedy about his dad. Did you know he was killed right here at the castle?"

"What? He was *killed*?"

"Yeah, apparently looters came by one night, turned off all the power, and went looking for valuables. Hamish hid away and was able to call Alex's dad, who came right over. He caught them by surprise and they shot him, and fled. They didn't even end up taking anything."

"That's horrible! Murdered right here in this castle?"

Dad nods and says, "So don't start giving me grief about supporting that poor boy's math habit."

"Sorry," I say, feeling like a schmuck.

He pats my knee. "Get dressed and come down for breakfast."

When he leaves, I quickly check my email and there's one from Justine's grandfather. Nervous about whether or not he believed my story, I just stare at it in my inbox for a minute before I open it.

From: stephen@professormiddleford.com
To: caitymacfireland@gmail.com
Subject: RE: RE: Ancient text

Dear Caitrina, Thank you for your email. I completely understand how one can get overly excited with a new discovery. I sent your email explanation on to Dr. Tenzo, the professor who thought he recognized the symbols. After examining the facsimile of the rubbing for some time, he said that this was not actually ancient Drocane script as he had thought. I beg you though, don't be discouraged by this, my budding etymologist!

Best,
Stephen Middleford

I'm so relieved that he and this Tenzo guy believed me! It's nice to have them off my case. Now I can concentrate on how I'm going to get those other spirals decoded. There's really no other way: I have to have Dad rewrite his program and decode another set. Once that happens, I can get a copy of the new program and decode the rest myself. I can't believe I didn't just copy the program before I deleted it—clearly I'm not cut out for espionage.

I trace another one of the rubbings exactly as I had done with the first one that I gave them. I roll it up and put it in the pocket of my "I ♥ SF" sweatshirt, then run down to the kitchen. Fortunately my parents are still there.

When I walk in, Mom gets up and gives me a kiss on the cheek. "Feeling better?"

"Totally. Must have been overtired or something," I say. Mrs. Findlay brings over a large Scottish breakfast, which means the eggs are barely cooked, there's lots of greasy sausage, and there's a big pile of pork and beans sitting unapologetically next to a broiled tomato.

I wish I'd said, "Just granola today, please," right when I'd walked through the door.

"Well, Caity, so much has happened since you pulled your Rip Van Winkle," Mom says.

"Really? What?"

"We have business!" she replies. "A small group of retired Berkeley alumni is coming next week to scout the place for a trip they might offer through the Alumni Association. Won't that be a riot?"

"Not sure if 'riot' is the word I'd use," I say. I've kind of enjoyed cruising around the castle without anyone around and I don't know if I want to share it. At least it's old people that are coming; they probably won't get around much.

"And when it rains it pours. Uncle Li is coming, too," Dad says.

"No way!" I scream. "That's so great!"

Uncle Li is my parents' Feng Shui Master, whom they've known forever. Years ago he'd tracked Mom down and had her crack an old Chinese safe for him and they've been good friends ever since. Even though he's a million years old, I think he's really cool. He has a way of explaining things that makes you just get it, and I never feel like he's talking to me like I'm beneath him just because I'm not an adult. We hung out a lot back in San Francisco.

"He's planning to stay awhile and help us get things arranged," Mom says. "He's done a couple castles in France and one in Spain, but he's excited to do one in Scotland. He says islands produce a much different energy than the mainland does."

Suddenly a guy I've never seen walks by the kitchen window. He looks like a business cherub; he's got the round, babyish face with rosy cheeks and pink lips that cherubs have but he's all business, packed into a black suit that's too small for him.

"Who's that?" I ask as I point to the window.

"Oh, that's Barend Schlacter," Mom says, "from the Scottish Tourist Board. They do mandatory inspections before you can open an Inn."

"'Barend Schlacter' doesn't sound very Scottish."

"He's Bavarian, actually. Seems very thorough. He'll be poking around so be really, really nice to him."

"Yep, the nicer you are, the more stars we get," Dad adds.

"How do you get rated before you even open?" I ask.

"Who knows?" Mom says. "We just do what we're told. We don't want to be the rude Americans who push back on everything. All we know is that he has to spend twenty-four hours on site and we're not supposed to bother him as he walks around inspecting the place."

"So how many guests will be here in all?" I ask.

"Well, there are four from Berkeley, right?" Dad says. "Plus Li, so that's five—"

"Oh, and don't forget that other guy who just emailed this morning," Mom says. "The professor from Princeton..."

"Did you advertise on that alumni website too?" I ask.

"No, not sure how he found us," Mom says. She turns to Dad "Honey, did you ask Professor Tenzo how he found the Inn?"

FIVE

id you say Tenzo?" I ask, trying to keep my voice steady.
Both my parents look at me. Dad says, "Yes, why? Have
you heard of him?"

"No. I mean, I don't know. I think maybe I've heard Justine's grandpa mention him."

"That's right, Middleford teaches at Princeton too," Dad says. "Well, we've got a blueprint of the castle in the library and we'll be figuring out where everyone will stay later today if you'd like to help."

Dad's mention of the library reminds me of what I was coming downstairs to do, so I excuse myself to go to the bathroom.

Walking quickly to the library, I try to piece this all together. My heart is pounding so hard I'm afraid they might just hear it. Why would Tenzo come all the way to the middle-of-nowhere Scotland if not to track down the rubbing? And why would he lie to Justine's grandfather, saying that it was "of no significance" as he put it?

The library is dark except for the eerie blue glow from all the computer screens, like a snowy Tahoe street before the sun comes up. I search for the piece of paper that I gave Mom and Dad the day before yesterday, the one with the symbols on it. I need to swap it with the new one so when Dad rewrites his decoding program he will start decoding this new set of symbols instead of the first one.

I pull the sheet of symbols out of my pocket and make a copy for Mom. I then exchange the original for the one on Dad's desk. Now they'll assume that this spiral was the same one that they were already working on; since they have to re-scan it anyway they'll never know the difference. I run up to Mom's study and switch out that copy of the symbols as well.

I stop in my room to burn the first tracing and its copy, trying not to think about my deception as I watch the paper turn into tiny glowing flakes that float like stars up the chimney.

When I get back to the kitchen, Mom and Dad have already left. Mrs. Findlay is busy cleaning up and has put my breakfast on the big stove, this thing called an Aga. There are four ovens below and eight burners on top and the gas is always on so all you have to do is lift the covers off the burners and turn them up a little. Above it is a copper stove hood that is as big as a VW bug and when the fan is turned on it sounds just as loud. This would all seem strange in any normal kitchen, but this one is the size of our whole house in San Francisco. There are two fireplaces in the kitchen and a huge table in the center—bigger than a public library table—with two long benches on either side. The sink is the size of a small bathtub and every inch of the floors and walls is covered in pale green tile, which is so retro it's hip again.

I pick up my breakfast, happy to see that the Aga has taken my eggs from gelatinous to over-easy and has dried out some of the greasy sausage.

"You ready for all the guests to arrive, Mrs. Findlay?" I ask as I sit to eat.

"Can hardly wait, dear. Have been planning the menus carefully," she says, drying her hands on her apron. Mrs. Findlay has bright red hair and is even taller than I am. She's not fat or anything but she definitely has a man's build; her wrists are thick, her hands are huge, and she has really broad shoulders. She wears these striped dresses with buttons all the way down the front like a man's shirt, and always has an apron on, like it's a permanent fixture. She had worked here before, years ago, so she was the only cook comfortable with having Mr. Papers stay in the little wood cubby by the far fireplace.

Mr. Papers loves her. In fact, the first time she came over to meet us (after two other cooks declined the job because they couldn't handle having a monkey living in a tiny tile cubby hole above the firewood in the far end of the kitchen) he hopped on her shoulders and started pushing on her bun like a kid with a jack-in-the-box.

"They'll love whatever you cook, that's for sure," I say.

"Aw, thanks Caity," she says. "You know, I'm going to ask your parents if they'd like to hire Alex to serve when your guests arrive."

"Really?" I ask, almost before she even finishes her sentence.

"Aye. Would do you good to have a mate your age around the castle too, methinks."

"People in this century still say 'methinks'?" I joke, trying to hide my excitement at the thought of having Alex here every day.

"Well, *methinks* you spend too much time alone, or with that little scoundrel," she replies as she points to Mr. Papers, tucked away in his cubby eating a big piece of honeydew. It looks like he has an enormous green smile.

"There you are!" Mom says, walking into the kitchen.

I'm hit with a brilliant idea. "Hey Mom, remember I agreed to do a private study with you or Dad? Maybe I should start that now, during the summer."

"What's this about private study?" Dad asks.

"Instead of being shipped off to boarding school, I told Mom that I'd do some kind of independent study with you guys. And this whole code-cracking thing seems interesting, so maybe you could show me how you went about decoding my symbols. You know, if it wouldn't interfere too much with your work—"

"I love it! Let's start this morning," he says.

"You really think you could decode it today?" I ask, excited at the prospect. "Don't you have to rewrite the whole program?" I'm twitching hard about Dr. Tenzo showing up here and the more I can find out before he arrives, the better.

"No problem," Dad replies, cracking his knuckles. "I was *so* close last time. C'mon, let's go."

Back in the library, Dad doesn't realize that the paper he holds is the one I just put there this morning. He scans in the symbols, separates them so each is a unique piece of data, and then launches into this spiel about writing code to decode. I'd say that I'm an above-average techie for my age, but this is beyond me. I get it only enough to know when to say *Really?* and *Wow!* and *Oh, I see.* Which makes for a long few hours.

After he starts the program, Dad gets up and stretches and says it could take minutes or hours, so if I have anything else I'd like to do I might as well go do it. I tell him I'm here to learn so I'll stick it out. He leaves to shower and get dressed for the day.

Settling in, I open up solitaire on a separate computer and play a few games. After awhile, from the corner of my eye, I see some action on the screen next to me. A word appears, and then another and another. It's like watching popcorn popping. Sometimes two will come at once, then there will be a lull and then another will pop up. Finally the cursor starts blinking like it's finished. It pretty random and doesn't say anything about me in it so I figure it's okay for Dad to see. I print out a copy for me and slip it in my pocket just as he comes back.

"You did it Dad. It worked!" I say as I point to the screen.

"Wow—faster than I thought! God, I'm good." He sits down, reads it, and says, "Oh nice, it's in verse. Let me break it correctly." Then he puts it in to four lines and reads it out loud.

> *Know chi is in everything, through and between*
> *Yet despite its great power it remains quite unseen*
> *Its quality transforms as we tread backwards 'round*
> *To the great year's ores we are fastened and bound*

He looks at me with a big smile on his face. "This is so cool Caity, I like that you did this in rhyme. And I think I recognize what you're referencing!"

"Really?" I say, both stunned and hopeful. "You recognize this?"

"Let me take it to Mom. I'll bet she can place it. She really is smarter than me, you know," he says with a wink as he prints out a copy. "But seriously, don't ever tell her I told you that."

I follow Dad, who is whistling the theme to *Doctor Who*, as he runs up to Mom's study. Her feet are up on her desk and she's reading *Safe and Vault Technician Monthly*, Barbie leg in hand.

"Fiona, take a look at this," he says proudly as he holds up the printout. "I still got it! I rewrote the program, decoded the symbols, and almost have the content pinned down."

Mom reads it and starts working the Barbie knee. "Well, the first part about chi is obviously about dark matter, the energy of the universe that remains unseen. Then this second part, '*Its quality transforms as we tread backwards 'round, To the great year's ores we are fastened and bound*' refers to the concept that the rise and fall of these ages are caused by the Earth's wobble backwards through the constellations, also known as the 'Precession of the Equinoxes' or, as Plato called it, The Great Year—and the seasons of The Great Year are represented by metals, or 'ores' as Caity so poetically put it."

"That's it! The Golden Age, Bronze Age, Silver Age, and all that," Dad says.

I don't understand a word Mom said but she looks mighty pleased with herself.

Dad whispers to me, "What did I tell you about your mother?"

"Yep, a certifiable genius," I say, hoping they won't ask me any questions right now.

Mom grabs my chin. "Look at you, studying Plato and astronomy!"

"So are we all finished with our first lesson?" I say, totally baffled by all of this.

Dad shakes my hand and says, "Yes, and you graduate with honors, my friend."

"St. Godehard's in Austria is still accepting prodigies for fall term," Mom yells after me.

"Great," I yell back. "Then I'm sure you'll get in."

I create a protected Word file (password: bigfatliar) and type both decoded spirals in it. I'm shocked that my parents recognized any of this, and now I have to find some info on this stuff in case they grill me on it. I search for "Plato" and "Golden Age" and find millions of mentions. In my sketchbook I jot down the interesting bits that make sense.

I need to see if I can find anything else in the secret room, but there's no way I'm going in there alone. I need to get Mr. Papers. (I know he can't protect me, but it's just nice to have someone else there.) Before I go, I send an email to Justine, hoping she reads it right when she wakes up.

From: caitymacfireland@gmail.com
To: justinemiddleford@gmail.com
Subject: SOS

Hi J! Something really weird happened—my parents told me that Dr. Tenzo from Princeton is coming to the Inn next week!!!!!!!!!!!!! Do you know anything about this? I'm kinda freaking out, would your Grandpa really tell Tenzo where I live? I mean I know he was

interested in those symbols and all, but then he
supposedly agreed that they didn't mean anything. This
is borderline stalking. What do you think? XO, Caity

Down in the kitchen, Mrs. Findlay is sitting at the table writing out a menu. I pick up an apple and sit down with her, hoping I can ask about Alex's father, her son-in-law.

"What do you reckon our guests from California would like to eat, Caity?" she asks.

"Old people love prime rib," I say. "And they like more old-fashioned desserts, like tapioca. And fruit pies."

She laughs and says, "Are you an expert on the elderly?"

"Remember, my mom doesn't cook so I've been eating out all my life," I say with a shrug. "Can't help but observe."

"Ah, I see," she says. "Okay then, what else?"

"They like lamb. Plain, with mint jelly, not on kabobs or curried or anything. Old people are 'meat and potatoes' types. And speaking of potatoes, they love them scalloped."

"Easy enough. That's the food I like, too."

"Oh, and soup. Old people *love* soup. They could have it before every meal. Given a choice of soup or salad, they almost always choose soup."

She starts writing all this down, so I continue, "They need lots of fiber, too. Especially at breakfast."

"Prunes and oatmeal along with the other breakfast items?" she asks.

"Yep. And speaking of breakfast, you know that Americans are totally freaked out by pork and beans at breakfast, right?"

"Really?" she says, genuinely surprised.

"Yeah, it's weird. Pork and beans are strictly for hot dog night or camping."

"You're quite a font of knowledge now, aren't you?" she says, as if I've offended her.

"Well, you asked …"

"Aye, you've been quite helpful. I thank you," she replies as she continues jotting down menu items.

"So, um, Mrs. Findlay? Can I ask you a question? About your son-in-law?" She nods, so I continue, "Was he really killed here?" I ask quietly.

"Aye, he was." Her lips get small and stiff as she speaks, trying to hold back tears. "Bloody shame, that. Such a good man."

"Did anyone ever figure out who it was or what they wanted?"

She shakes her head. "Nae, they must've had a boat; no one saw them come or go on the ferry. S'pose the castle seemed an easy target because of how isolated it is, but they didn't take a thing." She shrugs. "It's never made sense to anyone."

"I'm sorry, Mrs. Findlay. That must've been horrible."

She pats my hand and says, "It has never *stopped* being horrible, child."

"Can I help you with anything?" I ask, but she waves me off. I think she wants to be alone.

I feel terrible for upsetting her, so I just walk over to get Mr. Papers and then leave. Pulling him out of his cubbyhole where he had been napping, I cradle him like a baby—he's all cuddly and warm when he first wakes up, which I love. I suddenly wonder how old he is, and how long monkeys live.

"We've got a lot to do today, pal," I whisper in his ear. He butts his forehead against mine and sinks back into my arms as we make our way up the stairs.

Finding no email from Justine, I decide to check again after we explore the room. I gather a stack of origami paper, some white paper for tracing more symbols, my tape, and a couple pencils—once I'm in the secret chamber I don't want to have to keep coming back out.

An inventory of the carvings is in order, so I tack a piece of tape above one spiral to remember where I started. Then I systematically take a rubbing of each one that has not yet been traced, making sure to number them so they stay in order. As I pass by the very first one that I took a rubbing of, the one that mentions my name, I notice that there's a tiny carving underneath that says, *"In lak'ech, Fergus."* If he signed it there, that would mark the last spiral, so I put them all in order based on that one being the end.

Back at my computer, I do a search for *in lak'ech*, thinking it may be some important Gaelic saying. Turns out to be a saying from the Maya, the people who built all the cool pyramids in Mexico, that means "I am another yourself." Apparently this is how they greet each other, like we say hello. It's really strange that Fergus would use Mayan language, but then again Hamish gave me that clay Mexican symbol when I was born so maybe there's some connection.

Before going back, I check my email again and see a reply from Justine.

From: justinemiddleford@gmail.com
To: caitymacfireland@gmail.com
Subject: RE: SOS

OK CMF, that thing about Dr. Tenzo is sooooooo weird.
I've always thought he was creepy. He's one of those
guys with really really big red lips and kind of greasy
hair. I have no idea how he found you, honest. I'll call
Gramps this afternoon after summer school and ask
him about it. It's just really weird. I'll let you know when
I talk to him but until then, don't worry, I'm sure it's just
some freaky coincidence. XO, J

PS The reason I'm up at the crack of dawn is that today
is my first tutoring session with David von Idiot. I'm
excited to see his room—you can tell so much about a
person by what their room looks like. Remember how
we thought Sarah Finkler was so sketchy after we saw
that she had pictures of all the CSI actors around her
room? Anyway, I couldn't sleep so I was happy to see
your email. I'll try to go downstairs and fall asleep on the
couch watching infomercials. Ciao for now.

The Sarah Finkler thing makes me laugh out loud. We
became friends with her before we knew how much she was
into morgues and stuff; she had a serious "CSI" obsession. So I
told her about this computer-based class on crime scene inves-
tigation to keep her busy and then Justine and I slowly—very
slowly so as not to end up on an autopsy table—pulled away
from her.

SIX

Now that I have all the rubbings, I decide to trace each one so they are ready once I find a way to use the new software program Dad wrote to secretly decode them all. While I'm on the second set, I hear Mrs. Findlay announce lunch on the intercom so I pick up Mr. Papers from the bed and go downstairs. Mom and Dad are already there.

"Hello Professor," Dad says to me as I enter.

I give him a weak smile. I can tell they're going to run this thing into the ground.

Mom says, "Well, we've got some good news. Your friend Alex will be spending some time at the house when our guests arrive. Mrs. Findlay has offered his services."

"Yeah, she told me he might be doing that."

"Mrs. Findlay, you should invite him to dinner tonight so we can talk about the job," Mom says. "Oh, and we should have your daughter over as well."

Dad snaps his finger. "Good idea! I can give Alex that computer tonight, too."

Mom turns to me and says, "Caity, I got a call today on a job in Zurich. It should be a quick one, but I'll be gone for a couple days."

"What's going on in Zurich?" I ask.

"Oh, it's a safe in a lakeside chateau. One of those cases where the grandfather dies and leaves the house to his kids but forgets to ever write down the combination to the safe. It's a classic double-door Cyrus Price. Definitely won't take longer than a day."

"When do you have to go?"

"I'm taking the ferry to a train tonight."

"And after I take her to the ferry, I'm going to check out the scene in downtown Brayne," Dad says. "It's about time I met the locals. Thomas is going to take me to each pub to meet everyone."

"That should take about two seconds," I say as I finish my sandwich. After our first ferry ride from Scotland to the Isle of Huracan we docked in Brayne, the island's only town, and Thomas gave us a tour. There is a butcher shop; a very small grocery store; a building that says City Government that was completely dark inside even though it was a Tuesday afternoon; and three pubs. The priorities here are obvious.

After lunch, Mr. Papers and I go outside for a walk and to investigate the outside of the tower. It just seems that if Fergus worked so hard to build this thing in secret, there must be something inside of it. All I know so far is (a) that Fergus and the Chinese guy built it alone, (b) there might be some clue to all of this in the spirals, and (c) there's some Mexican connection with the *in lak'ech* saying. Now I just need to find out how all of this comes together.

Thomas is out with the clippers, shaping the hedges so tightly you can hardly believe they are living things. He looks up at us and waves.

"Just out for a stroll," I shout as I walk behind the tower to the water coming from the base. It runs out of a big pipe made of stone and then flows right into the little canal that runs around the castle.

Mr. Papers jumps off my shoulder and onto the ground near the spigot and sticks his tongue in the running water as if he's licking a Popsicle. He takes a mouthful, looks at me with his head cocked, and swishes the water around in his mouth like a pretentious wine snob looking for just the right adjective for the flavor.

I stick my cupped hand under the spigot and then take a sip. You know how the air is when you're skiing and there's absolutely no smells because everything is blanketed in snow? It's as if the water carries no flavor at all, yet its flavorlessness is delicious. I can't get enough.

Mr. Papers takes another scoop and then just stares at it like he's watching TV. I glance over to see what he's looking at, thinking he might have caught some little creature, and he immediately lets the water go as if his hands are on fire. I scoop up a big handful of water and examine it closely for bugs. When the ripples disappear and it becomes still, a weird image appears. I swear I'm not making this up; it looks like a picture of a snake eating its own tail.

I have the same reaction Mr. Papers had, releasing the water as quickly as I can. It must be some weird trick the sun and the trees are playing. I try it again, but don't see anything at all this time. I try to push the image from my head as I search the back of the tower.

Moving to each side searching for entry points, I find only tightly mortared walls. I sense in my bones that this tower sits on top of what I need to find, I just don't know how to get in. Then I remember the blueprint that Mom and Dad mentioned.

On my way in I pass the inspector, Barend Schlacter. I'm not sure why, but the guy gives me the creeps. He has this weird combination of a boyish face with sinister eyes. I give him a huge smile, just trying to be friendly, and in return he looks me up and down like I'm a side of locker beef he's examining.

Dad is at his computer in the library when Mr. Papers and I walk in looking for the castle blueprints.

"Hey Dad, whatcha doing?" I casually ask.

"A freelance project for World Bank," he replies, without looking away from his screen.

"They don't even care that you don't have a name and a face, just a number that you bill with?"

"Skill is king in the programming world," he says, twirling around in his desk chair to face me. With an arrogant shrug he adds, "When you're one of a handful of people who can do what I do, you can go by any name or number you want."

"You. Are. So. Cool," I say.

He sighs. "I'm so underappreciated around here. If I didn't have some of the largest financial institutions in the world licking my boots, I might just get a complex."

"Ah, you know we worship you," I say, as I lean over the big library table where the blueprints are sitting. "Well, I'll let you get back to work. I thought I might take a look at the blueprints; find out where everything is."

"Isn't it strange to live in a house that has almost more rooms than you can explore?"

"I know," I say. "It's like that dream I always have where I'll open a door I think is a closet and it's a whole other wing of the house I never knew about."

"I love when you tell me about those dreams. I wish I'd have one."

"Now you're living it—you don't need to dream it."

"I suppose I am!" he says, seeming amused by his own good luck. "Excellent point."

"So you don't mind if I borrow these blueprints for awhile?" I ask.

"Sure honey, whatever you need," he says as he turns back to his work.

I roll them up and skip up to my room. Mom pops her head out of her room as I pass by.

"Want to come talk to me while I pack?"

I set the blueprints outside her door, then go in and hop up on her big puffy bed.

"You're doing okay here, aren't you?" she asks as she folds clothes into her red suitcase.

"Sure. I mean, I miss Justine a lot, but I'm doing okay." I run my fingernail fast across the outside fabric so it makes a satisfying *zeet zeet* sound.

"That code you made up was so creative; maybe this solo time is expanding your mind."

"Yeah, maybe." I don't want to get into the boarding

school conversation again, so I change the subject. "What are you going to get for me in Switzerland?"

"What would you like?"

"A new sketchbook would be great." I turn over on my side and lean on my elbow. "And if they have a Gap, can you get me some jeans that are NOT capri length? I need the longest jeans ever made in the history of the world."

"No problem."

"Oh, and Mr. Papers desperately needs a new outfit. He's like a doll-size medium. Try to get something boyish. The circus look isn't really working for him anymore."

She sighs and rolls her eyes. "You and that monkey..."

"Hey, it's not my fault I'm an only child."

"Oh Caity," she says as she takes my face in her two hands and kisses me on the forehead. "I will miss you."

When she finishes packing I pick up the blueprints and go to my room. I gather my sketchbook, a ruler, and pencil before hopping up on the bed to spread them out and work.

I find my bedroom on the plan of the East Wing. In between my bedroom and the tower is a long skinny rectangle with an X through it, which must be my secret room. I draw it all in the sketchbook for when I have to return the plans.

When I'm finished drawing I realize that something is really off. In the plans, the room with an X through it runs the whole length of my bedroom, but I know it's smaller than that.

Or maybe the chamber is bigger than I think.

I spend all afternoon recreating the blueprints in my sketchbook; it may come in handy to have a plan of the whole castle sometime. Everything looks to be pretty straightforward from the blueprints; there isn't even one other small room with an X in it.

A car door slamming reminds me that Alex is coming for dinner. I brush my teeth, carefully apply defrizzer to every strand of hair, and glide on some lip gloss. I have to walk a fine line between looking cute and not looking so dressed up that my parents tease me about being in love with Alex. Then I grab my favorite accessory, Mr. Papers.

I decide to wait for the intercom; I don't want it to seem like I've just been sitting around for Alex to arrive. So I pace. I roll the blueprints back up and set them by the door. I pace. I rearrange the items on my desk. I pace. Finally Mom announces dinner on the intercom.

Mrs. Findlay is waiting for me outside of the dining room, where she removes Mr. Papers from my shoulder. "Inspector Schlacter mustn't see him anywhere near the food," she whispers.

"Stupid cherub," I mutter to myself as I hand over Mr. Papers.

SEVEN

Dad is at the head of the table, Alex is sitting on one side of him, and Barend Schlacter on the other. Alex's mom is sitting next to Barend and then my mom is at the end, which leaves one open place right next to Alex.

As I approach the table, Alex's mom stands up and offers me her hand. I can see where Alex gets his good looks. She's stunning—one of those women with black hair and very pale skin who actually look glamorous instead of ghostly.

"So nice to meet you Caity," she says. Her shiny chin-length hair is so silky that it almost looks liquid.

"Nice to meet you, Mrs.—" I look at Alex. "I guess I don't even know your last name. I'm sorry."

"It's Cameron. Ainsley Cameron." She stares at my eyebrows and says, "My, you do have the Mac Fireland arches!"

Dad laughs. "She looks a lot like the paintings hung all over the castle, doesn't she."

I'm dying here. This is just what I need, all eyes to be on

me as I walk to the table. Alex gets up and pulls out my chair for me.

"Wow, thanks," I say.

"So, Caity, how have you taken to living in Scotland?" Mrs. Cameron asks.

"It's been good so far." I am unable to come up with anything remotely interesting to say.

"It's tough with no one her age," Mom says. "Which is why it's nice that Alex will be around next week when all the guests come. At least she'll have someone to talk to."

"And when school starts you'll meet more of the local kids," Mrs. Cameron says.

I look at my parents. "I'm not really sure we're staying through the school year," I say. "This was supposed to just be for the summer."

"Oh, well, that's too bad. We'd love to have you year-round," she replies.

We make small talk as we eat each course of the Old Folks Test Dinner that Mrs. Findlay serves us. The dining room has been transformed; this morning it was dusty and cold and the table seemed enormous. Mrs. Findlay must have spent hours polishing the wood paneling because it now glows, and the big silver tea service on the buffet table looks like pirate's booty. With all the china and crystal and a fire in the fireplace—and our beautiful guests—it feels like a real castle dining room.

During dessert the hotel inspector, Barend Schlacter, starts quizzing my parents about their whole life story. He won't let up. I can tell Mom and Dad are only being nice about it because they want as many stars as they can get.

I keep staring at Alex's hands—the only part of him I can look at without being conspicuous. I'm absolutely mesmerized by the aqua blue veins running under his tan skin.

I try to think of something to talk about so I can look at more than just his hands. "So did you spend a lot of time here at the castle when you were younger?" I ask him.

"Aye, I used to come here with my dad whenever he had to repair the electrical."

It occurs to me that he might know the layout of the castle better than anyone. "Do you happen to know if there is a way to the tower from inside the castle?" I ask.

"Nae. Don't think there's really anything in there. This castle was never used for defense, so I'm not really sure why there's a tower here in the first place."

"Thomas said that Fergus, my super-great-grandfather who built the castle, put in the foundation to the tower all by himself, in secret."

"Aye, that's part of island lore," he says. "Hard to believe isn't it?"

"I guess he had help from one other guy, some friend he brought to Scotland from China."

"Oh, right. Forgot his name, I think there's an X in it? It's inscribed on the tower."

"What's inscribed?" I ask.

"The man's name. Fergus Mac Fireland and some Chinese name I can't remember are both carved in the cornerstone."

"Really?"

Alex takes a big swig of milk. I like watching his Adam's apple move as he drinks. "Yep, I'll show you sometime. I think it's covered with ivy now, but I know where to look for it."

"I'd love to see that."

Thomas walks in and says, "Sorry to disturb, Mrs. Mac Fireland, but we must leave in ten minutes to make the ferry and the train."

Mom looks at her watch. "Oh, thank god someone is keeping track of me!"

Alex and his mom leave at the same time as Thomas and my parents. Mrs. Findlay is staying overnight in the old servants' quarters off the kitchen so Dad can go out with Thomas after Mom gets on the ferry. Thomas goes to the pub every night and says that as the Laird, Dad has to get out and mingle; since they'll be in Brayne dropping Mom off it's the perfect opportunity for Thomas and Dad to have a guy's night out. They even invited Barend Schlacter but he said he cannot fraternize with Inn staff and said he was going to turn in very early anyway.

I haven't needed a babysitter in years, but the thought of being in the East wing alone for a few hours at night freaked me out, so I bit my tongue when Mom told me she was having Mrs. Findlay stay.

Once everyone is gone and Mrs. Findlay in the kitchen, I sneak off to the library. I take a blank CD and make a copy of Dad's decoding program. Happy to finally have what I need to decode all of the spirals by myself, I burst out of the library. I don't see Barend Schlacter standing behind the door and I almost knock him over as I run to the staircase. "Sorry, sir," I yell back as I bound up the stairs.

I install the program on my computer, pick up the page of symbols marked as number one, and try to remember Dad's sequence. *Scan the page, separate each symbol so each one is an independent piece of data, make sure the decoding begins with the innermost symbol, hit start.*

I can't stand the tension of watching each word pop up one by one, so I leave to put on my pajamas and go to the bathroom. That's when I notice the *huge* piece of mushroom in my teeth. My God, mushroom soup was the *first course*!

I close my eyes, letting the cringe work its way up and down my body.

After what seems like half an hour of teeth brushing, I go back to check on the code. It's already done. Man, have I got a smart dad! Between the fact that he called his program "littlegenius.exe" and my newfound respect for his brainpower, I start to feel guilty. I'm sure he'll be really proud of "littlegenius" if he finds any of this out.

I sit down to read the text, breaking it up and punctuating it as best I can:

> *With will and labor I built the great tower*
> *To sit atop this place of power*
> *Know this though, 'tis less for defense and more to*
>   *conceal*
> *What once was lore until I found 'twas real*

I knew the key to this was under the tower! Whatever is under there must be so weird that Fergus couldn't believe it until he saw it himself. The fact that this is a place of power is pretty intriguing. I wonder what that means. Just as I'm closing the document, I get an email from Justine.

From: justinemiddleford@gmail.com
To: caitymacfireland@gmail.com
Subject: RE: RE: SOS

Hey CMF, Just got off the phone with Gramps. I said
what's up with Dr. Tenzo from Princeton booking a
room at the Mac Fireland's Inn? You won't believe
this—Gramps said Tenzo left suddenly for a sabbatical!
He said he's supposed to be studying some ancient
language in China for a year. He has no idea why he
is going to Scotland instead and said that it seemed
"untoward." Then he got all upset because he said
he may have mentioned where you lived when he
forwarded your last email on to Dr. Tenzo. Maybe that's
how he found out who/where you were? He tried to call
Tenzo but got his answering machine that said he would
be out of the country for a while. Sorry I don't have
more info for you. I'm sure the guy is harmless. I mean,
you're way taller than he is. You could take him in a
fight! Ok, off to David's for a chem tutoring session. We
have so much chemistry! ha ha ha ha. XO, Justine

This does nothing to ease my mind!

Another email message pops up; this one is from Uncle
Li. It's to my parents but he copied me on it, telling us he'd
be in Brayne by 12:30 tomorrow. I am so relieved that he's
coming—maybe I can talk him into staying the whole time
that Tenzo is here.

I want to be able to recognize Tenzo, so I search the Princeton University site for him. Sure enough, there is a faculty
picture: *Tadashi Tenzo, Ph.D., Ancient and Extinct Languages.*
Justine was right; he does look creepy. Big glasses, huge red lips,
acne scars on his face. If Hollywood were casting for a villain,

he could walk in and steal the part. I shudder and finally feel like it might be time to tell my parents about all of this.

Dying to decode another set of symbols, I look for spiral number two. After going through all the tedious steps to input it, I then let it run in the background while surfing the web.

When my computer stops churning, I click over to the program to see the result:

> *You know of the hares and their unity knot*
> *Now find what the Flower of Life sits atop*
> *These symbols hold wisdom from tribes of the Earth*
> *Knowledge essential for new world rebirth*

These are starting to sound like fortune cookie messages. The Flower of Life? Huh?

I immediately search the Internet and find millions of results—guess maybe I *should* have heard of it. It's some weird geometric pattern found in ancient sites all over the world. No one knows its origin and it's a mystery as to why it shows up in all different cultures. I print out an example and then trace it in my sketchbook; it is way too complicated to draw from scratch.

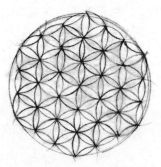

Just as I'm about to hop in to bed, I hear a knock at my door. Assuming it's Mrs. Findlay or Dad home early, I say, "Come on in."

To my surprise, it's the hotel inspector and resident cherub, Barend Schlacter.

"Oh, hi Mr. Schlacter. Sorry about running into you earlier."

"I need to check on one thing in here," he says as he closes the door and walks directly toward me.

"Well, um, this is my private room—no guests will ever be staying in this wing," I say as politely as I can, worried I might cause my parents to lose a star by being rude.

I start to get nervous and ask him to please come back in the morning, but he doesn't stop until he's only about a foot away. Then he looks right into my eyes and says, "You'd better be careful, *fräulein*, I've seen you sneaking around. Some secrets are better left untouched." His breath smells horrible, like mothballs in vinegar.

"What?" I say as I walk backwards away from him. I hit my ankle on my bedpost but the pain doesn't even register.

"Your father did such a good job of hiding that we lost track of the American line. But alas, we knew we'd find you when your uncle died. No one leaves a castle unclaimed."

"Look, I honestly don't know what you're talking about," I say. I'm trying to be forceful, but my voice, shaky and weak, is giving me away.

He lunges and grabs my wrist. I try to pull it away and he holds it even tighter, so tight that the tendons in his fat wrist bulge, causing the clasp on his metal wristwatch to pop open. As it dangles on his arm, I see a tattoo on the inside of his wrist. While still holding on to me, he reaches over with his other hand to snap it back together. "Let's keep it that way, hear me, *freund*?"

I nod and he finally lets go of me. As he adjusts his suit and pulls his shirt sleeves back down over his wrists, he says, "Good. I'd hate to see a girl your age orphaned..."

My horrified expression makes him smile. This is surreal; it is all so out of the blue that it's taking too long to register and I'm speechless, drained of all response.

Then he says, "And don't go crying to the old *frau* downstairs, either, or she might go the way of her son-in-law."

Now I'm not breathing at all.

Instead of turning, he walks out sideways and backwards, like some evil crab, never breaking eye contact with me. As he closes the door he says, "We never spoke, *verstehen*?"

I nod again and hold back tears until the door is closed. Then I run over and fasten the big iron bolt on the door. Falling to the ground, I unleash the silent, heaving cry that I haven't done for years. I cry until no tears are left, until I am cold and empty on the stone floor.

I don't know how much time passes before I am able to pull myself together. I try to wrap my brain around all of this, but it's not making sense. I can't put together what it means that he would have "lost track" of my dad, how he would know about Mrs. Findlay's son-in-law, and what he would think that I'm up to. Could this guy have found out what I've been decoding?

Remembering the tattoo, I jump up to get my sketchbook to draw what I can of it before I forget the image. It was all black, a spider web made from lines over a spiral, and then the letters "FRO" dangling from a piece of the web.

Once I've captured it, I go to my computer to see if I can find anything about FRO. I search a bunch of different ways, but only when I combine FRO + spider web + secret, do I find one small reference about a group called *Fraternitas Regni Occulti*. Supposedly formed way back in the days of the Roman Empire, this mythological *Fraternitas* is supposed to be the secret society of all secret societies. Their whole goal is to place the world's power in the hands of a few people who run banks, the government, and the military. Their symbol: a spider web divided into twelve segments.

It has to be the same group—it would be too much of a coincidence that their initials would be FRO and their symbol the spider web—but I can't figure out what on earth a supposedly mythological secret society would have to do with me, this place, or my dad.

My brain is so scrambled I can't think anymore, so I double-check the bolt on the door, lock all the shutters on my windows, and crawl up onto my bed. I fully expect not to sleep a wink, so I prop myself up with pillows and wait for Dad to get home.

Make me an orphan? What the hell?

EIGHT

I'm disoriented when I hear Mrs. Findlay on the intercom telling us to wake up already. It's still pitch dark in my room because of the shuttered windows, but when I look at the clock I see it's 9:30. It takes a moment to remember what happened last night, and when I do, I'm surprised I was even able to fall asleep.

I jump at a knock on my door. "Wake up sleepyhead," Dad mumbles. "We both overslept."

Excited to hear Dad's voice, I bound out of bed, unbolt the door, and give him a huge bear hug. I have *never* been so happy to see him.

"Easy, tiger, I'm a little fragile today," he says.

I look up at him; he's looking kind of scrappy. "What's up, Dad? You sick?"

He rubs his face with both hands and then runs them through his rumpled hair. "Thomas took me out to the pubs last night," he says with a gravelly voice. "I think everyone in the village bought me a draft..."

"Come on," I say, grabbing his hand. "You just need a big plate of runny eggs and a broiled tomato!"

Dad looks like he might barf and says, "I think I'll stick with dry toast and coffee."

I don't let go of Dad's hand the whole way down, but he's too groggy to think it's weird.

When we get to the kitchen, I peer in to make sure that Barend Schlacter isn't in there. Mrs. Findlay shakes her head when Dad walks in.

"Thomas told me you had quite a time last night," she says with a smile.

"Pretty rowdy bunch, for old men..."

"'Tis the scotch and ale that keeps them young!"

I glance over at Dad. "Looks like it put twenty years on you, though."

"Hot chocolate, Caity?" Mrs. Findlay asks.

"Yes, please. Hey, Dad, did you get that email from Uncle Li? He's coming today."

Dad drops his face into his hands, and then he looks back up at me. "I'm so embarrassed about this, but there is just no way I can go get him in the state I'm in. I was thinking, perhaps you could be the best daughter in the world and go with Thomas to pick him up?"

"Sure, no problem," I say. "I wanted him to check the feng shui of my bedroom anyway."

This will be good, I think to myself. Being with Thomas and Uncle Li will keep me safe from that psychopath Barend Schlacter in case he only pretends to leave Breidablik.

A look of relief washes over Dad's face and he gives me a

big hug. "You're the best, Caity," he says as he kisses the top of my head.

"And you're the stinkiest, Dad."

"Aye," adds Mrs. Findlay, plugging her nose. "I noticed the pub stench, too."

"That's my cue to have a bath and a long nap," Dad says, grabbing coffee and toast to go.

I walk over to the empty cubby. "Where's Mr. P?" I ask.

"Thomas put him in the library, the kitchen is being inspected this—"

The door opens and Barend Schlacter walks in. My whole body tenses and I have to concentrate in order to breathe.

"*Guten morgen*, ladies," he says with a smile. One of his front teeth is dead and has been capped so it's a different color than the rest of his teeth. He's so vile.

He walks over to me, squeezes my shoulder gently, and says, "Sleep well?"

I'm frozen and can't say a word. Mrs. Findlay, still working for the five-star rating, starts lavishing him with compliments and asks what he wants for breakfast; she says she'll cook him anything his heart desires. He takes full advantage of her sucking up and asks for blintzes.

I listen to this like they are speaking underwater, or like they are aliens that I'm examining. I am completely detached, watching from afar.

Who is this guy, anyway?

While they yammer on, an idea springs to mind. I walk over to the desk in the corner of the kitchen and pretend to grab a pen while sneaking a piece of tape from the industrial-sized tape dispenser. Fortunately Barend Schlacter's back is to me, and Mrs. Findlay is concentrating on making blintz batter. I reach up to the intercom panel and tape down the talk button for the guest wing. When I see that it's secure, I leave with a quick goodbye. Barend Schlacter turns and winks at me and I have to breathe deeply to keep my hot chocolate from coming back up.

I figure this is my one and only chance to get more information on this guy, so after I pick up Mr. Papers from the library, I suck up my nerve and walk to the guest wing to Barend Schlacter's room. I honestly don't know where I'm getting the courage to do this.

Turning up the intercom in the hallway outside his room, I listen to them in the kitchen arguing playfully about the best blintz fillings. I figure as soon as I hear him leave I'll still have a few minutes to scramble away.

When I open his door, Mr. Papers runs right in and perches on the window sill. There's not much to see, just a small overnight bag with his clothes in it. No briefcase, no laptop, no pad or pen, nothing. Then I peek into his bathroom and see gold; his cell phone is in there charging.

Sweating and shaking, I open his phone to look at his contacts. There isn't one single person or phone number listed! So I look at the last number dialed. Strangely, it has a San Francisco area code. I jot it down on my hand with the pen I took from the kitchen, then look at his call log and see that the last ten calls received are all from this same San Francisco number.

I put the phone exactly as it was and go back into the room. Mr. Papers has jumped up to the top of the tall armoire in the corner and he's trying to lift something heavy up there with all his might. Pulling the chair over from the desk, I get up to see what he's doing. Just over the crown moulding on top of the armoire lays a metal laptop case. I reach over to try to open it, but of course, it's locked. The only identification on it is a luggage tag that says "B.V.S. 415-555-1224." I jot the number on my hand next to the other, return the chair to the desk, and leave as quickly as I can.

When I'm back in the hall, I listen in on the intercom and hear Thomas telling Barend Schlacter that they have to leave for the ferry in about fifteen minutes. I know I'm safe because I can still hear them chatting away in the kitchen, but I can't help but run to get out of the guest wing and back to my room where I bolt the door. I won't feel safe here until he is off the island.

After giving Mr. Papers some origami sheets to busy himself, I do a reverse lookup on the phone numbers that are written on my hand. The number on the laptop case tag is not available, which means it must be his cell phone.

I try the other number and it comes up as unlisted, but available for $13.99 through some shady track-you-down company. My parents have set me up with a PayPal account that I can use for small purchases, so I immediately pay; it seems like a small price for some key information.

A few moments later, the name pops up: F.R.O., Inc., 600 Montgomery Street, San Francisco, California. Map-Quest shows the address as the Transamerica Pyramid building. These people are in my old backyard!

When I try to Google the company name, nothing comes up. Nothing. It seems almost impossible for a company to have not one single mention. Weird. I need Justine's help on this.

From: caitymacfireland@gmail.com
To: justinemiddleford@gmail.com
Subject: Spy job?

Oh my god Justine, you would not believe the CRAZY
that is going down here!!!! I'm trying to piece a bunch
of stuff together but I need a little help ... I can't stress
enough how important it is that you not mention any
of what I'm talking about to your parents, cuz if it gets
back to my parents I am in so much trouble you don't
even know. Seriously, the whole Tenzo thing seems like
playground games compared to what's been happening
lately.

This FREAK is here, posing as a hotel inspector and
while my parents were out he came to my room and
threatened me. We're talking like adult-level scare
tactics. I'm fine tho, and he'll be gone for good in a few
minutes, but I need to find out what his real story is. I
searched his room and got the only phone number that
he calls and that calls him, then I did a reverse lookup
and it turns out it's a company at the Transamerican
Pyramid building! Can you believe it? It's called F.R.O.,
Inc. and of course there is not one single mention of
it on the web. Type in dung beetle and you get like a
half a million pages but there's not one mention of a
company that works right there in the tallest building in
San Francisco! Anyway, here's my big favor—can you
go over there and pretend you're a bike messenger
delivering a package? You'll be totally safe in public.
Look in the lobby at the company directory and find
another company that's on the same floor as FRO, then
go up and take a peek. Just check if there's anything
to see, if they have like a tagline under their company
name about what they do or anything. I know that this
is a lot to ask, but I really need your help. THANKYOU
THANKYOU THANKYOU!!!!!!!!!!!!

I hear noises outside so I walk to my window just in time to see Thomas loading Barend Schlacter up to take him to the ferry. I stand in the window and watch the car drive away, not moving until it's out of sight.

The combination of the unusually warm sunlight streaming in and the relief of knowing that man is gone loosens me up. I look over at the loch, twinkling in the sun like a blue plate with diamonds on it, and feel a great urge to go swimming. I pull on my bathing suit and a hat, put a towel and my sketchbook in a bag, and grab Mr. Papers.

The loch is too big to swim across, but not so big that you'd think a monster could live in it. It's actually very nice. There's even a little sandy area where Mr. Papers and I sit and listen to waves lap the shore.

When I get warm enough from lying in the sun, I start wading in. Mr. Papers comes to the edge of the water and makes little screeching sounds. Guess he's not much of a swimmer. When the water hits my thighs I dive in; it's so cold that it takes my breath away. I do a few dolphin dives and then stand on my hands underwater and try some synchronized swim moves that I saw in the Olympics. I am always amazed at how much makeup those women can wear underwater and wonder if there's a whole line of cosmetics just for synchronized swimmers.

I hear a voice say my name in the distance. I look toward where it's coming from by the castle, and I see Alex.

Great! The last time he saw me I had mushrooms in my teeth and now I'm completely wet in my bikini. I shake the water from my hair, but see by my shadow that this has made it go full fro so I go back underwater to wet it. Alex is nearing the shore when I resurface.

Running for my towel, I wrap up in it before he gets too close.

"On holiday, I see," he says as he walks over.

"Just going for a swim."

"Surprising, that," he says as he skips a stone on the water.

"What? You didn't think I could swim?"

"Just didn't think you'd enjoy the cold water so much, being such a big city girl and all."

He never comes right out and says it, but I can tell he thinks I'm spoiled.

"Well, it's not like the San Francisco Bay is heated and I swim there," I say, even though I have never even stuck one toe in those shark-infested waters.

He doesn't answer, just nods and goes on skipping stones. I see he is wearing fishing waders so I ask if he caught anything.

"Aye. Some nice wild brown trout. You ever fish?" he asks as he flips his hair back from his eye. I'm already over being irritated.

"Not really. My dad's not too handy outdoors." I wonder what to do next; there's no way I'm taking this towel off while he's still here. Then I remember the cornerstone that he told me about and ask him if he has a minute to show me where it is. He agrees, so I pack up.

As we walk up the path, I think about talking to him about his dad. From what Barend Schlacter said, it seems like F.R.O. may have been involved with his death. I decide it's too touchy a subject; I'll wait for the right time, maybe when I have more information.

We approach the tower and Alex points to the far corner. "I think it's this one here." He feels through the ivy with his fingers, and then takes a pocketknife and starts slicing through some of the vines. A carving about the size of a file folder begins to show through. It says:

FERGUS MAC FIRELAND
XU BAO CHENG
12 . 8 . 17 . 7 . 6
1760 A.D.

"Cool! What's that string of numbers above the date?"

"Dunno. It's always flummoxed me."

I run my fingers over the carved name of my super-great grandfather and feel some kind of shock, a zing. I jump back.

"You okay?" Alex asks.

"Weird, I just got some kind of … shock," I say.

Alex points to my feet. "Those flip-flops can generate a lot of static."

"That was probably it," I say, though I know it wasn't.

"Well, I best head back to the farm," he says as he jumps on his bike. "Bye, then."

As soon as I see that he left through the gate, I go back to the names and write them down in my sketchbook. Then I pull at the ivy to hide the carving again; I don't know what Dr. Tenzo is looking for, but I'm certainly not going to make it easy for him to find *anything*.

After changing to pick up Uncle Li, I run into Thomas at the front door.

"I'll go get Uncle Li with you, Thomas," I say. "Dad's staying here."

"Your father not well?" he asks with a smile.

"You people are evil," I say. Thomas gives me a wicked smile.

"So what did you think about that inspector?" I ask on the way to the ferry.

"He's a wee sour man, isn't he?" he replies. "I didn't like him a'tall. Was happy to send him off."

"Me too," I say as I gaze out the window wondering what on earth would make me interesting to a Bavarian man and the secret society he might work for.

NINE

We arrive at the dock as the ferry is pulling in. I see Uncle Li waving his hand and yelling, "Caity! Caity!" like a kid who hasn't seen his mom in a long time. He's dressed in his usual uniform, a dark blue silk shirt—the Chinese kind that buttons up to the neck—black pants, and soft loafers. He's the only person I know who's old enough to have a lot of wrinkles but no gray hair; his hair is still a glistening blue-black. Seeing him puts me so at ease that I feel it all though my body, like a long soak in a hot tub.

The ferry docks and he hops off. I run over and give him a big hug. I can feel it already; he will make everything better. "I have so much to tell you, Uncle Li," I whisper.

As soon as we drive through the castle gates, Uncle Li has his hand on the door handle like he can't wait to get out. Thomas parks and takes his luggage, but I keep him for the tour.

We start in the formal garden. Not wanting to influence what he thinks, I don't give anything away before he checks out the property. As we walk around he says things like mmm hmmm, and uh huh, and at one point he puts out his hands in front of him, palms down, and starts walking like a sleepwalker in the movies as he checks for underground water currents.

Uncle Li stops at the tower and silently looks it up and down. He walks around to the back where the waterspout is, takes a sip, and nods his head. Then he looks at me for a few seconds. I look right back at him, still not giving him any information, even in my gaze. He walks around to the front of the tower, and then goes in the little door; he's so short he doesn't even have to duck. As we walk up the stairs he keeps one palm on the wall, dragging it along the whole way up. I scan each rock, hoping to find something with the Flower of Life symbol on it. When we get to the top, we stand and look at the loch and the forest and all the huge boulders. Finally he says, "This castle is not what it seems."

Staring straight ahead, I ask, "In what way?"

"You must be honest with me and I will be honest with you."

I turn to look at him. "But what's your first impression?"

"This castle is hiding something. Very unusual energy field here, along with odd subterranean water patterns. Also a sense of ancestry. A very strange combination of forces."

"You can just sense that?"

"You could too, it's not that hard. Become a receptor; information is available to all."

"What do you think it's hiding, Uncle Li?"

He shakes his head and says, "Something very powerful. Can't put my finger on it yet."

"I hope you can help me figure it out. This is getting…"

I want to say dangerous but then I think it may freak him out so I say, "complicated."

"Most the time *complicated* can mean interesting. Let's go sit down and you can tell me all about it."

Uncle Li looks tired when we get back to the castle. I ask if he'd like to rest. "I'm not as young as I once was," he says forcing a smile. "Travel exhausts me."

"Let's just talk later then. I'll walk you to your room." For the first time I notice that Uncle Li is getting older. When you see someone almost every day the little changes become incremental, but since I hadn't seen him for awhile, I notice that he is aging. Could I really burden him with what's going on?

Once Uncle Li is in his room, I run up to check my email. I haven't really had a chance since I sent Justine that email this morning. She's written back.

From: justinemiddleford@gmail.com
To: caitymacfireland@gmail.com
Subject: RE: Spy job?

OK, Caity, if weird men are coming to your room to threaten you I think it may be time to tell your parents or call the police. I mean, I'm totally happy to dress up like a messenger and check out that company, but you have got to get somebody to protect you. I'll let you know what I find out at FRO.

PLEASE promise me you will be careful. Isn't Uncle Li coming soon? Maybe he could help you figure out this big mystery if you really can't tell you parents. J

I know she's right, but I also have to trust my gut about when is the right time to tell Uncle Li everything. Now that

Barend Schlacter is off the island I feel a little better, although I know I need to stay on guard—who knows what he will tell the *Fraternitas* about me?

I still smell like sunscreen and loch water from my swim earlier today, so I pour lavender bubble bath in my big tub and fill it as high as I can. This is the longest bathtub I've ever seen; I am able to stretch out completely, which I do as I soak for a long time.

Uncle Li must have been tired because he doesn't come out again until morning. I find him at the kitchen table having breakfast and catching up with Dad.

Sitting down to have some oatmeal with them, Dad fills him in on the guests who are coming. When we're done with breakfast, Uncle Li suggests that I finish my tour of the inside of the castle.

"That's great," Dad says to Uncle Li. "I was a bit under the weather yesterday and didn't get any work done. I've got a project to wrap up and then I'm all yours."

"Take your time, Angus," he replies. "Caity and I can poke around here for days."

I finish showing Uncle Li around; he wants to see every inch. Then we go back to my room to talk and I make a fire as he looks around.

"Your room is very good, no major problems," he says. "It's a little big, but the oversized furniture fills the space nicely."

"Is the bed placement okay?"

"Yes, fine. It's on the solid wall, the dragon wall, and it has a good view of the door, two things that are key to a good bedroom."

He stands up and walks over to a window, sticks his head out, and looks both ways. Then he comes back in and sits down. He points to the carved panel and says, "What's behind there?"

"Are you psychic?" I ask, dumbfounded.

He laughs. "Just look out the window, you can see that distance between your back wall and tower is about eighteen feet. These walls can't be that thick."

"Ah. Right."

"Not everything is mystery with me," Uncle Li says with a wink. "So what is it?"

I take the carved metal key from my desk and lead him over to the panel. I slip the key over the rabbit ears and Uncle Li does not even seem startled when the wall gives away. "This is where it starts to get weird," I say as I lead him in and turn on the light.

Uncle Li walks slowly around the room. "What do you know about this?" he asks.

"Not much. There's this book I found, by accident, let me get it…" I take the book from under the tabletop and hand it to Uncle Li. "Look at this, and then look at the wall," I tell him. "It's a grimoire to some of those symbols."

He takes the book, smells it, and looks closely at the binding. Then I hand him the printout of the decoded poems. "It's a long story how I got these decoded, but this is what I've found out so far."

Sitting on the fainting couch, he starts to read the poem. Then he looks through the book of symbols. "You decoded this?" he asks as he thumbs through the pages of the book, looking carefully at each symbol and its sound. I watch over his shoulder. He smells like incense.

"Someone else decoded these ones in the book, but Dad decoded the poem that I printed out."

"So your Dad knows?" he asks.

"Not exactly … he doesn't really know he decoded all of these, he only knows about one. I kind of tricked him into helping me," I say.

"My, you're a crafty girl." His eyes sparkle.

"I'm not proud of it. I feel horrible about it actually, but I have to keep this a secret until I figure out some more stuff."

"Well, I'm flattered that you're telling me about it."

"You're different," I say. "You can't punish me and I know you wouldn't take over." I don't want to lay down the whole story about Barend Schlacter yet; I think it might scare him away from helping me, so I angle it a different way. "Do you remember in the seventh grade when I had my first big science project, that thing where I was making batteries? My parents kind of took over and got so involved that the teacher had to have a talk with them."

Uncle Li laughs. "I do remember that. They simply can't help themselves, can they?"

"Nope. They're dorks, it's what they do. And I'm telling you, this is the kind of thing they would *totally* take over."

"I understand completely," he says as he puts his glasses back in his pocket.

I point to the title and ask if he knows what *As Above, So Below* refers to.

"Yes, of course. It's a shortened version of 'That which is above is the same as that which is below' from *The Emerald Tablet*."

"What's *The Emerald Tablet*?" I ask.

"It's an ancient book of secret wisdom purportedly written by Hermes Trismegistus."

"Secret wisdom? Hermes Trismewhatsit?"

He says, "Where it comes from isn't as important as what it means."

"Give it to me plain," I say. "Pretend I'm in third grade."

"It means whatever happens on a large scale also happens on a small scale. The theory is man is a part of the universe but he also *can be* the universe. Just as each strand of DNA contains all the information about your whole body, each individual human mind contains all the information about the whole universe."

"So we know everything?" I ask.

"No," he shakes his head, "we *are* everything."

I roll my eyes. "How can we 'be' everything?"

"It's very simple, at the most basic level, everything—you, me, this castle, are all just a bunch of waves. Matter is just dense combinations of waves, vibrations."

"That's just too weird to believe…"

Uncle Li smiles. "It's not something you have to *believe* in. It's not a religion, it's science. Physical law. Look at water—it can be a gas, a liquid, or a solid. The form it takes is determined by how fast it's vibrating. When it's vibrating slowly, water becomes solid ice, when it's vibrating really quickly, it's steam. And when it's vibrating in between, it's liquid."

I look down at myself. "So I'm vibrating right now?"

Uncle Li nods his head. "That's all we are, masses of vibrating energy. Mystics have known this forever. With quantum physics, science is now catching up. Turns out ancient civilizations had a lot of knowledge that we're just now starting to be able to prove."

"So if we're all just vibrations, then there's no me or you. We're all in one big pool?"

"Exactly," he replies, "one big pool of possibility. Sometimes particle, sometimes wave, but always connected through *chi*."

"All that from four little words scribbled at the beginning of that book?"

"Often the least amount of words speak the most profound truths," he says with a smile.

"Thanks, Confucius."

He chuckles and looks again at the paper with the pieces of the poem. "I think our next step is to find the Flower of Life," he says.

"Yeah, and we need to do it quietly and fast—there's a guy named Tenzo from Princeton coming here to find these spirals."

Uncle Li looks surprised. "How does he know about them?"

"I know this sounds like a dumb thing to do, but when I first saw the spirals, I faxed a rubbing to Justine and she sent it to her grandpa at Princeton who is into that stuff."

"So then how many people have seen these?"

"Just Justine, her Grandpa, and this Tenzo guy, I think."

"And they knew what it was?"

"Well, this Tenzo guy recognized something about it but then when I told Justine's grandfather that it was nothing, Tenzo agreed, as if to end all examination of it. Then the next thing I know, boom, he tells everyone he's on a sabbatical and then books a room here."

"I can stay for a couple of weeks," he says. "We'll get to the bottom of this."

I sigh and look up so he won't see me tearing up. "It means so much to have you here."

"I know, Caity," he says as he picks up the paper with the decoded messages on it. He folds it four or five times and then puts it in his pocket with his reading glasses.

"Well, if I start now I can probably get another couple of spirals decoded today."

"Excellent. I have some work to do for your father; let's pick this up again in later," he says as he makes his way to the door.

I check my mail and see a message marked urgent from Justine—it says to call her cell phone, ASAP, any time of day or night.

My heart sinks. Has Barend Schlacter gotten to her, too?

TEN

While Justine's phone rings, I do the math and realize it's the middle of the night there. Justine answers groggily.

"Hey J, it's Caity."

"Oh, hi," she says, coming out of sleep. "I'm so glad you called."

"Are you okay? What's going on?"

I hear her covers rustling as she sits up to talk. "I'm fine. I just had the weirdest day—"

"What? What happened?"

"So I went in to the Transamerica Pyramid building with the whole messenger getup like you said, and tried to go to the floor that F.R.O. is on. They have the whole floor, by the way, and it's restricted access, so you have to have a special key to get out of the elevator there."

"So you couldn't even get in?"

"No, I didn't see their offices, but I followed two people who worked there."

"How did you know they worked there?"

"Well, it was around lunchtime so I waited on the floor below theirs. I watched for the elevator to stop on the F.R.O. floor, and when it did I punched the button so it would stop to get me. Then I got on the elevator with the people it had just picked up."

"Smart! Who were they?"

"Two older men. Suits, ties, pale skin like they live under rocks. They pretended not to know each other, but once they got out they kept walking together so I followed them."

"You are such a great spy!"

"I know, I totally want to be a P.I. now. It was perfect because I even had a change of clothes in my bag—I didn't want to have to wear those bike shorts any more than I had to…"

"Where did they go?"

"They walked over to China Palace for lunch. After they went in, I ran across the street to the coffee shop and changed clothes, then went in for lunch myself."

"Is China Palace the one with the really high booths?"

"Exactly. I sat in the booth next to theirs and eavesdropped as much as I could. Some other guy had joined them, but I never got to see him; I had to be careful that they never saw me."

"You don't know who the other guy was?"

"They called him Tremblay. I got the feeling that he'd been away for a long time and was coming back to work with them. They toasted to having Tremblay back at HQ."

"Did he have a German accent?" I ask, wondering if it could be Barend Schlacter using a different name.

"No, Canadian. You know how they say 'aboot' instead of 'about' and end every sentence with 'eh'?"

"What did they talk about?"

"They started by asking about the progress on the North-west Passage, that waterway above Canada that hooks up Asia and Europe. It's been frozen forever and is starting to thaw out."

"And?" I ask. Like a waterway in Canada has anything to do with me.

"What I read said that this thawing is a super-bad thing, but these guys were all excited saying how great it is that in just a few years it will make the Northwest Passage totally usable. They laughed about how with the billions they'll make on shipping stuff through there instead of going all the way down through the Panama Canal, they could make a freezer the size of Wyoming for polar bears."

"Strange."

"Then the new guy starts asking about Project Khymatos and they say it's obviously working really well, that they're going to have the biggest U.S. exposure yet with all the fighter jets doing their demonstrations over millions of people on the 4th of July."

"I don't get it."

"You know those white lines in the sky that come from airplanes? Well, supposedly some of those are really exhaust from the airplanes, but conspiracy freaks think most of them are metals and chemicals that are being sprayed over us."

"Gross. Why?"

"I don't know. I mean, there's tons of theories on the Internet. But the part that really freaked me out was when Tremblay asked how they are protecting themselves and their families, and the two guys say they have master filtration systems at the Pyramid and at their homes."

"The Pyramid meaning the Transamerica building?"

"Right, they call it the Pyramid. Then they talked about not going outside much, and how their home filtration systems help protect their families but doesn't totally stop exposure. Then Tremblay laughed and said, 'Like the rest, I guess it makes them a lot easier to control, eh?'"

"So, you think that what they spray controls us somehow?"

"That's what it sounded like."

"There's just no way," I say. "You can't just hire planes to spray people with chemicals."

"I know it seems like a stretch, but these guys were totally serious."

"Did they talk about anything else?"

"Then they started talking about HAARP."

"Wait—I've heard of HAARP," I say recollecting the name. "Haven't we heard of HAARP?"

"Sixth grade, Mr. Mattson was obsessed with it. It's that weird electrical station the government built in Alaska. The High Frequency Active Auroral Research Program."

"That's right! He said they're controlling weather and earthquakes and hurricanes with it!"

"Exactly," Justine says. "I did some more research on it when I got back and it's definitely creepy."

"But what did these guys say about it?"

"I didn't catch the whole thing, but it's something about using the 'Planetary Defense Shield' that everyone believes is to protect us from nuclear weapons to block something else."

"What I don't get is why anyone in the *Fraternitas* would be interested in me. What possible tie could there be?"

"I don't know. These guys were talking about stuff that happens on a huge scale. No offense, because *I* think you're really interesting, but I don't know why someone who works with this big creepy company would think you're worth flying to the other side of the world to scare."

"I don't either. Too weird," I say, still trying to place myself in this puzzle. "But hey, thanks for your help. That was huge."

"Anytime you need me to spy on anyone, I'm totally up for it."

"You're the best. Think you can fall back to sleep?"

"I'm halfway there. I'll email you tomorrow."

I stay in my room for the rest of the day, processing what Uncle Li was explaining and Googling all the stuff Justine told me about. There is so much information out there about chemtrails and HAARP and the Northwest Passage and it's all so terrifying.

I'm having trouble reconciling these two worlds—the world of energy and vibration and the world of corruption and control. I can't help wondering if the *Fraternitas* is using this ancient knowledge that Uncle Li was talking about to manipulate us. Is it possible that people would be so driven by greed and power? Is it possible that everything we know to be true is just an elaborate mirage?

After too much time in the labyrinth that is the Internet, I feel like I need to do something where I am in control, so I scan in two more sets of symbols to run while I'm sleeping.

My dreams are invaded by fighter planes and electrical

arrays and fleets ships all crewed by people who look like Barend Schlacter. It's a relief when my eyes open and it's light out.

I check the decoded spirals, which are cryptic as usual. I need to get these to Uncle Li, so I make my way down to the kitchen to see if he's up. Sure enough, he and Dad are talking with Mrs. Findlay. She has her hands way up inside some large bird, stuffing it for tonight's dinner. Mr. Papers jumps from his perch to the back of a chair and then directly onto my shoulder; we butt heads and then he takes my earlobe in between his finger and thumb and rubs it absent-mindedly.

"Hey, Uncle Li, have you seen Mr. Papers do his origami yet?" I ask. I set a few sheets of origami paper in front of Mr. Papers. "Do your stuff, my friend."

He starts slowly, as if he's not sure what to make, and then gets moving. After a couple of minutes he lays down a sheet of blue paper and then gently sets his creation on top of it. It's a beautiful pink lotus blossom with green stem and leaf, floating on the pool of blue paper.

"How exquisite!" says Uncle Li.

Dad rubs his chin. "It *is* quite amazing, isn't it?"

"He's a genius," I say as Mr. Papers picks up the blue paper and carries it, like a waiter carrying a tray, over to Uncle Li. Then he bows. Uncle Li nods and bows back, whispering something in Chinese.

"Well, Caity, what do you have planned for the day?" Dad asks.

"Following Uncle Li around as he checks out the feng shui of the castle."

"That okay with you?" Dad asks Uncle Li.

He brushes some crumbs off his silk jacket and says, "Of

course. Caity is actually very helpful. She has an excellent intuitive sense of feng shui principals."

"What time does Mom get home?"

"I'm picking her up at four," Dad says as he gets up, chugs the rest of his coffee, and then sets the cup in the sink.

Thank God, I think. I'm so excited to have her back. The whole Barend Schlacter thing has made two days without her seem like two weeks.

"Aye, and I'm making duck," says Mrs. Findlay, holding up the bird she was stuffing by its back legs. I can see Uncle Li's eyes light up. Mrs. Findlay winks at him and he looks down quickly and blushes. I take his hand and lead him out of the kitchen.

When no one is around, I whisper, "I decoded two more. I need you to look at them."

"Great work! Yes, let's go see."

We head upstairs with Mr. Papers in tow. Once in my room with the door closed, I pull out a printout of the two decoded spirals. He puts on his glasses and then reads out loud.

This birth may come like a storm or a dove
The outcome lies in how much we can love
Like gravity, love is a force of great might
True power comes when we connect and unite

Into arcane old knowledge you must delve
To find the secret to twenty-twelve
The oldest myths, the oldest sages
Point only upward to explain the ages

"The secret to 2012? Love a force like gravity?" Uncle Li says as he looks up to the ceiling and pulls on the skin of his neck "What do you make of this?"

"No clue. I'm going to start decoding another," I say. "Maybe you need them all to make any sense." I get the next set of symbols into the program and ask Dr. Li what he wants to do.

"We need to get inside that tower. Let's go back into the chamber." He walks over to the panel and I follow and open the door with my pendant.

"There just has to be another way out of here," he says walking around the room, his face an inch from the walls, looking up and down and feeling everywhere for some way out. I concentrate on the ceiling, thinking there might be some kind of hatch up there.

I hear Mr. Papers huffing and puffing and look down to see him burrowing under the enormous Oriental rug. Uncle Li and I look at each other, thinking the same thing. Moving the fainting couch and side table, we roll the carpet back and right there in the center of the floor is a round stone, like a manhole cover, with a pattern of circles carved into it.

"You found it," he says as we kneel down to touch it. "The Flower of Life."

"What do you know about this thing?" I whisper. Every hair on my neck is standing at attention.

"It's a symbol seen all over the world, but no one knows its origin. Many people believe profound knowledge about how the universe works is encoded in it."

I bite my lip. "Now what?"

"Open it!" he says. "You found it, you get to open it."

I am seriously freaked out. Too many horror movies. "Will you do it?" I beg. "Please?"

He laughs, pulls out his pocketknife, unfolds the longest blade, and slips it under the stone cover, prying it up enough to get his fingers under it. *I wouldn't do that in a million years,* I think to myself, imagining tarantulas and maggots scurrying around under his fingers.

We feel a whoosh of air when he lifts the stone. It's not musty or rotten at all; it actually smells good, like the inside of a cornhusk right after you peel it off the cob. Clean, but earthy.

The hole is pitch black. Uncle Li holds his hand over it like a psychic trying to feel what's in there, and Mr. Papers has his whole head down it. I try my flashlight, but all we can see is the top few rungs of an old ladder. There's nothing moving around down there and there aren't even any spider webs—it's the *lack* of anything creepy that seems creepy.

"We need more light," Uncle Li says and I tell him about the lanterns I saw out in the shed where Thomas used to keep Mr. Papers, then run out to get them.

Back in the chamber, I give them to Uncle Li. "I'll light them once I'm down," he says, holding the lanterns in one hand as he descends the ladder using the other hand. I shine the flashlight down to light his way. "Made it!" he yells up at me. "Come on down."

I figure since the air smells okay and there are no rats or snakes so far, I'll follow. Mr. Papers holds on tightly to my shoulder. Once I'm down, Uncle Li lines up the lanterns. I wave away the throat-closing smell of match hitting lamp oil, and then the room lights up.

It's slightly larger than the secret room above. Where the room above ends, this one goes on, as if my secret room is just nested and hanging inside this larger space. Other than that, there's nothing to see. We walk over to the wall that butts up to the tower and look closely for a way through, but can't find anything.

Mr. Papers grabs my flashlight and points it up. We follow the beam and see the outline of a door on the wall above our heads. Mr. Papers runs over to the ladder and hops on a rung, so Uncle Li moves the old thing over to the wall at the base of the high door. With the flashlight pinned under his arm, he climbs up then pushes the door as hard as he can.

It moves.

ELEVEN

I can't believe we're finally breaking through to the hidden core of the tower. More than a little bit nervous, I'm not going to tell Uncle Li that my legs are shaking so bad I can hardly stand up.

As I run each lamp up the ladder to Uncle Li, he pushes them through to the other side of the door. Then he climbs through and Mr. Papers and I follow. Once on the landing, we each take a lantern and leave one there so we can find our way back.

The space is too large to see much of anything from where we are, so we start down the stairs that lead from the landing to the tower floor below. I hear the sound of water moving; must be the spring that feeds out of the base of the tower. With each step a bit more is revealed, and we see that there are big boulders arranged in either two circles or a figure eight. Inside one of the circles is a flat round space, like a stage, and inside the other is a fountain.

Then as we walk around the circle of rocks, something

amazing happens: each rock lights up until the whole place is glowing dimly with yellow and pink light like a sunset. The whole scene starts to look like some kind of Maxfield Parrish painting.

"Phosphorescence!" Uncle Li says, excitedly. "The electrons in the rocks store the energy from our light and then play it back. Extraordinary!"

"It's beautiful," I say as I shine my lantern on each one for a few moments to get the whole group glowing strongly. It's hypnotizing, like a campfire. Their glow lights up the space below but is not bright enough to allow us to see the ceiling. Looking up is like looking into a dark well—it's pure black and makes me feel dizzy.

I walk over to the fountain. A tall cylinder, maybe eight feet high and a foot wide, has been carved from rock and made into a pipe for the water to flow up through. Then the water spills over the sides of the pipe and is caught in a stone basin. From there it flows down another stone pipe about a foot wide that goes directly out the side of the tower where I saw it the other day.

"Let's walk the perimeter of the tower," Uncle Li says. Always a slave to the power of Yin and Yang, he adds, "Clockwise, of course."

We start at the left of the staircase and walk slowly. As we hold the lanterns up, the walls become visible and we see carvings. Instead of symbols like in the secret room, these are just holes with rings around them, like bull's eyes, most about the size of my hand. Some overlap and some stand alone. I run my fingers over the cool, sanded carved circles.

"What's the deal with the circles?" I ask.

"You find these at ancient sites all over Scotland," Uncle Li replies, looking closely at one. "They're called cup-and-ring carvings."

"Do you know what they mean?"

"No one really does. They could represent the sun, as does the Egyptian symbol that looks like this. Or perhaps they represent the galaxy."

Mr. Papers starts jumping on my shoulders, pointing to the wall. He brings his hands together and then spreads out his arms, like people do when they say, "All this can be yours."

"What's going on?" I ask him.

He uses his finger to make figures in the air.

"Is he...writing something in the air?" Uncle Li asks, as if he doesn't believe it himself.

Setting my lantern on the floor, I take Mr. Papers off my shoulder and hold him out in front of me. He starts over, tracing letters slowly in the air, wearing the exasperated look that Mom gets when she's told me a million times to do something.

"Look," Uncle Li says, "he's making an R. And a U... and...a...an N!"

"Run?" I look around, terrified. It feels like someone shoved a shot put in my throat and it sunk right down to my gut. This is like a bad slasher film. "*Run?*"

Mr. Papers points to the wall and then makes that grand gesture with his arms again. Uncle Li's eyes are huge and he doesn't say anything, which makes me even more scared.

"There's no way this monkey can spell, can he?" I ask.

"Doubtful," Uncle Li says. "But, he could be tracing something he sees…" He backs up, holding his lanterns as high as he can.

When the wall lights up, I see it. "Look! Do you see it?"

"What? I don't see anything but the cups and rings."

"Look at the big picture," I tell him. "They're not random at all, they cluster together in letters." When you adjust your eyes differently, the ring carvings come together to make three letters that must each be twelve feet tall. It spells *Rùn*.

"Oh, yes! I see!" Uncle Li says. "Look, there's an accent mark over the U. Must be Gaelic."

Walking quickly to the next wall, I say, "Let's see if there are any more." We stand back a bit and adjust our eyes to see the big picture. Sure enough, there's another word: *Fuaigh*.

"Has to be Gaelic," Uncle Li says as he walks to the next wall. Again we step back and light it up. The word there is *Cruitheachd*. Each one is getting stranger than the one before. I wouldn't even know how to try to pronounce these—when's the last time you saw "chd" together in a word? We move on to the last wall, above the staircase. The word is written higher up and we can barely make it out. Finally Uncle Li reads off the letters: *Creid*.

"Let's go see what these words mean," he says.

We go straight to my computer, which has stopped decoding the last spiral. My stomach tightens when I see the word *Fraternitas*. I flash back to Barend Schlacter's foul breath and his fat fingers wrapped around my wrist.

"Can you read it?" Uncle Li asks.

Watch closely the Fraternitas and follow each lie
An animal is most dangerous when it knows it might
  die
Look who profits from war, who controls by fear
At the end of this age, their end too could be near

Uncle Li walks over to look at the page. "Did you say *Fraternitas?*"

"Have you heard of it?" I ask. I'm still terrified about what Barend Schlacter said he'd do if I told my parents, so I don't let on that I know what it is.

"Oh, no. It's so similar to 'fraternity,' I probably just recognized the word," he replies.

I search for Gaelic dictionaries, then type in *rùn*. It means *intention, love,* or *secret.* Then I try *fuaigh* and get *stitch, knit, connect. Cruitheachd* means *the creation,* or *universe.* And *creid* means *believe.* Uncle Li jots it all down. "So if we put it all together it's something liked *Secret connects universe believe.*" I say.

"Or, if it starts with creid, it could be *Believe love connects universe.*"

"Cool! That's kind of sweet, isn't it?" I like to think that's the right one. "Plus, that kind of relates to that spiral about love being a force or something."

"You are absolutely right," Uncle Li says. "We're getting more and more information that *seems* to relate, but we can't yet put this mosaic together in any meaningful way."

"So what now?" I ask as I look at the clock. "It's close to noon. Want to go back down?"

He looks at me with a twinkle in his eyes and says, "Don't you?"

Once back in the tower, Mr. Papers scampers off. He heads toward the circles of boulders that are still dimly glowing. I follow him over while Uncle Li investigates the walls a bit more. Mr. Papers goes to the side of the formation that does not have the fountain in it, the side with just a flat stage-like area where one enormous cup and ring is carved, then he pats a boulder like he wants me to sit down, which makes me laugh out loud. After I sit, Mr. Papers looks at me to make sure I'm watching and walks slowly to the center of the ring.

Then the strangest thing happens—it's so weird that for a second it really doesn't register—Mr. Papers starts to rise in the air. He keeps going until he is about fifteen feet up, lying back as if he's floating in a pool. Then he manages to sit up, look down at me, and wave.

"UNCLE LI GET OVER HERE!" I yell.

Uncle Li turns around to look at me and then runs over. He doesn't even see Mr. Papers; I mean, who would think to look for a monkey flying fifteen feet in the air?

I point and he looks. He staggers backwards like he's lost his balance. Mr. Papers motions to us to come in. I walk toward the ring, and as I get closer to the center, I feel a strange pulling sensation, the same kind of feeling you get on a spinning ride when you're forced to the edge of the seat and you can't do anything about it. This pull is as firm as that, yet gentler, not jarring. By the time I walk to the center of the ring, I'm floating upward too. I get about five feet off the ground, not nearly as high as Mr. Papers but high enough to really trip me out. My body naturally tips back like I'm sitting in a car with the seat reclined.

I look down at Uncle Li coming inside the circle. As he gets closer, he too starts to rise and ends up even higher than I am. This makes me think that I probably weigh more than he does, which would really depress me if I weren't, you know, levitating with a monkey and a Chinese man inside a castle in Scotland.

We all look at each other and start laughing. Honestly, monkeys can laugh, or at least Mr. P can. We don't stop until tears are coming from our eyes.

Mr. Papers starts doing somersaults in the air. I watch how he does it and give it a try. I make it over once, but accidentally kick Uncle Li. Then I try again but hurl myself too far and end up falling. Uncle Li inches his way over to me and then juts his body out of the ring and falls to the ground as well. Catching my breath, I look up to see Mr. Papers heading over to where we are. He throws himself out of the ring and falls gracefully into my arms.

Uncle Li is shaking his head. "I've read articles about this, but never seen firsthand—"

"Articles about what? Floating?"

"Levitation. There's a university in the Netherlands with some of the world's largest magnetic field labs, and they've managed to levitate a live frog."

"One little frog and that was big news?" Imagine what kind of story this would make! "So something magnetic made us float?"

"A magnetic field is the only reasonable explanation," he says, rubbing his eyes with his palms. "Although the force of this must be a thousand-fold stronger than any other discovered."

"Let's do it again!" I say. "You know, just to make sure…"

Uncle Li smiles and walks back into the circle. As he gets close to the center, he tips backwards and his feet leave the ground. I follow him in, start to rise, and then sort of "swim" to the center where I get back up to about five feet. Mr. Papers runs to the center and then jumps really high, and instead of falling he stops about a foot off the floor and then slowly rises again until he's way above both of us.

"This is officially the strangest day of my life," I say.

"Keep an open mind," Uncle Li says with a wink. "It may get stranger yet…"

Floating is a weird sensation. It's not as effortless as you'd think; you still have to balance your wobbly body. It's easier if you kind of curl up in a ball and hug your knees.

Once I find a stable position, I enjoy the ride. Taking a deep breath of the cornhusk air, I look down at the bright lanterns and the glowing rocks. I take in the cups and rings on the wall, and still shudder a little when I see the word *Rùn*. Now the accent mark makes it look even more sinister, like there's an emphasis on it. I try to keep reminding myself that it probably means *love*.

I look up at Mr. Papers and see him holding his arms out to each side and then spinning his body over and over. Uncle Li is a few inches above me; he has managed to get himself into lotus position and is sitting very still with his back straight and his hands on his knees, palms up with middle fingers touching his thumbs. He looks like a Buddha statue—if Buddha had hair.

I look down at the ground, but lean too far and tip over so I'm hanging there upside down. Once in this position it's hard to get back to sitting upright, and by the time I manage it I'm actually tired from the work. "I'm getting down," I yell up to Uncle Li. He flinches a bit, like I startled him. I think he was meditating.

"I suppose we should go," he says with a sigh, as if he could hang out here for hours.

I nod. "Mom's coming home soon and Dad's probably wondering where we've been."

We decide to leave the lanterns on the landing at the top of the stairs, no sense in dragging them up and down the ladder every time, and we use the flashlight to get down and back up the ladder into the secret room. It feels like I've come back from outer space. I touch the fainting couch to ground myself.

"I'll run some more symbols this afternoon," I say, regaining my composure. "Hopefully by tomorrow I'll have all of them done."

"Good work, my friend," Uncle Li says as he heads out the door. He turns around and says, "It's an honor to have this adventure together."

I smile and nod my head, feeling guilty for not yet telling him the whole truth.

Mr. Papers jumps onto my desk and I hand him the sandwich that Uncle Li had brought up for me. He chows down and then rolls a piece of paper and pretends to drink, so I get him a glass of water from the bathroom.

There's a knock on my door and Mom peeks in. I run over and give her a hug. So much has happened since she left that it seems like she's been gone for weeks.

My mom isn't the warmest, kissy-kissy person in the world, but when you want a real hug she's the one to go to. You could stand there for days because she'll never be the first one to pull away. "I'm so happy to see you," I say.

"Happy to see me or to see your goodies?"

I pull back and say, "Maybe both..."

She picks up a shopping bag from the hall and spills three pairs of jeans, a couple of T-shirts, a cool Euro sketchbook, and a tiny polo shirt and mini khaki shorts onto my bed. From another bag she pulls out a huge bar of Toblerone chocolate, almost the size of a baseball bat. "This ought to keep you busy," she says as she tosses it over. It's so heavy it sinks into the duvet. I pick it up, open one end, and slide the triangular bar part way out.

"God that's good," I say, sinking my teeth into the chocolate, chewy with honey and nuts.

"Evil good," she replies, breaking off a piece for herself. "So, ready for our big day?"

"What do you mean?"

"The Berkeley alums are coming tomorrow. And Dr. Tenzo. Didn't you know of him somehow?"

"No," I say quickly. "I mean, I've heard of him from Justine's grandpa. They work together." All of a sudden I worry that she'll bring up the subject of Dr. Middleford to Tenzo, and then Tenzo might mention the spirals, and then I'd have to explain everything. "But, they hate each other so I wouldn't bring up Justine's grandpa *at all*."

Mom laughs. "Grown men who hate each other? Now that's just silly."

"I'm serious! They have some sort of rivalry, so just don't mention Middleford. Please."

Mom's eyebrows go up and I wonder if I've made too much of a big deal out of this.

"Settle down honey, I won't mention a thing," she says as she slips the chocolate bar back in the box and hands it to me. "You keep this. Otherwise I'll eat the whole thing."

"Gladly," I say.

"I'm going to take a quick bath. See you at dinner," she says as she tucks my hair behind my ear.

I put away the clothes Mom bought and then dress Mr. Papers in his new outfit. He looks ridiculous in these normal clothes, like all the stupid preppy boys at the Academy of Cruelties. I liked him better in his old circusy outfit so I give them a good cleaning in the bathroom and set them on the window sill to dry. He deserves to look unique.

That night, I eat dinner as quickly as I can and then head back up to my room; I want to decode two more spirals before bed. After a lot of work getting them decoded, I'm a little frustrated that they seem just as confusing in English as they were in whatever weird language they were originally in:

The butterfly will emerge in three different ways
At the source, at your core, and by way of the days
Called feathered serpent when spoken of in code
Connected to all by the great white road

Remember this always, and above all other
The wise ones grasp the power of our great mother
The numbers, the stars, the cycles and days
Should all be counted, should all be praised

I print them out and write, "Make any sense to you?" on top. Then I sneak over to Uncle Li's room and slide the paper under his door. I hear a creak as I'm walking back down the hallway and run like a gazelle back to my room; I don't even feel my feet hitting the ground. Obviously I'm a lot more on edge than I thought if one random creak can get me this freaked out. I wonder if I'll have permanent nerve damage from all of this.

When I get to my room, I bolt the door and literally fly into bed. I'm so jacked up on adrenaline I don't even have to use the stairs. Drawing all the bed curtains, I enclose myself in my little velvet-tufted genie's bottle and try to calm down.

Mom taught me to say the Fibonacci series when I can't sleep. You start with one plus one and then you keep adding the previous number to the result. It works—believe me, nothing puts you to sleep faster than doing math in your head.

0, 1, 1, 2, 3, 5, 8, 13, 21, 34, 55, 89, 144, 233, 377, 610, 987 ... I'm out.

TWELVE

Waking up late and hungry, I pull on some clothes and make my way to breakfast. When I get downstairs, I hear voices and realize the alumni group from Berkeley must have arrived.

Slipping quietly past the dining room and into the kitchen, I see Mrs. Findlay folding apricot filling into crêpes and Mom making more coffee in the huge percolator.

"Hey, when did all these people get here?" I ask.

"Oh, they just arrived," Mom says, rubbing her hands together over the sink to dust off the coffee grounds.

"Was Tenzo on the train with them?" I ask, trying to seem unconcerned.

"Yes, he was. He wanted to take a look around, though, so Thomas is giving him the grand tour."

"What?" I blurt out.

"What do you mean, 'what'?" Mom asks.

"Nothing. I'll be right back." I bolt out of the kitchen to look for Uncle Li and find him in the dining room next to a tiny woman with a long grey ponytail. As I make my way over to him, I notice that Alex is in the room dressed in a crisp white shirt and black pants. He sees me before I can sneak away and I instantly regret not paying more attention in the mirror this morning.

"Isn't it nice to see this old place full of people, the way it was meant to be?" he asks.

"Yeah, but it's strange to hear all this noise after it's just been us." I pour myself some tea. He hands me the sugar bowl. "Thanks. So will you be here all day?" I ask.

"Nae, Gran is making up picnic lunches for your parents and the guests to take with them on their tour of the countryside. But I'll be back to serve at dinner."

Mrs. Findlay pokes her head through the door and gives Alex the stink eye.

"Hate to get fired by my grandmum," he whispers. "Excuse me, Caity."

I love hearing him say my name.

I serve myself a crêpe and some potatoes and sit down next to Uncle Li. He introduces me to grey-ponytail lady, Kimberly Slaton, and tells me she is a retired astrophysicist. "Oh how cool!" I say, pretending I know exactly what that is.

"How are you this morning?" Uncle Li asks me.

"Good, good. Thanks," I reply as I dig in to my crêpe. As nonchalantly as I can I say, "So, Tenzo is here. He wanted to see the castle so Thomas has him on a tour right this minute."

Dr. Slaton chimes in, "Oh, we met him on our way over from the train station. He's very serious! We couldn't figure out what a man like that would be doing on a vacation by himself."

"I guess everyone has a different reason for being here,"

Uncle Li says. He looks at me and motions to the door with his head. He stands up and tells Dr. Slaton what a pleasure it was to talk with her as I shove the last bites of potato in my mouth. "Caity, we really should be getting started with that project," he says to me.

Running into the kitchen, I pick up Mr. Papers before we go up to my room. I immediately change him back into his crazy circus clothes and he looks just right again.

"Okay, so what do we do about Tenzo poking around?" I ask.

He thinks for a moment and says, "We do nothing. We sit and watch."

"Really? You don't want to follow him? See what he knows?" I reach into my pocket for the last decoded message. "Here are two more I did last night. Something about the sky and cycles and stuff."

Uncle Li reads it and asks, "Are these the last ones?"

"I think there are two more," I answer. "What do you make of it?"

"Context is everything. We should decode those as soon as possible and read them all in order," Uncle Li says.

I get up to see if I can catch sight of Tenzo and Thomas from my window. Mr. Papers jumps up on the sill and starts sniffing the air and furrowing his brow. I scan the courtyard but don't see anyone. Then Mr. Papers starts jumping up and down, screeching and pointing, so I follow his finger. "Oh my God, they're on top of the tower!"

Uncle Li runs over to look, and Mr. Papers is still screeching. Not wanting them to see us, I grab Mr. Papers and close the window. I feel his heart racing under my fingertips.

"Is there any way he could know what's deep inside the tower?" Uncle Li asks.

"No, I don't think so," I say, trying to remember how this all came together. "All I did was fax some symbols to Justine, and she forwarded that to her grandpa. He sent it on to Tenzo, who's some kind of specialist in ancient languages. He asked Justine's grandpa where I sent it from. That's how he knew I lived here."

"Okay. Well, we're many steps ahead of him, so let's just relax," Uncle Li says.

"Relax? Are you serious?"

"There is an old Chinese saying, 'Give evil nothing to oppose and it will disappear by itself,'" he says, putting a reassuring hand on my shoulder.

Usually Uncle Li's words of wisdom work, but today they do nothing.

————

I'm fidgety and nervous and I try to think of something to do, but all I'm really interested in right now is looking at Alex, so I head back downstairs. Everything is cleared and cleaned from brunch, and Alex is nowhere in sight. Mrs. Findlay is in the kitchen, looking a little stressed. "What's up?" I ask.

"Oh, 'tis the first big dinner I've done in awhile," she says. A piece of hair has sprung from her bun and she pushes it out of her face with the back of a floured hand.

"Can I help? I can do basic stuff like chop or stir or something."

"Ah, thanks lassie, but I'll manage. Besides, the Laird's daughter shouldn't be found working for the cook."

"Hello? Is this not the twenty-first century? We're *so* past that," I say.

She gives me a crooked smile and goes back to her work. I hand Mr. Papers a banana and he takes it back to his cubbyhole.

"How long have you lived in Brayne, Mrs. Findlay?"

"Why, my whole life. Was born in the house that I was raised in and never left," she says as she sprinkles flour on the marble pastry slab.

"So this castle has always just been a home, nothing more?"

She punches her fist into a huge ball of bread dough. "Aye. It's only belonged to the descendents of Fergus Mac Fireland."

I search for the right way to ask. "Do people think it's unusual? Like haunted or anything?"

"Haven't you heard dear?" she says, laughing deeply. "Everything in Scotland is haunted."

I can tell she's preoccupied with cooking, so I stop my interrogation and ask again if there's anything I can do to help.

"Nae, child, Alex will be back to help before too long," she says with a wink. The whole master/servant thing bothers me, but at least I'll get to see Alex again today. "Why don't you just rest up for dinner?" she suggests. "These four-course meals can last hours."

"Is this something I should dress up for?"

She looks at me like I'm an idiot. "Most certainly. Didn't

your parents talk to you about this? Your paying guests have come to a castle; they're expecting the royal treatment."

Seriously? Sitting through a four-course dinner with old people after what we've discovered seems ridiculous. But, since Alex will be there, I have a long bath and try on every outfit in my closet. I end up choosing a sleeveless ice-blue linen dress with a silver chain belt.

Mom stops by as I'm getting dressed. "You look beautiful!" she says, slipping a tube of lipstick into a purse the size of a clamshell. She's wearing a green nubby silk dress with three-quarter sleeves and a square neckline. It looks retro, like something from a Hitchcock movie.

"Where have you been hiding that cool dress?" I ask.

"Just got it in Switzerland. You like?"

Dad pops in. "Can you believe I've forgotten how to tie a tie?" Mom turns around to look at him and whistles. He does look nice in a suit, a sight we rarely see.

Mom shakes her head. "I've never known how to tie one. I don't think I've seen you in one since … well, I don't remember."

"Thomas gave me this one; it was my grandfather's," Dad says. "It's the dress plaid for the Mac Fireland clan."

"When're you going to bust out the kilt?" I ask as I Google "how to tie a tie."

"Might be awhile, don't think I could get used to the draft …" he says.

"You want the windsor, four-in-hand, or half-windsor?" I ask.

Dad comes over. "Ah, my little genius," he says. "I'll take the windsor, please."

I hold up the printed instructions so he can read and tie at the same time.

"Alright! When have the Mac Firelands ever looked so good?" he asks as Mom and I thread our arms through his.

The guests are already in the parlor having cocktails. Thomas is behind the bar, dressed in a white shirt and black vest. He has his hair slicked back and I hardly recognize him. Alex is wearing the same, and is passing out hors d'oeuvres. He looks amazing, amazing, amazing.

His whole face smiles when he sees me. I'm sure it's because I'm the only person here within 50 years of his age. "Smoked salmon with crème fraîche, Miss Mac Fireland?" he says. Then he leans in and says, "You look stunning tonight."

All of a sudden I'm dizzy and need to sit down. I blush and say thanks and then sink in the nearest chair. Thomas brings me a glass of fizzy water with lime, which I drink all at once. I turn to my right to set the glass on a side table and jump; Tenzo is sitting in the chair next to me.

"Good evening," he says as he extends his hand. I reluctantly give him mine and he shakes it in that floppy way where you only grab fingers. "I'm Dr. Tenzo."

I pull my hand away and covertly wipe it on my lap. "I'm Caity."

"I know," he says as his thick red lips curl into a smile.

Within seconds Uncle Li is standing by my chair. He offers his hand to Tenzo and says, "Hello, I'm Zhong-Shan Li."

Tenzo stands up to shake. "I'm Dr. Tadashi Tenzo. Are you here with the Berkeley group?"

"No, I'm a family friend," he says as he puts a hand on my shoulder. I like that he seems to be saying, *This is my territory.*

I rub it in by saying, "I've known Dr. Li my whole life. He's our Feng Shui Master."

"Oh, *Doctor* Li is it?" Tenzo says with a smirk. "Do Feng Shui Masters get such titles?"

"Actually I have a Doctorate in Philosophy from Columbia University."

Tenzo seems embarrassed, "Oh, fantastic. Well done." He looks into his empty glass, and shakes the ice. "I think I'll freshen up my drink before dinner," he says as he heads off to the bar.

"What a jackass!" I say.

"He is quite annoying, isn't he?"

Dad comes over and walks me around the room by the elbow, introducing me to the guests. I feel like a poodle at a dog show—I expect Dad to pull a liver treat out of his pocket and reward me at any minute.

There's Dr. Slaton, the grey-ponytail astrophysicist who can actually pull off wearing orange lipstick; Mr. Inada, a tall, willowy chemist with a beard that looks as soft as rabbit fur; Dr. Frasse, a gorgeous Italian-looking college professor who is as tall as my dad; and Mr. Dressel, an ex-pilot who is missing two fingers (didn't ask). Plus Tenzo, of course.

When Mom announces dinner, Dad and I follow the others into the dining room. Thankfully, Uncle Li has saved me a seat as far from Tenzo as possible.

Each place setting has three crystal glasses of varying size, three forks on one side, two spoons and a knife on the other, and another spoon across the top. Three huge silver candelabras sit along the length of the table, and each one holds ten candles. I'm sitting near one and can actually feel the heat from all the flames. Between the candelabra are two big flower arrangements. I wonder where Mrs. Findlay is going to put all the food; there's no room left on the table for anything.

Once we're all seated, Alex pours the adults wine and me sparkling cider and then brings in a big tureen of soup on a wheeled cart. After we've all been served, Alex comes back in with rolls and puts one on each bread plate using silver paddle-like tongs.

The formality of the dinner causes an awkward silence. Mom uses me as an icebreaker and says, "Dr. Frasse, didn't you teach Classics? Our Caity has become quite interested in Plato and the Ages of Man."

All the old heads turn toward me and I turn as red as their wine.

Dr. Frasse's face lights up. "Oh, that's wonderful!" she says. "At such a young age, too. What have you been reading?"

I give Uncle Li a desperate look, and he says, "Actually, I have been tutoring her. We're studying preliterate myths and how they all boil down to one thing: how astronomy affects man. I'm sure you all know that the rise and fall of cultures is closely tied to where we are relative to other stars and planets and the Galactic Center."

Dr. Frasse nods. "It's true. All ancient myths are about cycles of time and how human development is tied to the movement of the heavens."

"Cycles as in Light and Dark Ages?" Dr. Slaton asks.

"Precisely," says Uncle Li. "As the Earth takes its twenty-six-thousand-year trip through the constellations of the zodiac, each sign reflects an age. Some ages are dark, some are light."

I didn't realize Uncle Li knew so much about this.

"So you actually believe there has been a Golden Age?" Mom asks. She seems as surprised as I am that Uncle Li knows so much about it.

"Absolutely. And we're emerging from a Dark Age now," he replies.

"Really?" Dad says skeptically. "With the amazing technology we've developed over the last hundred years I'd call *this* a Golden Age."

"You know what's driven most of that technology?" Uncle Li asks.

"Military research," Mr. Dressel answers. "How to control and or kill more people more efficiently."

Uncle Li nods and says, "Even the Internet was developed by the military. A civilian named Licklider wrote a paper about the concept of the Internet in August of 1962 and two months later he was snatched up by the United States Department of Defense to develop it."

I can tell Dad is getting freaked out and he makes some comment about the conversation getting heavier than the leek soup. Mom uses distraction and says, "So, what would you all like to do tomorrow? Go walking? Fishing?"

I'm glad my parents have to show these Berkeley alums every possible thing there is to do here; having them so involved with the guests keeps their eyes and their minds off of me.

As they all discuss what they want to see and do, I whisper, "Nice save, thanks," to Uncle Li. As I look up, I catch Tenzo watching us talk.

The door from the kitchen opens and Alex rolls in a cart with the biggest leg of lamb you've ever seen. He raises his eyebrows at me and I realize this must be the poor creature that Mrs. Findlay and I picked up from the farm the other day.

THIRTEEN

I wake to a knock on the door and promptly roll over and put the pillow over my head. A few moments later there's more knocking. "Who is it?" I yell through the pillow.

"Caity it's me, Uncle Li."

I put on my robe and unbolt the door.

"Tenzo is creeping around," he says as he closes the door behind him.

I rub the sand from my eyes, "Already? Where? Inside the castle?"

"No, outside. By the tower," he says quickly. "I was out for my walk this morning down by the loch and as I was coming back up the path, I saw him by the tower drinking from the water spigot with a large object in his hand."

"What was it?" I ask as I sit down on the edge of the bed.

"It was a disc the size of a Frisbee with a digital readout. As I made my way up the path—quietly so he wouldn't notice me—I saw him running it over the walls of the tower."

"What could he be doing?"

"Well, when I came up behind him and said hello, he nearly jumped out of his boots. I asked him what his machine was and he stalled before telling me that it was a metal detector."

"A metal detector? Do you believe him?"

Uncle Li shakes his head. "I asked him why he was using a metal detector on a stone wall and he gave me some fool story about finding interesting 'ores' in the rocks around these parts."

"Ores! Yeah, right. What do you think he was doing?"

Uncle Li scratches his head and then shoves his hands in his pockets. "I think it was a radar-type device to detect depth. I think he was trying to find a way into the core of the tower."

"What I don't get is how he knows about the tower."

"I suppose if you looked through the castle you'd realize the tower is the only place anything could be hidden," Uncle Li says. "All other space is accounted for in common areas and bedrooms."

"I guess you're right—but that means he's been poking all through this place."

"We'll just have to keep an eye on him," he replies. "But now you must excuse me, I have a meeting with your parents to present my initial feng shui analysis of the property."

I give him a wide-eyed look but he smiles reassuringly. "Don't worry Caity, I won't let on about any of this. There are definitely enough interesting features to talk about even without mentioning the tower."

Uncle Li leaves and I take a bath to wake myself up. Mom bought tons of cool Swiss bath products for the guests and gave me a whole basket of them too. I use a big brick of creamy white soap that has wildflowers from the Alps mixed in, and every so often a tiny yellow or purple flower springs from the bar and floats up. As I slip all the way under and stare at the ceiling through a veil of water and wildflowers, I hear Alex's voice from last night: *You look stunning tonight…* I remember that he'll be here for breakfast, so I pop up, rinse off, and get out of the bath.

Breakfast is over by the time I get downstairs, but Alex is still there, carrying the big silver trays in from the dining room. "Hey Alex," I say casually.

"Caity! We missed you at breakfast, mate."

Before I can even reply, I feel a clammy hand on my shoulder and look around. Tenzo. "Good morning, Caity," he says with a smile.

I can't take my eyes off his thick yellow teeth. I shrug my shoulder from under his hand.

Alex turns to him and says, "Dr. Tenzo, I'll be done in a few minutes and then we can go."

"Fine, fine," he says, looking at me with a smile. "I'll just talk to Caity while you're finishing up."

I breathe in sharply. "Oh, I have to help Mrs. Findlay. Bye."

Alex looks at me sideways as I run to the kitchen. He says to Tenzo, "Ten minutes tops, sir. I'll come find you."

When Alex comes in I try not to yell as I say, "*What* are you doing with him today?"

"Who, Tenzo?" he asks. "He just wanted a guided tour of the castle grounds."

I point to the dining room. "That guy is *trouble.* Thomas

already gave him a tour yesterday, you know. What more could he want to see?" I realize I sound hysterical.

Alex puts his hands up in a surrender position. "Easy Caity, 'tisn't a big deal; I don't mind showing him around again. He *is* a paying guest."

Mrs. Findlay comes over and stands in front of me with her brow furrowed. "What do you mean by 'he's trouble' dear?"

"I know him. He works with my best friend's grandpa. He's a well-known kleptomaniac."

Mrs. Findlay looks at Alex and says, "Hide the silver, boy!" and they both bust up laughing.

"I'm dead serious you guys. Just be very careful about what you show him, Alex. No hidden doors, no secret spots, nothing," I say, irritated that no one is taking me seriously.

Mrs. Findlay tousles my hair like I'm a two-year-old. "Aw lassie, I'm sure a professor from Princeton University is not going to ruin his reputation by taking a trinket from Breidablik."

"Alex," I say as calmly as I can, "just promise you'll tell me everything he asks about."

"Absolutely, Caity," he says with a smile, backing away like I'm a lunatic hobo asking him to donate a kidney to me.

I walk over to Mr. Paper's cubby, but it's empty. "Is Mr. Papers with Thomas?" I ask.

The two of them look at each other. Mrs. Findlay says, "Oh, uh...Dr. Tenzo wanted to play with him a bit this morning."

"You allowed—" I feel myself getting hysterical so I take a deep breath and collect myself. "Okay then," I say slowly.

"Where is Mr. Papers *now?* When I saw Dr. Tenzo in the dining room, he was alone."

Mrs. Findlay bites the corner of her lip. "I'll go ask; 'twas me who agreed to let him take Mr. Papers."

When Mrs. Findlay is gone, I put both my hands on Alex's shoulders and look him in the eyes. It's a bold move, but I need him to listen to me. He looks a little perplexed as I pin him in place and say, "I can't tell you everything right now, but you must not tell Dr. Tenzo *a thing* about this place."

He doesn't say anything, but I sense he's getting it, so I continue, "You can talk about general stuff, weather, dates it was built, the community, stuff like that, but *nothing* about the family, or the tower, or that Chinese guy who helped Fergus build it. Got it?"

He nods like I'm a cop asking him to stay out of trouble.

"Thanks," I say, releasing him from my grip. Once out of the kitchen, I can't help but put my hands to my nose. *These hands have touched Alex's shirt,* I think as I breathe deeply.

I drop them immediately when I see Mrs. Findlay.

"It's all sorted out," she says, seeming pleased with herself. "Dr. Tenzo told me he put Mr. Papers in your room. Since you weren't there, he just slipped him through the door and left."

"He went into my *room?*" I yell. This guy has nerve!

Mrs. Findlay looks bothered by my shouting. "Child, you really must calm down." She puts her arm around my shoulder. "Really dear, what could a grown man want in your room? It was a harmless mistake, returning Mr. Papers to your room instead of the kitchen. I'm sure he thought he was doing both of you a favor."

"Whatever," I say under my breath as I walk away.

The door of my room is closed, and I'm almost too scared to go in. I crack the door an inch and say, "Psst, Mr. Papers. You there?"

A squawk relieves my tension, so I throw open the door and run over to hug him. He's on my desk by yet another origami creation: a man in a robe with a tiny monkey. This one isn't made from origami paper, though; it looks like it might be a page from a magazine. I pick it up and point to Mr. Papers. "You made this?" I ask and he nods and points to his chest.

I gently unfold a corner so I can see what magazine it's from. At the bottom of the page it says *Journal of Ancient Near Eastern Languages*. Tenzo!

What is that guy trying to get Mr. Papers to tell him with origami? I'm too creeped out to be up here alone, so I take Mr. Papers downstairs and wait for Uncle Li to finish with my parents.

All the guests are sitting in the parlor, reading newspapers and drinking coffee. Seems like old people can read newspapers all morning. I pass them and walk toward the library, but then decide not to go in and interrupt. There's a nice velvet-covered chair outside the library door with a small, shiny wood table next to it. Mrs. Findlay has placed a crystal dish full of those little puffy square pastel-colored mints on it. Mom calls them pillow mints. They're only good when you're absolutely desperate for candy. Sitting in the chair with Mr. Papers on my lap, I start melting mints in my mouth as I listen to their conversation through the open door.

"The site is nearly perfect, from a feng shui perspective,"

I hear Uncle Li say. "The hill behind the castle acts as a good protective dragon. The castle itself sits just at the flat spot beneath the hill; you see, energy gathers where the momentum stops and that's right where we are. The forest on the left makes the Dragon, or Yang side, stronger and the Tiger, or Yin side, weaker—as it should be. The tower is rightly placed on the Yang side, and the wing with the restful guest rooms is on the Yin side. The stream that circles the inner wall of the castle is perfect; it reminds me of the Inner Golden River at the Forbidden City in Beijing."

"Wow, really?" Dad says. "I never considered the feng shui of the Forbidden City."

"Oh, the Forbidden City is the largest feng shui project in the world!" says Uncle Li. "The best feng shui masters in China helped design it back in the 1400s. What surprises me," he continues, "is how many feng shui principals were used when building this castle."

Dad says, "You know, Fergus spent a lot of time in China before he came back to build the castle. Maybe he picked up some tips."

"And I'll bet that fellow who came back from China to help Fergus had some feng shui knowledge as well," Mom adds.

"I didn't know someone from China helped build this castle. How did that come to pass?" Uncle Li asks, pretending never to have heard of this.

Dad explains, "Well, my great-great-great-great grandfather Fergus left Scotland when he was just eighteen. He traveled around China, learning the languages and customs. He was able to get his good friend Xu Bao Cheng to come back with him to build the tower, and then later the castle.

"Why would Cheng do this? What was his motivation for coming here?" Uncle Li asks.

"Who knows?" Dad says. "He must've been a good friend—he wasn't paid and this was hard labor. After all, it was just the two of them who built the tower, if you can believe it."

"The fact that good feng shui was employed in its construction makes this castle very auspicious," Uncle Li says. "And the island as a whole is very good, too. Lots of old, low hills, very nourishing. And a surprising number of springs and clean streams."

Mom sounds cheery "That's great; let's hope we can make it pay for itself so we can keep it. We're probably idiots to try and run an Inn in this economy." I can hear her knock the wood table for luck.

"Plus, Caity's doing so well here; it's as if her brain has expanded," Dad says.

"Really... how so?" Uncle Li asks, trying to see how much they know.

Mom says, "She's been doing the most interesting work, making up this code—"

"And she's finally taken an interest in what Fiona and I do. She asked me to teach her about encryption technology."

"Well, the energy of a natural spring under the tower is a great feature for fostering intellectual growth," Uncle Li says. "That might be what's going on."

"Whatever it is," Mom says, "we like it."

"I'll do a detailed analysis of each room next," Uncle Li says, trying to wrap things up.

"We should get going, Angus. These guests are expecting

a walk around the grounds with the Laird and Lady of the Manor."

"Aye, aye matey," Dad replies.

"That's pirate, honey, not Scottish."

I pop another mint in my mouth and scramble over to the parlor where all the guests and their newspapers are so they won't know I've been eavesdropping. Mom and Dad come out of the library and seem surprised to see me reading *The Scots Independent* among the older folks.

"Hi Caity, are you going to join us on our walk today?" Mom asks hopefully.

"Oh, I was going to go with Uncle Li to do more analysis on the castle," I reply.

Mom and Dad look at each other with raised eyebrows as if to say, *See, she is so much more intellectual here in Scotland.* "We'll see you at dinner then," Dad says.

Taking Uncle Li by the arm, I escort him out of the room. "We have a problem," I whisper. "Tenzo came in my room. Mrs. Findlay let him take Mr. Papers from the kitchen this morning, and he had Mr. P doing origami for him! I think he's trying to get info from him."

"How do you know this?"

"Because the piece—a guy in a robe with a monkey on his shoulder—was made from a page of a magazine called the *Journal of Ancient Near Eastern Languages.*"

"Do you know where he is now?" Uncle Li asks.

"He asked Alex for another tour of the grounds."

"The houseboy?"

Somehow that word sounds demeaning. "Alex is not really

the houseboy. I mean, he's helping us while the guests are here, but he's a friend, too. And he's Mrs. Findlay's grandson."

"Have you told him or Mrs. Findlay anything?"

"No, just to watch out for Tenzo because he might be a thief. I asked them not to give him any information about the place other than the stuff he could get out of a guide book."

"Well done, Caity."

"Hey, since everyone is going out walking today let's head back into the tower," I suggest. "We should take lunches, so Mrs. Findlay doesn't try to come find us."

I take two of the boxed lunches in the kitchen. Mrs. Findlay always has a pot of water on the stove, so Uncle Li removes a thermos from the shelf and fills it. He carries this small tin of tea with him; he never goes anywhere without his personal stash. His sister who still lives in China has a tea plantation and she sends Uncle Li the cream of the crop. He is a total tea snob and says that the stuff in tea bags is the garbage they sweep off the floor at the tea factory. His tea leaves are hand rolled into little pearls, and after sitting in water they unroll themselves and become leaves again. The tea is so pale you can hardly tell it from water, but *man* is it good.

Once in the tower, I walk Mr. Papers over to the magnet area so he can play while we look around. Then, as I head toward the fountain, I see that it isn't a figure eight, it is two interlocking circles, one with the magnet and one with the fountain. Kind of like the Venn diagrams we studied last year.

As I step between the two circles where they overlap, something happens.

I feel the ground move.

FOURTEEN

"Hey, Uncle Li, come here," I say, trying to keep balanced. It's like being on a surfboard.

Uncle Li walks over and looks down. "Well look at that! A *vesica pisces*," he says.

"What?"

"A *vesica pisces*. It's that middle part of two overlapping circles—an old mystical symbol that ancient cultures thought to be a source of immense power and energy."

"I don't mean look at the symbol, I mean look at it move!" I shift my weight a bit so it wobbles.

"Oh, my—"

"Step on it, it feels weird," I say, crouching down to keep my center of gravity low. Mr. Papers is perched on my backpack, tightly holding on to my shoulders.

When Uncle Li steps on the slab, it begins to sink. We both instinctively drop to our knees. It lowers as slowly as an elevator and stops about eight feet below the floor above. I hold up my lantern to look around, and see that we have been lowered into another dark chamber. The walls are rock, like a cave, as if this had been carved out below the tower.

Uncle Li gets on his stomach and holds his lantern over the edge. I do the same. We both turn them up as high as they will go and look down; beneath us is a massive set of stone gears.

"What is it?" I ask Uncle Li. "Some kind of machine?"

"I have no earthly idea," he replies. "How many pieces are there?"

We start counting. They're all different sizes, some are nested inside each other and others are interlocked so that they could move together. We count twenty.

"Do you see the faint carvings on them?" Uncle Li asks.

"I can barely even see the wheels. Do you think we should go down?" I ask, wanting to check it out more closely. "It's only about seven feet. I could jump that."

"As much as I'm anxious to find out what this is, I'm afraid that if we get off this *vesica pisces* it will rise again and trap us down here."

"Oh my God, you're right." A shudder goes through my body.

"This platform seems precisely weighted. I think it's just a viewing station."

"I wish we could lower our lanterns to light it up." Dying to see what's down there, I try to think where we could get rope and then remember the long elastic cord laced through the front of my backpack. I remove the toggle, pull out the cord, and tie it to the lantern.

Because the cord is stretchy, the heavy lantern lowers almost to the floor and illuminates the wheels. "Look, you're right; there really are carvings on them!" I say.

"They aren't anything like the carvings in the chamber; this is a true pictographic script."

"Like Egyptian writing?" I ask, scooting over to light up a different wheel.

"Not Egyptian, more like South or Central American," says Uncle Li. Then he snaps his fingers. "Of course! I think I know what this is!"

"What, what?"

"Back when I taught philosophy, I had a graduate student who was doing his thesis on Mayan cosmology."

I sit up to listen. "And…"

He pauses and looks up at the ceiling trying to remember. "I don't recall much about it—this was years ago, you see—but I do remember that much of the Maya's focus was on advanced astronomy and these elaborate calendars. And," he says with emphasis, "there were twenty of them!"

I point down. "You think that's what's down there?"

Uncle Li sits cross-legged on the platform. "I recall this fellow's paper describing how these twenty calendars that measure cycles of things, from insects to humans to the solar system and everything in between, work like a bunch of cogs together. While they are separate measuring devices, they all move together."

"You know, of all the things I expected to find down here," I say as I pull up my lantern, "a calendar was not one of them." I was hoping for something a bit more exciting. Treasure. A time machine. Something *radical*.

"I think this is a profound discovery," Uncle Li says emphatically. "Let me hold the lanterns and you sketch some of what's down there."

Uncle Li illuminates the floor while I try to sketch. It's actually quite beautiful when you look at it as a machine.

It's hard to sketch lying on my stomach, so I'm only able to get three of the gears drawn before we decide to break for lunch. To get back up, Uncle Li gives me a boost and I pull myself up with my arms. Once my weight is off, the platform moves up a bit. I watch Uncle Li rising up on this eye-shaped platform and realize it's an image that wouldn't be out of place in one of those cheesy sci-fi movies from the sixties that Dad is so in to. It stops a few feet below the floor, so Uncle Li pulls himself up like he's getting out of a swimming pool. Once he's off, the platform comes level with the floor.

We sit for a moment looking at it. "So what's the deal with the *vesica pisces*?" I ask.

"Pythagoras thought it represented the beginning of creation—it's symbolic of the intersection where the divine world meets the world of matter. Plus," he adds with emphasis, "it's the second step in making the Flower of Life, that intricate carving that covers the hole in the floor of your secret chamber."

"So the first step in making the Flower of Life is one circle, right?" I ask. "That means the beginning of this story started when we entered through the hole in the floor of the chamber."

"Excellent deduction!"

"And the second chapter started under the second step in making the Flower of Life—two overlapping circles—when we lowered ourselves into the cog room."

"I think you're right," Uncle Li says. "Which means the next step would be to find three overlapping circles."

I'm itching to do some research on these cogs, so after we finish our box lunches and Uncle Li goes to his room to rest, I do a search on Mayan stuff. It's weird how much there is on the Internet about the Mayan calendar. They were way ahead of their time when it came to astronomy and could even predict when planetary things would happen in the future. Plus they tracked astronomical stuff like eclipses back millions of years that have proven to be totally accurate. Then I see something weird that stops me cold. The Mayan calendar for human cycles ends in 2012.

Why would a calendar *end*? That's not really the point of a calendar. I remember that spiral about the secret of twenty-twelve: *Into arcane old knowledge you must delve, to find the secret to twenty-twelve.*

The intercom buzz makes me jump. Alex says, "Caity? You there? May we have a word?"

Running over to the intercom to hit the reply button, I say, "I'll meet you at the stairs," while trying not to sound out-of-breath or overexcited.

Alex is waiting at the bottom of the stairs for me, and when Mr. Papers catches sight of him he leaps from my shoulder, springs off the banister, and then lands on his shoulder. Alex looks worried. When I get to him, he looks around and whispers, "You were right about Tenzo."

"What?" I grab his arm and lead him to the library, closing the door.

"Tell me everything," I say, taking a seat.

"Well, first he wanted to walk around the perimeter of the castle, following the canal. And the whole bloody time he had this long stick that he was dragging along in the water, like he was trying to find something in that little *burn*."

"Did he?"

He shakes his head. "Of course not. Just the odd clump of moss. And then he had me walk him around every building on the grounds."

"Including the tower?" I ask as casually as I can.

"Aye," he says, rolling his eyes. "You'd think the man was doing a building inspection the way he was walking around that tower, poking at it with his stick, looking over every rock."

"What happened when you finished the tour and he didn't find anything?" I ask.

Alex sits on the arm of the chair next to me. "To be honest he seemed quite perturbed."

I give him the I-told-you-so shrug. "The guy is a freak."

"What do you reckon he wants?" he asks. "Why's he obsessed with the bloody tower?"

I shrug and shake my head, weighing whether or not I want to tell him all I know.

Alex reaches for my hand, places it on his open palm, and then puts his other hand over it like a sandwich. "I'm sorry I doubted you this morning."

I feel myself blushing. "No big deal," I stammer. "I must have seemed kind of psycho." I don't want to pull my hand away so I wait for him to drop it. He holds on for a moment. Then he lets go and gives me a big smile. If I look at him any longer, I swear I'll blurt out I LOVE YOU! So I turn away, becoming very interested in the upholstery on the chair next to me.

"Caity, what's up?" he asks.

But being this close to him, with his pale-blue wolf eyes and pineconey smell, it all makes me want to just come clean and tell him what I'd found out about his father.

"Alex, uh, can I ask you something kind of personal?"

"I suppose so..." he says reluctantly. I shouldn't have used the word "personal." I think he's expecting me to ask him about body odor or something.

"I was wondering if you know any of the details of how your dad...well, what happened here the night your dad passed away?"

"Aye," he says as he looks down and moves the edge of the Oriental carpet with his foot. "The castle was being burgled. Hamish managed to call over to our house and Dad came by to help. He was a hero, shot dead by cowardly thieves."

"But you never found out who it was? What they wanted?"

"They vanished before help could get there. Why're you asking?"

"I've just been discovering some weird stuff. I actually don't think it was a burglary. I think whoever shot your father might have thought they were killing Hamish instead."

He looks at me as if I'd been speaking Japanese. "What?" he says.

I start to repeat myself and he shakes his head. "Nae, I heard you. I mean, how could you say such a thing?"

"Well, it's just that some of the information I've found here—"

"Listen, Caity, you don't know *anything* 'bout my father," he says, cutting me off. He points his finger at me like a dart and speaks slowly and quietly, which for some reason freaks me out more than if he were to scream. "Whatever you think you're doing here, making up little detective stories to pass the day, leave my father out of it." I see tears welling up in his eyes. He tightens his face to control them, then looks down.

Uncertain of what's going on, Mr. Papers jumps to the floor and paces nervously. This is not at all how I thought Alex would react. My throat closes up like I'm going to vomit and my face feels white-hot. How could I have been so callous?

"Oh, my God, Alex, I didn't mean to—"

He stops me by putting up his hand. "I don't want to hear it. Just leave me and my family out of your silly made-up adventures." He keeps his hand up as he walks out of the room.

I feel exactly like I did on a childhood field trip to a farm when I accidentally grabbed onto an electric fence: fried to the core.

FIFTEEN

I'm wallowing facedown in a pillow when Mom knocks on my door and pops her head in. "Hi honey, how was your day?" she asks.

I don't want to answer that question, so I ask, "How was the walk?"

She flops on my bed. "Everyone had a great time. We walked to town, had a couple of drams at a pub and walked back. I'm exhausted and I'm thirty years younger than all of them!"

"Guess you shouldn't have tossed that Tae Bo tape..."

She rolls her eyes at me. "Anyway, dinner is not far off, so we need to get cleaned up."

I look at my watch. "Wow, it's later than I thought," I say.

She groans as she lifts herself up and says, "This place makes me forget time altogether. I never seem to know what day it is. Without the bustle of the city, it's easy to lose time."

"I've noticed that too," I say, getting up to try and do something about my puffy eyes.

Before dinner, the guests mingle in the parlor sipping drinks. I spot Alex with a tray of little quiches. He doesn't look at me. How do I apologize for something like this? How could I have been so dumb to push away my only friend here, not to mention my potential husband?

I see Tenzo walking right toward me. I look around but don't see my parents or Uncle Li, so I dash for the kitchen. "Can I help with anything?" I breathlessly ask Mrs. Findlay.

She waves me off. "Don't be silly Caity; you shouldn't even be in here right now."

"Okay, I won't do any work; I'll just sit and watch." I take a banana to Mr. Papers, who's sitting cross-legged on the pillow in his cubby like he's going to start a yoga class.

Alex comes in with an empty tray. "The savages have eaten them all," he says to Mrs. Findlay. It's as if I don't exist; I am officially dead to him.

"Nothing quite like a long walk in the glen to get the appetite up," replies Mrs. Findlay. "Will you ask the Laird to call them to dinner, son?"

I wait in the kitchen until I hear them taking their places. Uncle Li is saving a spot next to him and I'm happy to see Tenzo is at the far end of the table. I take a seat. While the guests are talking to one another, I whisper to Uncle Li, "Remember that line about twenty-twelve?"

"Vaguely," he replies.

"Well, I was surfing for info on Mayan stuff and guess what. Their whole calendar thing *ends in the year 2012!*"

"That's right! Now I remember. That was part of the thesis I was telling you about!"

"If they tracked eclipses and stuff back millions of years, why end it all in 2012?"

"I wish I could remember. This was so many years ago," he says. "It was something about moving into another plane of consciousness or something."

Talk is dying down and it's getting quieter, so Uncle Li and I end our conversation.

Alex walks around the table ladling seafood bisque into everyone's bowls. Mom picks up her spoon to eat and everyone follows.

"So Caity, what did you do with yourself today?" Dad asks.

"I kicked around with Uncle Li a bit, then I helped Justine with a summer school project."

"What a good friend you are!" he says as he pats me on the back. "What's the subject?"

"Well, she has to do this paper on Mayan Cosmology." I feel super smart saying "cosmology" even though I just learned what it means today.

"Wow! Well, you've finally found a subject that stumps me." He turns to Mom at the other end of the table. "Fiona, now Caity is studying the Maya!" he says loudly so that everyone at the table hears him. I just shake my head. It's *so* obvious that my parents have only one child.

"Oh Caity, that's wonderful!" Mom says. "Didn't they have an advanced civilization back when the Europeans were still living in muddy little villages?"

"Quite true," says Mr. Inada. "An amazing culture. My wife, Marcella, God rest her soul, taught Mesoamerican Studies at UT Austin."

"Well, you must know a lot about the Maya then," I say.

He wipes the corners of his mouth with his napkin. "Yes, quite a lot actually," he says. "We took many a sabbatical down in Guatemala, Belize, Mexico. Fascinating culture."

"So what's up with the 2012 thing?" I blurt out, wishing I'd said it more elegantly.

Dad asks, "What do you mean by 'the 2012 thing'?"

Tenzo looks at me and raises his eyebrows. "She means the end of the Mayan calendar."

I look away fast. What a creep.

"The *end* of a calendar? Enlighten us, Caity," Mom says.

I shake my head. "I don't know, that's why I'm asking. I just know that they were really good astronomers and they made these different calendars that end on December 21, 2012."

Tenzo lifts a finger and says, "Only one calendar, the Long Count calendar, ends then."

"Have you studied this much?" Uncle Li asks Tenzo, with a tinge of irritation.

In his snooty tone Tenzo replies, "I teach ancient languages, so of course I have studied the Maya. Though it's not my primary area of expertise."

The door from the kitchen opens and Alex rolls in the cart. There's a salmon the size of a toddler surrounded by lemons, crispy roasted potatoes, steaming rolls, and peas with chopped mint. I'm trying to catch his eye but he avoids looking in my vicinity. It's worse than I thought.

"Is the fact that the end date of this calendar—December 21—is winter solstice significant to the Maya?" asks Dr. Frasse.

"Absolutely," replies Mr. Inada. "Not only is December

21, 2012, the winter solstice, it's also when the sun rises in the middle of the dark bulge in the Milky Way." I notice that his eyes are watery like old people's eyes get, but something has lit them up.

Dr. Slaton nods and says, "Interesting. That part of the Milky Way is the center of the galaxy. Where everything originates."

"What's this now?" asks Dad, trying to keep up. It's weird to see him uncomfortable because he doesn't know something. "Is this alignment rare?"

Mr. Inada nods and says, "Well, I'd call once every 26,000 years or so pretty rare."

"Actually it's 25,920 years," corrects Tenzo, the big know-it-all.

Mr. Dressel says, "Oh, then this must have to do with the Precession of the Equinoxes."

"And we're back to the Ages of Man, that we talked about last night!" Dr. Frasse says.

"Wait, what's the 2012 thing have to do with dark and light ages?" I ask.

"All ancient cultures knew and mythologized what a profound affect Precession has on the human mind; the Maya just put dates to it all," explains Mr. Inada.

"Precession is caused by the Earth wobbling, right?" Dad asks. "Like in addition to orbiting the sun we also make this other little wobbly orbit?"

"Wow, really technical terms, Dad," I say.

Mr. Dressel adds, "That's right, Angus. Our wobble moves us backwards through the zodiac, causing the sunrise to move one degree every seventy-two years."

"But how exactly can this affect our brains?" I ask.

"One theory is that based on how close we are to the Galactic Center, we are pulled in and out of 'dark ages' when knowledge is lost, and 'ages of enlightenment' that cause evolutionary leaps," explains Mr. Inada. "It's just like our relationship to the sun, in summer there's growth, in winter there's death. Except the center of our galaxy has a bigger effect as it has the mass of more than *three million* suns."

"Let me put it plainly," says Tenzo, condescendingly. "Basically we're moving into an alignment with the Galactic Center that will profoundly change the Earth's electromagnetic field. The Maya predicted that this would cause some sort of... *evolutionary event*."

Mom goes for the hard facts and asks Dr. Slaton, the only one here who really studies space, if this is true.

Dr. Slaton shrugs. "Well, here's how it may be possible. We all know that the sun's activity influences *us* right? But what influences the sun? What triggers solar activity?" She pauses for a moment and wipes a bit of lipstick off her glass with her thumb. "The sun's cycles are triggered by energy that comes from the Galactic Center. So how the Earth and the sun are positioned to this center source greatly affects humans. And we're definitely noticing changes in the sun."

"What kind of changes?" asks Dr. Frasse.

"Well, there have been more sunspots in the last sixty years than for the past 1,150 *combined*. And the biggest solar flares in recent human history are predicted for—drum roll please—the year 2012."

"Really?" Mom says desperately, as if she's just been told there's rat poison in her wine.

"They call this time The Quickening," says Tenzo.

"But what's going to happen?' I ask. "I mean, why would the Maya track all these star and planet happenings back millions of years and then just end the whole thing in 2012 when we face the galaxy's center? Is that like the end of the world?"

"Or is it the beginning?" Tenzo asks mysteriously.

"Both," says Mr. Inada. "The Maya say it's the end of the Fourth World and the beginning of the Fifth World."

"The beginning of what?" Mom asks.

"Even before the fifteenth century, Mayan Elders knew—through the prophecy of their calendars—that they would be invaded in 1519. That started 468 years of what they called the Nine Periods of Darkness." All eyes are on Mr. Inada as he continues. "Because the Maya predicted it, they were prepared. Daykeepers hid in remote mountain caves to save the prophetic calendar systems. The ancestors of these people are still hidden today, counting down the days."

"And we are now in the final *Baktun*," says Tenzo. "The final cycle. A tenuous time."

Directing my question to Mr. Inada so that Tenzo will stop butting in, I ask, "Do you really believe that the world will change in 2012?"

"I'm just a chemist; I'm no scholar. But my wife spent her life studying the Maya, and she believed with every fiber of her being that 2012 would be one of the most important years in human history. Such a shame she won't be around to see it." We all see that Mr. Inada is getting emotional. People start scooting peas around on their plates and fidgeting with their wine glasses.

Dad eases the tension by raising his glass and saying, "To

Marcella Inada!" and everyone clinks glasses. Mr. Inada smiles and dabs at his eye with a tissue. Then Dad announces that they'll be boarding a coach for a special treat—a whisky tasting—and the room erupts with applause. Dad rubs his hands together and adds, "There are five distilleries just a short ferry ride away and we'll visit them all tomorrow. Be prepared to be away all day."

While everyone else gets up to leave the dining room, Uncle Li and I stay seated. Mom comes up behind my chair and puts her hands on my shoulders. "Caity, you're welcome to come along tomorrow. See the countryside. And Uncle Li, I hope you'll join us."

"Blech," I say. What is it with old people and whisky?

Dr Li shakes his head. "Thanks Fiona, but since I don't drink I'd be better off here."

"Uncle Li and I are working on something. Don't worry about us," I say.

Mom smiles and then grabs my hand. "Let's go, honey. I'll tuck you in."

"I'm taller than you, you know," I say, smiling at her as she walks me upstairs.

When she's gone, I bolt my door and hop into bed with my sketchbook. I have to write some of this stuff down before I forget it.

I turn to a sketch I'd done of Alex. If we're all just vibrations, maybe I can send some apology vibrations out to him.

I stare into his eyes and say, *I'm sorry, Alex. I'm so, so sorry.*

SIXTEEN

I hear the tour van pull up in the morning to take the guests on the whiskey tour. Leaning out my bedroom window, I say goodbye to my parents. Uncle Li is down there too; he motions that he'll come up.

While I'm waiting, I check my mail and see that there are three connection attempts from Justine flashing on my screen:

Justinem: KT-u there? Haven't heard a peep!
Justinem: Ok, maybe u r roaming around the castle or swimming in your moat or something
Justinem: Just wanted to fill u in on the latest w/David von Lovesme

My interest is piqued. I write fast.

Caitym: Justine, u still there?

Almost immediately a new message pops up:

Justinem: Hey KT! Yes, still here!
Caitym: What r u doing up?

Justinem: can't sleep. what r u up 2?

Caitym: oh, just ruining my future with mr. perfect.

Justinem: ?

Caitym: can't even go into it or i'll spiral down. what's the news with David von Lovesyou?

Justinem: OK, I know I'm a big hypocrite cuz I said he was a complete idiot in chemistry, but all of a sudden he's way in2 me

Caitym: Like throwing grapes at u in the cafeteria kind of in 2 u or asking u out kind of in 2 u?

Justinem: went to a movie last night… although he did throw a few pieces of popcorn at me

Caitym: u GOT 2 tell him that the throwing food thing isn't really considered flirting

Justinem: I'll get right on that, since we're going shopping 2GETHER in exactly 10hrs and 38 minutes!

Caitym: so weird that he likes 2 shop

I try to picture Alex shopping at high-end stores like the dweebs at the Academy of Cruelties. Thinking about the whole commercialism of my San Francisco life kind of creeps me out. I'll admit I was a shopper, but I wasn't even one of the bad ones. Some kids went shopping every single day after school.

Justinem: I know—I swear the boys in r class like to shop more than the girls

Caitym: get a hobby David

Justinem: well we know it won't be chemistry

Caitym: HA!

Justinem: he IS pretty smart in english though, so maybe he's a left-brainer. or is that a right-brainer?

Caitym: Good try… grasping for straws?

Justinem: I know. do u think I'm pathetic? just going out with him because he's beautiful?

Caitym: and popular

Justinem: and smells good

Caitym: No, I prefer 2 think u r dating him in an ironic way …

Justinem: Right, like wearing my mom's puffy-sleeved blouses from the 80s?

Caitym: xactly!

Justinem: ok, so I'm ironic. I feel better—think I may be able to sleep now. beauty rest for tomorrow …

Caitym: as if u need it!

Justinem: XOXOXO infinity …

Caitym: save the kisses for your new boyfriend ☺

After I sign out, I remember the square spiral I have left to decode. I dig it out of the bottom drawer and scan it. As I'm getting Dad's decoding program rolling Uncle Li knocks on the door. I unbolt it and find him holding hands with Mr. Papers.

We go straight down to the tower so I can draw the rest of the cogs, and make our way over to the center of the two interlocking rings. Mr. Papers can't resist playing in the magnetic field; I watch as he takes a flying leap off a boulder into the ring, falls almost to the floor, and then begins rising.

Just as we are about to step on the lowering platform, we hear a door slam followed by the grinding slam of a bolt locking. Chills run up and down my body and I find it hard to breathe. "What was that?" I whisper.

He looks at me. I look side to side. Then he heads back to the door. I hold on to his sleeve. "Uncle Li? What's going on?"

He places a finger on his mouth. "Shhhhh," he says, almost silently. A snake's hiss.

We walk quickly over to the door. There's a strange box

sitting at the top of the staircase. Uncle Li jumps the stairs two by two to get to the door but when he turns the knob, nothing happens. Even when he pushes it with his shoulder it doesn't budge. "Locked," he says.

No one knows where we are, there are no other doors out, and the place is soundproof. When my protein bar runs out we'll simply wither up and die here. I feel my throat tightening up, I don't want to cry but I don't think I can stop it. My lip starts quivering and then the tears come.

Uncle Li comes down the stairs and puts an arm around my shoulders that are now fully shaking. I can't stop crying.

"Oh, Caity, we'll work it out," he says in his calm steady voice. "Here, let's have a look in the box." By this time Mr. Papers is freaked out seeing me cry, so he wraps his arms completely around my neck. It's constricting but oddly comforting.

We sit on the last step and examine the wooden box that is about the size a pair of boots would come in.

"You want me to open it?" Uncle Li asks.

I wipe the tears from my eyes. "Well, I'm not! What if it's a snake or something?"

"Hmm, hadn't really thought of that …" Uncle Li stands back a few feet and gracefully extends his leg, then quickly kicks it open with his foot. All those years of Qigong have paid off.

Nothing pops out of the box. Uncle Li moves closer with his lantern and peers inside. "It's a note," he says as he bends over to pick it up. "Oh, and look here. There are books under it." He picks them up and comes back over to the stairs to sit by me. Then he removes his reading glasses from his chest pocket, puts them on his tiny nose, and reads aloud, "*Read.*

Translate. Write English translation in blank book. At this time tomorrow, knock three times on door and go to far wall. Remain facing wall until you hear door close again."

"Translate what?" I ask, still sniffling. "Do you think Tenzo did this?"

"Has to be Tenzo," he says, shaking his head in disgust.

Uncle Li opens the top book. It's really old and covered in leather, but hand bound with needle and string. The writing is small, and since it's pretty dark I can't really read it.

"Hmm," Uncle Li says. "This is old Sanskrit. Ancient text."

"Sanskrit? Like from India?" I ask.

He nods, then sits for a few minutes, paging through the text and not saying much.

"So," I say, unable to handle the suspense any longer. "Can you read any of it?"

"I'll get the lay of the book first. I want to know what I'm looking at."

"Is there anything I can do?" I ask, wanting some kind of distraction.

"Perhaps you should sketch the interior of the tower so we'll have it for future reference," he says. I know he's making busy work for me, but I'm grateful to have something to do. I sketch while he reads, but I find it hard to concentrate. Who could?

"Eventually they'll come looking, right?" I ask.

"Excuse me?" Uncle Li replies, not looking up from the book.

"For us! You know, they'll come looking, right?"

"But who would look down here? We are the only ones

who know about it!" Then I think of Barend Schlacter. Had he found this place? I think it's time to come clean.

"Um, Uncle Li?" I say with a wince. "There's one thing I haven't mentioned yet."

He looks at me sideways and says, "What?"

"Okay, first let me say that I wasn't trying to keep secrets from you or anything. I just thought that you might think this was all too dangerous for me and then tell my parents."

"What?" he asks firmly.

"Well, this guy came here a few days ago. His name was Barend Schlacter and he was pretending to be from the Scottish Tourist Board to approve us opening the Inn."

"Pretending? When was this?"

"The night before you got here. Mom and Dad were both out, so I was upstairs alone."

"He came to your room?"

I nod. "He said that I need to leave secrets alone and that if he finds out that my parents know anything he will..." I can't say the rest out loud.

"What? He will *what*?"

I look down. "He will make me an orphan," I say quietly.

"You really should have told me, Caity," he says, shaking his head. "You really should have told me."

"I know, I'm sorry. I thought you'd tell my parents or the police or—"

An air bubble in the fountain makes a loud gurgling sound and we both jump.

"Did he say who he really was, who he worked for?" Uncle Li asks.

"Well, that's the other thing... remember the spiral that

mentioned the *Fraternitas*? I think that's who he works for. He had the letters FRO tattooed on his wrist."

A flash goes off in my head. "Wait a minute!" I say as I get up and run over to the fountain. I push my whole arm through the pipe that carries water outside.

Uncle Li comes over. "Ah! Are you thinking of sending a note through the pipe?"

Mr. Papers jumps up onto the fountain to see what we're looking at. "No," I say as I point to the little monkey. "I'm thinking about sending *him* through the pipe."

"Do you think he would go?"

"He can definitely fit," I say, sizing him up next to the pipe.

With both of us staring at Mr. Papers, he gets that something is up. His little eyes go from me to Uncle Li and back again without moving his head. He takes a step back, so I kneel down until I am eye level. "Okay pal, you need to get help. Mrs. Findlay—go find Mrs. Findlay."

He nods his head up and down and runs to the door. I follow him and show him that the door is locked. "No door," I say, carrying him back down the steps and putting him on the edge of the fountain. I make that gesture like your hands are fins, and say, "Swim? In water?"

Mr. Papers cups his hand and draws some water to his mouth.

"No, *swim*," I say, plunging my whole arm into the pipe. He looks at me with his head cocked and then glances over at the water again like I'm crazy. He points to the water, then to his chest and looks at me to see if that's really what I mean. "Yes! Good!" I say. "Swim!"

He puts a foot in and then draws it out quickly and shakes it with disgust, like a cat that has just stepped in a mud puddle.

"Can monkeys swim?" I ask.

"Sure. But whether he wants to or not is another story," he says, skeptical eyebrow raised.

I remember that he'll need the rabbit-ears key to get back in here, so I take it from around my neck and put it around his. I have to wrap the string twice for it to be secure enough. Then I put my hands together and plead, "Please, Mr. Papers, please. We need your help."

He seems to understand my desperation and gets a little closer to the water.

"Swim?" I ask one more time and he nods.

The pipe is more than big enough for a small monkey, and since there's a current I figure he will get pushed out even if he doesn't use his arms. Still, though, I feel terrible seeing the last of his tail, now wet and a fraction of its normal size, go down the pipe. We notice the water slowly backing up behind him and I hold my breath until it flushes through.

"That was good thinking, Caity," Uncle Li says as he puts a hand on my shoulder.

"Thanks," I say as we head back to the stairs and the book. "I just hope it works."

"Can we talk more about this Barend Schlacter now?" Uncle Li asks.

"I'm sorry Uncle Li, I just can't right now. Can we discuss it later?"

Uncle Li nods, but doesn't look happy about it.

I dive right back into sketching so I don't have to think about what I just did to that poor little monkey. By the time I finish drawing the inside of the tower, I figure at least an hour has gone by. Turning back to the beginning of the sketchbook, which I started on the trip out here, I leaf through my first drawings: San Francisco as we were leaving, our lion's-head door knocker, the café on the corner, the Golden Gate Bridge at dusk, the front of our tall skinny Victorian house.

Pages later are some sketches of the big dark castle in Edinburgh, which (you can tell just by looking at it) has to be haunted, and some sketches of the train station there. Then there's my first sketch of our castle. Now knowing it as well as I do, I can tell what's out of proportion and wrong about the picture.

I hear someone fumbling at the door and instinctively run for the darkest corner and Uncle Li turns off his lantern and joins me. Because the two other corners are lit up, we are invisible in the dark where we are. I see the door open and the dim light of a small flashlight.

I can't tell who it is until he says, "Hello? Hello?"

"It's Tenzo!" I whisper. He must hear me because the flashlight swings around to the corner we're in and shines directly on us.

SEVENTEEN

aity? Dr. Li? Is that you?" He shines the flashlight on his face so it lights up and I see that Mr. Papers is on his shoulder. "Look, it's me, Dr. Tenzo."

I'm now totally confused about how he is behaving, and I'm pissed that Mr. Papers is with him; Tenzo must have grabbed the poor little guy on his way to find Mrs. Findlay.

"Why did you lock us down here?" I ask.

Uncle Li holds my hand as the flashlight comes back in our direction.

"What are you talking about?" Tenzo says as he comes down the stairs toward us.

Uncle Li and I take a step back, which puts us against the wall. The flashlight beam in our eyes makes it impossible for us to see him.

"Let's not play games here," Uncle Li says.

Tenzo replies, "Listen, I don't know what you think I've done—"

"So you're denying you locked us down here to translate these Sanskrit books?" I yell.

Tenzo laughs. "I'm one of the preeminent scholars of ancient languages. Why would I need *you* to translate anything for me?"

"Oh," I say, deflated and confused.

Uncle Li strikes a match to light his lantern and the room brightens up again. Tenzo looks around, amazed. I look at Uncle Li and shake my head—I hadn't wanted him to see the tower.

"Well, then how did you end up down here? And what are you snooping around for all the time?" I ask. I look at Mr. Papers on Tenzo's shoulder and wonder why he's not running over to me. Maybe he's mad at me for shoving him into a wet pipe. When I pat my thigh he finally hops off of Tenzo and into my arms, still damp.

"Look, I didn't go on the whisky tour. I was in the parlor reading the newspaper and having some tea and your monkey ran in soaking wet, grabbed my newspaper, and tore it up. He started building an origami tower, and then he made two people and put them inside the tower. After that, he motioned for me to follow him and I did. That's the whole story."

Tenzo is wearing a blue button-down shirt and there are long, dark sweat stains coming from his armpits. His glasses slip a bit down his nose, which are also beaded with sweat.

"And Mr. Papers was able to open the panel?" Uncle Li asks.

"He showed me where to put the key—fascinating that the three hares were used, by the way. Then he led me into the chamber, where, I must admit, I saw all the Drocane writing."

"You know what those symbols are? The writing in the square spirals?" I ask.

"Yes, it's a little-known script called Drocane. It's actually my specialty," he replies.

"What are the chances of that?" Uncle Li asks as he looks at me. "So if you had nothing to do with this, then who locked us down here?" he asks.

"I have no idea. Honestly, there is quite a lot I haven't told you about why I'm here, but I had nothing to do with locking you in." His eyes wander to the books Uncle Li is clutching. "I would like to look at the ancient Sanskrit books though."

I want to get out of the tower while we can so I suggest we leave and meet in the parlor. I hustle Tenzo through the chamber and my room as quickly as possible, then lock my door and take a moment to catch my breath.

By the time I get to the parlor, Uncle Li and Tenzo have already requested tea. Mrs. Findlay brings it in along with a three-tiered tray of goodies. Once she leaves, Uncle Li starts right in. "I believe you were going to explain yourself?" he says.

Tenzo takes a deep breath, then looks up and rubs his hands together. "Where to start?"

"You tell me," I say. "How about why you came here in the first place?"

He looks right at me. "Well, that was entirely because of *you*, my dear." I shudder as he calls me dear. He continues. "It all started when Dr. Middleford emailed me a copy of a rubbing you had taken. It was a beautiful sight, one I had been waiting to see for many, many years."

"Where had you seen Drocane before?" Uncle Li asks.

"At home. My mother has one of the only Drocane codices in existence," Tenzo says, grabbing a scone. He sets it on the napkin draped over his knee. "Before my mother changed our names back to her maiden name of Tenzo, my last name was Xu," he says, as if this is supposed to mean something. We both look at him blankly.

Tenzo's eyes move from me to Uncle Li and back again. "Have you not heard of Xu Bao Cheng?" he asks.

Uncle Li gasps. "No! You're related to the man who helped Fergus build the tower?"

"He was my grandfather's grandfather," Tenzo replies.

"You could have just seen Xu Bao Cheng's name on the tower and made that up," I say. "Or maybe 'Xu' is as common as 'Smith' in the United States."

Tenzo shrugs. "What do you want to know? How can I prove that I am a descendant of Xu Bao Cheng?"

"What do you know about the tower?" I ask.

"Very little. My mother never told me where this was, for fear I'd go looking for my father when I was too young," Tenzo says.

"Where was your father?" Uncle Li asks.

"My father," he says as he picks up the scone and then puts it back down again. "My father died here at the castle when I was just a small boy."

"Died?" My voice comes out shrill and high. "Here?"

Now two people's fathers have died at this castle?

"My father was here working with your great-grandfather, Robert Mac Fireland, during World War II. Although he was Chinese, my mother was Japanese. As soon as the Japanese became allies of the Germans, he had to go underground. He would have been thrown into prison or worse had he been found." He pours more tea. "Robert was kind enough to risk his life to help my father—and both gave up much in order to protect what is in this tower."

"So what was your father doing with Robert?" I ask. "I mean, why was he here?"

"*'Preparing the way'* was how my mother put it," he says, removing his glasses and wiping his greasy face with a napkin.

"Preparing the way for what?" I ask. I sip my tea, which has gotten a little cold.

Instead of answering, Tenzo looks at Uncle Li and then at me. "So what do *you* know about the tower?"

I feel like it's a standoff: *How much do you know? No, how much do* you *know?* Neither of us say anything.

Tenzo breaks first and says, "Let me tell you how this all started, centuries ago. Xu Bao Cheng lived in Dunhuang in the western Chinese province of Gansu. Although it's obscure, you may have heard of this place—it's been in the news recently as one of the oldest sightings of the three hares symbol."

"Like the three hares carved on the panel in my room?" I ask.

He nods. "Like the Flower of Life, it's a very old symbol that's been found all over the world yet has not been accurately decoded. Anyway, Dunhuang was once the beginning of the Silk Road, the trading route through Asia to Europe. There is a massive network of caves in Dunhuang that archaeologists are just beginning to discover. Of course, Xu Bao Cheng had known of them all his life."

"And this is where he met Fergus?" I ask.

Tenzo nods. "One day Fergus showed up at Xu Bao Cheng's house and said, 'I think we're supposed to meet.'"

"In China?" I ask. "How did he get there? Why did he pick Xu Bao Cheng?"

"Crazy as it seems, Xu Bao Cheng had been waiting for him," Tenzo replies. "He was the Keeper of the Caves."

"What's the Keeper of the Caves?"

"The Dunhuang Caves are full of documents, fabrics, paintings, and relics, kind of like a library. But in addition to things cataloged for history and reference, a secret part of the cave holds..." he pauses, looking for the right word, "I suppose you would call it 'esoteric' information."

"Chinese esoterica?" Uncle Li asks.

Tenzo shakes his head. "Not exactly. This information belongs to the world, but much of it came from the Maya."

"Another Maya connection..." Uncle Li says.

"I don't get why Fergus would go there and how he would know to look for this Xu Bao Cheng guy," I say.

"Well, it's all part of the prophecy." He looks at me, then Uncle Li, and then me again. "Do you know anything about this?" he asks.

I'm about to say yes, but Uncle Li says, "What prophecy?"

"Remember at dinner we were talking about how the Maya predicted, to the day, when Cortez and his conquistadors were coming?" Uncle Li and I both nod. "Well," Tenzo continues, "because by their calendars they could predict when things would happen, the Maya had sent many of their Elders to caves to keep their most precious information safe. But they also sent a few groups of Elders far away, to all ends of the Earth, so keeping the Mayan prophecy alive would be guaranteed."

"So Mayan Elders made it to Dunhuang?" I ask.

Tenzo nods and says, "And to the Isle of Huracan."

"Right here?" I say, pointing down to the ground. "In this place?"

"Yes. But they were old, the journey was arduous, and they didn't last long here. They had just enough time to find this energy center—where the tower is—and place their relics."

I glance at Uncle Li to see if he will give away anything about the calendar, the cogs below the tower. At this point, knowing what I know, I'm starting to trust Tenzo, but I don't think Uncle Li is. His face gives nothing away as he asks, "What happened to the Elders in Dunhuang?"

"Three of them arrived in 1518. They were very strong and lived there for years. The knowledge they imparted has been handed down to one person in each generation. Since then each man, the Keeper of the Cave, has passed this information to his first son. The last one was Xu Bao Cheng."

"Why did Xu Bao Cheng leave the caves and come here with Fergus?"

"The prophecy said that a man from the west would come when the Mayan Long Count Calendar read 12-8-4-2-0."

Uncle Li asks, "Did he make it on the date?"

"That was the summer of 1780. Fergus had been robbed of everything a couple weeks earlier. They'd even taken his shoes. But he made it to Dunhuang with bare feet the day of the prediction. Of course he knew nothing of this, he was just compelled to keep going, driven to find this person and this place he had been dreaming about."

Mrs. Findlay stands in the entryway to the parlor and says, "Knock knock."

She must know something intense is going on because she doesn't move until Uncle Li says, "Yes, please come in."

She wrings her hands together. "Forgive the interruption, but the Laird just called. The van's axle has broken—no injuries, the driver just backed into a rock while parking at a whisky distillery. Perhaps the driver was tasting as well …"

"But everyone is okay? Are the guests upset?" Uncle Li asks.

Mrs. Findlay laughs. "Quite the contrary. They have had a lot of drink and are thinking of this as some sort of adventure! Being stuck in Ballamorgh overnight is like being shipwrecked in heaven; a quaint little town with fine inns and, most important, a lot of single malt Scotch."

Uncle Li and Tenzo laugh and I try to smile, but I am seriously worried about tonight, without my parents here. Remembering the last time my parents were not home at night, a chill runs down my spine like ice water. "Will you be staying the night?" I ask Mrs. Findlay.

"Yes, of course dear. I just sent Thomas off minutes ago to find a replacement part, so it should be all sorted out by tomorrow."

"Wait, Thomas just left from *here*?" I ask.

"Aye," she answers. "Why, did you need him for something?"

I shake my head. "No, but I thought he was driving the van."

"Nae, lassie, the tour van comes with a driver. Thomas has been here all day."

Uncle Li and I catch eyes, thinking the same thing. Would *Thomas* have locked us in?

"Can I get you anything else, then?" Mrs. Findlay asks.

"No thanks," I reply. I pull at a string on the hem of my T-shirt and it starts unraveling. I find it impossible to stop, even though I know it will ruin the shirt.

When Mrs. Ferguson is gone, Tenzo asks, "Were you thinking that Thomas may have locked you in?"

"It's a possibility," Uncle Li says. "He does seem like a man who is hiding something."

"Obviously *someone* other than the three of us knows about the tower," he says.

Uncle Li nods in agreement. "It couldn't be any of the guests; they were all gone by the time we went down there. And Mrs. Findlay wouldn't know anything about that—your parents hired her, right? She wasn't a fixture at the castle?"

"No, she wouldn't have anything to do with this," I say. Now that Tenzo is no longer a suspect, I think it has to be either Barend Schlacter or Thomas.

"And her grandson, that fellow you're so fond of...what's his name?" Uncle Li asks.

I instantly turn red. "What? Alex? I'm not..." I stammer for the words. "He doesn't know anything either. They're all totally *not* involved."

I cradle my forehead in my hand. "If my parents knew what was going on, they'd freak out." I've never been a part of something big before. I mean, a *prophecy*, for God's sake! Do

I bag it because I'm scared, or do I trust Uncle Li and Tenzo to keep me safe?

Uncle Li closes his eyes for a moment and pinches the bridge of his nose with his fingers. "Buddha help me when your parents find out I kept any of this from them—"

"I'll take all the blame," I say. "Really. All of it."

Uncle Li shakes his head. "Doesn't matter. I'm the responsible adult in this situation. But I do agree that our efforts to get to the bottom of this would be thwarted if we told them."

"They already want to send me to boarding school. If they found out any of this they'd send me to a locked-down military school." If I'm going to trust Tenzo to keep me safe, I might as well tell him what we know. Looking Tenzo in the eyes I say, "So, you want the full scoop?"

"Absolutely," he says, eyes wide with surprise.

Uncle Li gives me an approving nod so I take a deep breath and dive in. I tell him about the grimoire I found in the secret room, the rubbings I took of the square spirals on the wall, about how I conned Dad into decoding the symbols in the spirals and then copied his program, how I found the way to the tower and the stuff we discovered there, like the fountain and the glowing rocks and the cogs and wheels down below. "Am I forgetting anything?" I ask.

Uncle Li raises his hands up to the air and makes that floating gesture. "Oh my God, that's right," I say. "There's a huge magnetic field or something that makes you float!"

Tenzo looks at me and then at Uncle Li and says, "Okay" in that long drawn-out way that really means *I'm not sure I believe you.*

"Really! Mr. Papers showed us. You stand inside the circle of rocks and you start floating."

Tenzo leans forward in his seat. Then he asks, "Have either of you ever been to the United Nations Headquarters in New York?"

We both shake our heads.

"There's a very interesting room there, the Meditation Room," Tenzo says. "In the center of the space is a six-ton block of solid iron ore—said to be the largest natural piece ever mined."

"So you think they're trying to *create* a place of power there?" I ask.

"Well, you have to wonder why the architects of the U.N. Meditation Room would import and install such an expensive material if it didn't do anything."

"Can you float above the United Nations one?" I ask, more interested in the amusement-park aspect of it than the weird theories.

Tenzo chuckles. "No, there are different types of magnets and magnetic fields. I don't think this one is like the one in the tower."

My legs are falling asleep under me, so I shift. Mr. Papers lifts his head and screeches with irritation because I wake him up. When I settle, he curls back up like a cinnamon roll. "You know," Tenzo says, "my father was responsible for bringing Mr. Papers here."

"Seriously?"

"Yes, he's from a rare pygmy lineage of white-throated capuchin monkeys, brought to Dunhuang from the Mayalands by the first Daykeepers. There was an extensive breeding and training program in the caves to produce helper monkeys with special skills. Basically they were using the same type of electromagnetic energy from the Galactic Center on monkeys and they found a leap of evolution happened. Mr. Papers is from this lineage."

"But that would make him really old, wouldn't it? How long do they live?"

Uncle Li says, "Capuchin monkeys can live fifty years or more in captivity, and the pygmy variation lives even longer. Based on what I know, I'd guess he was about sixty-five."

"So did you know Mr. Papers when you were a kid?" I ask, petting the fur on his head until it's slicked back, soft and shiny. He looks too young to be sixty-five.

"No, but he knew my father. He'd send me letters with stories of Mr. Papers. It's delightful to finally meet him." He takes a deep breath through his nose and exhales quietly.

The fact that Tenzo doesn't seem to be the bad guy any more doesn't change the fact that he still looks creepy. I want to get over it because I know he can't help it, but it might take more than a day.

I try for a kind gesture. "Would you like to spend some time with Mr. Papers?" I ask. He seems touched. I put Mr. Papers in his lap and he jumps up to his shoulder and puts one hand on Tenzo's head. His eyes say *thank you*.

Looking weary, Uncle Li suggests that we rest and reconvene for dinner. I agree, wanting to go back to my room to see what the newly decoded spiral says.

Once back in my room I rush over to my computer and read:

When the masses, by bondage and slavery are torn
Eight Batz, the Last Daykeeper, will then be born
This beginning of the end before the new beginning
*   will arrive*
The twelfth of November, nineteen hundred ninety-five

I gasp. November 12, 1995? That was the day I was born.
I feel dizzy and taste metal in my mouth.

EIGHTEEN

I'm overwhelmed so I do what any overwhelmed girl would do: I lay face down on my bed and crash. When I wake up a little later feeling chilled, I'm too tired to get up and crawl under the covers so I reach over to grab the comforter and fold myself up like a burrito.

That's when I see the man standing at the foot of my bed.

You know in dreams when you're too scared to run or scream? That's how I feel: paralyzed.

The man walks to the side of my bed. "Do not be afraid," he says.

I assume I must be dreaming because all of a sudden I'm not scared.

He sits on the edge of my bed. His poncho looks like a rug, woven with really bright colors. His skin is dark and weathered and he has very high cheekbones and small square teeth; I get a feeling he's Mexican, although he almost looks Asian. He's wearing old black sandals and thick pants made out of some kind of heavy linen cloth.

"It's good to see you," he says with an accent I can't place. "My name is Bolon. It has been a long day, yes?"

"You have no idea," I reply.

He is silent for a long time, but it doesn't seem weird. We just look at each other.

Then he says, "You are doing well. You are on the path and we are very proud of you."

"Wow... thanks, I guess. But who do you mean by 'we'?"

"The Elders on The Council who help guide the prophecy."

I prop up on one elbow and wonder if I could be aware of myself like this if I were actually dreaming. "Is this a dream?" I ask.

He smiles, "Isn't it all? What is the difference between a dream and waking life—both are created by you, so which is real? Or are they both?"

I lay back down on the pillow with a thud. He shifts a little and I get a whiff of a complex smell—wood fire, spices, tree sap. I don't remember ever smelling anything in a dream, but if this is real, why aren't I scared?

He seems to know what I'm thinking. "I am not here to frighten you, or to make you uncomfortable. I am here to answer any questions you have."

I sit up again. He has this incredibly kind face with the type of small, squinty eyes that make a person look like he's always smiling.

"I just don't understand any of this."

He puts his old hand over mine and I feel the same jolt of energy I did when I touched the names on the tower, which seems like forever ago. He looks me straight in the eyes and starts to speak, although I feel like he could tell me everything I need to know without saying it out loud.

"The world is changing very fast right now, and will only get faster as we head toward 2012. The Shadow Forces are gaining momentum. From an evolutionary perspective, things have not moved this fast in the billions of years that the Earth has existed. Imagine how lucky you are to be living here, now, at this moment."

"But how am *I* involved in any of this?" I ask.

"You will help overcome the Shadow Forces."

I can't help but laugh.

"Caity, you and the hundreds of millions of other young people on the planet are the midwives of a new world."

"We can't do *anything*! We don't run the world. Old white men run the world."

Bolon smiles. "Oh, so you've met the *Fraternitas*?"

"What do you know about the *Fraternitas*?" I ask.

He shrugs. "The *Fraternitas* has been around for ages. It's an elite group of people who rule together. They control banking, commerce, and military organizations at the highest level; together they run the invisible world government—the Shadow Government."

"Oh come on! Some of my dad's geek friends are deep into conspiracies, so I've overheard conversations like this before. Mom says you can make anything look like a conspiracy if you want to."

"This is truly the most powerful and dangerous group in the world," he says.

When I see that Bolon is serious, my heart rate bumps up and my fingertips go cold. "Oh my God. I sent Justine to their office in San Francisco! And that's who that freak Barend Schlacter works for—"

"I heard he had been here to visit. I hope he didn't scare you too badly."

"Are you kidding me? He scared the crap out of me! He said he was going to make me an orphan! This is who doesn't want me to do what you're telling me I'll do?"

Bolon takes a deep breath and simply says, "Yes."

"And you don't feel bad putting a girl my age in huge danger?"

"It is not up to me. This is your path. But if there is no risk, there is no reward."

What kind of comeback can you use on that?

"So why do they want to hurt me and my family?" I ask.

"Because you can impede their progress. You can stop them from controlling the masses. You see our consciousness has been declining so we have been easy to control. Now, because of changes in electromagnetic energy coming at us, our consciousness is elevating and it will be more difficult to be controlled by them. They know this and are getting desperate."

"So it goes back to the Galactic Center thing? That's where this energy is coming from?"

Bolon nods. "Our relationship to the Galactic Center affects us deeply. We are on the verge of a leap in evolution, but this time it's an evolution of *consciousness.*"

When it comes right down to it, I think to myself, I'm not even sure I could define what consciousness is. Awakeness? Awareness? Brain power?

"How does that happen?" I ask. "I mean, how does consciousness *evolve?*"

"Did you know that more than ninety percent of your brain is not being used? And more than ninety percent of DNA is classified as 'junk' because scientists cannot figure out what it does. And more than ninety percent of space is considered 'empty' even though it's teeming with energy? It's as if we are wearing blinders. We understand almost nothing! This change in electromagnetic energy will allow us to access parts of ourselves we didn't even know we had, to understand things that seem inexplicable."

"So pretty soon these vibrations from the center of the galaxy will make us … what … smarter?"

"If the *Fraternitas* doesn't destroy us before then, yes. Our minds expand as we get higher-dimensional energy from the Galactic Center."

"See, this is exactly why you got the wrong person— space is really not my thing. To tell you the truth," I admit, "I didn't even know there *was* a center to the galaxy."

"Scientists have only recently discovered exactly where the center of our galaxy is, and only a few years ago discovered that it is a massive black hole. But the Maya knew where the center of the galaxy was thousands of years ago—*and* they knew it was a black hole."

"Wow, that's amazing," I say. I sit up and draw my knees to my chest. "But how does a black hole out in the galaxy have any effect on us here on Earth?" I ask.

"Doesn't the moon affect us?" he replies. "The moon moves oceans and it's billions of times less powerful than the Galactic Center! We've begun moving into a special and rare alignment of the Earth, the sun, and the Great Mother that will do more than just move tides—"

"The Great Mother?"

"The center of our galaxy—where new stars are born and where everything, including us, comes from."

"Us too? People?"

Bolon bursts out laughing. "You are very funny," he says, reaching over and gently patting my hand. "Do you realize that you are in the ultimate recycling center? Every atom in your body has been processed in at least one star and has gone on to be a part of various other things—you have atoms that may have been part of dinosaurs, fireflies, flowers, lava—even other humans. *Every* part of you came from the Galactic Center, and every part of you has been, and always will be, connected to everything else. You will see this more clearly as your dormant DNA wakes up."

"But how?"

"Picture only being able to see this one room. You live in this one room for hundreds of thousands of years because it's all you know, it's all you can see. Then all of a sudden a door opens and you find out that there has always been an enormous building attached to the one room you have been living in."

"I have that dream all the time! I'll be in a house that I believe I live in, although I just made it up in the dream, and then I'll open a door that I'd thought was a closet or something and it turns out to be a whole part of the house I never knew was there. And it's always something amazing like an indoor garden or a ballroom."

"That is a perfect metaphor for what is happening. You are living in five percent of a mansion. And you will not believe what's behind the door you're about to open…"

This thought gives me chills.

"Can you lay out the nuts and bolts here, like exactly how does this brain evolution, or whatever you called it, work?"

"You know a lot about computers, yes? The ones and zeros that tell your computer what to do are just a series of magnetic charges. There are many things that can make these magnetic charges go haywire and make the computer slow and prone to crashing—things like air pressure and electrical surges. Just like a hard drive, we are magnetic beings and we are fundamentally changed by the electromagnetic energy that surrounds us. Think of it as if we're about to get a major hardware upgrade."

"And the *Fraternitas* doesn't want us to upgrade?"

"The *Fraternitas* will do everything in their power—and that power is considerable—to *stop* this upgrade. Only weak, fearful, indebted people can be controlled. If your goal is to control the masses, having people wake up and open their eyes is the worst thing that could happen."

"But you said this upgrade is related to where we are in the universe. The *Fraternitas* can't do anything about that, can they?"

Bolon shakes his head. "They cannot change where we are relative to the Galactic Center, but they're trying other extreme methods; they've been spraying metals and compounds in the air to block the magnetic energy coming to our planet and they've built a network of arrays in Alaska that can change the nature of our ionosphere, greatly affecting what comes through."

"That's HAARP and Project Khymatos! Justine heard them talking about that!"

Bolon doesn't look a bit surprised. "They think this, in combination with physically weakening us by putting chemicals in the water and genetically modifying the food we eat, emotionally weakening us by keeping us in a state of fear about our safety, and financially weakening us by keeping us in a state of perpetual debt, will help stop the upgrade and keep us easy to control."

"But you're talking about big-time world-wide conspiracy..."

"You need only to look at the two things that the *Fraternitas* care most about: war and money. There are eight to ten wars happening on the planet right now. Follow the money funding these wars and you will find the *Fraternitas* on both sides."

This makes no sense. "Why would they pay for *both sides* of a war?"

"Wars make people fearful and easier to manipulate. They control population. They take the focus off other sinister things that are happening. They put countries in debt while making the FRO billions of dollars each year. Wars will continue to escalate until 2012 while *Fraternitas* members from various industries can put things in place to exert their control."

"Then what?"

Bolon shakes his head. "We do not have to worry about that because we have *you*."

"Why can't you Elders stop them?" I ask. "You're these all-powerful shamans and I'm a totally inexperienced kid who doesn't know much about anything at all."

"It is your path. Did you know there are more people on

the planet under the age of twenty than there ever have been before? It will be the young who will see that we can manifest great things and create a different world. And it will be you who shows them."

Me? In a way I secretly want to be the person who could change the world. Seriously, how cool would that be? But realistically, it's crazy.

"You will use your machine," he says as he points to my desk.

"My computer?" I ask, finally happy to have some concrete instructions. If I can do anything well, it's use a computer.

He nods. "We have created computers as helpers and companions—yours even helped you decode text, no? Now you will use your computer to help unite the youth."

I'm trying to run through my mind how I could possibly do this, what I could possibly do with a computer to unite kids besides creating a game better than World of Warcraft.

"This is not a game," Bolon says, looking me in the eyes to make sure I am paying attention.

"I know that. Believe me—Barend Schlacter drove that point home. And speaking of him, what do I do about my parents? Should I tell them about all of this?" I ask.

Bolon shrugs. "That is entirely up to you. Your parents are good people—they prepared you to be the smart, independent, capable girl you are. It is up to you to decide whether they would interfere, or whether they would support you in doing this yourself."

I know that their worry would drive them to do something crazy, like home school me until I'm 38, and then I'd never see this thing through. But more important, if Barend Schlacter and the *Fraternitas* found out that I told them...well, I can't even think about that.

"But enough of this for now. You need to rest." At that he gets up and walks out the door.

"Wait, Bolon—" Too late, the door clicks shut. I don't follow him out because I'm not sure what I would ask anyway. I just didn't want him to go yet.

Seeing that it's almost dinnertime, I head to the bathroom to clean up. I turn the hot water on full blast until the sink starts to steam, throw a washcloth under the spray of water. I lay it over my face, holding it down with my fingers. It feels good to have the hot pressure on my skin.

When I take it off and look in the mirror, I'm surprised at what I see. Maybe the heat of the towel has messed with my eyes, or maybe it's something else, but it's as if I have a bit of a glow—kind of like a halo, but instead of floating above my head it's all the way around me.

I put my face over the sink and splash it with water that's so cold it stops my breath. Looking up again, I see the glow is gone. This both disappoints and relieves me.

I gaze into my eyes and say, "Finish it. Finish what you started." My voice comes out clearly though I have no idea who is pushing the words through my mouth.

NINETEEN

I hear Mrs. Findlay announce dinner so I run as fast as I can downstairs; I'm still scared to be alone in the castle unless I'm in my room with the door bolted.

"So did you meet Bolon yet?" I ask Tenzo and Uncle Li at the bottom of the stairs.

They both look at me blankly. "Who is Bolon?" Uncle Li asks.

"That guy in a poncho ..."

Tenzo and Uncle Li look at each other and shake their heads. Uncle Li says, "No, but I haven't been out of my room since we left each other earlier."

"Oh, I guess you'll meet him later," I say.

We go into the kitchen and see Mrs. Findlay. "Thought I'd serve you in the parlor tonight since it's just the three of you."

A game table in the parlor has been set for dinner.

"Now that all the spirals are decoded, I printed you each a copy of the whole poem," I say, handing them each a sheet of paper.

With will and labor I built the great tower
To sit atop this place of power
Know this though, 'tis less for defense and more to
    conceal
What once was lore until I found 'twas real

You know of the hares and their unity knot
Now find what the Flower of Life sits atop
These symbols hold wisdom from tribes of the Earth
Knowledge essential for new world rebirth

This birth may come like a storm or a dove
The outcome lies in how much we can love
Like gravity, love is a force of great might
True power comes when we connect and unite

Into arcane old knowledge you must delve
To find the secret to twenty-twelve
The oldest myths, the oldest sages
Point only upward to explain the ages

The butterfly will emerge in three different ways
At the source, at your core, and by way of the days
Called feathered serpent when spoken in code
Connected to all by the great white road

Remember this always, and above all other
The wise ones grasp the power of our great mother
The numbers, the stars, the cycles and days
Should all be counted, should all be praised

Know chi is in everything, through and between
Yet despite its great power it remains quite unseen

Its quality transforms as we tread backwards 'round
To the great year's ores we are fastened and bound

Watch closely the Fraternitas and follow each lie
An animal is most dangerous when it knows it might
   die
Look who profits from war, who controls by fear
At the end of this age, their end too could be near

When the masses, by new bondage and slavery are torn
Eight Batz, the Last Daykeeper, shall then be born
This beginning of the end before the new beginning
   will arrive
The twelfth of November, nineteen hundred ninety-five

As is writ in the prescient fable
Told to me 'round a far Eastern table
'Tis me, Fergus who would begin the story
But one named Caitrina will usher in the glory

                              —In lak'ech F.G.M.

When he's finished reading, Tenzo asks, "Is November 12, 1995, your birthday?"

Every hair on my arm stands up and I nod.

"Let's just get this all out right now," I say to Tenzo. "Can you please just tell us everything you know about this place and what's going on here?"

"I brought something," Tenzo says as he reaches into his inside jacket pocket and removes an old envelope. Inside is a letter written on thin paper that has yellowed with age.

"This is a letter from my father, Shan-Tung. He had given

it to your great grandfather Robert to send back to me in China when he passed away, which happened when I was very young."

He pushes his glasses up with his finger and begins.

"Dearest son, If you are receiving this letter it means that I have left this physical realm, but know that I am always with you. Just as the stars shine brightly even though they cannot be seen in the daytime, so I shine for you. Even at your tender age you already show a keen interest in ancient history, and this will serve you well, for at some point in your future you will be given the opportunity to continue what I have been doing. I cannot tell you where I am; the location will be revealed to you at the proper time. You will know you are in the right place when you see my good friend and companion, the origami monkey. I am sorry I cannot tell you more than this, but it is for the good of all that the prophecy reveals itself when it is time. In lak'ech, Father."

"Well, I guess you're in the right place," I say quietly, scratching Mr. Papers' head.

Tenzo nods as he puts the letter back in its envelope. "As soon as Dr. Middleford showed me the rubbing of the spiral with Drocane script, I sensed it was all beginning. I booked my trip not knowing what I would find once I got here. Things have just fallen into place so far."

"So your mother didn't tell you anything?" Uncle Li asks.

"Just what I've told you. She encouraged me to study the

Maya and their calendars and she showed me the Drocane script, but even on her deathbed she would not give up the location of this castle. The only thing she told me about the mysterious place where my father went was that it was the pineal gland of Mother Earth."

"Pineal gland? What is that?" As I say it out loud it sounds kind of nasty and I hope that it's not some guy thing.

Uncle Li taps a finger between his eyebrows and says, "It's the seat of the third eye."

Mrs. Findlay rolls in a huge cart of sandwiches, salads, and soup along with a pitcher of iced tea. "Would you like me to serve you or would you prefer to do it yourself?" she asks.

"We've got it," I say. After she's gone I ask, "So what does the pineal gland do? Like what's its purpose?"

"It's a gland the size of a pea that lives in a little cave in the geometric center of your brain," Tenzo says as he pours himself some iced tea. "Because of its location in the body, I was prepared to look for this place in Egypt, by the pyramids."

"Why? Is it shaped like a pyramid?" I ask.

"No, because the Great Pyramid at Giza is in the exact center of gravity of the continents," Tenzo replies. "See, if you pushed all the continents together you'd find that the Great Pyramid divides all of our land mass into four equal quarters."

"I didn't know that," says Uncle Li. "It's rather extraordinary, isn't it?"

"I think we'll discover that ancient civilizations were far more advanced than we gave them credit for," Tenzo replies.

"But what does this gland *do*?" I ask.

"It's the timekeeper of the body," Tenzo replies. "It regulates day and night cycles."

"So that's why Fergus and your ancestor came from the Dunhuang Caves to the Isle of Huracan? Because it was some special place on the planet?" I ask.

"That's what my mother told me. She said that when Fergus got to the caves, Xu Bao Cheng described a mythical place to him and Fergus knew exactly where it was. He stayed on with Bao Cheng for several years, learning what he could about the prophecy and his role in it, and then the two of them set off for this place. And that's where my mother stopped—she wouldn't tell me about Breidablik or the Isle of Huracan. Like I said, I had originally guessed it was in Egypt. But I still don't know what to make of it all, especially your part in all this, Caity."

"Well, one thing Bolon told me is that what I'm going to be doing will involve the computer," I offer.

Both look at me "Sorry, what did you say?" Uncle Li asks.

"Bolon, the Mayan guy. He said I'll be using my computer as this thing unfolds."

"What else did this 'Bolon' say?" Tenzo asks.

"He was just telling me that the Elders think I'm doing a great job so far, and then he explained the Galactic Center thing."

"Caity, I'm worried about this stranger being in your room with you," Tenzo says. "I'm going to ask Mrs. Findlay what she knows about our new guest."

I try to protest but he just walks out. I turn to Uncle Li and say, "I know it seems weird, but wait until he explains it to you, you'll totally get it."

"I'd love to meet him," Uncle Li says. It seems weird that he doesn't seem concerned at all, while Tenzo is freaking out.

Tenzo walks back into the room with a stern look on his face, and says, "Caity, Mrs. Findlay knows nothing of a new guest. She said that your parents never mentioned there would be anyone checking in while they were away."

"What, you think I made him up? Like an imaginary friend or something?" I ask.

"I *wish* he were an imaginary friend. No, I worry that he's real. He could be the one who locked you in the tower."

"There's no way. You shouldn't even worry about him; he's the nicest, most gentle old guy I've ever met."

"And you're certain you weren't dreaming?" Tenzo asks as gently as he can.

"Maybe I was," I say just to get them off my back. My brain hurts. I'm tired of talking to these guys, I wish I could talk to someone my own age. I wish Alex were still speaking to me.

"Are you all done with dinner?" I ask. "I'll help Mrs. Findlay clean up before bed."

I pile the plates on the rolling cart and Mr. Papers runs over and crawls on the lower rack for a ride. When I get to the kitchen, I'm happy to see Mrs. Findlay sitting at the table playing solitaire.

"Hello dear," she says.

Papers jumps from the lower rack to the table and Mrs. Findlay nearly has a heart attack.

"Up to your cubby you scoundrel!" she says to him.

"Hi." I plop down next to her and put my head on her shoulder. "Would you mind if I slept in one of the twin beds in your room tonight?"

"Course not," she says. "It's your castle; you can sleep wherever you please."

It's so nice to be near someone comforting that I decide to confide in her, but only halfway. "Mrs. Findlay, if I tell you something will you promise not to tell my parents?"

She looks at me to see if I'm joking around or serious. "S'pose I would," she replies.

"Really, you have to swear you won't tell."

"Right then, I swear," she says. "What is it dear?"

I decide to tell her a modified version of the story. "Well, earlier today Uncle Li and I were in the shed, um, looking for something for Mr. Papers, and someone slipped a couple of books in and then locked the door."

She looks at me as if she doesn't believe me.

"I'm serious! Someone locked us in with a note that said to translate the books, then we'd be let out."

"And what were the books?"

"Some old Sanskrit books. Uncle Li said he can read them. Anyway, we managed to get out, but we think Thomas might have locked us in."

Mrs. Findlay takes a deep breath. She picks up her cards, even though her game is not over, and neatly stacks them, shaking her head slowly the whole time.

"What?" I ask.

"Well, I reckon we'll have to have an agreement that goes both ways—if I tell you something then you must promise not to tell your parents. They'll probably find out sooner of later, but I'd like it to come from Thomas, not me."

"What is it?" I ask.

She puts the cards back in their box and then sets her hands on them before she begins.

"Thomas has a twin brother named Donald. They're identical—even their parents had trouble telling them apart."

"Really? Thomas has a twin?" For some reason I associate twins with young kids. I never think of old people as being part of a twin set.

"Yes. They were quite the pair growing up, thick as thieves. But one day at the age of about sixteen, they had a falling out. It was as if on that day Thomas became the golden child and Donald became the bad seed, always getting into trouble. Then one day, not long after I started working here, *poof*! He up and disappeared. Hamish's father, Robert, had always taken a likin' to the twins and they were allowed to roam freely in and around the castle, which was a rare treat for anyone outside the family. Aye, but after the falling out, Donald only came back here once—to steal two rare old books from Robert. Robert, Hamish, and Thomas looked all over for that boy and those books but no one could ever find him, nor the books."

"And in all those years he's never returned?" I ask, mesmerized by her story.

"Not that anyone has been aware of. But," she says looking at me sideways, "the books he took were two ancient Sanskrit texts."

"Oh my God! Do you think Donald is back? That these are the books he stole?"

She puts her arm around my shoulder. "I don't know dear. But when you told me what happened, all I could think of was Donald."

"Is he crazy? Would he hurt us?" I ask.

Instead of answering my question she says, "You know what? I'd sure feel better if we had Hans, my German shepherd, here with us tonight."

She stands up and goes to the phone. "I'm sure Alex won't mind bringing him out, what with having the night off and all."

I wince when I hear his name. He definitely wouldn't want to do *me* any favors. She dials a number and speaks quietly; Alex must not have put up any resistance because she quickly hangs up the phone.

"You'll love Hans. He looks vicious but he's a sweet, sweet creature."

When I was a kid I saw an animal show about wolves taking down a huge moose and since then I've been afraid of dogs. It shocks me that people let these animals that are capable of total savagery sleep in their beds. However, tonight I am thrilled to have a savage on my side.

While Mrs. Findlay prepares for breakfast, I play a couple of games of solitaire with her cards. I've only ever played solitaire on the computer and it's kind of nice to play it in real life. I like the snap of the cards against the table as I lay them out and the way they never stay completely straight in their rows. Lost in the game, I don't realize how much time passes before the kitchen door swings open and a huge German shepherd runs in. Mrs. Findlay bends down to greet Hans and slips him half of a sandwich, which he swallows in one gulp without chewing. Mr. Papers has crammed himself as far back as he can inside his cubby; this would be like me encountering a grizzly bear or something.

Alex walks in and sits next to me at the kitchen table. I keep looking down, ashamed and embarrassed by what I'd said to him about his father. While Mrs. Findlay is distracted by the dog, Alex taps me on the shoulder and mouths the words, "I'm sorry."

I put my hand to my chest and whisper, "No, no, it was my fault. I'm *so* sorry."

He takes a napkin from the dispenser on the table and waves it like a surrender flag. I do the same. My heart feels like a chocolate chip on a hot cookie sheet.

When Mrs. Findlay looks over at us he puts the napkin down and says, "So you girls need a bit of protection tonight?"

Mrs. Findlay scratches Hans behind the ears until his whole body shakes and says, "Don't be silly! I just thought Hans would be a bit lonely without me."

Once Alex is loaded up with a basket of cookies and scones, Mrs. Findlay sends him on his way, bolting the kitchen door behind him. I follow her and Hans to the guest room off the kitchen that used to be a servant's quarters. I'd always thought it was so depressing that there weren't any windows in this room, but now I'm glad there's only one way in—through the door that I'm locking.

There's no way I'm going upstairs alone, so I decide to sleep in my T-shirt. Mrs. Findlay disappears into the small attached bathroom and comes out wearing a long white nightgown. She pulls down the covers on one of the beds, gets in with a big sigh, and says, "Ah, lovely."

Despite my fears, as I look down at Hans lying on the cold floor I feel the urge to have him on the bed with me.

"Mrs. Findlay?" I say quietly. "Would it be alright of Hans slept on my bed?"

Mrs. Findlay makes the *tsk tsk* sound but then looks at my pleading eyes and shakes a finger at Hans. "Only tonight, mister."

I get in, pull the covers up, and then pat the foot of the bed. "Come on pal!" I say, and Hans hops up gingerly, as if he knows he's doing something he shouldn't. He looks over at Mrs. Findlay and she nods. "It's okay, boy," she reassures him, "it's okay."

I roll over and fall deeply to sleep with my toes tucked under the weight of the big savage.

TWENTY

wakened by the sounds of Mrs. Findlay in the kitchen, I roll over and bury my face in the pillow. I don't feel like bouncing out of bed yet. Hans' nose is twitching like crazy; when he can't stand it anymore, he hops off and trots into the kitchen. His toenails make an interesting noise on the tile, like a million tiny high heels clickity-clicking.

I follow Hans and pour a cup of tea while toasting two slices of bread. Passing the big cast-iron pan of bacon, I can't resist pulling out a couple of pieces to slip between my toast, sandwich style. I walk over to Mr. Papers' wood cubby to check on him, but because Hans is in the kitchen, he's backed himself as far back into his little space as he can. "Here Hans!" I yell as I toss piece of bacon and open the side door. As soon as the meat is launched in the air, Hans runs out and catches it like a Frisbee and I quickly close the door.

Mr. Papers finally emerges and hops on my shoulder. By the time we get to my room, Bolon is already there sitting in one of the leather chairs.

"Good morning, Caity," he says.

"Hello Bolon," I reply as I walk over to the chair next to him. Mr. Papers hops on back of the chair that Bolon is in and then climbs up his shoulder and then onto his head. He just sits there as if he is a monkey hat, with his tail curled around himself like he's settling in. Bolon doesn't even seem to notice.

"So where are you staying, anyway?" I ask.

"Oh, just a little place in town." Then he leans forward in his chair and says, "Today I would like to discuss the specifics of your role in the unfolding of this plan."

"Finally!" I'm good with specifics.

"I've brought you this," he says as he hands me a CD. "It's one of the Mayan calendars; the one for the human cycle, called the '*Tzolk'in*.'"

"Wow, thanks!" I say, surprised that Bolon even knows how to burn a disc. "Zol-keen? That's how you pronounce this?" I ask as I look at the word *Tzolk'in* printed on the disc written on it.

"Yes. It's a Mayan word that can be translated as either 'Count of Days' or 'Pieces of the Sun'."

"Pieces of the Sun," I repeat. That's beautiful.

Bolon says, "The *Tzolk'in* is one of the twenty Mayan calendars explained on this disc. It will help synchronize your youth, help ease the transition that the world is going through."

"Seriously?" I say. "Can a calendar really matter?"

Bolon closes his eyes for a moment as if I have just personally insulted him. "The calendar is the *center* of any civilization.

It's the agreement we all make about *what time is*. The *Tzolk'in* is a different kind of agreement."

I'm trying to hide it, but Bolon sees that I still don't buy into a calendar as this huge and radical change-maker.

"Your calendar was devised by a Pope for religious and agricultural reasons. It has nothing to do with humans and our particular cycles. A serious error in time happened when Western Civilization decided to view time as a straight line heading into the future, rather than as a cycle."

"So you want me to somehow make everyone start using a different calendar?" I ask.

"Not everyone, only those who are ready. But you will be shocked by how many people, especially people your age, will embrace the *Tzolk'in*." He looks at me like he's deciding whether or not to say something before he continues. "There will also be many who deny what you say. Some will be working for the Shadow Forces and will want to put out your light, some will just ignore you. Remember: it is not your job to *convince* anyone."

I'm relieved to hear this. "Good, because I had a hard time even selling Girl Scout cookies, and if you've ever had a Thin Mint you know those things practically sell themselves."

"This is not a product—it is a highly sophisticated synchronization tool," Bolon says. "Do not come to this as a warrior or a salesperson; come to it as a flower opening to the sun. Walk away from those who are not open or those who align with the Shadow Forces."

"Every time you mention the Shadow Forces you scare me," I admit.

"The Shadow Forces want people to remain off balance,

put off-kilter by mechanical time and chaos, so that people are easier to control. When you are balanced, it's more difficult for someone to push you over, yes? Stay balanced and you will not be controlled; stay soft and openhearted and evil will have nothing to oppose."

Didn't Uncle Li use that same line? I hold up the CD. "So I give this away to anyone who wants it? Like shareware or something?" I ask, trying to define my actual job.

He shrugs. "How you distribute it will be up to you. The most important thing is that you must make it *resonate* with people your age."

"Resonate?"

"Yes, *resonate*. If you do not make it resonate, it will be like handing out books to a blind person; it will mean nothing."

We both freeze when Mom's voice comes over the intercom. "Caity, we're home!"

"We'll continue this talk later," Bolon says. "There's one more thing you'll need to do."

"I hope it's easy; this is starting to sound like a full-time job," I say.

Bolon laughs. He says, "I'll find you later," and walks out the door.

When I get to the kitchen, Mom runs over and gives me a huge hug. "Oh, Caity, I just had the weirdest feeling about you yesterday. I know it's probably because we were stuck and I couldn't get to you, but I'm still glad to see you."

As she's hugging me I wonder whether she picked up on my vibe while Uncle Li and I were locked in the tower. God was that just yesterday?

"So how was the big tour?" I ask. "Were any of the guests upset?"

"We might just fake a bus breakdown with every group—they *loved* it!" Dad says.

"So Thomas came out and rescued you guys?" I ask. I'm dying to find out where he is and talk to him about his brother. "Is he here now?"

"Thomas saved us. He picked up the part we needed and brought it out," Dad says. "We told him to take the day off, after all his help. Why, do you need something?"

I shake my head. Dad musses up my hair like I'm a six-year-old and I shrug and duck away from him.

"We've had an overwhelming request for fly-fishing today," Mom says, cheerily. "Want to come?"

"No thanks, I'm good here. Uncle Li is teaching me so much about feng shui."

"Angus, aren't you proud of how we raised such an independent girl?"

They have no idea just how independent, I think to myself.

Mom hugs me again and then she and Dad go to the parlor to join the guests.

When I get to my room I check out what's on the *Tzolk'in* disc from Bolon.

The Tzolk'in
(Pronounced *Zole-keen*)
The ancient Maya knew that humans have a specific rhythmic cycle, which is why they devised the Tzolk'in, a 260-day calendar that has 20 months of 13 days.

Each day has 1 of 20 energies (pictures) and 1 of 13 forces (numbers). The combination of the number and the picture tell you what to focus on that day. For example, a day called 8 Imix (pronounced ee-meesh) would look like this:

Imix represents creation, or beginning, and is a great day to start something new. The number 8 brings the force of integrity, so whatever you begin with, have honest energy behind it.

Though deceptively simple, the Tzolk'in is a highly advanced DNA synchronization tool that reconnects humans to the natural cycles of the universe. Like a room full of tuning forks, if you strike one the others will resonate without even being touched.

Sounds interesting, kind of like one of those daily meditation calendars. I scroll down to see how it works. It looks like a regular calendar, but there's a number and a picture and a word on each of the days in addition to the normal date that we use. At the end there's this key to the thirteen numbers and the twenty pictures so you can look up the deeper meaning of each day. I print out the whole year so I can use it myself and see what it's all about.

Now for the web. I start by securing the web domain www.mayatwentytwelve.com that I register to "Bolon" in the Bahamas, and pay for from my PayPal account. I put up the basic info about the *Tzolk'in* on the top of the page. There's a formula for how to figure out what your birthday is, so I whip out a JavaScript calendar converter and embed that into the page as well because just like with horoscopes, everyone wants to know how the day they were born is different. Then I use the calendar engine to generate which of the 260 day files comes up, depending on what day it is when you check the site. It's no design winner, but a pretty serviceable website, if I do say so myself.

I decide to send the link to Justine, just to see what she thinks of it. I still have the email addresses to everyone at school, so I could send it out to a huge group if I wanted to, but I'm afraid to pull the trigger until I get some feedback.

From: Caitymacfireland@gmail.com
To: justinemiddleford@gmail.com
Subject: Ever heard of the Tzolk'in?

Hi J, I know this may seem totally out of the blue, but check this out. It's an ancient calendar created by the Maya. They were amazing astronomers way before anyone else even had telescopes. Anyway, I just started looking in to it and it seems pretty interesting. Let me know what you think…

PS—Still have not heard about date with David von Shopping. How was it?

I spend some time tweaking my website, then I hear my new mail chime.

From: justinemiddleford@gmail.com
To: caitymacfireland@gmail.com
Subject: RE: Ever heard of the Tzolk'in?

Weird! You know how when you learn a new word then all of a sudden you hear it like fifty times a day? Just yesterday I was in that coffee shop we used to go to

in the Haight to pretend we were in college, and I was
eavesdropping on this trippy conversation about Mayan
people and how they have a calendar that predicts
something or other to happen in 2012. And then you
send me the exact thing they're talking about! How
freaky is that? I printed it out and will use it every day.
Is it okay if I forward this on? My cousins Chris and Jeff
would be so into this. I'll totally give you the cred, of
course.

David was kind of a gentleman for the first time ever.
After shopping we even ate lunch at this little cafe and
A) he didn't throw any food at me and B) he actually
paid although all I had was a scone and a mocha cuz
I was too worried about getting sandwich or salad stuff
stuck in my teeth.

I'm a little surprised at how easy that was. Maybe Bolon was
right; maybe people will be into this thing. I email her back.

From: caitymacfireland@gmail.com
To: justinemiddleford@gmail.com
Subject: RE: RE: Ever heard of the Tzolk'in?

So all of a sudden he's David von Manners? Sounds
suspiciously like he is totally and completely in love with
you… More details puhleeeze. Freaky that you had
heard of this Mayan thing! Send it to whoever you want,
apparently the more the merrier. Maybe the two of us
can change the world! Ha ha. I might just send this to
everyone at Cruelties, too. If you get a weird email from
an unknown source at your school email address, you'll
know who it's from… Heart ya. Caity

Since Justine was so into it, I decide to go ahead and send
it to everyone at Cruelties. I'm afraid of getting in trouble if

someone forwards this to a teacher, so I register a legitimate-looking fake email address to use.

> From: SFAcademyofHumanities@gmail.com
> To: Student Body
> Subject: New policy-Mayan calendar
>
> Dear Students, we hope you are having a restful summer. We are getting a jump on our upcoming study of the Maya by sending out a mystery they left behind, their calendar. Please use this calendar for the rest of the summer and throughout the school year. Part of the study will be how students adapt to the calendar without adult supervision, so there is no talking to teachers about how to use it. You may reply to this email if you have specific problems, otherwise follow your own intuition.
>
> Click **here** to start.
>
> Thank you from the San Francisco Academy of Humanities Staff

I hesitate only slightly before I click the send button. Well, Bolon wanted me to get it around, and here's to the first 900! I feel a hand on my shoulder and freeze.

TWENTY-ONE

"Well done, Caity," I hear Bolon say.

"Geez, Bolon you just took ten years off my life!"

"Sorry, you know I meant you no harm. I was just pleased to see that it had all started."

"Since my friend Justine thought it was interesting, I figured I'd send it out to all students. If viruses and bad jokes can fly around the web millions of times a day, maybe this can too."

"It's a fantastic start," he says.

"Even if a bunch of kids at school start using this, I can't guarantee anything will happen. Especially with these rich snobs—they're not what you'd call *deep*. They like to shop. A lot."

"Then they are looking for something. They are like hungry ghosts, gorging on food and never feeling full," says Bolon cryptically. "What's important is that you have started the shift."

I look at the corner of my laptop at the little box of head-line news. Most of the articles are about violence and war and corrupt politicians and the failing economy. I point to it and say, "Bolon, look at the world. Look at this mess. You think we can really influence anything?"

"Chaos is necessary for order. Any scientist will tell you that chaos is at its worst right before a higher level of order is about to emerge. Crisis is often an evolutionary cattle prod, the force that moves us ahead."

"Weird," I say. "Now what's the other part you were going to tell me about?"

"Come and have a seat," he says as he walks over to the two leather chairs. This sounds serious. He sees the look on my face and says, "Don't worry, Caity, you can take it."

Once we're seated I say, "Give me the bad news first, then the good news, please."

"There is no bad news," he says, looking baffled. "You're going to have an adventure." He gets up and grabs the old globe on my desk. "Close your eyes for a moment, please."

I close my eyes and put my hands over them so I can't peek, which I always try to do.

"Open them now," he says.

I look at the globe. There's this weird band of light cir-cling it. He's holding the base, but the globe is slowly rotating with what looks like a greenish-yellow glow stick around it. "How did you do that?" I ask.

"This band of light circling the Earth like a tilted halo is a line around the Earth where most of the world's most important ancient sites are situated."

"A physical line?"

"No, it's kind of like a dot-to-dot puzzle. When you connect the dots between ancient monuments, you get a very precise circle around the Earth."

"Which monuments?" I ask.

"The enormous rock faces at Easter Island, the massive Nazca Lines engraved in the Earth that can only be seen from the sky, the gigantic monoliths in Ollantaytambo, the Pyramids of Paratoari, Machu Picchu, the temples of Malta, the Angkor temples, the ruins of Perseopolis, and the most impressive of all monuments, the Great Pyramid of Giza— and many more I haven't even mentioned—all of these are *exactly* 6,291 miles from one central axis."

"All of these are aligned on *one* circle around the Earth, like to the mile?"

He nods and sets the globe on the small table between us. The glowy line fades away.

"How did these people know exactly where to build all these monuments so many thousands of years ago?"

"They are all places with unusual magnetic energy. You see, humans have ferric iron in our sinuses that allows us to detect magnetic fields."

How cool that we have magnets in our faces!

"Okay, so there's a ring around the Earth with a lot of important places on it. What does that do ... or mean?" I ask.

"We need you to get young people to resonate powerful, positive energy worldwide along this circle," he says, as casually as telling me to go to the store to pick up a box of Special K.

I have a good laugh. "You know, sending out email and posting shareware is one thing. I mean, those actually match my skills, being kind of a computer person and all. But world-wide chanting or whatever? There's no way."

Bolon looks at me as if I just told him that his dog died.

"Look, it's not that I'm not willing," I say. "Seriously, haven't I been open to everything you've thrown at me? It's just that it's not *possible*. How am I going to leave here all alone and travel to God-knows-where and get kids to 'reso-nate' along some invisible line at places that I had never even heard of before this week?"

"You will," Bolon says calmly. "And you know that you know that you will."

If anyone else had said that sentence to me I would have been pissed; I have huge issues with this kind of you're-gonna-do-it-no-matter-what thing. But the way Bolon says it is different. He says it like he's showing me a new possibility or something, and it actually gets me thinking that maybe I *could* do this—whatever "this" really is.

"But what if I don't?" I ask. As soon as the words come out I feel cold, as if my body has turned to metal, and I feel like I'm being sucked down a whirlpool. As quickly as the feeling comes, it goes again but it leaves a residue of fear. "So what exactly do you want me to do?" I ask.

"In a few hours you will see that this calendar has spread like fire through a dry forest. Kids will set up study groups and build meeting places on the Internet to talk about it. All you need to do is put out the word that you are doing a kick-off for the *Tzolk'in*. List the places and times, which will be different everywhere, obviously, because of worldwide time zones."

"Okay, so far it doesn't sound too hard," I say.

"Then you will be at one of these places, preferably a place you don't think many others will be able to get to; perhaps Easter Island—"

When I start laughing really hard, Bolon looks confused. "Wait—you're serious?" I say.

"Of course," he answers. "Why is that funny?"

All of a sudden it's not so funny. "You really want me to go to those big heads? I don't even know what country they're in…"

"Chile," he replies.

I shake my head and laugh again. "Going to Chile, to Easter Island without my parents? I spell that C-R-A-Z-Y."

"Your friend Alex will join you," he says with a knowing smile.

I look down at my hands and pick at a hangnail. He found my weak spot. He pulls a thick manila envelope out of his poncho and hands it to me. I open it and see a wad of money.

"Wow, this is very *mafioso*," I say. "Is this my hush money or something?"

"Clearly you have watched too much television," Bolon says flatly. "This is what you'll need for travel. If you come up short I'll make sure you get more. I think you'll find all the various currencies you'll need so that you can pay in cash. And there's a slip of paper in there with information on how to access money online through Banco de Maya."

"Nice work Bolon. Thanks for thinking ahead," I say.

"That is what we Elders do," he says with a smile.

I leaf through all the weird-looking bills. "Okay, let me get this straight: I'm supposed to use the computer to stir up interest for kids to show up to this gathering, and tell them the various places around that great circle they can go. But then what?"

"Then you talk," he replies. "You talk to the world, to your young brothers and sisters."

"About what?" I ask.

"About change," he says, as if that was supposed to be obvious. I feel stupid, like I haven't been paying attention, so I change to subject.

"So you want me to do some kind of webcast?" I ask, surprised that he is asking me to get so technical.

"Exactly. You will announce the time and date and then at the appointed moment, you will talk through your technology. You don't really need to use all these gadgets, but since you all *believe* you do, we'll let you proceed that way."

"Wow, Bolon. Shareware, online money accounts, webcasts—I didn't know you were such a techie."

He waves his hand and says, "Compared to the complex math and astronomy we Elders must learn, this is nothing."

"What exactly do you want me to say?"

"You will know what to say when the time comes. The important thing is that you talk, and unite, with nothing else in your heart and mind than love."

"How will I know what to say?"

"All information is accessible to those who are open. At the time you speak, we will make sure you are open."

This idea sounds interesting, yet freaky in a demon-possession kind of way.

"We're not taking over your body," Bolon says, again

answering a question I didn't ask out loud. "It's more like tuning your radio to the Information Channel."

"Okay, so say I do it. Then what?" I ask.

"Then we measure the effectiveness. Talk to your friend Tenzo about PEAR."

"What's PEAR?"

"It's a lab. Tenzo will know someone there who can measure the effects of your work."

I laugh. "Tenzo just *happens* to know someone who can do that?"

"Coincidence is merely a fleeting glimpse at wholeness," he replies.

I'm not even going to touch that one. "So when do you want me to go?"

"Summer solstice," he replies.

"When is that? I know I should know but—"

"June twenty-first," he says without blinking.

I laugh. "Um, isn't it June sixteenth right now?"

He shrugs. "Is that a problem?"

I rub my face with my hands. "I'll do what I can, honest. But if it doesn't happen, I don't want you to be mad at me, okay?" I say.

"We would never be mad at you. We only have love for you."

I excuse myself to the bathroom, where I wipe my face with a cold washcloth and drink a full glass of water. This is all catching up with me. Bolon has a way of saying things that makes them sound like they'll be a cinch, but with all that I have to do I am seriously scared that I'll let these guys down.

Suddenly I feel sick and throw up the whole glass of water that I just drank. I don't want Bolon to see me this upset, so I pull myself together, brush my teeth and wash my face, and walk out trying to look normal. But Bolon is gone.

The fat envelope of cash sits on my desk with a note: *Dear Caity, You can do this. Above all else, have fun; love is expressed at its fullest in true joy. —In lak'ech, Bolon*

I hide the envelope in my drawer under the printer paper. Then I sit down at my desk with my sketchbook and make a list of everything I have to do.

TO DO

<u>Today, June 16</u>
1. Email Justine about visiting scam
2. Register fake email addresses for our moms
3. Brief Li/Tenzo about all of this
4. Reserve plane tix online
5. Convince Alex to come across the world with me!

<u>June 17</u>
1. Announce times/places of group meeting via email
2. Get Dad's satellite phone
3. Find out what PEAR is

<u>June 18</u>
1. Pack clothes, sat. phone, xtra batteries, laptop
2. Ferry from island, overnite train to Edinburgh

<u>June 19</u>
1. Fly to SF
2. Stay overnite w/Justine

June 20
1. Board flight to Easter Island—see big freaky
   heads!
2. Test equipment
3. Try not to freak out ...

June 21
1. Summer solstice
2. Do it!
3. Don't get caught or will be grounded for life and
   any afterlife there might be ...

A to-do list always makes me feel better; I love being able to check things off. It's my driftwood log when I'm lost at sea.

I start by emailing Justine, asking her to IM me ASAP. Then I register some fake email addresses that will allow me to pose as Justine's mom and my mom so I can communicate back and forth with their real email address to set up a "visit." I send the first piece of mail from Justine's mom's fake address to Mom's real address with some stuff about Justine being lonely and needing me to visit. Within minutes she takes the bait and says it's a great idea, that she thinks I'd love to take a trip back to San Francisco.

My God, it's going to happen.

TWENTY-TWO

As I'm about to scratch some things off my to-do list, I get an IM from Justine. There's no time like the present to ask a friend to go to Peru for you...

Justinem: Wassup? U still there?

Caitym: omg, thank u for being there! Things have taken a really weird turn and I need your help with some stuff. We have to IM so there's no email trail...all covert

Justinem: r u joking?

Caitym: no, totally serious. Swear on r friendship

Justinem: what can I do? what's going on?

Caitym: that rubbing I sent u was what got this whole thing started. It's some old code and when we decoded it we found it was a poem, like a prophecy...

Justinem: a prophecy?

Caitym: yeah, like one of those things that was foretold years ago and is now going to come tru

Justinem: like Nostradamus?

Caitym: kinda—but not really. Different kind of prophecy

Justinem: about what?

Caitym: about me
Justinem: u?
Caitym: Yep. And yes, I know I sound crazy. anyway, this has to do with that mayan calendar I sent u. I guess my part in this thing is to get kids to use it
Justinem: that shouldn't really be a problem—after u sent it to me I got the email that u sent to the whole school and I immediately got a bunch of emails from people who want to get together to talk it over.
Caitym: really? all since I sent that a couple of hours ago?
Justinem: Yep. so if u r supposed to get people interested in it, it looks like u succeeded.
Caitym: now I have to get it out worldwide. I have to have some sort of, like, gathering to kickoff using the calendar.
Justinem: from Scotland?
Caitym: No, here's the tricky part. i have to go to Easter Island
Justinem: those big heads?????????????????
Caitym: xactly
Justinem: and parents are ok w/ this?
Caitym: No, they don't know a thing.
Justinem: how?
Caitym: This is where u come in…
Justinem: ?
Caitym: can I say that I'm @ your house?
Justinem: of course! U don't think they'd find out?
Caitym: I think I have it covered, I just may need some help from u.
Justinem: No prob.
Caitym: & one other thing…
Justinem: ?
Caitym: Do u feel like going to Machu Picchu?

Caitym: u still there?
Justinem: wait, u r joking, right?

Caitym: uh, no…but from your answer I get the picture.
   it's too crazy
Justinem: wait wait. where is that, anyway? Mexico?
Caitym: Peru…south america
Justinem: Hmmmmmm
Caitym: honestly, I know how insane this sounds and I
   would not even blame u if u sent the psych ward 2
   come get me, but u KNOW me. I'm totally serious
   about this and would not ask if it were not so totally
   important.
Justinem: what do I tell my parents?
Caitym: I'll set it up so they will think u r here.
Justinem: if u can get them to believe it, then I'll go
   to Machu Picchu. I can't believe I just typed that
   sentence.
Caitym: u have no idea how much I love u for this…
Justinem: when?
Caitym: need to be there june 21, so fly in2 peru on the
   20th
Justinem: AS IN 3 DAYS FROM NOW????????????
Caitym: Yep
Justinem: u ARE crazy
Caitym: certifiable. but hey, I'm not making the
   deadlines here, I'm just following orders. I'll plan
   a layover in SF so we can hang & I'll fill you in on
   everything
Justinem: alright, sister, it's a go. bsides what else have
   I got going on?
Caitym: God, this has been too e z…
Justinem: r u calling me e z?
Caitym: ha ha. Okay, so I'll be @ the freaky heads, u
   will be @ Machu Picchu I'll try to get Amisi Mhotep
   to organize the pyramid one. u know anyone from
   Cambodia?
Justinem: Duh. The whole Huy family from your favorite
   vietnamese Pho soup shop!

Caitym: Oh my God, u r a genius. Is Chantrea still in
    Cambodia visiting her grandparents?
Justinem: Yep. I was just @ the restaurant 2 days ago.
    They asked about u, btw.
Caitym: Oh, I'd pay a million $$ for a bowl of Pho
    right now. Can u do me a huge favor and ask for
    Chantrea's email address?
Justinem: Si senorita
Caitym: Practicing for Peru?
Justinem: Si senorita
Caitym: u r the best.
Justinem: no, u r
Caitym: no, u r. hey, guess what? I'm going to ask J
    Crew to come with me.
Justinem: If u can pull that off u really r the best…
Caitym: doing it tonight, will let u know how it goes.
Justinem: I can't believe how weird your life got since u
    left.
Caitym: u and me both. Thanks for trusting me.
Justinem: anytime…
Caitym: ok, I'll be in touch
Justinem: ciao baby.

Now that Justine has agreed to go, I email her mom with
my mom's fake email address and ask if Justine can come for a
visit. This is going to be a harder sell with summer school and
all. But Justine is acing chemistry and with her extra tutoring
I'm sure she's scoring huge points.

There's one more thing I have to do before I go down to
dinner, and it's the hardest of all.

I sit at my desk and force myself to do it. I write on a
small piece of paper, "*Alex—Can you meet me at the tower by
the hidden names as soon as dinner is over? Very important. Very*

secret." As I slip it in my pocket my nerves start; it feels like caterpillars are crawling around inside my stomach.

As I'm putting on my shoes, Mom pops her head in the door. "Come on in," I say, glancing over at my computer to make sure my screen saver is on.

"I have a big surprise for you ..." she sings.

I try to fake excitement. "What is it?"

She takes my hands, "Justine's mom, Erin, has offered to fly you to San Francisco for a few days to surprise Justine as an early birthday gift!"

"And you said yes?" I say, jumping up and down. "Please please please?"

I may be overdoing it.

"Of course we said yes! Dad and I will take you to the Edinburgh airport and then you'll be on a direct flight to San Francisco."

"Oh my God, I'm so excited! Thank you, Mom!" I say as I hug her.

"You should thank Erin; she's the one who arranged all this."

"So when do I leave?" I ask.

"We'll get on the overnight train late tomorrow night and be in Edinburgh in the morning. I'm glad it's only a few days," she says as she gently pulls on one of my curls and lets it spring back up again. "I miss you already."

"Me too." For some reason my eyes well up. I walk away mumbling something about leaving my sweater in the bathroom and dab my eyes.

During cocktail hour I corner Uncle Li and Tenzo and tell them my plan. They have all sorts of reasons I shouldn't do this, of course. But what can they do? Neither of their names or birthdates is carved in the wall upstairs.

"So will you cover for me?" I ask Uncle Li. "You have to distract my parents with some big feng shui project they have to do or something."

"Certainly," he replies coolly. "I'll do what I can."

"And Tenzo, Bolon said to ask you about PEAR."

"The Princeton Engineering Anomalies Research lab?" he asks.

"I don't know, he said you would know somebody at something called 'PEAR' that could measure whether or not this worked. But to be honest, I'm not really sure what you would measure. Do you even remotely know what I'm talking about?" I ask.

"Of course. The PEAR lab runs the Global Consciousness Project that gathers information about whether there is this sort of 'collective mind' that all people are plugged into. Bolon told you about that?"

"Yep."

"I'll send an email to my friend at PEAR tonight. You said summer solstice, right?"

"Just like *that* you can get someone to use a big lab at Princeton?" I ask.

He nods. "If it's too short notice for a formal experiment, he'll do it off the record for me."

"Must be a good friend," I say. It's hard to imagine that Tenzo has many pals.

"Actually, he is the only person at the University I could

call a real friend," he replies. "We grew up on the same block. Happy coincidence that PEAR is where you need the favor!"

"Coincidence is just a fleeting glimpse at wholeness," I reply. They both look at me like flames are shooting out of my nose. "That's just Bolon talking."

The three of us sit together at dinner, and while all the guests re-live their super exciting "stranded for a night in Single Malt Scotchland" experience, I explain quietly to Uncle Li and Tenzo about the emails and the plane reservations and all that I've done so far to make this trip happen. At one point, surprised at how well I am deceiving the authority figures in my life, Tenzo asks if I think all of this is ethical. I don't really know what to say, but Uncle Li immediately defends me by saying, "If ever there were a case of the ends justify the means, this is it!"

Then, as if my trip to Easter Island isn't shocking enough, I tell them about what Mrs. Findlay had told me about Thomas and his brother Donald. Their mouths hang.

"So do you think it's Donald who locked us in?" whispers Uncle Li.

"Has to be. It can't just be a coincidence that Donald stole two ancient Sanskrit books—"

"We should talk to Thomas tomorrow to see what he says about all this," I say.

When Alex reaches for my plate after dinner, I slip my note into his hand. He walks to the kitchen, comes back a few seconds later to clear my glasses, and then nods his head discretely. My stomach does roller-coaster flips and I stop breathing for a moment at the thought of being alone in the moonlight with this beautiful creature.

And then the nervousness sets in. How can I ask a guy I've only known for a couple of weeks to run across the world with me?

When my parents rise from their chairs and the guests get up and mingle, I slip out the side door into the kitchen. Mrs. Findlay is making a racket washing an enormous pot so I am able to pick up Mr. Papers and creep out the back door without even being noticed.

In Scotland, the midsummer sun never goes far enough below the horizon to get really dark, so even at ten o'clock it's still twilight—dark enough for stars, but light enough to see your way. When I arrive, I see Alex is already there, leaning against the tower.

I take a deep breath to keep my cool.

"What's this all about then, Superspy?" he asks with a grin. His teeth shine in the moonlight like glowing Chiclets. "It's all very 'cloak and dagger' now, isn't it?"

I'm glad to see he's amused and not annoyed.

"Hey, about the other day, I'm just so sorry, I really—"

"Stop," he says, holding up one hand. "I'm the one who needs to apologize, mate. I had no right to say those things."

"You didn't say anything that wasn't true," I reply.

"Let's just forget about it, shall we?"

"Great, I'd love to. Because there's something I have to ask you, and I'm not sure . . ." My voice trails off. "God, where do I start?" I say under my breath.

"The beginning?" he says.

"Okay. Right. The beginning." I exhale. "When I first got here I discovered this hidden room off of me bedroom. And in that hidden room is a passageway into the tower."

Alex points to the small door on the outside of the tower. "There's one right here, too ..."

Does he think I'm an idiot? I shake my head. "The one upstairs goes to a different place. You know how this door leads to stairs that go up around the outside of the tower? Well, they're twisting around a hidden inner core, and in this core is a huge room with all this crazy stuff in it."

"What kind of crazy stuff?" From the look on his face I assume he is picturing medieval torture devices.

"It's not dungeon crazy. It's more, I don't know, new-age crazy? I'll take you there sometime when this is all over. But let me get to the important part ..." I pause for a moment while I try to figure out how to put this without sounding totally insane. I decide to bring some adults into the picture first so he doesn't think I've made this all up in my head.

"Tenzo and Uncle Li have been helping me figure all this out. It's very complicated and involves this weird code and stuff. But the bottom line is that this whole castle was built to protect a prophecy." I look in his eyes to make sure he's following me, and then I say, "A prophecy that I'm supposed to carry out."

Alex looks totally confused. "What kind of prophecy? And how do you know you are involved?" He asks this in just the right way, not with a tone of disbelief, but in a way that tells me he is genuinely curious.

"Seriously, I know how crazy this seems. But we found this book, this poem that Fergus Mac Fireland wrote way back in the 1700s, and it mentions my name and my birth date. And the year 2012. Remember the heavy conversation at dinner about the Mayan calendar and stuff? Well, it all has to do with that, too."

Alex crosses his arms and rubs his biceps with his hands like he's warming himself. "You're giving me goose bumps, Caity."

"Believe me; no one is more freaked out by this than me. But here's the deal, and I know this is way too much to ask, but I have to give it a shot." I look him in the eyes again, trying to get a read on how receptive he'll be.

"Go on ..." he says, "I'll help in any way I can."

"Would you ever consider going away for a few days? We'd have to fib about some things, but in the end everyone would understand why we did it. It's for the good of the world, although I know that sounds like something a schizophrenic would say."

"Where exactly?"

"Have you heard of Easter Island?"

"Are you *mad*?" he says, looking at me like I just told him I eat live babies for breakfast.

I'm crushed. I don't know what to say. "I've wondered that myself," I mumble.

We stand there silently for so long that it becomes uncomfortable. He is just staring at me, examining me like I'm some prehistoric creature that's just been unearthed.

"I reckon we need to back up even further," he says. "Let's start at the very beginning; tell me how you even came to the Isle of Huracan in the first place."

I'm not sure how this is going to help him, but I start at the beginning, in the spring, when my dad first got the news.

"It really came out of the blue," I tell him. "Mom and Dad came into my room while I was studying one night, and I remember thinking something was up because Dad sat in my desk chair, which he only does when he needs to 'come down to my level.' I don't know about here, but that's classic behavior that adults use on kids and dogs in the states."

Alex nods like he knows exactly what I mean.

"So anyway, Dad sits down and tells me that his Uncle Hamish had just passed away and had left us some property in Scotland. Then he said they were planning on selling it, but then that very day they got a *sign*."

"A sign?"

I nod. "This is so embarrassing to admit. The 'sign' thing should have been my first clue that it was all going to get weird, because my parents are *not* the kind of people who talk about getting signs. They're the kind of people who make fun of people who talk about getting signs."

"So what was the sign?" Alex asks.

"Oh, God, it was this obscure thing about some guys at UCLA discovering a double helix nebula near the center of the Milky Way."

"You mean a double helix like in DNA?" he asks.

I nod. "Yep. Seriously, my parents are the only people in the world who would see a DNA-shaped cloud of gas and dust as a sign to keep property."

Alex looks confused. "What was the connection? How did this become a sign?" he asks.

"They thought that the universe was telling them to keep the property—Hamish's fascination with the Milky Way and then the big DNA cloud next to it told them to keep Breidablik in the bloodline." When I say this all out loud, it sounds as crazy as finding an image of the baby Jesus on a grilled cheese sandwich.

But Alex looks like he gets it. "Aye, when you put it that way I can see their point."

"Hard to believe this all came down to space dust," I say, wondering what would have happened had Mom *not* read that very article on that very day.

"And what's the Mayan connection? It's odd enough that there's a Chinese element."

"Back in the 1500s before the Maya were invaded by the Spanish, they took their secret knowledge of space and calendars and cycles of time and hid it all over the world. Some went to China, some came right here. They built something on this island that Fergus and Xu Bao Cheng concealed with the tower."

"So why is this all coming out now? And why you?"

How did I think he was just going to say, *Yeah! Right on! Get me a plane ticket and let's roll!* I give him an out. "Look, I get that you don't want to go. Let's just forget it."

He looks pissed. "Have I said no?" he asks. "Can you blame a bloke for wanting some background before hopping a plane to Chile?"

I am so in love with him for knowing that Easter Island is part of Chile.

"Sorry," I say as I cross my arms across my chest. "You have no idea how weird this all is for me."

"Then imagine how weird it is for me, hearing it all in a five-minute conversation."

"I know. Sorry. So anyway, I'm supposed to unite kids

by getting them to use this *Tzolk'in* calendar and having this worldwide kickoff of it. That's where Easter Island comes in."

"It sounds bloody interesting and I'd love to help, but I couldn't possibly get that kind of cash anytime soon," he says, looking down and rolling a rock around with his foot.

"Oh, no no no, it won't cost you a cent. Honest, I've got this huge wad of cash that Bolon gave me. All I need is for you to go with me. I'm a little scared to do this on my own."

"Now who is Bolon?" he asks.

"He's the Mayan guy, the Elder, who's helping me with this prophecy thing."

"Geez Caity, this sounds serious." He bites the inside of his lip. "But your parents don't know anything about it?" he asks. "Your father has been so good to me, I really hate to—"

I put my hands up. "I've got it covered. I've set it up so they think I'm going to visit my friend Justine, so all you have to do is tell your mom and your grandma that you're going camping or fishing or something. They won't even know we're together."

We're together. I say it again in my head.

"Well, you've got it all figured out, haven't you?" He looks down and pulls at his chin as he thinks. "Alright then. I'm sure I could come up with some reason to be gone."

"Really?" I ask. "You're really saying yes?"

"Against my better judgment," he says as he closes his eyes and shakes his head, "aye."

I spontaneously hug him and then quickly pull away.

"So may I see some of this stuff you've discovered?" he asks.

"Right now?"

"I have to go help Gran finish with dinner cleanup, then I'll come up. Unless, of course, you don't trust me in your room all alone," he says with a smile.

"Very funny," I say as I hit his shoulder with my fist. I'm embarrassed that I make such a fifth-grade move.

When he turns and jogs back to the kitchen door, I step over and press my back up against where he was leaning. The wall is still warm from his body. I look up at the stars winking in the twilight and tell myself I can't move until I see one falling through the sky. After a few minutes one streaks by and I think about how it's possible that Alex and I had, at one time in the past few billion years, been atoms in the same star soaring through space.

TWENTY-THREE

"Anyone see you come up?" I ask as I close and bolt the door behind Alex, who has Mr. Papers balanced on his shoulder.

"Nae, they're all getting snookered in the parlor," he replies.

"Thank God for Scotland and all that whisky." I lead him over to my desk, open the file from Bolon, and then give up my seat to Alex. "Have at it."

I fake being cold so I can light a fire, which both gives me busy work and adds to the romance of having Alex in my room again.

As he scrolls through the pages, he quietly says things like *hmm* and *interesting* and *I see*, as if talking to someone on the phone. Once the fire is lit, and I can't give him space anymore, I stand behind him to read over his shoulder. He's looking at the grid representation of the *Tzolk'in*.

"You read it top to bottom, starting in the upper left corner," I tell him. "These little pictures on the far left are the twenty daylords and the numbers of their weeks of thirteen days are made up of dots for ones and bars for five."

"Caity, this is amazing."

"Amazing how?" I ask, not wanting to shape how he interprets this thing. Maybe he sees something I hadn't. I mean it *is* really cool looking, this grid, which is why I'd printed it out and taped it into my sketchbook.

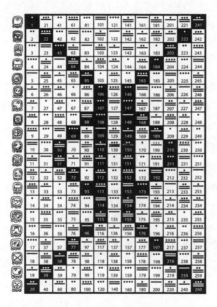

"Between this and the Long Count calendar that ends in 2012, there's some really interesting math here," Alex says.

"Oh yeah? There is such a thing?"

"What?"

"There's such a thing as really interesting math?"

"Aye, all math is interesting to me. Got a problem with that?" he asks with a grin. "Because if you do, I s'pose I couldn't possibly go with you to Easter Island and bore you with all my math talk."

"Nope, no problem at all. Love math, always have. Don't make me get out my 'I heart Math' T-shirt..."

"Now you're just torturing me!" he says with a laugh. "We can go ahead and get engaged this minute if your homepage is set to www.mathworld.com."

Oh how I wish that I could stop time right now to reset both my homepage and my blushing face.

Alex turns back to the screen. "Now what exactly are you supposed to be doing with this information?"

"Getting it out to kids. Getting them to use the Mayan calendar—or 'resonate' with it was how Bolon put it. But I really don't get how a calen—"

Alex interrupts. "Resonate? Seriously?"

"Yeah, why?"

"Because the whole time I was looking at this stuff, I was thinking that the underlying math looked harmonic."

"Like music?"

"Maybe notes, or maybe just a tone..."

Mr. Papers waves his hands at us and jumps, but we're too engrossed in the calendar to pay attention to him.

"So you're saying take Bolon's suggestion literally—*literally* resonate—with some kind of sound?" I ask.

Mr. Papers suddenly jumps in between the computer screen and Alex, then taps Alex on the nose like a reprimanding teacher.

"What?" Alex asks, seeming irritated.

Mr. Papers grabs a hair band from my desk and three newly sharpened pencils from my pen cup, binding the pencils together about an inch down from their points. Then he fans them out into a tripod and sets this contraption, eraser-side down, on my desk so that it looks like an upside-down teepee. Finally, he sets a sheet of origami paper on top of the pencil tripod.

"What on earth are you doing?" I ask.

He raises one finger to me as if to say, "Just a moment," and then hops over to an old tea tray by my bed. He takes a spoonful of sugar from the sugar bowl and with expert balance he walks back to the desk and hops up without spilling a grain. Very carefully he shakes some sugar on the piece of paper.

"C'mon Papers, what's this about?" Alex asks.

Mr. Papers takes a deep breath, bends down so that one side of the paper is touching his chin, and then bursts out with a weird sound, like someone singing the note "ti."

The grains of sugar hop around on the paper from the vibration of his voice.

"Bloody hell, Caity! Look at what the sugar is doing!"

He doesn't have to tell me to look; I can't even talk for fear of missing a second of what's happening before me. The sugar is forming a pattern on the paper, a beautiful image somewhere between a zinnia flower and a stylized sun.

When Mr. Papers is out of breath, he sits back and looks at the paper, then smiles at us.

Quickly Alex Googles "shapes from sound" and some articles pop up, which Alex reads out loud.

"The study of the wave phenomena of physical patterns produced through the interaction of sound waves in a medium such as sand is called cymatics. Sand activated by sound can form itself into standing wave patterns from simple concentric circles to traditional mandala designs."

"But how does Mr. Papers know this?" I ask.

"Haven't a clue," he replies, lost in an article on cymatics. "Oh, Caity, listen to this. A Russian research team of geneticists and linguists is using the theory behind cymatics to *modify DNA*."

"No way … the right sound can change DNA?" I'm stunned. "So I guess Mr. Papers is saying that you're right, that this must have something to do with turning the *Tzolk'in* into sound."

We both jump back when Mr. Papers lets out a deafening screech, again placing his chin on the paper.

"Damn it Mr. Papers," Alex says, covering his ears. "Ought not do that to a pal!"

"But look what it did to the sugar!" The crystals have morphed from the pretty, symmetrical arrangement into what looks like broken glass.

"Freaky!" we both say at the same time.

I add, "Jinx, you owe me a Coke," but Alex looks at me like I'm speaking Martian, so I let it drop. Must be an American thing.

"I reckon he's telling us that there are good tones and bad tones," Alex says, still looking at the sugar on the paper.

"Or damaging tones and healing tones," I add.

He shrugs. "I s'pose, if you want to get all new agey."

"Brace yourself, Alex, this thing may get very new agey."

He gets up from the chair and puts a hand on my shoulder. "As long as I have my math to hang on to, I think I'll be fine."

I could kiss him. Really. We are in position—one of his hands is touching my shoulder and I can feel the heat of his palm though my T-shirt. All I have to do is lean in.

I am a wuss.

"So what next?" I ask instead.

Alex picks up the *Tzolk'in* disc. "I'll look more deeply at this and try to find some way to make it resonate."

I lean over my desk and jot down the website URL. "Here's the website I put up. Definitely not my best web work, but—"

"My, you work quickly!" he says, pocketing the paper. "Should we check on some air and train schedules while we're here?"

I love how he pronounces *schedule* like shed-u-all.

"Oh, good idea," I say, as eager to have him stay as I am to get everything lined up. I take the driver's seat and pull up my favorite travel site.

I'm glad I have a big wad of cash from Bolon because travel prices have gone up even more. Pretty soon only the elite with private jets will be able to travel, which is probably exactly what the *Fraternitas* wants: keep the people down on the ground, broke and pathetic.

We book our flights and then I print out all the plane ticket information and give him enough of Bolon's money for the ferry, train, airfare, and other stuff that might come up.

"Okay, you just get yourself to San Francisco and then we're off to Easter Island for this...gathering," I say.

Alex smiles. "You know this is the most exciting thing that's ever happened to me, don't you?"

I want to ask if *I'm* the most exciting thing or if *the situation* is the most exciting thing, but I'm afraid of the answer so I just say, "Me too."

"Do you need me to bring anything special? Herbs, potions, eye of newt?"

I laugh. "No, got it covered. I just need to sneak Dad's satellite phone…"

"Ah, you going to do one of those fancy teleconference things where everyone calls a number on their phone and you talk to them?"

"Genius! I hadn't even thought of that! I was thinking I'd webcast, but I hadn't figured out how they were going to get Internet access at all these funky places."

"And there's cell service pretty much everywhere."

"Have you done this before? How do you know about it?" I ask.

"I've called in to some football teleconferences; they have famous footballers talking about their strategies and such, and you just listen in."

"Very cool. I'll check it out."

After Alex takes the CD and goes home, I check the fake email account I set up for Mom. There's a reply from Justine's mom: She bit! We're on!

I immediately reserve a plane ticket for Justine to Peru, one that flies to Los Angeles first so that her parents won't see her board a plane to South America. I pay for it from Bolon's Banco de Maya account and then I email Justine's mom with all the information.

Justine has to be in the know, so I forward all the emails to her so she can see what I'm doing. She responds:

From: justinemiddleford@gmail.com
To: caitymacfireland@gmail.com
Subject: Chantrea's email

Dude, you nailed the email momspeak. I just called the
Pho shop, Chantrea is in Cambodia all summer with
her grandparents like I thought. Her email address is
chantreahuy@gmail.com. I can't believe I'm going to
peru. If you get to take jcrew can I invite David to come
with me? You wouldn't have to pay, he could probably
buy a plane ticket with his weekly allowance, you know
how loaded the von Kellermans are…

For a moment I hesitate about the David von Kellerman
thing, but then I think about how much I am asking of her. I
mean, making your friend go alone to South America is a lot
to ask. Plus I'll feel better about her safety if someone else is
with her.

From: caitymacfireland@gmail.com
To: justinemiddleford@gmail.com
Subject: RE: Chantrea's email

THANKS for getting me Chantrea's email address so
quickly. As for David, why not? You think he'd want to?
I arrive around noon on the 18th, then leave again the
next day right around the time you do. I'll get a hotel
room in SF when I get there. Then we can spend the
day together before we both have to go do this…

All this scheming has me completely exhausted. I really
want to go to bed, but I figure I better set up this phone thing
and try to get in touch with Chantrea and Amisi. With the
time-zone weirdness, the hours that I'm asleep could be crucial
in this whole plan.

The teleconference setup is pretty easy. I get assigned an 800 number and book a block of time for my call. As long as it's listen-only and no one but me is going to be actually talking, it looks like there is no maximum number of callers. Now I have to email the girls.

From: caitymacfireland@gmail.com
To: chantreahuy@gmail.com, amisi@yahoo.com, justinemiddleford@gmail.com
Subject: Hello from Caity Mac Fireland

Hey girlies, it's Caity! Amisi and Chantrea, I don't think you two know each other, but you both know me and you both know Justine. Amisi, let me introduce Chantrea—her parents own the best Vietnamese restaurant in San Francisco called Lucky Pho (oh how I miss it!). She's spending the summer in Cambodia with her grandparents. And Chantrea, Amisi is from Egypt. She lives in Cairo but went to school with us at the Academy of Cruelties last year while her dad was in San Francisco with that huge mummy exhibit (he's the main guy in charge of the pyramids).

Anyway, as you both know my parents moved me out to Nowhere, Scotland this summer, to this very strange island. Well, it turns out that my relatives or ancestors or whatever were involved in a big mystery that is kinda unraveling right now. Anyway, one of the things I'm supposed to do is sort of unite kids. I don't even know the whole entire story yet, but I know it has to do with kids and this ring of sacred places around the Earth and with the Mayan calendar (see website **here**).

OK, so let me get to it—would either of you be able to be the point person on a gathering? Amisi, you'd be in charge of the one at the pyramids and Chantrea, you'd be doing one in Cambodia at Angkor Wat (which I never even heard of before I moved here!) Anyway, it wouldn't require much work, just your cell phone and a poster with a phone number on it. We're supposed to do this event at the same time all over the world, on summer solstice (I know that is only a few days away! Yikes!) Justine is going to Machu Picchu and I'm going to Easter Island (double yikes!). I'll be calling from Easter Island and all you have to do is call this 800 number and listen. There might be no one there with you, there might be ten or twenty people. Who knows? This is all new to me too.

If you're up for it, cut and paste the message below, along with the Mayan calendar website attachment, in a new mail to as many kids as you know, and encourage them to send it to more. Let's see how many people we can get! So here's the mail you can send around:

Dear friends,

Did you know that if you have a room full of silent tuning forks all you have to do is strike one and its vibrations will make all the other tuning forks sing too? You can be that tuning fork!

Join us (no one over 19, please!) as we come together at special places on Earth to get everyone our age to start changing the world. It doesn't matter if you can't vote—as long as you feel like we need to change the hellish course the adults have sent us on, then join us.

We're kicking off the use of the Mayan calendar (the website is attached to this mail). Check it out; if it makes sense to you, then use it and meet up with us on summer solstice. Here are the times:

Egypt/Pyramids @ 7:00 PM on June 21st
Angkor Wat Temple @ 11:00 PM on June 21st

Machu Picchu @ 11:00 AM on June 21st
Easter Island @ Noon on June 21st

Bring your cell phone! Join us! We CAN make a
difference.

I hit the send button and realize that they may just think
I've totally lost my mind. I know Amisi really well; she had
English class with Justine and me and we stalked her until she
would talk to us because she was so beautiful and exotic looking. Chantrea goes to a different school and I only know her
from the restaurant. I was a seriously regular customer but we
never had any big deep conversations or anything. But I do
know that she considers herself a closet anarchist so this kind
of thing might be right up her alley.

I guess I'll just have to wait until tomorrow to see what
they think.

TWENTY-FOUR

In the morning the first thing I do is check my email. I can't believe it, both Amisi and Chantrea have responded.

From: amisi@yahoo.com
To: caitymacfireland@gmail.com, chantreahuy@gmail.
com, justinemiddleford@gmail.com
Subject: RE: Hello from Caity Mac Fireland

Hello to you! For some reason I am still on the Academy's email list and I received an assignment on the Mayan calendar just a few hours before I got your email! Quite a strange coincidence, no?

I would love to help! The day of the gathering I will ask my father to tell the guards that I am permitted to have a few students come into the restricted area around the great pyramid for a class project. It will be a beautiful place for something like this, especially at that time of the evening. I'm sure I can get a few people to show up.

Thank you for including me. I love that it's all girls doing this—and you and Justine are quite brave to go so far!

Chantrea, good luck at Angkor Wat. I was there once on holiday with my parents and was awed by the beauty of Cambodia. In Peace, Amisi

I just love Amisi! It's obvious from her email she has had a seriously fancy education. She writes like an adult and English isn't even her first language. I wish I could be with her right next to the pyramids—now that I've heard Tenzo talk about them it's got me very interested.

Next I open Chantrea's email.

From: chantreahuy@gmail.com
To: caitymacfireland@gmail.com, amisi@yahoo.com;
justinemiddleford@gmail.com
Subject: RE: Hello from Caity Mac Fireland

Hey you, I knew all that spicy chili oil you always put on your Pho would go to your head. You are crazy but I love it! I haven't been to Angkor Wat yet but one of my cousins has been wanting to take me there. I don't know what you're talking about with the whole phoning in thing but I'm sure my cousin can help. He's so into technology it's insane, like he has pictures of Bill Gates all over his walls and stuff. Hello, dork?

I sent the email out to about 13 people I know here and I think I can get them to go. I'm like a rock star here already just because I live in the US. Seriously, all my cousin's friends try to dress exactly like me and ask me questions like "Is Brad Pitt short?" as if I'm his best friend because we both live in California. If they only knew I am pretty much a band geek at home! Keep me posted on what else I need to do ... Chantrea

A wave of relief washes over me. Now I just have to be able to pull off the big one—going to Easter Island without my parents knowing.

Tiptoeing out of my room, I sneak to see if Mom and Dad are still in their bedroom. Their door is cracked and I see them in bed talking about their plans for the day. I run back into my room for my backpack so I can get Dad's satellite phone from the library. He bought it right when they decided to come out here, thinking he'd have to use it for Internet access while they got this place wired. Before we left, Dad and I had taken it to the top of Mount Tamalpais and used it to call Mom, pretending we were on Everest. He hasn't had to use it here so he shouldn't miss it.

I make it to the library without seeing a soul. I pull out the satellite phone from the cabinet in the corner where dad stashes his portable electronics and slip it in my backpack. Back upstairs, I bolt my door and roll up the phone in a sweatshirt and put it in my suitcase. Then I hear Dad ask if I'm ready for breakfast.

"Sure," I say as I quickly slip the suitcase under my bed.

In the hallway Dad takes my hand. "I hear you're leaving us for a few days, kiddo. We're going to be so lonely here since the Berkeley alums are leaving tomorrow as well."

"They are? Will they be on the same train to Edinburgh tomorrow?"

"Indeed they will," Dad says.

"Well, if they're all going to the airport I could just go with them. You guys wouldn't have to take a two-day round-trip train just to take me to the same place they're going."

Dad looks over at Mom. "I hadn't thought about that. Fiona, what do you think?"

Mom stops walking. "I suppose it's more about how Caity feels," she says as she looks at me. "You really don't want us to take you there?" she asks.

"It's not that I don't want you to; it just seems silly. I definitely want you to come on the ferry and get me settled into my train car, but really all I'm going to do is lock the door and go to sleep. When I wake up we'll be in Edinburgh and I'll just take the train to the airport with all the Berkeley alums. I mean, who could be more responsible than a bunch of smart old people?"

Mom and Dad look at each other and shrug, wondering if it's an okay thing to do. I don't want it to come off like I don't need them so I add, "I totally insist you pick me up when I come back, though. I want to see you the second I get off the plane!"

"Of course, Caity," Mom says, grabbing my other hand. We walk down the wide staircase, all holding hands like we did when I was little.

I see Tenzo and Uncle Li at the breakfast buffet in the dining room. "You want to eat in the parlor?" I whisper to them. "We should try to talk to Thomas about you-know-what."

Alex walks out with a pitcher. He sees me and then motions with his head for me to follow him over by the coffee urn. While he fills the cream pitcher he says quietly, "I worked it out with my mum and I'm free; turns out most people are leaving tonight anyway."

"Perfect!" I say, amazed that this is all falling into place. "Hey, have you seen Thomas?"

"Aye, in the kitchen."

I see Mom and Dad watching me and Alex whispering, with grins on their faces. Whatever. Let them think I'm in love with him; it will distract them from what's really going on.

"When you go back in the kitchen, would you mind asking Thomas to meet me and Uncle Li and Tenzo in the parlor?" I ask.

He nods as he walks back to the kitchen. I slip out the side door to the parlor. Tenzo and Uncle Li are already there, and when I get to the table they both stop talking. "Are you talking about me?" I ask, sounding kind of paranoid.

They look at each other. Uncle Li says, "We're worried that all of this is going too fast."

"You're not going to put a stop to it are you?" I ask. I have to admit that I'm thinking as much about losing a trip with Alex as I am about stopping the gathering.

"Perhaps one of us should go with you, for protection" Tenzo adds.

I shake my head. "It would look super suspicious if you left with me. Plus I need you to be a distraction to my parents so they don't try to call me 24/7 while I'm gone."

"Do you think we could at least meet Bolon?" Tenzo asks.

"Look, even I don't know how to get a hold of Bolon," I say. "If he's not staying here I don't know where he's staying. He might even be camping. Who knows?" I say. "Next time he comes by, I'll have him stay in my room until I can get you guys so you can meet him." Their nervousness has transferred to me and I feel all agitated inside but I don't want to let them know.

Thomas walks in and says, "Did you folks ask to see me?"

Uncle Li says, "Please, have a seat."

Obviously nervous, he sits down and says, "So how can I help you, then?"

"I'm not sure where we even start?" Uncle Li replies.

"How about here: Thomas, we know about Donald and the Sanskrit books."

He looks up, his eyes like golf balls. "Do your parents know about this? Mrs. Findlay?"

I don't want to get Mrs. Findlay in trouble so I shake my head. "Only the three of us."

He closes his eyes for a long moment, then opens them and says, "There are things you need to know, Caity."

TWENTY-FIVE

enzo and Uncle Li and I all look at each other. Everyone seems on edge. "What is it?" I ask Thomas.

He takes a deep breath and says, "There's a room, off your bedroom—"

I interrupt. "I know all about that, Thomas. I know about the room, the poem, the tower."

"Bloody hell, you work fast!" he says. "So you know how deeply you're involved?"

"Sort of. But we don't know anything about how you or your brother are involved. And yesterday someone locked us in the tower to translate the Sanskrit books."

"Donald?" he asks, wincing as if he's just about to watch two cars crash.

"We think so."

"Can you tell us how much he knows?" Tenzo asks. "And why he wants those books?"

Thomas shakes his head. "There's a lot more to it."

"More to what?" I ask.

"Ah, Caity. I don't want you to feel betrayed by not knowing this sooner," Thomas says as he puts his hand over mine. "I didn't know you'd find out so much so fast."

"What?" I say, my voice getting shaky. "Thomas, you're scaring me."

After a pause he says, "We are related, Caity. I am a Mac Fireland. Your father's uncle."

"But how is that possible? Why would you hide something like that?"

"And what does that make Hamish?" Tenzo asks.

"Let me explain," Thomas says, taking in a deep breath as if preparing to go underwater. Then he exhales and begins, "There came a point when my father, your great-grandfather Robert, was the only surviving Mac Fireland. His sister died quite early and being the only one left in the lineage, he was very concerned about the prophecy not coming to completion. In fact, he became downright obsessive about it. When his wife, my mother Elspeth, became pregnant he talked her into organizing something very ... how shall I put it? Unorthodox."

The three of us lean in, dying to hear what he's going to say next.

"He and Elspeth went to a home for wayward girls in Edinburgh and found a young pregnant woman called Beatrice who looked about as far along as Elspeth. They talked the home into letting her come live with them. Beatrice was delighted to have such an upstanding patron, and to move somewhere where she could start anew. My father had a nice lad in mind for her, Tobey, and they were wed when they got back to the Isle of Huracan. Beatrice and Tobey lived in the little room off the kitchen while she was pregnant; she was a cook, he a groundskeeper. "

"Why did Robert go to all that trouble?" I ask.

Thomas holds his hand up as if to say *I need to finish* and continues. "When it was time for the babies to come, the castle was closed off, and nary a soul was to come or go. My grandmum was there to help with the births, and the mothers helped too, as the deliveries were thirteen days apart. My mother Elspeth gave birth to twins: me and my brother Donald. Beatrice gave birth to one child, whom they called Hamish."

We all gasp.

"So Hamish is not a Mac Fireland?" Tenzo asks.

Thomas shakes his head.

"Why would your parents switch you at birth?" I ask.

"My father came to believe that the prophecy was being threatened; he thought the Shadow Forces would come in and snatch his children to put an end to it all. So he hid us."

"Hid you in the tower?" I say, horrified.

Thomas laughs. "Nae, lass, I don't mean he locked us away, he just hid the fact that we were Mac Firelands. He gave Beatrice and Tobey a house in town and took care of them well. My brother and I were raised like all other island folk, not suspecting a thing."

"When were you told?" Uncle Li asks.

"I reckon I should have guessed earlier, what with all the time Robert spent with us. But since both my parents worked at the castle, it was natural to spend most of my time here. When Donald and I were sixteen Robert took us up to the hidden room and told us the whole story."

"Were you pissed?" I ask. "I would have been so mad!"

"We were well loved by our surrogate parents, so I was more amazed than angry," he replies. "Not so with my brother. He didn't take the news well. Some people feel entitled to things, and Donald felt robbed of his upbringing as the son of the Laird in a castle."

"Was Hamish totally in the dark?" Tenzo asks.

Thomas nods. "For his own safety, he never knew a thing about the prophecy."

"What about the silver three hares key he sent me? The one I used to get in to the secret room?" I ask. "And that weird Mexican plaque and the photo of the Milky Way?"

"That was me, Caity. I sent those."

"But what about my grandfather? He would have been your younger brother, right—or was he not really a Mac Fireland?"

"Aye, your grandfather Aeden was indeed a Mac Fireland," Thomas says. "After Donald and I were tucked safely out of sight, Aeden was born. Father felt strongly that Aeden would be the one to keep the lineage going."

"You mean to have Dad and then me?"

Thomas nods. "So at a young age your grandfather was sent off to boarding school in Edinburgh and then to university in America under a false name. For his own protection, your grandfather was never told anything until after your own father was grown. Not long after he was told, Aeden was killed in a car accident."

"So no one thought it was weird that Hamish stayed here his whole life and my grandfather was sent off to boarding school?" I ask.

"As the eldest son, it was expected that Hamish would stay on the island with the castle. Most folks were impressed that father was preparing his younger son for life in the real world."

"Where has Donald been all these years?"

"Haven't a clue," he replies. "He left the Isle of Huracan when he was about seventeen. Once we knew the truth, Donald assumed that at a certain age he and I would move into the castle and take over. When we were told that Hamish would remain the perceived heir for all our lives, Donald became enraged. He took the two books that Robert, our father, guarded most closely and left, never to be seen again. Until now, apparently."

"Why wouldn't Donald have had someone else translate the books?" Tenzo asks. "He could have found any number of scholars to read this ancient language."

"Nae. He would've been too timid to do that. I don't think you understand the power of this information; any scholar who could read this text would understand how valuable it is. No one would translate without questioning where it came from or wanting to publish it."

"Have you found this to be true?" Tenzo asks Uncle Li.

Uncle Li pauses, and then replies. "I haven't read them through yet, I'm just getting reacquainted with the language—"

"Can you read them?" I ask Thomas. "What's so special about them?"

"I can't read ancient Sanskrit, but Robert told me what they were: the collected wisdom of what was called the 'Nine Unknown Men' in India."

"The 'Nine Unknown Men' were not just a myth?" Tenzo asks.

"Nae," replies Thomas.

Suddenly I'm lost. "Wait, who are the Nine Unknown Men?" I ask.

"Over 2,000 years ago, after witnessing a gruesome massacre in war, the Indian emperor Asoka gathered together nine lads to preserve ancient knowledge that would be dangerous to humanity if it fell into the wrong hands," says Thomas.

Tenzo looks astounded. "If this is true, Caity, it means that thousands of years of secret study have been distilled into these books, kept hidden so that methods of destruction would not fall into the hands of the unqualified or evil-minded."

"Thomas, if you knew about this, and me, the whole time, why didn't you just tell me about it?" I ask. "Why'd I have to sneak around and do all of this by myself?"

"If I learned nothing else in this life, I learned timing; everything in the proper order. Time is a spiral that must unwind."

"So where is Donald now?" I ask. "Is he for sure the one who locked us in?"

"Aye, that'd be my guess," he says. "Don't think the Shadow Forces have been here."

I look at Uncle Li. He nods. "Well, they uh, they kind of have," I say, leaning away from Thomas like a dog who's about to get hit with a newspaper.

Thomas puts his head in his hands and says, "Ah, this is not good. Not good at all." He looks up at me again. "Who was here?"

"Remember that inspector, Barend Schlacter?"

"Bollocks! I knew that man was a weasel."

"But you took him to the ferry a couple of days ago. Could he still be here on the island?"

"You don't understand," he replies. "These people can do *anything* they want, be *anywhere* they want."

"Could Barend Schlacter have gotten the books from Donald?" Uncle Li asks.

Thomas shakes his head. "Actually, if Barend Schlacter and the *Fraternitas* had them, they'd be translated already. They'd have just killed the translator once he'd finished the work. Li, I'd keep those books hidden while you do the translations if I were you."

We all look down, not wanting to acknowledge what Thomas just inferred.

"So what now?" I ask. "You were protected so that you could make sure this prophecy happened, but what's next for you?"

"You tell me," he replies. "What do you feel you need to do next?"

"Well, first of all, my parents don't know anything about this, so keep it on the down-low. But I guess I'm supposed to start this movement, kicking off the use of the Mayan calendar for kids. Get us united around some ancient equator. I'm going to be in Easter Island, and three of my girlfriends are going to be at the Giza pyramids, Machu Picchu and Angkor Wat."

"Ah, berries! That's great. Good start." Thomas says. He looks at Uncle Li and Tenzo and asks, "So which one of you is going with her then?"

They both shake their heads and Uncle Li says, "Neither, against our better judgment."

"Alex is going," I say. "It would be *way* too suspicious if either of them went with me. My parents just think I'm going back to San Francisco to see a friend."

"Well, now you're just a mad rocket, child!" he says. "You two can't go to the far corners of the world alone! Why don't I come along? I'll tell your parents I have a bit of a family emergency I have to sort out in Edinburgh, but really I'll slip away with you."

As much as I want this adventure with just Alex, all this new information and talk of Shadow Forces has me on edge. I'd probably be more comfortable with Uncle Li going, but since Thomas is the rightful heir to the island, not to mention a blood relative, who am I to stop him from going along? He's been involved with this whole thing for decades.

"Okay," I say with a nod.

"Brilliant," Uncle Li says, putting a hand over his heart. "That relieves me to no end."

"But Thomas, I leave tonight and Alex leaves tomorrow. Can you make it happen?"

"Aye, I'll tell your parents straightaway. Then I'll call the airlines and book a ticket. If I can't get on the same flight, I'll just meet you two on Easter Island."

Once Thomas leaves, Tenzo says, "How about that story? Imagine finding out that your mother and father were fakes, and that your real parents lived in this castle."

"Thomas is a saint!" I say. "Can you believe he does all the grunt work around here without complaining and he's really the heir to the whole place?"

Uncle Li nods. "But I can also appreciate Donald's side of the story. It would be a bitter pill to swallow, to know that you would continue to live out your days in anonymous toil. The human ego is so fragile."

"Well, I'm glad you feel sorry for him, because you may just run into him! You've got his books and apparently they're pretty valuable," I say. "I'm dying to know what's in them."

"I hope to have them both translated by the time you get back," Uncle Li says.

Tenzo raises his hand. "Please, I'd be more than happy to help."

Uncle Li says, "Thanks... perhaps," but I can tell by his face that the answer is no. I wonder for a moment if I'm reading something into the situation or if Uncle Li doesn't yet fully trust Tenzo.

"Listen, I gotta go pack and send a million emails and stuff," I say, taking my plate to the kitchen. Mrs. Findlay is at the stove cooking more scrambled eggs for the buffet. Through the window over the sink I see Thomas and Alex talking outside.

"We're goin' to be so lonely the next few days," Mrs. Findlay says. "What with you and the guests gone, and Alex off on a fishing trip. I don't know what I'll do!"

"Maybe you could take some time off, too," I say. "Just have Mom cook for Uncle Li and Tenzo." I look over at Mrs. Findlay and when she sees that I'm joking she laughs really hard; apparently she's caught a glimpse of Mom's kitchen skills. My mom is this technology genius who can't even make a pancake without it having that bitter burnt taste on the edges.

Alex and Thomas walk in the door and each one gives me a very slight head nod. My life has morphed into a spy movie.

I run upstairs to finish my last task: emailing the girls with final details.

From: caitymacfireland@gmail.com
To: chantreahuy@gmail.com, amisi@yahoo.com,
justinemiddleford@gmail.com
Subject: Last-minute details

You all ROCK! I can't believe you are so willing to help me with this project, crazy as it sounds! Now all that's left to do is make some sort of poster or sign with the 800 number on it to call at the designated time. The password is KIN.

Things are getting so bad—the wars still rage, the economy sucks, and we're going to bear the brunt of it if we don't change things. Can't wait to see what happens! Thanks so much. XO, Caity

Once I finish the email, I get to packing. I'm not going to need much since I'll only be gone a few days and most of that time will be spent in an airplane.

Suddenly I'm dizzy and overcome with fear.

I sit down on the floor because I feel like I might even fall off a chair.

What am I doing? What am I *doing?*

TWENTY-SIX

I lie back on the floor and try to breathe. Curious about why I'm on the ground, Mr. Papers comes over and stares at me. Then I hear the door slowly open. I'm on the other side of the bed, but because it's so tall I can see all the way under. Leather sandals with tire-tread soles—Bolon. Mr. Papers hops up on the bed, squawking, happy to see him.

Bolon walks around the bed right to me as if he knows exactly where I am. He looks down and says, "Hello, Caity," as if it's not at all strange that I'm flat on the floor.

He sits next to me with his legs crossed, then grabs my hand and pulls me up to a sitting position. I'm feeling a little steadier now. "How are you?" he asks.

"How do I look?" I reply.

"Is there something I can help you with?" Bolon asks.

His eyes are so dark that you can't tell the iris from the pupil. When I was nine I went to horse camp and was assigned a horse named Pearl who became my best friend for the summer. She was all white except for these huge, glossy black eyes.

Bolon's eyes remind me so much of Pearl's that I burst out in tears. For the first time I feel like I want my old life back.

"I'm sorry," I say. "I'm just having a ... moment."

"Why should you be sorry?" he says. "I cry every day."

I look up. "You do?"

"How can you not? Look around at the world. I would be ashamed if I did *not* cry."

I nod like I know what he's talking about, but then I come clean. "Bolon, I think maybe I'm crying more for myself," I admit. "I'm just kinda overwhelmed by all of this."

"I know, Caity," he says quietly as he takes my hand and puts it between his. I am always surprised by how smooth his skin feels because it looks so leathery. "Is there anything I can do to help you? If I could do this for you I would, but it is not possible. It is not *my* path."

"I just feel like such an imposter. I mean, I didn't even know where the Maya were from until this week. I think it would be so much better if you got a Mayan girl. I'm a white girl from San Francisco. How can I represent these people and this calendar and the whole 2012 thing?"

"You are representing information, not people. And it is *because* of your differences, not despite them, that you have been chosen," he replies. "People will listen. Just because you have not been born in Mayan clothing this time around does not mean that you are not one of us."

"Really?"

"Certainly. You are as much a Maya as I am. And as this unfolds you will remember more," he says with a certainty that makes me believe him. "You must keep in mind that we are all just vibrations, just information and possibility. What you *look like* has nothing to do with your great purpose in life."

I use the sleeve of my T-shirt to wipe my tears away. "And everyone has a great purpose?"

"Yes. You may think that you are special because your task seems so huge, but your great purpose is no more important than that of a nomadic child in Siberia, an orphaned child in Africa, or a wealthy child in Norway. What is most important is that you *remember* your great purpose."

Hearing this actually relieves instead of offends me; somehow it takes the pressure off.

Sensing my relief Bolon says sternly, "You still need to fulfill your purpose; I just mean to tell you that all humans are equal when it comes to this. Every single human being is a lead in this play. All you young people have purposely come here at this time to shine light on the darkness, to help the spiral unfold."

I am finally able to get air all the way into my lungs. "Okay," I say. "I can do this."

"It will be dangerous, you need to know that." He pulls out a piece of paper from his pocket and puts it in my hand. "Here is an address in San Francisco. If you feel you are unsafe, go there."

I look at the address and then fold it up. This kind of talk isn't helping my confidence.

"But you also need to realize how powerful and dangerous *you* are," he says with a smile. At that he gets up from the floor and walks out the door.

When I'm feeling steady again, I stand. Mr. Papers has curled up inside my suitcase. "I wish I could take you with me,"

I say. "I won't be gone long. I promise." He looks down and plays with the zipper as I pet the soft fur on his chest. Instead of moving him from my bag, I just pack around him.

We both look up when we hear a knock at the door. Uncle Li lets himself in and says, "I just came to say goodbye and wish you luck, my friend."

"Thanks. Any last words of advice?" I ask.

He replies, "As the prophet Zarathustra said, *Think good, do good, speak the truth.*"

I laugh. "I'll try. Bolon keeps telling me I'll know what to say when the time comes, but I'm not so sure."

"I believe you will," he says, leaning against my bedpost. "Easter Island, how about that? You're going about as far away from here as you can!"

"Let's not talk about it. I just got over a panic attack," I say. "So is there any information from those books that could be helpful?"

Uncle Li pauses and then says, "It's all very … esoteric … so far."

"Must be important if Donald would run off with them and never come back."

"It's fascinating," he replies. "Lots of information that has only recently been discovered by modern science."

"So do you know what it has to do with the Mayan calendar?"

"It all seems to be pointing in the direction of some sort of evolutionary event having to do with this Galactic Center energy and its relationship to human DNA."

"I keep hearing about this evolutionary event, but what does that even mean?"

"Well, if it's true that to help you must unify a large percentage of young people, then it means for the first time the task of evolving has been placed on the organism itself."

"So we have to *help* the evolution process?" I ask. Suddenly this whole picture seemed like a nearly finished jigsaw puzzle that I was in sight of finishing. "Maybe that's why there are more kids alive on Earth now than ever before—like maybe we have to hit a certain level for consciousness to change!"

"It's possible. To be conscious the way humans are, an organism has to have ten billion nerve cells in the part of the brain that develops conscious thoughts; any less than that—like dogs that have only one billion—are not capable of being self-reflective in the way that humans are."

"So maybe humans are like one big organism, one big brain, and once we hit a certain number of people with raised consciousness, then we'll change everything…"

"You've got it. Now you just have to figure out how the tools you have, like the Mayan calendar, fit into the picture. And how to implement them without the Shadow Government stopping you."

"I really wish you could come along," I say.

Uncle Li nods. "I'll be more use here, keeping your parents distracted," he says as he gives me a hug. Then he holds me at arm's length and looks into my eyes. "You can do this, Caitrina. Remember you are well loved; become that love and share it with others."

"I think I would have gone insane if you hadn't helped me through this," I say.

Uncle Li looks at me for a long time, as if trying to memorize my face. Then he says, "Thank *you*," and bows deeply at his waist before leaving.

I finish packing and then take the suitcase downstairs and put it in the Land Rover so my parents will only touch it once when I go from the ferry to the train; I don't want them to have any reason to open it up and see the satellite phone.

Everyone is out walking so I head to the kitchen for lunch. Just as I enter I see Thomas quickly pulling his hand away from Mr. Papers' cubby. "Ya wee monster!" he shouts.

"What happened?" I ask, running over to the cubby.

I see Mr. Papers hovering in the back of the cubby like he did when Hans was in the kitchen.

"The little scoundrel bit me!" Thomas says. "Reckon I startled him when I woke him."

I look over at Mr. Papers and he's shaking a little. "Mrs. Findlay had her dog here yesterday and it totally scared him. I think he's just freaked out," I say.

Thomas walks over to the big sink and sticks his hand under the cold water, sucking air through his teeth from the pain. The water runs pink from his blood.

Mr. Papers looks at me like a child waiting to receive a punishment. "What's up pal?" He scoots ever so slightly closer to me, but still won't come out of the cubby. "It's okay," I say, "no one is going to hurt you." He motions his head toward Thomas and then looks at me with pleading eyes.

"Thomas I think he's afraid you're going to put him back in the shed. You're not mad, *right?*" I say, indicating with my voice that he needs to say no.

Thomas wraps a towel around his hand, looks over at Mr. Papers, and says, "Nae, of course not. Fault was all mine."

I decide to leave Mr. Papers in his cubby until he calms down. Making myself a sandwich, I ask Thomas if he'd made his plane reservations yet. "Aye, it's all set," he replies.

Mrs. Findlay walks in and sees the blood and Thomas says, "Oh, just had a wee fight with me pruning shears." He looks at me and winks. I guess he thinks Mrs. Findlay might want to have Mr. Papers go if she knew he bit Thomas.

"Those trees don't prune themselves," I add. I don't want to see Mr. Papers taken away any more than he does.

A van comes to get the guests and Mom and Dad and I follow in the Land Rover. My hands are freezing no matter what I do to try to warm them, and my stomach feels like it's filled with fluttering goldfish. At this point I'm just hoping I can get to the train without melting down.

I try to calm myself, leaning my head back and closing my eyes. I keep seeing that thing I saw in the water outside the tower with Mr. Papers, an image of a snake in a circle eating its own tail. Like an annoying song, the picture keeps playing in my head.

We arrive at the ferry dock and drive onto the boat. It's windy so we decide to stay in the car for the crossing and the choppy waves do nothing to calm my stomach. I turn around and take a last look at the Isle of Huracan out the rear-view window. It sits up like a round mole on the otherwise open sea.

"Why is the captain waving his hands?" Dad asks, straining to see the guy in the little cabin that sits atop the ferry.

Then we see all the guests in the van get out, pointing at the water. I jump out of the car and see a school of dolphins jumping and swimming alongside the ferry.

"Look!" I yell. "Dolphins!"

Mom and Dad hop out, as do the other few people in cars on the ferry. I'm the youngest on the boat so the captain motions for me to come up to the small cabin. From up there I can see all of the dolphins, which have formed a "V" around the boat, like they're birds and we're in their flock.

"I didn't even know there were dolphins in Scotland!" I say to the captain.

"Aye, we've our Scottish bottlenose dolphins here. But they're usually pretty shy. I've been helming this ferry for twenty-eight years; never seen anything like this." The captain points ahead. "Look! Perfect formation, that! Like they're escorting us in…"

We follow the dolphins as they swim ahead of us all the way to the mainland and then they disappear into the cold, dark water.

The train station is right next to the ferry dock, so the guests and I walk off as the cars follow us. Mom and Dad park and I run over so I can be the first to open the back of the Land Rover and get my suitcase.

When the train pulls in, Mom and Dad board with me to get me settled in a cabin between Dr. Frasse and Dr. Slaton. Before they leave, they both hug me at once and I have to think about algebra so I won't cry. I don't want them to sense that I'm too young to travel without them or they might rethink this whole thing.

"Goodbye, baby," Mom says, holding my face in her hands. "Be good."

Dad hugs me again and says, "She's always good."

Dagger in the heart.

The whistle blows and Mom and Dad rush to get off, saying their last goodbyes to me and the guests. I open the window of my sleeper car and hang out of it. "I love you guys!" I say as the train pulls out of the station.

There is no turning back. I watch out my window as the sun slowly sets, illuminating the sky with the pinks and oranges of the glowing rocks inside the tower.

Dead to the world minutes after the porter made my couch into a bed, I don't open my eyes until I hear someone knocking on my door.

"Caity, time to get up," I hear Dr. Slaton say. "We'll be in Edinburgh in twenty minutes."

"Thanks," I reply, trying to sound awake.

The guests all wait for me as we disembark and transfer to the airport train. It's still really early in the morning so the city is quiet and the air is crisp. The creepiest castle you've ever seen sits on a massive rock high above the train station in Edinburgh; it makes Breidablik Castle look like a friendly little playhouse.

Once we're at the airport, all the guests walk me to the airline counter to make sure I get my ticket and then we go through security together. Since they are traveling to Paris and I'm going to San Francisco, we have different gates and have to part ways after security.

I wave to them as they turn to leave. I feel ten pounds

lighter and ten years older. I am alone at an international airport with adults buzzing around me not even paying attention—no one cares, which is both exciting and frightening.

I'm more than two hours early so I buy some magazines and candy and wait at my gate.

Once the flight takes off and we are safely in the air, I feel a strange sensation in my chest. It's the weirdest thing, like I can't take enough air into my lungs. It's not as if I can't breathe, it's more like my lungs have expanded beyond what my breath can fill. I have to actually arch my back and sit up straight to get enough air, which really bugs the guy next to me who's working on his laptop.

I wonder for a moment if I'm having another panic attack and try to calm myself down. I force myself to breathe steadily as I look out the window into the endless sky. I think about the letter from Tenzo's father, how the stars are still shining brightly just above the blue even though we can't see them. And then it hits me—this is about pulling away from my parents. I see it plainly now. It's always been as if my parents were Saturn and I were their rings; hazily separate from them but still a very close part of their system. But now I see them as their own planet, and I, their moon. A broken-off piece of them now orbiting independently.

This realization makes me intensely sad and I have to bite my lip to keep it together. I continue gazing out the window so my seat-mate, who already thinks I'm a freak, won't see me holding back tears. My eyes become heavy and trying to keep them open is like doing bicep curls; each time gets progressively harder until I can no longer do it.

I have another of those amazing house dreams that Bolon and I were talking about, this one is in kind of a Spanish mission-style house, stucco with big dark beams. I feel like I've lived here all my life, but then I open what I think is the kitchen pantry door and instead I find this incredible room. The walls are painted an iridescent blue-green, and a metallic gold peacock head is painted on the ceiling, with this crystal-clustered light fixture as its eye. All the furniture is plush and velvet, in blue-green peacock shades. I walk around looking at all the beautiful gold objects, amazed that this room has been sitting here the whole time. I see another door and I walk over to it. It has a tarnished door-knocker on it that I think is just a ring until I get closer and see that it's a snake eating its own tail. I reach for the knocker, but the minute I touch it I wake up with a start.

It takes me a moment to remember where I am until the guy next to me exhales loudly and leans away like I'm a leper. I try not to do anything weird for awhile, and between the meals and movies, the rest of the flight goes fairly quickly.

I'm glad I have the window seat as we land in San Francisco. As soon as I see Coit Tower and the Golden Gate Bridge and the sparkly blue water my heart caves in on itself. I can't take in enough of the scenery and I keep my nose pressed to the cold window until all we see is tarmac.

When the plane door opens I breathe deeply, sucking in the moist air. I wonder if there is any place on Earth that smells like this, the intense combination of salt water, fog, muddy bay, and eucalyptus trees. This first breath of air makes me more homesick for my old, uncomplicated life than anything yet.

TWENTY-SEVEN

Walking directly to the cab stand, I make my way to the city. On the way, I call Mom to let her know I landed safely. The connection is clear but she sounds so far away.

I ask the driver to drop me at the coffee shop across from the Transamerica Pyramid where Justine and I had agreed to meet. As I step out of the taxi I see her in the window of the café and I run toward her; it honestly seems like years, not weeks, since I've seen her. My whole life has changed, but here she is, same old Justine, just as excited to see me as I am her.

"I can't believe how crazy your life is turning out to be!" she says, pulling back from our hug to look at me, I guess to see if I've changed at all.

We order mochas and before we can even sit down, Justine says, "Okay, I can't wait any longer. I have new news."

"What is it?" I ask, hoping that this is not about backing out of Peru.

"I stalked that Canadian guy who works for F.R.O. last

night when he left the Pyramid. Look." She reaches for something in her pocket and then sets a Montgomery Grand Hotel key card on the table with a snap like she's laying down a winning poker hand.

"You got his room key?"

"No! I got the room next to his. I told you, I'm total spy material. I have found my calling." She leans in and starts to whisper, "I waited outside the Pyramid all afternoon and then followed him. He had one of those metal briefcases and although he was trying to hide it with his jacket sleeve, I saw that it was *chained* to his wrist."

"Like handcuffed?"

"Yup."

"Because the info is so top secret?"

"Exactly. Which means that if you want to find out what this creepy guy who threatened you is up to, we need to get that briefcase."

I look at her closely to see if she's joking.

"Come on—obviously these are not good people, right?" she says. "So getting some answers about why they'd be harassing you is completely justified."

I'm leaning so far forward in my chair that the back two legs are off the ground. I lean back so the chair doesn't come out completely from under me. "You don't think he saw you follow him to his room do you?" I ask.

"Do I look like someone he'd be worried about? I followed him to the hotel, got into the elevator, and off on the same floor. I walked in the opposite direction and when I heard his door click, I ran down and got the room number." She taps the key card on the table to punctuate her sentence.

"I listened at the door for a minute to hear if anyone else was in there, but then I heard the shower start up and that gave me the perfect idea for how to get into his room."

"So what's your plan?" I ask.

"You mean *our* plan," she says, tipping what's left of her mocha back steeply to catch all the gooey bitter chocolate at the bottom. "Let's go to the hotel and I'll tell you everything."

In our room, an enormous suitcase sits in the corner and two outfits are laid out on the bed. "What's up with the schoolgirl thing?" I ask. "Does Cruelties have uniforms now?"

"No, this is my disguise. Have you ever looked around a hotel lobby? There are a bazillion little cameras down there, especially at the desk. When this dude finds his case missing and tells the management about it, the first thing they're going to do is look through the video tapes to find out who asked for a second key."

"Ah, good thinking." I pick up a frumpy old maid outfit. "So I guess that makes me the ugly housekeeper?"

"Hey, just be glad I didn't get one of those totally inappropriate maid costumes that Ashley Levinger wears every Halloween."

"Yeah, thanks. I do like that this one will actually cover my butt."

"It's not exactly Montgomery Grand Hotel regulation, but how will this guy know anyway? There's almost zero chance he'll even see you."

"So run me through the process," I say as I slip the scratchy polyester dress over my head.

"At about 4:30 I'll hide in the corner of the lobby. I'll call you when he comes into the hotel to give you a heads up, then you listen for his door to close. I'll ask for another key to his room but when they give me a new key, then the key he has no longer works, so it's *really* important that he is already in his room when I request a second key."

"Got it. But do you really think they'll just give you a key?"

She makes the look-at-me gesture with her hands and says, "Who would deny this child a room key?" Then in a small voice she says, "Um, I just came down to get a candy bar at the gift shop and forgot my key. My dad is in the shower so he doesn't hear me knocking. Room 2013? Under Tremblay?"

"Can I just say you are a genius?"

"Yes. Yes you can," Justine says, getting into her fake school outfit. She pulls a long brown wig out and puts it on. "Real hair," she says, braiding it tightly, "I splurged."

I look at the clock. "It's 4:20."

"Okay, gotta run. I'll call you when I see him come in."

I flip on MTV so I can turn off my brain. At 4:35 she calls and says, "Ground squirrel on the move."

My mouth instantly goes dry. I hang up the phone and put my hands over my face. Am I going insane? The way I just nod and say okay to crazy schemes until I have to actually act on them and then I freak out, like right now?

I look at myself in the mirror, jet-lagged and scared in a two-sizes-too-big maid outfit and wonder what I am doing. What if I get caught? Why didn't I stop this train earlier? *Could* I be going crazy and not know it?

I practically jump out of my skin when I hear the faint ding of the elevator stopping on our floor. Bolting over to the door, I press my eye to the peephole. A tall guy with Raggedy Ann red hair walks by. He looks exactly like Slugworth from the original *Willy Wonka & the Chocolate Factory* movie, same sunken cheeks, waxy skin, and dead eyes, except with red hair. The hair is really strange—it looks unnatural for a grown man to have red hair and wrinkles at the same time. Hair like that should only be on kids.

As soon as I hear his door close I call Justine.

"It's go time," I say. That lame line seems appropriate right now.

Hoping to control him from my side of the wall, I sit on the edge of the bed and chant, "Don't get in the shower, don't get in the shower, don't get in the shower."

When Justine comes back in the room, I hop up from the bed. "Thank god you're back. Did you get the key?" I almost hope the answer is no.

She looks insulted. "I can't believe you even asked me that!"

"Sorry, I knew you would. I'm just freaked out; I didn't want him to get in the shower before you got back in case he took a really short one."

She points her finger to the ground next to the wall. "Sit here and listen while I get changed again and then we can switch."

I sit and put my ear to the textured wallpaper. Then Justine comes back and sits next to me holding the wig and a brush. "Let me take out the braids for you."

"Oh, I'm going to wear it too?"

"Absolutely. We have to have a security video plan for you as well."

"So once I get the briefcase, I can't come back here, right?"

"Not in this outfit, at least. See that big boy?" she asks as she points to the mammoth rolling suitcase in the corner of the room. "When we hear the water turn on, you get in it."

"Okay..."

"We don't want them to ever see you leaving this room in a maid outfit, so I'll roll you to the stairwell and then you get out and do your thing."

"Got it. I'm going to hang one of these hotel robes over my arm, that way once I get the briefcase I can hide it under the robe before I walk back out the door."

"Perfect. Just make sure to go back to the stairwell, not to this room. I'll have a change of clothes for you and we'll slip the briefcase into the suitcase."

"Then we'll just go down a floor and come back up the elevator?"

"Yup. And no one will suspect a—" she doesn't finish because we hear the water turn on.

I must look seriously scared because she puts her hand on my knee and says, "Caity, you can do this."

We both stand up and Justine unzips her suitcase. Without saying a word I curl up inside it, clutching a Montgomery Grand Hotel robe from the bathroom. She tosses in the pants and top I was wearing before I got changed and then zips me in. It actually feels kind of good to be safely curled up inside. Justine wheels me out of the room and into the stairwell and then she unzips the case and I reluctantly get out. "Here's the key," she says. "You'll do great."

My hands are shaking. I try to steady them by clenching my fists as I walk. I get to Tremblay's room and listen at the door. The shower is still running.

I very gently slip the key card through the slot and open the door. I hold the door open with one foot as I lean forward to look into the room for the case and see it's under the desk.

I can't reach it without going all the way into the room, so I have to let the door close. Praying to all my dead relatives to help keep Tremblay in the shower, I creep over to the desk. There's a chain attached to the handle of the case so I quietly gather up all the links, grab the briefcase, and run toward the door, stopping to flip the robe over the case before I leave.

I try to walk through the hallway so I don't look suspicious, but as I get closer to the door of the stairwell I can't help but run. In fact, I run all the way in and then straight down one flight of stairs, taking them three at a time. I feel like I could run all the way across the Golden Gate Bridge right now, my adrenaline is pumping so fast.

Justine comes flying down the stairs after me. We don't even speak; she unzips the suitcase and I roll the briefcase into the robe and then put it in. I shake off the wig, pull my pants up under my maid dress and then rip the dress off. Justine is ready with my shirt and slips it right over my head, then scoops up the dress and the wig and puts them in the suitcase. We open the stairwell door and walk out, directly to the elevator, which we take back to our own floor.

Once back in the room, we listen at the wall for the shower. It's still going. I can't believe we did all that within five minutes. We set the briefcase on the bed and stare at it.

"Now what?" I say.

"You're the safecracker's daughter," she replies. "You tell me."

"Dad actually has a laptop version of this briefcase; it's called a Zero Halliburton."

"Your dad totally wants to be in covert ops, doesn't he?"

"Yeah. What a joke." The lock is a three-digit rolling one. I push one of the wheels with my thumb. "I think we have to just go through all the possible combinations, 1-1-1, 1-1-2, 1-1-3, on and on until you run through all nine numbers in all three positions."

"That will take forever!"

"Got any other ideas? I can't exactly call my mom and ask how to break into a Zero Halliburton."

We hear a shout and a glass hitting the wall next door. Justine's olive skin goes white. I can't feel my feet on the ground. We both push our ears to the wall and listen.

He's on the phone with someone. We catch bits and pieces, "been a breach...seconds ago...complicated situation... dripping wet...by the time...dressed...locked down..."

The minute I hear *locked down* I know we have to leave.

"Oh my God, we have to get out of here!" I whisper.

We throw everything, including my small rolly suitcase and backpack, into Justine's massive suitcase and run to the elevator. As much as time sped up while we were taking the briefcase, time is moving in slow motion now as we watch the numbers on the elevator. I'm anticipating the ding so desperately that when it finally does sound, it actually hurts my ears. We scurry on and as the elevator doors close I see Tremblay's door handle move. We back up as far as we can into the elevator, but he sees me just as the doors close.

I reach into my pocket to make sure I still have the address that Bolon gave me.

We make a swift exit to the street, straight into a taxi. The driver tries to get us to put the suitcase in the trunk but we just cram it in next to us.

"It's okay, please, just go, we're really late..." Justine says.

I start to hand him the note with the address on it, but then realize we should cover our tracks a little better. Instead, I say "Chinatown, please."

We're really close to Chinatown and could probably walk faster than this guy could drive us through the one-way streets, but at least we're safely in a car.

Then Justine says, "Look behind you."

I turn slowly around and see a black car with two older men in it, both in suits. Their car is practically touching ours, they're following so closely. "Do you think they're..."

She nods.

I lean forward to the driver. "Sir, do you watch those race-around-the-world TV shows?"

He looks at me like I've asked him if he eats earwax. He shakes his head.

"Well, we're on a show and we're racing against our dads who are in the car behind us." As he looks in the rearview mirror, I pull a $100 bill out of my pocket and show it to him. "If you can ditch our dads and drop us by the Stockton Tunnel, that would be great."

The driver takes the money and nods. We're at a stoplight waiting for a cable car, but right as it's about to pass us our driver hits the gas. Justine and I are thrown back and I know that we'll be hit by the cable car. I close my eyes and wait for the impact, but it never comes.

I peek over the back of the seat—the men are still there. The driver is shaking his head and the passenger is talking on a cell phone. Our driver is taking my hundred-dollar offer very seriously and is all over the road. For a moment I almost hope we get pulled over by the police; at least we'd be *safe* in jail. The cab goes so fast down Filbert Street that we catch air, and when we land and bounce a few times I wonder if the old cab can hold itself together. Then we do a speedy turn that throws Justine and me at the door. My lip hits her shoulder and splits open. I have to keep my tongue on it to keep it from bleeding everywhere.

We're getting farther and farther from Chinatown, but we manage to get two cars ahead of the men. Then our driver reaches for his cab radio and says something in another language. We're in an industrial area that I've never been to before, driving ridiculously fast because there are no pedestrians. The men are trapped behind a slower car, and we see them veer right and left, trying to find a way to pass or intimidate the driver in front of them into going faster.

Then our guy hits the brakes and skids into a cab garage. We see the bumper of the other car just before the tall metal door comes down behind us. The garage is a pass-through style, so another door opens in front of us and our driver zooms through, tires screeching. He weaves his way back to the center of town, not going more than a block before turning. We never see the car following us again.

"Nice job!" I say.

He shrugs and says, "I am from Bombay."

"The parking garage on Kearny, please."

The smell of Chinatown hits us before we even see it. Over the years, I've spent many afternoons here with Uncle Li visiting his friends, mostly herbalists and doctors of Chinese medicine. They'd always serve me tea and cookies and give me weird things to look at like pickled snakes and dried animal organs. Sometimes if I had a cold or a headache they would do acupuncture on me or give me funky-tasting herbal remedies. If this place Bolon told me about doesn't work out we can always come back here and stay with one of Uncle Li's friends.

We get out at the garage, hail a different cab, and slide in, suitcase and all. I show the driver the address on the paper and then Justine and I slump down in our seats, partly to hide and partly because we are so overwhelmed by all of this.

"Where exactly are we going?" Justine asks.

I show her the paper. "Muchuchumil Imports. Bolon gave me this address and said to go there if I needed help in San Francisco."

We both take turns peering out the back window, and every time we're surprised that no one is following us. "Do you think they knew we took the case or do you think they followed everyone who left the hotel?" Justine asks.

"I think Tremblay caught a glimpse of me in the elevator. Did you use your real name at the hotel? I guess you'd have to with a credit card—"

"What kind of crappy spy would I be if I used my real name and Mom's credit card? I went to the bank and got one of those pre-paid American Express traveler cards. You load money on it and it looks and works like a credit card."

"You are so smart." I look at my loyal, brilliant friend. "Does this all make you not want to go to Peru now?" I ask. "I will completely understand if you want to bag it."

"You have got to be kidding me! I am *so* going."

The driver pulls up to a plain concrete building with one door and no windows. The words "Muchuchumil Imports" are carelessly stenciled on the door over a peephole.

Justine says, "Sketchy," at the exact same time that I say, "Shady."

"I guess I just have to trust Bolon," I say as I knock on the door.

TWENTY-EIGHT

The door opens immediately, as if someone had been waiting behind it. A dark woman with short grey and black hair pulls us inside quickly and then bolts the door.

"Welcome," she says with a warm smile.

"Thank you," we reply.

As my eyes adjust to the low light, I see the room is full of fabrics and baskets and other import-type things that smell like they'd ridden too long on diesel trucks.

Leading us past the stacks of goods to another door, she pulls a key on a chain out of her blouse and opens the lock. We follow her into another room, and then she bolts that door. Justine and I exchange freaked-out glances.

"Do not be afraid," the woman says.

I extend my hand to her and say, "I'm Caity."

She laughs and shakes my hand. "Oh, we know who you are."

"And this is my friend Justine."

She takes Justine's hand in both of her hands and says, "Justine, it is a pleasure to meet you."

"Thanks so much," Justine says. After a pause she asks, "And what is your name?"

"Forgive me, I am so excited to see you that I have forgotten myself. My name is Chasca."

She is beautiful in that weird way where the sum adds up to way more than the parts. In a picture she would probably just look like a wrinkly Mexican woman, but something about her smile and her eyes and the way she carries herself makes her unusually beautiful.

She breaks the awkward silence and says, "It's rude of me to keep you all to myself; come and meet the others."

Justine and I get up and follow her to a different door. She knocks on it in a pattern, then someone knocks back and she knocks again with a different pattern. Obviously they have some security issues here.

We walk in to a semi-dark room that is hazy with bitter-smelling incense. It takes a minute to adjust my eyes, but when I do I see several people sitting in a circle on the floor. They are all staring at me. Chasca says, "Caity, meet The Council. Council, this is Caity."

They all bow their heads and say hello.

"And this is Justine," she adds.

One woman motions to us and says, "Come here, sit." The people scoot together to make room for the two of us and then Chasca goes to the other side of the circle and edges in.

The woman next to me reaches for two cups and a teapot. She fills the cups, hands them to Justine and me and says,

"Welcome, I am Nima. We are happy to see you, although this must mean you are in some danger."

I take the tea. "Thank you. Yes, we got in to a bit of a … situation earlier."

"Well, you are safe here. For now." Nima passes the pot to the man next to her, who has the darkest skin I have ever seen. He's very small but powerfully built and he has a big round face with wide-set eyes. While he refills his cup, Nima says, "Please meet some of our Council leaders. This is Apari, an Aboriginal Elder from Australia."

Justine and I bow our heads and say hello. He says, "Yow," which I assume means "hi."

The person next to him is a woman with long black hair in a braid as thick as a boa constrictor. She looks similar to Chasca, but a little younger and taller. "This is Ichtaca, she is a Nahuatl Daykeeper."

She looks at me with hypnotic brown eyes and says, "Niltze."

Next to her is a man who has that ageless quality; I can't tell if he's forty or eighty. His skin is the color of red modeling clay and he has the most beautiful hands I have ever seen. "This is Tawa; he is a Hopi Elder."

"Um pitu?" he says in a voice that is much lower than I expected.

"And you have met Chasca," Nima says. "Chasca is a powerful Q'ero Elder from Peru. Next to her is Mabudu, a Shaman from the Dogon tribe in Africa."

Mabudu, a small, bald black man with a white beard says, "Diganai po."

"It's an honor to meet you all," I say.

"The feeling is mutual," Nima says.

Again there's weird silence as they all stare at me.

"So you guys know Bolon?" I ask, not exactly sure how I can get to the subject of who they all are and why they're sitting in the dark in the back of a warehouse waiting for me.

"Bolon is a member of The Council, yes," Nima answers.

"Are you allowed to tell us about The Council?" I ask.

Nima pours more tea into my cup and says, "We are simply called 13:20—I hope you have never heard of us. We are the ones who preserve the knowledge that the *Fraternitas Regni Occulti* is trying desperately to destroy."

"You know about the *Fraternitas?*"

"Of course. They have been trying to annihilate us for centuries."

"You guys?" I ask.

"The Council, yes, but also our communities. The effort to wipe out indigenous people has been systematically deployed for as long as anyone can remember."

"Like pilgrims killing the Native Americans?"

"Before that and after—all the way to present day. Look around, China is trying to kill or oppress all Tibetans. The United States financially backed the killing of millions of Maya in Guatemala. Europeans all but extinguished the Aborigines in Australia. You see it everywhere: Asia, Africa, the Americas."

"Why are they so threatened by you?" Justine asks.

"Because we all know what is about to happen. We all know a change is coming and we all know that the Shadow Government, the *Fraternitas Regni Occulti,* is trying desperately to maintain the control they have had for so very long."

"And are you trying to destroy them?" I ask.

"We do not destroy anything," she says.

I try to change the subject. "So it's you guys and Bolon?"

"There are thirty-three of us actually, thirteen women and twenty men."

Just as I'm thinking it's not very progressive to have more men than women, Chasca says, "We need fewer women because women are far more powerful than men."

All the men nod in agreement. I like these guys.

"Where are all the others now?" I ask.

"It's too dangerous for us all to be in one place. We gather in small groups and only meet together when it is absolutely necessary. The Council has survived for centuries by remaining very secretive. We have our own version of the World Wide Web; one that needs no hardware."

"Cool! How does it work?" I ask.

Nima shakes her head. "Maybe another time. Now tell us about the trouble you are in. You are on your way to Easter Island are you not?"

It's hard to believe that for the last couple of hours I haven't thought once about the fact that I'm going all the way to Easter Island tomorrow! "Oh, yeah. I wanted to have a lay-over in San Francisco to see my friend Justine; she is going to Machu Picchu for me."

Chasca reaches for Justine's hand and squeezes it. "You will love Peru," she says.

"But we got a little carried away," I say, "and we took a briefcase from someone who works for F.R.O."

Justine immediately says, "It was all my doing; I take the blame." It's sweet of her to not want to get me in trouble.

"Brave girls," Tawa, the Hopi man, says.

"Have you opened it?" asks Apari.

I'm mesmerized by his face; I've never met an Aborigine before. He looks unlike anyone else I've ever seen. "Not yet, it's going to take awhile. It's a three-digit combination," I reply.

He waves his hand and says, "You can do it in no time. Bring it so."

"You mean right now?" I ask.

He nods. I go over to Justine's big rolling suitcase, unfurl the robe, and remove the briefcase. Then I place it in front of Apari.

"No no, you will open it," he says as he points to my spot in the circle. I sit back down where I was, with the case on my lap.

"Everything leaves its imprint in the universe," he says, "that case carries with it the imprint of its code, even if it had only been opened once. Put one palm over the number and one palm over the case. Now close your eyes, clear your mind, and take a few very deep breaths." After a short pause he claps once and says, "Now! What is the first thing you see?"

I try really hard to see numbers, but all I see is a flash of the initials on Barend Schlacter's tattoo: FRO.

I shake my head. "I only see letters."

"Then you have the code. Count out the letters in the alphabet."

I'm embarrassed that I have to use my hands to do this; I look like a first grader. "F is the sixth letter, R is the eighteenth letter, and O is the fifteenth letter. Six, eighteen, fifteen... but I only need three digits..."

"Combine the two-digit numbers," says Mabudu.

"Okay," I say, thinking aloud. "Eighteen is one plus eight, which makes nine. Fifteen is one plus five, which makes six. So it should be six, nine, six."

I set the case upright and turn the wheels on the lock, which is hard because they're tiny and my hands are sweating. I line up the six. Then the nine. As soon as I put the last six in place I know it will work. Call it genetic, call it Barbie-knee syndrome, but I know by the feel of the six rolling in to place that when I push the button it will open.

Click.

"No way!" Justine says. "I can't believe you just did that."

No one else seems the least bit impressed.

"And what do you have in there?" Nima asks as she leans in.

It's a binder of information. "It looks like a manual," I say as I open it up.

Justine looks disappointed. "Did you think it would be something more interesting?" I ask her. She nods. I feel the exact same way. We risked our lives to get this guy's home-work?

I open to the index of tabs and read it out loud.

Ongoing Priorities—
2nd Quarter Fiscal Year

A) Knowledge Suppression

1. Continue stirring the Mayan conflict in Guatemala

2. Debunk Mayan Astronomy/Calendar

3. Widen Project Khymatos exposure

4. Increase funding to large religious groups

B) Continued Northern Projects

1. Finish destruction of remaining icebergs in Northwest

Passage (N.P.) and assess potential Collateral Damage to keep N.P. project quiet

2. *Fund expansion of HAARP array through Scientific Grants*

C) Expansion in Third/Fourth World Country

1. *Ramp up lending to Third/Fourth world countries*
2. *Continue steady buy-out of utilities/natural resources in Third/Fourth world countries*

D) Distraction/Fear

1. *Begin phase three of debt plan/recession triggers*
2. *Introduce new Middle East conflicts*
3. *Assess need of natural disaster*

"This is terrifying," I say. "Can they really do all that?"

"They've been doing things like this—and worse—for several centuries," Chasca says. "It's wonderful to have all this information in one place, though."

"I'm just glad I didn't make it onto their list," I say.

Mabudu says, "Look under Debunking the Mayan Calendar—I suspect you are there."

I flip to tab A-2 and the first thing I see is a photo of me in the kitchen at the castle. Barend Schlacter must have secretly taken it when he was there.

My heart feels tiny and prickly. "I'm in here..."

"Read it!" says Justine, leaning over to see.

"It says, 'Target: Caitrina (Caity) Mac Fireland, born November 12, 1995, in San Francisco, California. After death of Aeden Mac Fireland (target's grandfather) lineage went underground for two decades, only resurfaced earlier this year when Angus Mac Fireland (target's father) came forward to claim the Breidablik Castle on the Isle of Huracan, Scotland.

Unknown why this girl or this family is so important in the next stage of development of the *Tzolk'in*. Second Degree Praetor, Barend Schlacter (F.R.O., Bavarian Sect), reports that Caitrina is odd, weak, and incapable of mounting a campaign of any consequence at all. Parents of target are both extremely intelligent but seem to know nothing as of yet. In addition, they are reportedly self-absorbed to such a degree that they would likely never be involved. Target will remain on periphery watch, but is not considered a threat.'"

"Wow, harsh," Justine says.

Chasca shakes her head. "They do not know you."

"I don't know whether to be insulted or overjoyed," I say. "I hate being called 'odd and weak,' but at least they don't think I'm a threat."

"Yet," Nima says.

"So what do I do with this?" I ask.

Apari answers, "You would do us, and the world, a great service by allowing us to analyze this information."

I scoot the book across the rug. "It's all yours. I hope you can do some good with it."

"You have no idea how helpful it is to have these plans," Chasca says. "We have never been able to get concrete information like this."

"Justine was the mastermind behind getting it," I say. She beams with pride; this spy thing might just be her calling. I lean back and my stomach growls. Everyone hears it and laughs. "Sorry, all I've had today was a disgusting airline omelet and a mocha."

"There is a good Vietnamese restaurant around the corner, it is very secure," says Nima. "Follow me out the back door. You can have dinner together, enjoy yourselves, then come back and sleep here. We will take you to the airport in the morning."

"Thank you so much. I would definitely feel safer staying here than at a hotel," I say. I want to jump up but my left leg is numb and useless after sitting cross-legged for so long. I feel like an idiot shaking it out so I can walk. Here I am: odd and weak!

Nima lets us out the back door. It's already getting dark. Justine and I hold hands as we walk through the alley to the street. I don't realize Nima has followed us until we're in the restaurant; I look out the window and see that she is watching from across the street, sitting on the sidewalk with a cup pretending to be homeless. I'm touched by her protection.

The hostess leads us to the back office, which holds one small table. She leaves us menus and a pot of tea.

"One rule," I say as we open up the menus. "We can't talk about any of *this*. I am so overwhelmed right now that if I don't just talk about dumb girl stuff my head will explode. Give me the latest dirt."

"Well, you're not going to believe what Rina O'Kelley told me about Kira Honeycutt and Doug Ostenson," Justine begins.

Just for a moment I feel normal again.

TWENTY-NINE

Stomachs full and feeling safe for the moment, we bed down in the back room of Muchuchumil Imports on stacks of scratchy blankets and rugs.

"So where do your parents think you are right now?" I ask Justine. "Did they want to take you to the airport in the morning?"

"No, since I was going to 'Scotland,' Mom tagged along on a business trip with Dad. God forbid she ever spends a second alone. They left yesterday and asked Esmeralda to watch me and take me to the airport."

"They left you alone with that crabby housekeeper?"

"Yes, and get this: when I told Esmeralda I was going to spend the night at a friend's so she wouldn't have to take me to the airport, she didn't even care. She was just psyched to have the house to herself. She'd be so fired if my parents knew what happened to me today."

We both laugh at the thought. "If any one of our parents

found out what we did today we would be under house arrest for decades," I say.

It doesn't take long before we are both sound asleep on the blankets that smell like faraway places. We don't wake until Nima brings us tea and bread in the morning. She tells us we need to go in a few minutes; they let us sleep in because we seemed so tired.

"Are you meeting David at the gate?" I ask Justine as she packs just what she needs for the trip into a backpack.

She nods. "I wish we were in the same terminal. I'm sure he'd love to see you," she says, brushing her long gorgeous hair.

"Thank you," I say. "For doing this. For everything."

"You'd do the same for me," she replies. "I know you would."

But I have to wonder if this is true. I'm not sure I'm that good of a person.

We part ways at the airport. When I get to the gate, Alex and Thomas are already there. I want to hug them both but that would be too weird. Alex stands up like a gentleman when I get over to them, and he's looking more incredible than ever. His worn corduroy jacket brings out the pale blue of his eyes, and his skin, tan from fishing, is set off by his white button-down shirt. He's a little rumpled from the long flight, making him all the more attractive.

"Can you believe we're really doing this?" he says as he sits beside me.

"I hope I can pull this off," I say. "You would not believe what's happened since I left Scotland. Pardon the funky smell; I slept in an import warehouse last night."

"Want to fill me in, mate?"

"Maybe later, I'm too … I don't know … I just can't talk about it right now."

An announcement is made that we will begin boarding in five minutes. Thomas gets up and says, "I'm going to hit the cludgie one last time."

"Oh, I almost forgot: look at this," Alex says, fishing a piece of paper out of his backpack. "Last night I got an email from a lad at school about the *Tzolk'in* calendar!"

I unfold the paper and read, hardly believing my eyes. It's the email I sent to all the kids at Cruelties! The text his friend added was, "Alex, got this from my cousin who lives in New York. Looks interesting—have a peek."

"This is incredible!" I wish I had checked the website count to see how viral it had gone.

"This is your old school, right?" Alex says, pointing to the email address.

"This is *me*! I registered that email address to look official. Can you believe I started an email on the Isle of Huracan and within days it came back to *you*, one of like twelve people who lives there? I mean, what are the chances?"

"Wow, that is quite a coincidence," he says, looking a little freaked. I resist the temptation to use Bolon's line, *Coincidence is merely a fleeting glimpse of wholeness.*

I see Thomas walking toward us, cradling his hand. "That still really painful?" I ask. He just nods. Being hurt has put him in a black mood.

We stand up and get in line to board. I'm glad when he has to go to the back of the plane. Alex and I are up front, near business class.

After we take off and get settled, I pull out my laptop to read more about the *Tzolk'in*. Alex leans in to read along.

"So I made big progress on the conversion of numbers to notes," Alex says.

"Really?"

"Aye, they're lousy with fractals and harmonics."

I try to recall what a fractal is. I sort of remember it's a small piece of something that looks like the whole but just in case, I ask a question that doesn't immediately show my stupidity, "Like what's an example?"

"Well, take the *Tzolk'in*, it's a cycle of 260 days—that's a fractal of the 26,000-year cycle of precession. And the Long Count Calendar, the one that ends in 2012, is a cycle of 5,200 days, and then there's another calendar that's fifty-two years. This goes on and on between the twenty calendars. The numbers 13, 20, 52, 260, and 144 all seem to be important."

For the first time I am more stunned by his brain than by his looks. Both of our arms are on the edge of the shared armrest, with just millimeters between us. As I feel the warmth coming off his skin and seeping into mine, I imagine my vibrating atoms jumping over to bump into his.

"That's amazing," I say, a little too gushy like some kind of fan girl.

"There's something really beautiful about all of these cycles of time nested in one another. These guys were such elegant mathematicians, thousands of bloody years ago!"

Elegant is one of those buzzwords that computer and math people use. For Dad it's the highest compliment he could get, that his code was elegant.

"So how does music fit in?"

"Well, I wrote a little music algorithm app that converts sets of numbers into notes."

"Are you like a closet genius?" I ask.

"If I were a genius, I wouldn't be hidin' it in a closet." He shrugs. "It's just math."

"*Just* math—"

"Hey—you're no slouch. How long did it take you to make that website? Or write that Mayan birthday converter?"

"That's just HTML and JavaScript."

"Aye, well, then we're a good team aren't we?" he says as he nudges me with his elbow.

I carry all these touches around with me; I can still feel the time he sandwiched my hand between his in the library, still feel his hand on my shoulder, still sense the warmth from his back on the castle wall after he'd stepped away from it. Even this nudge I'll catalog and save.

He pulls a thumb drive from his pocket. "Reckon you'd like to see it?"

I slip the computer onto his tray table. As he installs it he says, "Okay, today is 12 *Chicchan*—perfect because twelve is the pulse of understanding and *Chicchan* is all about human evolution and forward movement, aye?"

"Isn't that amazing? I mean, that's exactly what we're doing this minute—trying to understand this human evolution puzzle!"

"It's bloody cool is what it is," he says, his face full of excitement. "Okay, now let's plug the long count number into the music algorithm app and I'll play you the tones of the day. Today is 12.19.17.8.5 in the Long Count."

"Those numbers seem so random."

"They are random by themselves, but each number is in relation to another—like this first number in the string, I take that as a fraction of the total it could be, which is 144,000 days. That's all built into the algorithm, though."

"God, you have really done your homework on this thing!"

"I set piano as default," he says as he clicks the play button. "But we can change it to whatever instrument we want."

A beautiful string of notes plays.

"That sounds…I don't know…"

"Haunting?" Alex says, finishing my thought.

"Yes! It's both beautiful and eerie at the same time."

"So if sound really has something to do with changing DNA, we just have to figure out how to get kids to hear the daily tone," Alex says.

I lay my head back for a moment to think.

"Ringtone?"

"Pardon me?" Alex says.

"What if there was a way to subscribe to a cell service that changes your ringtone to the *Tzolk'in* tune of the day?"

"Right! We could make a widget! Every time the phone rings the tone plays and the daylord and bar-and-dot number come up."

"And like a daily astrology download, there would be a sentence describing what that day means!"

"We could easily do this, Caity. Seriously."

"Hey, have you heard about the ringtone kids are using now that's in the hertz range that only people under twenty can hear?" I ask.

"Yeah! That's the mosquito tone that was developed for shopkeepers to blast so kids wouldn't loiter."

"Exactly. But kids have hijacked it to use in school, so teachers can't hear their phones ring. So if we wanted to keep it quiet, we could just translate your tones into mosquito hertz level," I say.

I am overwhelmed with what feels like a déjà-vu, but isn't. It's not exactly as if I've *seen* this before, it's as if I feel like I am exactly where I need to be.

"As soon as we get back I can start on that," he says. "I've an idea on how to do it but I'll have to do a bit of research first."

Before long, the food service and movie start. When the flight attendants darken the cabin and give everyone pillows and blankets, I pretend to fall asleep and slowly lower my head until it is resting on Alex's shoulder. I expect it to stiffen as my cheekbone touches it but there's no resistance, he just shifts a little to make it more comfortable for me. I can feel each skin cell in contact with his shirt. Before I know it, I really am asleep.

By the time I wake up, Alex is sleeping. I carefully pull out my sketchbook, trying not to disturb him. I want to draw that peacock room that I dreamed about yesterday, before I forget all the details.

Well into the sketching, I realize that Alex has woken up and is watching me. "Reckon you can draw me?" he asks, stretching as well as he can in the veal pen we're confined to.

I look at him as if I'm considering it. "I don't know, maybe," I say, as if I had never sketched him before. Turning to a clean sheet of paper, I'm nervous that my complete adoration for him will ooze out in the drawing. But I realize this will give me an excuse to *really* look at him for an extended amount of time.

Things to take note of: (1) There is not one ridge on his nose. It's as if it's been sculpted rather than grown. (2) His eyelashes are freakishly long, like a doll's. (3) The channel between his lip and nose is exquisite and it is extremely, extremely hard not to lean over and put my lips to it.

I take my time sketching, because we've got a lot of it, and it turns out to be one of the best portraits I've ever done. Of course, it's the best subject matter I've ever had, too.

When we land in Chile, I am blown away by the Santiago airport. I was expecting something small and rustic, but it's massive and modern and really clean. Boarding our last three-hour flight, I'm feeling both anxious and weary; I want to take a long shower and sleep in an actual bed for awhile.

Alex closes his eyes and I open up the CD again so I can get a better grasp on what I'm going to say. I spend the whole three-hour flight absorbed in the calendar. The more I read, the more I understand that there is some sort of strange power in this system.

The captain starts talking in Spanish so I look out the window. The island is in the distance and as we get closer, we see what it is famous for. At first they just look like dots, but then they come into view—hundreds of those big carved heads. I get goose bumps on my arms; this is just something I never thought I'd see in person. Pulling out my sketchbook and pen to take it down, I start to commit what I see to the page.

My fifth-grade teacher, Ms. Lea, was the one who first told me about Easter Island. She was kind of a hippie and really into stuff like this. She used to show us weird movies from the seventies like *Chariots of the Gods* and this other one about how much your soul weighs after you die until she got in trouble for it because some parents thought it was pagan. She had a bouquet of different feathers in a jar on her desk and wore long jangly skirts that looked like they could be used for belly dancing. The very first day of class she made us write this quote eleven times:

The larger the island of knowledge, the longer the shoreline of wonder —Sockman

The eleven times thing worked because I have always remembered it. I don't know who Sockman is and I never really thought about what the quote meant, but now, as I see the island in the distance, it seems to make sense. The more you know, the more you realize you don't know.

Alex motions to the back of the plane with his head. "Thomas is knocked out again," he says.

"Poor guy," I say, looking back over my shoulder. As I see him—face slack, head cocked, mouth slightly open—a wave of nausea passes through me.

That is not Thomas.

THIRTY

N o ... no, no, no!" I say. "This can't be—"

"What?" Alex asks. "What's wrong?"

"Oh, hell no!"

I look back again. How did I not see it?

"Caity, what is the matter with you?"

"That's not Thomas!" I hiss.

"Well, then who on earth would it be, mate?"

I cover my face with my hands. "No. No. No. No."

"Caity, you're scaring me," Alex says. "What is *wrong* with you?"

I tell him the whole story, everything Thomas told me. He turns white.

"Bloody hell!" Alex says, looking back. "I've known that man all my life."

"Well, that's not him, that's Donald!"

Alex gets up. "I'm going to check it out."

I watch as he walks back through the tiny aisle, slowly like a cat creeping up on a bird. He stops right by Thomas and takes a good long look at his sleeping face. Then he picks up the customs form sitting on his tray table, reads it and sets it back down.

"What did it say?" I ask when he returns.

"It has Thomas' name on it, but surely Donald just took his passport."

"What do we do?"

"We don't have many options at this point, mate. We need to just be on high alert, keep him within our sights at all times."

"But you have to share a room with him—doesn't that freak you out?"

"Nae, it'll give me a chance to keep an eye on him for you," he says. "Besides he's an old man and I'm a strapping young lad!"

He is trying to sound brave but I can hear a tinge of fear in his voice. All I can think about is what Barend Schlacter said to me in my room. I try to push the thought from my mind but it keeps popping up again, like a dandelion through concrete. The only bright spot is that those books had not been translated, which probably means he's not totally connected to the *Fraternitas*. Yet.

For the rest of the flight, both of us keep looking back at the man with Thomas' passport.

The Mataveri airport is what I expected the Santiago airport to look like: very small and pretty sketchy. While we wait for our luggage, I find a quiet spot and call my parents. After traveling all this way you'd think it would be a totally different day or something, but it's only a five-hour time difference between here and Scotland.

Time is so weird.

We have a short and pleasant conversation in which I totally and completely lie to my loving and trusting parents. Nice.

It's early evening by the time we check into the hotel, so before we head up to our rooms, we have an awkward dinner at the hotel restaurant; I'm glad that Donald is hurt because he doesn't seem to notice that no one is talking or making eye contact. When I see him move his hand and wince, something brilliant occurs to me.

"Thomas, they probably have a doctor they can call. Do you want to get some antibiotics or something?" I ask.

He looks down at the hand, which is so swollen from travel and infection that the skin bulges on either side of the gauze wrapping and says, "Aye, s'pose I should have someone take a look."

Before he even finishes the sentence, I'm out of my chair and on my way to the front desk where a man sits picking his nails with a staple remover. He's small and nervous—has the look of someone who is just about to be asked a question that he does not know the answer to.

I point to Thomas and tell him that my friend is really hurt and needs to see a doctor who can prescribe very strong painkillers. "Oh, and Thomas is very macho," I add. "He probably won't want to ask for painkillers himself, so please just tell the doctor he must *insist*."

The man nods nervously and says, "Of course," and makes a call, speaking quickly in Spanish. After he hangs up he holds up one hand and says, "Five minute."

"And he has pain medicine?"

"*Sí, sí.*"

"Thank you! *Gracias! Muchas gracias.*"

I walk back to the table. "They might have a doctor they can call," I say casually to Donald before ordering dessert to hold them there longer. As I'm picking at some weird cake that I ordered, the doctor appears.

"Come with me?" he says to Donald. I'm glad he's wearing a white coat and is carrying one of those old-school doctor cases—Donald might not go if he didn't look totally legit.

As soon as they disappear into a room by the front desk, I lean over to Alex. "Okay, here's the deal," I say. "Donald is going to get some really strong painkillers. We need to get him totally drugged up so he can't do anything but sleep."

"How?"

"Put it in something he eats, I guess? Oh, I know! Order room service first thing in the morning and slip a few of the pills in his tea. Did you see how much sugar he just put in his tea? I don't think he'd taste *anything.*"

"How many?"

"I don't know—maybe double the dosage? I mean, we don't want to kill the guy, just put him in a stupor."

"Aye," Alex says, clearly—and for good reason—nervous about drugging an imposter he has to share a room with.

When Donald returns to the table, he's gripping his upper arm. "Antibiotics shot," he says. "Biggest bloody needle I've ever seen."

"Did he give you anything for the pain?" I ask.

"Aye. Not going to take it until bedtime though, the doctor said it will make me drowsy."

I resist the urge to look at Alex.

"Well, I'm going to head up," I say.

"Wait, lass," Donald says. "What are your plans for tomorrow?"

"First I'm going to sleep in as long as humanly possible. Then have some lunch, look around, and find a good place to do my talk tomorrow night."

"Night?" he asks.

"Yeah. It's scheduled for 5:00 at night," I casually reply. For once it feels good to lie to a scumbag instead of my parents. "Meet here for late lunch? Say, oneish?"

"Aye," they say in unison.

I walk to my room on autopilot, so wiped out from the travel and the Donald thing. I barely muster the energy to set the alarm before I sink into bed, wondering how on earth I am going to get through tomorrow.

The curtains on the sliding glass door in my room are open so the first rays of the sun blast me full force. I get up to close them, but once I look outside the sunrise mesmerizes me in that weird way that you can get hypnotized by something completely ordinary, like a sprinkler.

I open the door and walk out on the small balcony. Waves are lapping the shore and the sun is peeking over the ocean. As more of the sun is revealed, I am filled with an amazing sensation. I don't think I can explain exactly what it is, but it's most like a feeling I had as a young child when I would fall asleep on my dad, with my ear on his chest so I could both feel and hear his heartbeat. Total comfort, total warmth, total love.

I remember a conversation I had with Dr. Slaton about how there's a sudden surge of magnetic energy when the sun rises, something about the solar wind changing the Earth's field as it turns to see the morning sun. I suppose that's what I'm feeling.

I instantly want to call Justine. I try her cell phone and after just two rings she picks up.

"Your phone works!" I say, happy it's as clear as if she were in the next room.

"Caity! How was your trip? How are you?"

"Great!" I say, not wanting to lay the Donald stuff on her. "I'm on Easter Island watching the sun rise over the ocean and it's so beautiful it makes me want to cry. But what are you doing up? How was *your* trip?" I ask.

"Oh my God, do you know how far this place is from San Francisco? It feels like we've been traveling for a week!"

"I know, me too. But you're there? You're fine? What are you doing?"

"Yep, we're fine. We're actually at Machu Picchu right now."

"Really?"

"Yep, and when the sun rose this morning it came through this hole in the wall of the Temple of the Sun and lined up with a groove in a huge rock. It's like some adventure movie or something, it was *so* cool."

"That's amazing!"

"Oh, and thanks for arranging for Eduardo to meet us at the airport, we'd never have made it without him."

"Wait, who?" I ask. "I thought you were with David—"

"Yeah, David flew down here with me and then Eduardo met us at the airport."

I can't think of anything to say. I have no idea who Eduardo is and wonder if Donald arranged for him to be there.

Justine says, "He said he was a friend of Chasca's."

"And you're sure he's legit?" I ask.

"Completely. He's great, and he shares a room with David so there's no weirdness about what to do with sleeping arrangements."

"So Eduardo got you guys to Machu Picchu?"

"Yeah, by planes, trains, buses, and foot. Plus he arranged for us to come up here late yesterday and stay overnight here so we could watch the sunrise. I guess he's a shaman or something. Whatever he is, he can definitely pull strings. Anyway, we all had to promise to be very quiet and very respectful, which is pretty easy because this place is incredible."

"So it wasn't creepy there at night?" I ask.

"No, it was beautiful. The moon lit the whole place up all night, and then that crazy sunrise thing happened."

"I wish I were with you," I say. "So do you think anyone else will show up?"

Justine pauses. "Well, I was going to wait until after the event to tell you …"

"It's okay, seriously. You and David and Eduardo being there will still be a good start."

"No, you don't understand, there are like hundreds of kids here now and more coming."

"What?" I say as I sit down on the corner of the bed.

"Caity, that email has gone all over the place," Justine

says. "Eduardo told us there was a huge underground movement of kids planning to hike up the last part of the Inca trail from a little town below Machu Picchu. They should be here in a couple of hours."

"Oh my God."

"Caity?" Justine says. "What's wrong? Wasn't this what you were supposed to do?"

"Yeah, I guess maybe I just didn't expect it to really happen…"

Justine slaps me into reality. "Well, it's happening, sister, so you better get yourself together! Lots of people are counting on you to say something worth hearing."

I walk back over to my glass door and step out on the patio to look at the sun. The fact that we are looking at the same thing comforts me.

"Caity, are you there? I didn't mean to—"

"No, you're totally right. I've got to get a grip," I say. "Hey, Justine, do any of those kids have cell phones?"

"Not too many, but it turns out that David is a genius," she says. In the background I can hear David say, "This should *not* have been a surprise…"

"What do you mean?" I ask her.

"Well, when I told him what we were going to do he was totally into it, but then when I got to the part about the cell phones he laughed so hard he almost fell down."

"What was so funny?" I ask, feeling stupid. I hear David saying. "Here, let me talk…"

"David wants to talk to you," Justine says, quickly passing the phone over.

"Hey! Cracky Mac Cracken!"

This is something I could have gone without hearing for the rest of my life. "Hey," I reply.

"Yo! Quite a little event you got going on. I'm shocked; I never pegged you as the worldwide-movement kind of girl."

I roll my eyes. "Hey, David. Thanks for traveling with Justine," I say, trying to be polite. "So what's the deal with the cell phones?"

"Love the teleconference idea, great work on that. And the fact that it's listen-only will really boost sound quality and keep the hecklers from bringing you down. But come on, kids with cell phones in Peru? What kind of low-grade crack are you smoking?"

"Oh," I say quietly. "Well, to be honest with you I wasn't expecting that many—"

"No worries, I got it under control."

"How?" I ask.

"You know that my dad owns a communications company, right? Well, we make this little adapter that connects your cell phone to any portable music player that has a mic input."

He pauses like I should clap or something. "Oh, okay, kind of like ghetto karaoke?"

"Exactly. We brought a small high-amp portable CD player, the adapter, and the cell phone. You'll be playing Machu Picchu *live*, baby!" he says, ending with that 'waaaere waaaere' sound that guys make when they play air guitar.

"Great, thanks a lot David," I say. I forgot what a cheese ball this guy was. "God, I wonder what they're going to do in Cambodia and Egypt, though?"

"Cambodia will be no problem; one of my dad's biggest

markets. More cell phones than land lines. Any kid that wants to should have no problem getting her hands on a cell phone."

I'm really impressed that he used "her" instead of "his" and it makes me rethink my cheese-ball judgment.

He continues. "And Egypt, well, you've got Amisi on that, right? She's kick-ass smart and her dad being who he is can set her up with anything she needs."

"Well, that's a relief," I say. "Thanks, David."

"Hey, no problem. Just remember: You need worldwide communications, you think von Kellerman ..."

There's no doubt about what he'll be doing when he grows up.

"Hey, thanks again, David. Can I talk to Justine one more time?"

"Sure. Great talking with you, Cracky. Can't wait to hear your speech!"

I gasp when I hear the word *speech*. "It's not a speech!" I say too late; he doesn't hear.

"What?" Justine says as she comes back on.

"I just want him to know it's not a speech," I say, pacing the room.

"Then what is it?" she asks, genuinely confused.

"Let's just call it a ... a conversation. Yeah, it's a conversation."

"But no one can talk back, only listen right? Isn't that what a speech is?"

"You're stressing me out!" Then I try to compose myself. "Oh my God, I'm sorry Justine, I just really need to think of this *not* as a speech."

"Jeez, Caity, are you okay?" she asks.

I look at the sun for as long as I can before my eyes water and twitch shut.

"I'm fine, really. Alex has been great and—really, I'll be fine."

"No, you'll be amazing," she says in her calming Justine way.

After we hang up, I take the longest shower ever. As I stand there letting the water beat down on my head, more and more ideas about what to say flood into my mind.

I get dressed and put the satellite phone and all the other stuff I'll need in my backpack. With how clear the cell phone was I realize I could use that, but the satellite phone is super reliable and less likely to lose a signal.

Alex is already downstairs when I arrive. Smiling with every tooth showing he says, "He's sleeping like a baby."

"You did it! You're the best!"

"Doubt he'll be up for hours."

As we walk through the lobby to the restaurant, two young girls approach me. They are beautiful, with brown skin that has a purplish undertone and shiny black hair. As they get close I realize they must be sisters; they walk the same way and have the same chin.

They stop in front of me. In a very thick accent the older one says, "Are you the one?"

THIRTY-ONE

xcuse me?" I say.

"Are you the one to talk?" the younger one says.

I look at Alex; he shrugs.

"What do you mean?" I ask. "Talk about what?"

"About kids. Change world," the older one says as she holds up a printout of my email.

I take a deep breath. My phone call with Justine should have prepared me for this.

"I guess so," I say.

"We help. We have car," the younger one says as she reaches for my arm.

"You want to take us somewhere?" I ask.

They nod. "Good place for talk."

I make the gesture for eating. "We need to eat first," I say.

"No no, we have food in car. Very good empanadas. Sweet coffee. You come?"

I turn to Alex. "Aye, let's go!" he says.

"What are your names?" I ask the girls.

The older one points to herself and says, "Catherine," then to her sister and says, "Maria."

I hold out my hand to shake. "I'm Caity."

"I'm Alex," he says, extending his hand. They look at him shyly and smile. Clearly Alex has worldwide appeal.

They lead us to the smallest, most beat-up car I've ever seen. The ceiling fabric is dangling down like tree moss and the seats are draped in blankets that are covered in dog hair. They offer me the front seat but I give it up to Alex.

Catherine starts the car, which is no easy feat because there are levers and pulls and things that have to be done, it seems, in just the right order. I ask where we are going. Maria replies, "Ahu Vinapu," as if this was obvious. "Vinapu special place for winter solstice."

"*Winter* solstice?"

Alex looks back. "Did you forget that we're on the bottom half of the world?" he asks, which makes me feel like an idiot.

As we drive away from town, we pass an enormous stone sculpture, about as tall as a two-story house, that's facing in toward the island. It's just a long head on a short torso, sticking out of the grass like a tree trunk. Maria points to it and says something that sounds like "Mo eye." I repeat, "Mo eye," and she nods yes.

"Do you ever get used to them?" I ask. "I mean, do they ever stop being strange?"

Both shake their heads. "Always strange," Catherine says as she points to another with almost everything but its cheeks and nose buried under the ground as if he's drowning in grass.

I'm surprised at how barren the island is. Aside from grass

it seems like the Moai are the only things sprouting from the earth. The early settlers and the animals they brought destroyed the island's plants and trees and soil, so now nothing but grass covers the island. I wonder, for a moment, what they were thinking those hundreds of years ago when they cut down the island's very last tree.

It doesn't take long to get where they're taking us, which is good because I'm really hungry. After we get out of the car, Catherine and Maria start pulling things from the small trunk.

We don't venture far from the car as we take in the scene. There are a couple of structures that look like stone walls and then the ground is scattered randomly with toppling Moai, as if some giant had shaken them in his hands and then thrown them like dice.

"Kind of sinister, eh?" says Alex.

"Yeah," I say quietly. I don't know exactly why, but it seems we should be quiet here.

The girls lay out a blanket and motion for us to sit. In the center they set down mugs, mismatched and chipped, but clean. From a huge thermos they fill the mugs with light-colored coffee, and hand us each one. I take a big sip; it's really good, very sweet and creamy. Then they bring out a big tin and set it in down on the blanket. Maria lifts the lid and an amazing smell escapes.

"Please, eat," she says. "Empanadas."

They look like small calzones, or like extra-big Hostess fruit pies, and are stuffed with meat and cheese. I bite into the warm pastry crust. "These are great, thank you," says Alex, the consummate gentleman.

We each have two empanadas and lots of coffee and I feel

the sugar and caffeine flooding my brain. "So how did you know where I was staying?" I ask.

"Our uncle drives taxi," Catherine says.

"Taxi driver knows all that happen here," Maria adds.

"And you knew about today because of the email?" I ask.

They nod. Catherine says, "I have email pen pal in Hong Kong. She know I live here so she send me your email message."

I look at Alex. "Can you believe this? From the Isle of Huracan to Hong Kong to Easter Island?"

"You're definitely doing your job."

We hear some honking in the distance and an old truck overflowing with kids comes barreling down the road toward us. "The others are here!" Maria shouts.

"Wow," I say. "Did you know they were all coming?"

"We make sure of it," Catherine says. "My brother and friends all get trucks to bring kids."

"Do kids here have cell phones?" I ask.

"No, only two or three," she says.

I think about David von Kellerman's idea but I seriously doubt there's anything like a Radio Shack or Circuit City anywhere within a million miles of this place. Suddenly I have an idea. "Do any of the restaurants here have karaoke?" I ask. They nod. "Do you think we could borrow a machine?" They both nod and run over to the car to run and get one.

A load of kids jumps out of the truck, then the truck turns around and goes right back to town as another one pulls up and drops off a load. I don't understand a thing they say as they mill around our blanket pointing at us and chattering away.

I am still in a state of disbelief that anyone showed up.

After a few more truckloads of kids get dropped off, Catherine's car pulls up. Alex and I run over to the car to see if she was successful. She pulls a small karaoke machine out of the trunk.

"Perfect!" I say as I give them each a hug. "Let's set this up."

We head over to one of the walls and place the machine on it.

I ask Catherine to find someone with a cell phone; I need to keep mine as a backup in case something happens with the satellite phone.

She nods and says something to the crowd. One girl raises her hand and Catherine motions for her to come up to the front. I tear out a page from my sketchbook and write down the 800 number on it. I say to Catherine, "When it is time will you call this number? Then put the microphone on top of the phone just like this," I say as I show them what to do. Catherine nods and says "Si, si."

"Maybe we should test it out, to make sure you can hear me," I say. I hand my phone to the girl who has offered her phone. "Will you please dial your phone number using my phone?" I ask her. She dials and after a delay, the phone rings. I answer it and start walking away.

"Okay, now put my phone down on the stone and put the microphone on top of it," I instruct the girl over the phone. Saying, "Testing, testing, testing," I motion to Alex to turn the volume up. It works! I can hear myself talking over the little karaoke machine even a few hundred yards away.

Maria has been getting all of the kids to sit in a semicircle around the stone wall where the karaoke machine sits. I walk in front of them and say, "Thanks so much for coming!" and then they all start clapping. This is just so weird.

I pick up my stuff and tell Alex that I'm going to set up and take a couple minutes to myself. I find a nice spot behind a fallen Moai head, above where the kids are sitting, and I take a seat. I definitely can't be someplace where anyone can see me; I don't want this to be a "performance" of any kind.

I pull out the satellite phone and make sure it's working. Then, to calm down, I pull out my sketchbook and start drawing the Moai I see around me.

The sketching chills me out for awhile. When I see that I have eleven minutes until I have to make the call, I put away my sketchbook and pencil, set my backpack to the side, and arrange the phone in front of me.

I close my eyes and sit quietly.

I try to breathe deeply. In and out, in and out.

Slowing my racing heart, and with only minutes to spare, I make a silent plea to The Council, or to whoever is watching over me, to give me the right words.

I repeat what Uncle Li said, *"Think good, do good, speak the truth."*

With four minutes left, I dial in to the teleconference. I'm relieved that the connection is good. An automated voice says to press five if I'd like to have music playing while the callers get set up, so I do and an instrumental version of *You Are My Sunshine* starts playing. I smile; this is one of Dad's standard whistling songs.

I give the others until 12:02 to dial in and then I begin, trying to speak as slowly and clearly as I can.

THIRTY-TWO

Hello, everyone. If you are listening to my voice right now then you have read the email my friends forwarded and felt drawn to what was said. I am not here to become your leader or anything creepy like that. I'm just here to pass on some important information I was given."

I can hear my voice coming out of the karaoke machine down the hill; there's a long delay and I have to consciously stop listening so it doesn't mess me up.

"There is so much to tell you, it's hard to even know where to start. I guess I'll start with the bad news: we are not, and have never been, free people. There is a Shadow Government, very high up in world politics, banking, and business that control us. And I mean this literally—they control us. Wars, poverty, financial crisis, drugs, these things are all orchestrated by a small, elite group of people. They've been able to control us by keeping us weak, physically and mentally. More kids are on drugs right now than ever before. Genetically modified food is in pretty much everything you eat. They're poisoning the air, playing with the climate, start-ing wars, and keeping us in debt. Economic meltdown doesn't just happen, it's planned. At every level. We have essentially been sold into debt slavery because *we* inherit this mess! At this rate there will be no money for innovation for our gen-eration, no money for *freedom*. This is not a coincidence or a mistake. They want to bind us in debt so we slog along, scared and broke and easy to control. And for what? Power and money.

"This Shadow Government is very powerful and very determined—but we are their worst nightmare. Because in all of history there have never been as many people under twenty on the planet as there are right now. Which means that if we can work together, we can make great changes. But they will do everything they can to keep us from uniting. They want us to be tuned out, detached from each other and not paying attention to anything important.

"We can change that. We *have* to change that. When it comes down to it, we are all just a bunch of vibrations, all just energy putting out waves. When we're isolated or think-ing negative thoughts our waves cancel each other out, kind of like the ripples of two separate rocks being thrown into a pond. But if we intentionally connect with each other we become *one wave*. And that's where our power is.

"What the Shadow Government doesn't factor in is how connected we are. Adults look at us with our phones and computers and think we're isolated and antisocial, but in real-ity we're totally and completely linked. Wired together. Look at the web—we are in a constant state of creativity and con-nectedness. When we want to make a change it will be quick and efficient because we can communicate almost instanta-neously and move as one."

My voice is getting shaky like it does when I'm nervous, so I take a really deep breath and push the air all way down to my belly.

"Does this make sense? Do you see how powerful we are, what we can do if we all share a common goal? We *have* to come together and reject the greed and hatred and fear and ugliness that we are inheriting. What they are doing is sys-tematic, it's planned, and it's designed to keep us under their control—and it's been going on for centuries.

"You may wonder how we can do this, how you and I, people so young we can't even vote, can change anything. But we can—both alone and together. Just as one powerful ocean wave is made up of billions of individual droplets of water.

"So now for the good news: Humans have gone through a lot of cycles and changes, all leading up to where we are now: sit-ting on the edge of a major transformation. Thousands of years ago the Maya of Mexico predicted that December 21, 2012, would be the start of a new era. *We are going to own that era.*

"A rare alignment of the sun, the Earth, and the Galac-tic Center—where all the energy and matter in our galaxy comes from—is happening. This will have a big affect on us, both physically and mentally. It's like having our computers rebooted. But we have to be ready, can't be broken and off-balance the way the Shadow Government wants us.

"The first thing we need to do is to get synchronized, or unbrainwashed. For this we can do one very simple thing: use the *Tzolk'in*, a calendar the Maya created thousands of years ago.

"If you haven't yet done it, get on the website and try using the daily *Tzolk'in* for awhile. It really is as simple as looking at the day's picture and number, and spending a few moments focusing on the intent of that particular day. Today is 13 *Cimi*; *Cimi* represents death, or transformation. This is the day we kill the old way and develop a new way of our own. *Cimi* days are good for tapping into community consciousness. And thirteen, the pulse of the day, is the energy that propels any new effort forward. Today is the day to propel transformation. And here we are.

"This synchronization tool also has a sound associated with it. We're developing a ringtone widget that will download the daily picture and number, along with the day's tone—it just couldn't get easier to use. Check the website for that.

"I know it seems crazy that a calendar could make any difference at all, but just try it. The Shadow Government had been keeping us easy to control by messing with our natural relationship with time. Our twelve-month calendar is an artificial thing, made up by the people in power to turn time into something that is *outside of us*, something we are a slave to. We even wear a time handcuff in the form of a watch. All of this keeps us off-kilter.

"Believe this, if nothing else I say today: there is important information encoded within the *Tzolk'in*.

"I look around here on Easter Island and I have no idea why they spent so much time and energy on these big statues. But it almost looks like an omen, a warning. Like this is a small-scale Earth where people and animals were out of balance with the environment and they devastated it. The trees are gone; all that's left are hills of grass and these statues, scattered around like broken toys. It's creepy to think the Earth could be like this someday if we continue down the current path.

"But this is *our* dream, and we can make it go any way we want. In a dream, every person, every texture, every sound is created in your mind, second by second. Well, scientists say that that's exactly what happens in waking life too—the future hangs in front of us as *pure potential*, waiting to become real based on how *we* observe it. So if the universe creates itself second by second based on how we interact with it, then it is not just exactly like a dream, it *is* a dream. And we—you and I—are the ones dreaming it into being.

"Sorry if I'm getting too heavy. Honestly, some of what's coming out of my mouth I didn't even know I knew. Anyway, I think I've talked long enough. I wish this could have been a two-way conversation. I can't wait to get on the web and see what you all think about this.

"Thanks so much for coming today, and for listening. The fact that we got together at these ancient sites of power is no accident; we are making a complete circle around our planet, a glowing halo of our clean, powerful energy. So that's it. Keep thinking good thoughts, look into the *Tzolk'in*, and stay tuned for more instructions on our next steps.

"Remember, it's up to us. As the Hopi say: *We are the ones we have been waiting for.*"

I hang up the phone and feel shaky and cold. I remember everything I said but I don't know how I knew some of that stuff.

Standing up to stretch, I look down at the group of kids by the half-wall and feel a strange jolt, like when the dentist accidentally hits a nerve. And then something really bizarre happens, probably from all the stress: instead of a group of people I start seeing something that looks more like a mirage. The group has blended together into kind of a vapor of light.

I quickly close my eyes. When I open them I can see clearly again.

I pack up the satellite phone and my sketchbook and walk back toward the group of kids. As I get closer the mass moves, like a swarm, toward me, shouting "*Unidad! Unidad!*" I am totally touched by their enthusiasm, but a little freaked. I bow deeply to them and say "*Gracias, amigos, gracias,*" with heartfelt thanks. As they disperse, Catherine runs up to me and gives me a big hug. I ask if she thinks they all understood.

"Oh, yes. We watch American shows, learn English from TV. We know almost all we hear, just not speak it so good."

"I can understand everything you say," I tell her.

Alex comes up behind me as I'm loading my backpack. "Caity, that was … amazing."

"Thanks for being here, Alex. I honestly could not have done this without you."

Alex and I help fold up the blanket and pack up the mugs and coffee and empanada tin, and then the girls take us back to our hotel. We exchange email addresses and hug goodbye, then they chug off in their little car.

Once in the lobby, we see no sign of Donald. "Are you nervous to go to your room?" I ask Alex.

He pulls out four pills from his pocket. "I won't be, after I make him another cup of sleepy tea …"

"Awesome. Stick it to him."

We get a big mug of tea from the lobby bar and I stir in

three huge scoops of sugar and a lot of milk while Alex grinds up the pills with the back of a spoon and slips the powder in.

I wait outside Alex and Donald's room; he said if anything looks weird he'll come right back out, but he doesn't so I assume all is okay.

When I get to my room, I take off my shoes and sit on the chair on my balcony. I want to call Justine but I just can't muster the energy yet, I feel like I just need to be silent and think about what I said, whether I got all the stuff out that I planned on saying.

The ring of the hotel phone makes me jump. I scramble over to get it. "Caity, turn on your TV," Alex whispers. "Look at CNN, right now. I'll be down in a minute."

I turn to CNN International and see pictures of the Great Pyramid with swarms of people around. I think maybe a bombing happened, but then I hear the newscaster.

"The organizer has not yet been identified, but apparently this person was able to mobilize kids across the world. Authorities are looking into whether or not this is the activity of a cult leader.

"There were four major centers of activities, and each had a significant show of young people. Nearly three thousand showed up at Machu Picchu, five thousand at the temples at Angkor Wat in Cambodia, and seven thousand at the Great Pyramid at Giza. Easter Island had the smallest crowd at about three hundred, but that's an astonishing number when it includes every single minor on the island.

"Gatherers were listening in on some sort of cell-phone teleconference. CNN is trying to track down a tape of that call. More after the break."

Seconds after the commercial starts, I hear a knock at my door. It's Alex.

"Can I watch with you?" he asks, out of breath from sprinting down the hall.

"Yes! Maybe I'll believe it if someone else is here with me—it's too weird." I lock the door behind him. "So what's up with Rip Van Winkle?" I ask.

"He barely opened his eyes when I walked in. I offered him the tea and he gulped about half down and then fell back asleep."

We sit on the edge of the bed facing the TV. Alex says, "Isn't it funny that they assume it's a cult?"

"Right, like we're not smart enough to organize anything ourselves. You know, because any organized movement of kids would have to be done by an adult with a Jesus complex..."

The newscaster comes back on and now there's a red bar at the bottom of the screen that says "Cult Watch."

"No way, we've got a news label!" I squeal.

"You're right up there with hurricanes and political scandals."

The newscaster says, "And we're back to the top story: An unnamed cult has lured thousands of young people to ancient sites around the globe. Barbara Hutchinson has been working on this story; Barbara is there anything new to report?"

"Well, we've just received some interesting data from Princeton University's Global Consciousness Project."

"Barbara, can you first explain what the Global Consciousness Project is?"

"The Global Consciousness Project was started by a lab at Princeton known as PEAR, and it uses sensitive equipment around the world to determine whether human consciousness can be measured. They've shown that when people around the world focus on the same event or idea—such as the events of 9/11—patterns form in otherwise random 'quantum noise.'"

I hit Alex on the chest. "PEAR is the place where Tenzo knows someone! *Tenzo* made that happen!"

"And what does this tell us?" the newscaster asked.

"Well, Janice, the data lead scientists to speculate on whether humans have a 'collective mind' of sorts."

"And they had something to say about what happened today?"

"The Global Consciousness Project reported a strong and distinct pattern in the otherwise random output, a coherence they say they have not seen since news of Princess Diana's death."

"Barbara, does this indicate that there were more people involved than just those at the four sites we mentioned?"

"That has yet to be seen, but according to experts, quality is more important than quantity. If these young people were able to really connect, to quite literally 'get on the same wavelength' so to speak, then they could have had this kind of effect."

"Fascinating, Barbara, thank you. Now to add yet another interesting twist, apparently there was an unusual response in animals that use sonar, such as bats, dolphins, and whales. Joining me via satellite is Carol Countryman, a specialist in animal sonar."

Alex puts his hand on my knee and says, "Bloody hell, Caity, you've managed to disrupt the whole animal kingdom!"

I try to focus on what they're saying, but it's hard while

also trying to catalog the feeling of Alex's hand on my knee in my database of Alex touches.

"Carol, what went on today?"

"Well, it was a strange day for those of us who study animal sonar and echolocation; today we found that these animals were, for lack of a better term, humming along together."

"And this coincided with this teleconferencing event that so many young people dialed into today?"

"It began precisely when the phone call started, according to the teleconferencing site, but lasted much longer than the call. These animals were in phase with each other for nearly an hour, the equivalent of us chanting the same word in unison for sixty minutes."

"And this was found all over the world?"

"Yes. I collect live streaming data from labs all over the world and it only took me a few minutes to see the coherence. Although these were all at different frequencies—each species has its own—but because the frequencies were coherent, they formed a *pulse*."

The screen goes black for a moment and Alex moves his hand from my knee. When the news comes back on the newscaster looks flustered and the "Cult Watch" label at the bottom of the screen is gone.

"For those of you who have been following this story, we're just received information that this was all an elaborate hoax. I'm not sure what parts, if any, are true, but we'll deliver the news to you just as fast as we get it. Back in a moment."

"That's bizarre," Alex says. "What would make them say it was a hoax? There was actual footage of the kids in Egypt!"

Would the *Fraternitas* be able to snuff a story like this? "Every time I think it can't get stranger, it does."

"Aye," he says with a laugh. "You never know what's going to happen next with you…"

"I'll tell you what's going to happen next with me: a huge tray of room service and then bed. I feel like martians have sucked my brain from my body."

"Well, I best be getting back to the room to check on Donald. Make sure he drinks the rest of that tea."

"Hey! You know what? Maybe you could get him to miss the plane tomorrow! How perfect would that be?"

"Nice," he says with a big smile. "Consider it done."

"So then I'll meet you and only you in the lobby tomorrow morning at 7:00?"

"Aye," he says, pausing for an awkward moment while he's looking at me.

Slowly he reaches up and holds my face in his warm hands. My body goes into some sort of shock mode and all I hear is the sound of the blood rushing through my ears like a busy freeway.

He looks in my eyes and says, "Caity Mac Fireland. Master of dolphins and bats the world over."

Then he slowly bends his face down to kiss me. Our noses touch first, for a split second, and then I feel the soft, warm pressure of his lips. I have to concentrate so I don't hyperventilate.

Time both stops and speeds up and I savor every millisecond.

When he pulls away I stand still as a statue. Frozen.

"Sleep well," he says as he leaves the room, walking out backwards.

I am too stunned to say anything back.

Just as I sit down on the edge of the bed to process the weirdest day in my entire life, my cell phone rings. I see Justine's number pop up.

"He kissed me!" I say into the phone, instead of hello. "Like a hands-on-face-deliberately-slow kiss..."

"Duh! Who wouldn't after that speech? I mean, uh, *talk*?"

"Really? Honest? It made sense?" I know Justine will tell me the truth.

"Are you kidding me? You don't even understand how many kids showed up—seriously, there are like thousands of people here all hanging on your every word."

"Three thousand, CNN said."

"Oh my God! We made the news?" Justine screams. "I was so proud of you, I yelled to the audience, 'That's my best friend!' and they cheered. These people are amazing. I *love* Peru."

"I'm so glad you had fun because I still can't believe you went there for me."

"Anytime, my friend," she replies.

"Hey, guess what?"

"What?"

"He kissed me."

"So I've heard..." she replies. "Now it's my turn, wink wink."

"Ha! Well, have fun."

"Sweet dreams, Caity. Heart ya, mean it."

"Heart ya more," I reply.

The only other person on earth I want to talk to is Uncle Li. I dial his number but only get his voicemail, so I leave a message to call me back as soon as he can.

After a weird room-service meal of Easter Island's twist on American food, I fire off a quick email to the girls.

From: caitymacfireland@gmail.com
To: chantreahuy@gmail.com, amisi@yahoo.com,
justinemiddleford@gmail.com
Subject: You pulled it off!

Holy hell, did you see that we made international news? I would never, NEVER have been able to pull this off without your help. THANK YOU. I hope I didn't sound like too much of a lunatic; hope the kids wherever you were understood some of what I talked about. Honestly, I don't know where a lot of that came from. It was like my brain was reading a ticker tape or something. Anyway, I hope you all get home safely and I am in deepest debt to you. ANYTHING you ever need, please ask! Big big hugs, Caity

Finally, I settle in to bed to make my last call of the evening—my parents. It's late there and I'm hoping I'll just get voicemail, but Mom answers, sounding totally awake.

"Hey, I was just about to call you!" she says. "How are you?"

"Good! So nice to be back in San Francisco. What are you doing up this late?"

"Having a good laugh over the news. Have you been following this cult thing?" she asks.

"Pretty crazy, huh?"

"Isn't it amazing that we were just talking about the Mayan

calendar at dinner and now it apparently had something to do with it?"

"Really? That's part of it?"

"Well, this might be part of the hoax too, but they said there's a Mayan calendar website that was the most visited site on the web today. Developed by a company called 'Bolon' that no one knows anything about."

I have to cover my mouth with my hand to keep from laughing. "Wow, I'll have to check that out," I say. "Well, just wanted to say hey. I know it's late, you probably want to get to bed."

"Love you, Caity."

"Love you too," I say. My voice catches and I'm afraid I might cry if I'm on the phone much longer. "Give Dad a hug for me. And lock your door."

"Excuse me?" she says.

"Bolt your door tonight. Please? For me?"

Mom laughs. "Okay, I'm walking … walking … hear that? I just bolted the door. For you."

All I can think about is getting home to see my parents. I know that Tenzo and Uncle Li are both there and aware of what's happening, so they could help if Barend Schlacter came back for my parents, but I still have a horrible, acidic feeling in my gut.

Just as I'm drifting off to sleep, the hotel phone rings and I bolt upright in bed and answer. Before I even say hello, I hear, "Caity, this is Bolon. You need to leave immediately."

THIRTY-THREE

hat time is it? What do you mean?" I say. My jaw clenches so tightly it feels like my teeth might disintegrate.

"The *Fraternitas* is on its way to Easter Island. You must leave the hotel until I can get to you."

"But where do we go?"

"Not *we*, just you. Write a note for Alex. Tell him you had to take an earlier flight for security reasons."

"I can't leave Alex! He's sharing a room with a spy."

"I'll handle that. You just get out of that hotel."

I am silent.

"Caity, this is important. Get a pen. Get a piece of hotel stationery. Write the note."

I set the phone receiver down on the table and do what he says.

"Okay, now what?" I ask. I've turned into a robot.

"Take only what you need, slip the note under Alex's door,

and walk down the staircase. Leave from the staircase door, not through the lobby. I will call your cell in a couple of minutes."

I pull on some clothes, throw what I can in my backpack, and scribble a note for Alex that I wrap around my room key in case he wants to move to my room. I leave it in front of Alex's door, knock quietly, and then run down the stairwell like Bolon told me. The staircase door leads out to the side of the hotel property, which is undeveloped. Just lots of lava rock and a path down to the sea.

As I wait for Bolon's call I start to hear something in the distance. At first I think it may be thunder, but as it gets closer I realize it's the *fwap fwap fwap* of a helicopter propeller. I try to think of all the things this could be other than the *Fraternitas*: Medical evacuation? Army training? Food drop?

The sound of my phone ringing startles me so badly that I bite my tongue. I should have put this thing on vibrate. "Hello?" I whisper.

"Stand with your back to the staircase door. Now walk straight to the outcropping of rocks directly ahead of you."

"Bolon, I'm scared! It's completely black out and I heard a helicopter a minute ago."

"I know. Just follow my directions. Walk to the rocks."

I walk like in a nightmare when you're in slow motion; each step takes concentration. "Okay," I say when I finally get there. "I'm at the rocks."

"Do you see the big flat one? Step over it and jump down to the sand. Now look to your right—you will see a small opening, a lava tube cave. I want you to kneel down and crawl in."

"No way! I'm not getting in a cave in the dark!"

"Caity, this is serious. Get in the cave."

I stand for a moment contemplating what to do. In the distance I hear dogs barking.

"Caity, I can hear the hounds. I'm on my way, but they will get to you before I do ..."

Tears stream down my face as I crawl into the small cave about the size of a tube on a playground, just big enough for me to get into and almost sit upright. "Okay, I'm in," I say.

"Good, Caity. Now keep going,"

"Going? Going *where*?"

"There's an extensive lava tube cave system under Easter Island. This cave will go about a quarter mile inland and then come up through the grass. I'll have landed when you get there."

"How do you know?" I scream. "How do you know I'm even in the right cave? I could be lost down here forever!"

"I just know, Caity. I do, I promise you that. I'll tell you *how* I know later. Right now I just need you to crawl as fast as you can through that cave."

I peek my head out of the cave to see if I could swim out into the ocean, but then I hear the dogs getting closer. I look back into the darkness of the cave and decide I have no choice.

The glow of my cell phone is the only source of light, so I hold it in my mouth as I crawl on all fours. After a few feet I stop to see if Bolon is still there. "Bolon? You there? Bolon!" There's no answer; the cave is blocking the signal.

I keep my front teeth on the phone keys so that the light will stay on, but it makes that horrible shrill sound, which, in the small cave, reverberates like a fire alarm. But at least the faint green glow helps me along.

I crawl on all fours as fast as I can. The bottom of the cave is mostly sand, so it doesn't hurt too much. Thankfully the tunnel gets larger and I'm able to walk upright if I duck a little. It feels good to straighten my legs and really run. Then it gets small again, even smaller than it was at the beginning and in some places I have to scoot through on my belly.

I am somewhere underneath one of the world's most isolated islands and only one person knows vaguely where I am. If anything happened I would never be found. *Never.* My stomach convulses but thankfully nothing comes out. I just dry heave.

When will this end? I try to work out in my head how long I've been crawling and walking so I can figure out how far I've gone, but between my crying and the key-tone noise, I can't keep a train of thought going long enough to do it.

Then I hear the barking of dogs echoing in the tunnel—they sound far away but I know how fast dogs are. When I get to a really small spot, I scramble around for rocks to block the way and I'm able to make a pretty solid wall that would probably stop dogs but if there are any people with them it will have been wasted time.

The cell phone light is slowly fading and the once-shrill tone winds down like a toy with a failing battery. This sound is even more disturbing than the shrill one, with its connection to something dying. I crawl as I've never crawled before.

The glow gets dimmer and dimmer and dimmer until there is no light at all. It is completely black and completely silent except for the echo of my sobs and my uneven breathing. I have to slow down to feel my way through.

Then the sound of the dogs returns, distantly at first and then closer, which means that people are with them! Some sort of autopilot takes over and I get mechanical about feeling my way through. My brain turns off and my body takes over.

THIRTY-FOUR

Finally I feel air moving; it's subtle at first but all my senses are on hyperdrive. Nothing has ever felt so good. About twenty feet later, a sliver of grey light becomes visible. As I get closer I see a small hole in the roof of the cave.

I pull myself out of the hole and Bolon is standing there. Throwing all my weight at him, he says nothing, just puts his arm around me and holds me up as I heave and sob.

Both of us stiffen when we hear the echo of barking dogs.

Bolon puts a finger to his lips and takes my hand. We run around the mound of rocks that I just crawled out of and I see an enormous, strange-looking metal thing—it's almost like a submarine, without propellers. Three retractable legs hold it about eight feet off the ground.

We climb up a skinny ladder and board through a hatch at the bottom. When I'm inside and Bolon is on the last rung, I finally see the dogs. Three of them are looking up into the hatch, jumping, barking, and snarling.

Once Bolon is all the way in, he pushes a button and

the ladder silently retracts. Then he closes the submarine-like hatch and it becomes freakishly quiet. We're in a small metal room with nothing but the hatch and one other door. Bolon goes to the door and says something, then the door slides open and I see a small staircase that we climb.

The staircase opens into the body of this plane, or helicopter, or whatever it is. Two men sit at the control panel in front of the only windows in the entire craft. The shorter one turns to me and says, "Please, sit and put your strap on. We are in quite a hurry."

Bolon shows me to a seat and helps me buckle up, then sits next to me. I feel a strange roller-coaster sensation in my stomach but I don't feel any movement or shaking and all I hear is a whirring noise. "When can we take off?" I whisper, anxious to get off this island.

"We already have," Bolon replies. "We're probably a thousand feet up by now."

"What is this thing?"

"It's called a Vimāna."

"Never heard of it. Is it new?"

Bolon laughs. "No, it's actually very, very old. Designed thousands of years ago."

"Right, this is thousands of years old—"

"No, the *plans* are thousands of years old. The oldest surviving scripture in the world, the Indian Vedas, actually describe how to build these."

"Then why aren't they used all over?"

Bolon shrugs. "No one has ever taken them seriously. Except for Hitler's program, of course..."

I don't want to get deeper into Bolon's conspiracy world.

"Okay, whatever, as long as it gets me home. The bigger deal is, I almost died back there!" Now that I'm relatively safe I feel anger welling up inside me.

"But you accomplished your goal."

"That was so not worth it—I gave some lame talk over the phone for a few minutes and now people are coming after me with *helicopters* and *dogs*?"

"You didn't hear the results? You even affected Princeton's sensitive PEAR equipment."

"I heard the results; I'm just saying that those results were not worth me risking my life!"

Now the sensation in my stomach changes and seems as if we are moving sideways instead of up. Still I hear nothing but a whirring and there's no shaking or tipping of any kind.

"I am sorry you feel this way. But understand, I did not choose your path, *you* did. This is what you were meant to do, I am only here to help."

"Well, I want a different path," I say as I cross my arms like a child.

"Let me get you some calming tea." Bolon unbuckles his seat belt, walks over to a small galley kitchen, and returns with a glass of lukewarm tea. I'm so thirsty from crawling through the caves that I gulp down the bitter liquid as fast as I can. Then Bolon shows me how to recline my seat and spreads a blanket over me.

"What will happen to Alex?" I ask. "Will they try to hurt him?"

"He'll be fine," he replies, as he puts a pillow behind my head. "We dropped someone on Easter Island to escort him home."

My eyes start to droop and I feel that subtle inner gear-shifting in my brain, like after taking allergy medicine. I know I'm about to drift off and I don't fight it.

Later I awaken to my own voice screaming, "Mom!" My whole body is shaking like an old person. Bolon puts his hand on my shoulder, which stops the shaking. "She's fine. Your parents are fine," he says. "They're being watched right now."

I sit up and find my whole body is sore; it feels like I've been in a car crash.

"Do cell phones work in this thing?" I ask.

"Who do you want to call?"

"Barend Schlacter."

"Let's talk this through, Caity."

"I don't want to talk it through," I say.

I don't even need to dig out my sketchbook to find the number; the image of his luggage tag is etched in my brain. His phone rings seven times and then a recorded message plays in German. I can't understand a word, but when I hear the beep I know it's time.

"Barend Schlacter, this is your *freund* Caity. I've written a letter detailing all that I know about you and the *Fraternitas Regni Occulti*. I also have a binder of information that links the *Fraternitas* to all sorts of atrocities. All of this is at a safe and secure site. If anything happens to my parents or to me, the people holding this information will go to the media and the police and you will go *down*." Before I hang up I add, "How's that for odd and weak?"

I've never seen Bolon look so worried. "Caity, that is not how we prefer to handle things," he says.

"Can we please change the subject? It's done, and I feel a lot better."

Bolon looks down at his hands, making me feel guilty, as if I have done something that will get him in trouble. I see the sky lighten out the front windows. "Where are we going?" I ask.

"Scotland. We'll put you on a commuter flight that comes in at about the same time as the flight you are supposed to be on from San Francisco."

It's mind-blowing to think of keeping up this charade. Would my parents even believe it if I told them? Would they ever let me out of their sight again? Could I go to jail for any of this?

"You've done nothing wrong, Caity," Bolon says.

"I'd like a little privacy with my thoughts, please," I snip. "Where's the bathroom?"

Bolon points to a small door behind us. I take my back-pack, which has a change of clothes in it. When I see myself in the mirror I can't help but laugh. I'm so dirty that I look like a soldier with a cammo-painted face.

There are real towels in the bathroom and I have to use up all of them to get presentable. I throw the clothes I am wearing away because they are beyond repair; the knees of my jeans are black and the sleeves of my shirt are frayed from crawling through the cave.

I don't even realize we've been descending until I feel a slight thud on the floor.

When I come out of the bathroom, Bolon is standing right there waiting for me. "I've been in touch with Easter Island, and Alex is safely on his flight home," he says. "Donald was on pain medication and could not be woken. We've arranged for his ticket to be extended."

I squeeze Bolon's hands and thank him. This information relieves me even more than I thought it would.

"We must go now. Our car is waiting."

Once outside, I see that we've landed in a desolate little valley. When we get a few feet away from the Vimāna, I turn around to get a good look in the daylight. Copper colored and shaped like a cigar, it's definitely not like any aircraft I've ever seen. "Do people think this is a UFO?" I ask.

"Most of the time," Bolon replies. "That is why we try to use it only for emergencies when great speed is necessary."

"Well, thanks for coming to get me," I say. "I'm sorry if I was rude."

We drive over a big hill and see a small town in the distance. Bolon points to the airstrip to one side of the town. "That's where you'll fly out of," he says.

As we make our way down, Bolon tells me how proud he and The Council are of my work. I try to take it in but now that a day has passed it doesn't register that it was me out there talking. It seems like some hazy dream.

When Bolon drops me off at the airport and gives me a hug, I want to stay mad at him but for some reason it's hard. Maybe I'm having that reaction where people start to love their captors.

"I'll be in touch with further instructions," Bolon says.

Is he insane? There will be no further instructions! I am *out*.

I shake my head, take his worn, soft hand in mine, and say, "Goodbye Bolon, take care of yourself," like this is the last time we will see each other. As soon as the words are out of my mouth, I know this is not true; the look on his face tells me he knows this, too.

The short flight on the small plane seems rickety and terrifying after the smooth ride on the Vimāna. When we land in Edinburgh and I'm able to turn my phone back on I see a new text message from a strange number. Nervously, I open it, not sure what I'll find. It says, SAFE IN SF, HM SOON. DON'T RTURN TXT, USING STRNGRS PHONE. AC

I don't realize I say, "Oh, thank God!" out loud until I see the person next to me try to read the text.

When the plane door opens I rush out and try to get through security as quickly as possible. I run to my parents and we all hug for a long time.

"Welcome home, kiddo." Dad says.

I don't know if Breidablik is my home, but right now I don't care. At least we're all safe.

"Let's head down to pick up your luggage," Mom says.

The truth is, my rolly suitcase is back in Easter Island, along with Dad's satellite phone. I couldn't take it with me when I had to evacuate. "Oh … you know what? I didn't feel like lugging all that stuff back, so I left it with Justine. I just brought my laptop with me."

"Smart girl," Mom says, kissing my forehead.

They suggest we stay over in Edinburgh and do some sightseeing, but I tell them I'm anxious to get back to the castle and sleep in my own bed. We make it to the station just in time to catch the early evening train.

After a good meal in the dining car, we go to our connected sleeping cabins where the couches have already been made into beds. I slip into a T-shirt of Dad's, triple-check that both our outer doors are locked, and use my backpack to prop open the door that connects our cabins. Then I drift peacefully off to sleep watching my parents read by the dim light above their bed.

In the morning we disembark the train and wait in the Land Rover for the first ferry to arrive; a few minutes later we see it chugging toward us. It's chilly on the water, so my parents stay in the car. I get out and stand at the front of the boat with the wind blowing my dirty curls into dreadlocks. As the Isle of Huracan comes into view I cannot help but yell, "The larger the island of knowledge, the longer the shoreline of wonder!" But my voice is no match for the sea, and the wind and the waves steal the sound of the words right out of my mouth.

The early morning sun glowing pink on the horizon makes for a beautiful sight. Taking a deep breath of the misty morning sea air, I try to box up the comfort I feel at this moment, safely back together with my parents. Like a squirrel burying a nut for the winter, I store this feeling deep inside—I sense that I will need that comfort not so very long from now. Things are expected of me. I have only just begun.

Then it hits me: my Discovery Fantasy has come true. *I have been discovered.*

Not by some talent agent or art critic, but by the universe. I gasp at the enormity of this thought, and the saying *Be Careful What You Wish For* comes immediately to mind. I finally accept the full weight of it: this is my path. And my future lies in a state of pure potential.

I touch a cut on my wrist from the lava cave, already working hard to close itself up. We are wondrous beings, aren't we?

THIRTY-FIVE

When we arrive at the castle, I go straight to the kitchen and give Mrs. Findlay a big hug. Then Mr. Papers hops up and I squeeze him probably harder than I should squeeze a 65-year-old monkey. He takes my earlobe in his fingers and rubs it a little. I make a promise to never leave him again.

I want to go straight to my room and see if I have email from Amisi and Chantrea and check what the latest news is on the event, but Mrs. Findlay motions to the table, laid out with sticky buns and eggs and thick-cut bacon, and says, "Eat, Mac Firelands, eat!" Mr. Papers scoots up right beside me on the bench and Mrs. Findlay doesn't even get mad.

"We missed you, little one," Mrs. Findlay says.

"I missed you guys, too," I say. "I mean, it was so great to hang out with Justine and all, but I'm *really* happy to be back."

"Glad to hear it," Dad says as he pats my hand.

"So where are Tenzo and Uncle Li?" I ask.

"Oh, they were both on the train with us to Edinburgh," Mom answers. "We parted ways at the airport."

I think I must have misheard. "Wait, you mean Tenzo is gone, not Uncle Li?"

"Yes, Li is gone; he had some sort of emergency and had to leave," Dad says.

I can't hide the fact that I'm stunned by this news.

"I think he left a note in your room," Dad adds.

"But where did he go?" I ask, my voice cracking.

"I'm not sure," Mom says, looking over at Dad. "Angus, did he tell you?"

Dad shakes his head. "No, he just said an international client of his had an issue and needed him right away."

I finish breakfast quickly so I can go see the note for myself.

Searching my room turns up nothing but Tenzo's business card with, *"Well done! Call or email anytime, day or night. I am at your service,"* written on the back in small, precise handwriting. I even look under the bed and in the bathroom and all through my desk drawers.

Then Mr. Papers hops over to me holding the key to the chamber. *Of course! Uncle Li would leave his note in the chamber so my parents could not find it.*

I put Mr. Papers on my shoulder and slide open the panel. It seems like months since I was last here, so much has happened. As soon as I turn on the light, I see an envelope sitting on the side table. I pick it up and am immediately filled with a feeling of dread.

I sit down on the fainting couch, and pull the letter from the envelope.

Dear Caity,

I suppose you are wondering why I left, and why I have taken the Sanskrit books. Perhaps one day I'll be able to explain. I know you will feel gravely betrayed, and rightly so. But nothing is as it seems. The Way of Heaven plays no favorites; it is always on the side of the good.

At this time, all I can say is that each one of us has our own path to walk, and however dark it may seem, this is the way of my path. I am deeply sorry that it interferes with yours.

Always, Uncle Li

He's left and taken the books?

I reread it three times looking for something new each time; it's just not sinking in that Uncle Li would steal the Sanskrit books from me! What's this garbage about "the way of heaven plays no favorites"? If he were on the side of the good he'd be *here* now, with the books, helping me figure all this out! Why would a close family friend, a man I have known all my life, someone who promised to help me and protect me, do this?

I lie on the fainting couch for a long time trying to think it all through, going over every step we made together, but nothing leads me to believe he would do this. What could be so important that it could make him betray me? And where would he go? Not back to his home in the states, or I could easily find him. Maybe back to his family in Shanghai? He has clients all over the world. He could be anywhere.

I don't realize I'm even crying until Mr. Papers' small hand wipes away a tear. I scratch him behind the ears and say, "Where would he go?"

Immediately, Mr. Papers goes to my desk and gets a piece of origami paper that he folds into the shape of a cave. Inside of it he puts my rabbit-ear key.

"Oh my god, you're right! *Of course.* He's gone back to the Dunhuang Caves, the archives where this all began!"

Hearing some commotion outside, I look out and see Thomas raking the gravel in the big circular drive. I'm so relieved to see that he is okay and run downstairs to talk to him.

"You're okay!" I say as I give him a huge hug.

"Aye," he says, looking around to make sure we are alone. "Now I am."

"What happened? How did Donald end up with us?"

"Where is he now, lassie? Did he hurt you at all?"

"No, we were able to keep him down. But what did he do to you?"

He shakes his head. "Somehow Donald found out that I was going with you. After we had that conversation in the morning, I went about my day. Was out in the shed getting my clippers when suddenly I felt a pain in my shoulder. That's the last thing I remember."

I gasp. "Did he shoot you?"

"Only with a needle. Drugged me and left me there on the floor of the shed, then locked it. I didn't come to until the next day."

Donald got what was coming to him on Easter Island.

"And no one came looking for you?" I ask.

"Nae, 'cause I'd told Mrs. Findlay and your folks that I was going to Edinburgh. No one even noticed I was gone. 'Twas not 'till I had the mind to turn off the fuses that Mrs. Findlay came to the shed."

"What did you tell her?"

"That I'd had too much whisky and slept there. By the time I got out, Alex was well on his way to meet up with you. I couldn't have made the train or the flight to Easter Island."

"I think Donald tipped off the *Fraternitas* to where I was," I tell him as I take a seat on a little stone bench. My whole body is numb and my brain is buzzing. "But you are not going to believe what else…"

"What?"

"Uncle Li. He betrayed us too," I say. "He ran off with those old Sanskrit books."

Thomas shouts, "Egad!" He uses his hands to guide his body down to the bench like a blind person.

"I'm so sorry I got him involved," I say, putting my face in my hands. "It's all my fault for being too scared to do this alone, but I *trusted* him! I mean, I've known him all my life…"

"Do you think he's working with Donald?" Thomas asks, looking out in the distance.

"What? I hadn't thought… Why do you think that?"

"What's been bothering me is how Donald would know that Li could read ancient Sanskrit, back when he locked you in."

My head starts to hurt like I'm chewing on tinfoil.

"I should've suspected something—he was so cagey about what was in the books.

He brushes the thought away with his hand. "Don't worry,

we'll sort it out," he says, without enough confidence to make me believe him.

We sit silently for a few moments, both trying to make the pieces fit. I actually wish I could talk to Bolon right now.

"Any idea where Li would go?" Thomas asks.

"Mr. Papers thinks he's gone to the Dunhuang Caves," I reply. "To the archives."

Thomas tips his head back and looks at the sky. "Of course," he says, "the archives."

We both turn toward the castle when we hear the sound of pebbles underfoot. Mom and Dad are walking toward us with a look I've never seen before—it's like a terrifying mix of anger and sadness and horror. They must have found out. I am now their greatest disappointment.

I brace myself for the worst as Mom sits next to me and puts her arm around me. "Caity honey," she begins.

I swallow hard.

"We just got a call from San Francisco..." She stops and breaks down.

"What?" I ask, now thinking the worst. "Is Justine okay?" I scream.

"It's not her, Caity. It's the house," Dad says, gently setting his hand on my shoulder. "It burned down last night. Honey, it's ... gone."

All I can manage to say is, "No, no, no, no, no!" before I can no longer talk.

We're all crying, even Thomas. He must know that the *Fraternitas* was behind it. After a few minutes Dad collects himself. "Mom and I have a lot of calls to make and a trip home to plan," he says. "Do you want to come back to the office with us?"

"I'll be in a minute," I say, forcing myself to breathe steadily.

"We still have each other and that's all that really matters," Mom says, bending down to kiss the top of my head before turning to go back. She turns around and adds, "And this place."

Seeing them walk away, their heads hung, totally oblivious to why this was done, my shock and sadness turns to rage. I look at Thomas. His skin is the color of a heavy rain cloud.

"They can't take everything from me! We have to find Uncle Li and get what he's stolen," I say coldly. "We have to go to the Dunhuang Caves."

Thomas looks shocked. "Caity, I'm not sure—"

"You know what today is?" I ask, interrupting him.

"One *Manik*," he replies.

"*Manik*, the daylord of balancing freedom with security."

"And One, the pulse of force and possibility," he adds.

"I *know* I have to go to the Dunhuang Caves," I say.

"Aye," he says, nodding his head and looking down as if he knows I'll do it no matter what he says. And I will.

A warm breeze blows by, carrying the scent of saltwater and grass. The loveliness of the smell makes the rage I'm feeling inside even uglier.

Uncle Li is one of them.

Joan Kleen

About the Author

Christy Raedeke's love of mysticism and thirst for ancient knowledge has led her around the world—trekking in the Himalayas, floating down the Ganges, cathedral hopping in Europe, studying feng shui in Kuala Lumpur, cloistering at a hermitage in the Sierra Nevada Mountains, and looking for shaman among the Maya ruins of the Yucatan and Chiapas. She and her husband Scott currently live in Oregon with their young children.

![glyph]												
• 1	••• 21	•• 41	•••• 61	••• 81	═══ 101	•••• 121	══ 141	 161	•• 181	• 201	••• 221	•• 241
•• 2	•••• 22	••• 42	══ 62	•••• 82	═ 102	── 122	•• 142	• 162	••• 182	•• 202	• 222	••• 242
••• 3	═══ 23	•••• 43	• 63	── 83	•• 103	• 123	══ 143	•• 163	• 183	••• 203	•• 223	•••• 243
•••• 4	• 24	── 44	•• 64	• 84	••• 104	•• 124	• 144	••• 164	•• 184	•••• 204	••• 224	══ 244
── 5	•• 25	• 45	••• 65	•• 85	• 105	••• 125	•• 145	•••• 165	••• 185	══ 205	•••• 225	• 245
• 6	••• 26	•• 46	• 66	••• 86	•• 106	•••• 126	••• 146	── 166	•••• 186	• 206	── 226	•• 246
•• 7	• 27	••• 47	•• 67	•••• 87	••• 107	══ 127	•••• 147	• 167	── 187	•• 207	• 227	••• 247
••• 8	•• 28	•••• 48	••• 68	══ 88	•••• 108	══ 128	── 148	•• 168	• 188	••• 208	•• 228	• 248
•••• 9	••• 29	── 49	•••• 69	• 89	── 109	•• 129	• 149	••• 169	•• 189	• 209	••• 229	•• 249
── 10	•••• 30	• 50	── 70	•• 90	• 110	••• 130	•• 150	• 170	••• 190	•• 210	•••• 230	••• 250
• 11	── 31	•• 51	• 71	••• 91	•• 111	• 131	••• 151	•• 171	•••• 191	••• 211	══ 231	•••• 251
•• 12	• 32	••• 52	•• 72	• 92	••• 112	•• 132	•••• 152	••• 172	══ 192	•••• 212	• 232	── 252
••• 13	•• 33	• 53	••• 73	•• 93	•••• 113	••• 133	══ 153	•••• 173	• 193	── 213	•• 233	• 253
• 14	••• 34	•• 54	•••• 74	••• 94	══ 114	•••• 134	• 154	── 174	•• 194	• 214	••• 234	•• 254
•• 15	•••• 35	••• 55	══ 75	•••• 95	• 115	── 135	•• 155	• 175	••• 195	•• 215	• 235	••• 255
••• 16	══ 36	•••• 56	• 76	══ 96	•• 116	• 136	••• 156	• 176	•••• 196	••• 216	•• 236	•••• 256
•••• 17	• 37	── 57	•• 77	• 97	••• 117	•• 137	• 157	••• 177	•• 197	•••• 217	••• 237	══ 257
── 18	•• 38	• 58	••• 78	•• 98	• 118	••• 138	•• 158	•••• 178	••• 198	══ 218	•••• 238	• 258
• 19	••• 39	•• 59	• 79	••• 99	•• 119	•••• 139	••• 159	══ 179	•••• 199	• 219	══ 239	•• 259
•• 20	• 40	••• 60	•• 80	•••• 100	••• 120	══ 140	•••• 160	• 180	══ 200	•• 220	• 240	••• 260